TYNE O'CONNELL

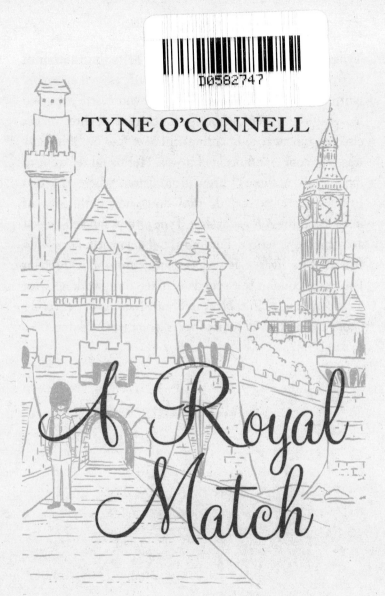

A Royal Match

PICCADILLY PRESS • LONDON

Tyne O'Connell is the international bestselling author of thirteen books including *A Royal Match*, as well as having written articles for *Marie Clare*, *Vogue* and *Elle*. Tyne loved her all-girls convent school so much that all three of her children ran away to boarding school to find out if it really was that cool – and decided it was. Her daughter went to school just a stone's throw from Eton, where the two Princes were educated, providing her with lots of inspiration for *A Royal Match*. Tyne always fancied herself as a bit of a fencer, but mostly she fancied boys who fenced. She lives a few doors away from Buckingham Palace in London but spends her free time working with local community initiatives in South East Asia, delivering books to children in remote areas along the Mekong.

To my divinely regal,
wildly intelligent, stunning daughter,
Cordelia, because she is my role model and the most
inspirational muse any writer could wish for.

Pulling Princes

THE CALYPSO CHRONICLES

by Tyne O'Connell

Piccadilly Press • London

You have to pull a boy
from the pond and kiss him
before you'll know if he's
frog or prince . . .

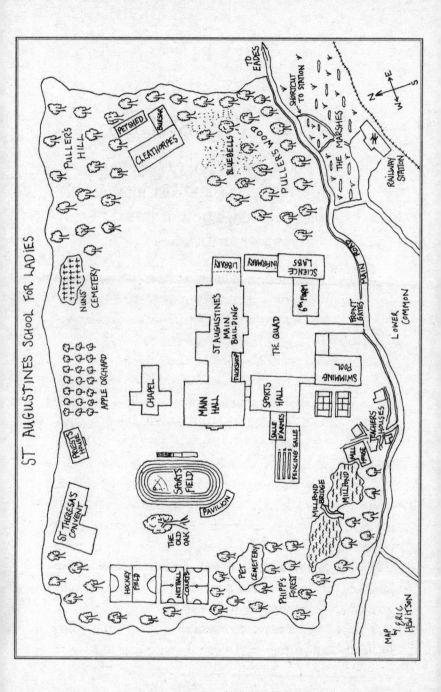

ONE

Saint Augustine's

Talk about random. This was the *worst* worst-case scenario in my long history of worst-case scenarios. But then, my entire life is a random series of worst-case scenarios.

At fourteen, you start to realise these things.

On the flight back to school after the Easter break, wedged between an enormous professional-mom type and a smelly backpacker, I had weighed up my tactics for turning my life around during the summer term at Saint Augustine's.

Life at Saint Augustine's had been hell since Day One, which was why I'd made a decision that I would do everything I could to get the cool crowd to accept – if not respect – me. I mean, OK, so I suppose I knew deep down they were shallow and mean, but . . . well, there is only so long you can spend as the form freak before you actually go mad and start wanting to be part of the cool set.

I knew I had a tough term ahead of me if I was going to finally start fitting in. I knew I was going to have to reinvent myself. That is, become the sort of girl who can pull boys – particularly really fit ones.

So it was sorted; I was on the case.

I knew radical action was needed.

But it was cool – I had a radical plan.

I had even factored in the possibility of things getting worse before they got better.

In short, I was prepared.

But even I, The Queen of the Doomsday Prophesies (my mom's nickname for me – what can I say, she's hilarious), hadn't considered the possibility that I would be forced to share a dorm room with The Honourable Georgina Castle Orpington . . .

The girls, all dressed in the hideously evil Saint Augustine's uniform – maroon pleated skirt and green ruffled shirt – were all crowded, with their toff parents and toff valets in tow, in the dimly-lit, wood-panelled entrance hall, peering at the noticeboard to find out which dorm they were in and who they'd be sharing a room with that term.

'Oh great, I'm with the American Freak,' I heard Georgina whisper sarcastically to Honey O'Hare, a member of her cool pod of friends.

That's what they called me – American Freak. They do these horrendously bad piss-takes of my accent, which is ironic, really, because when I go back to Los Angeles during the holidays everyone starts talking like Dick Van Dyke, imitating what they perceive to be my proper English accent. You can't win, really.

Standing at the back of the crowd, waiting for my

chance to see the list, I pretended not to have heard Georgina's lament and tried to think of something really cutting to say in reply. (I rarely actually say the cutting things that I think up in my head, though, because I have discovered that it is better to stay under the radar and keep my witty remarks to myself.)

Both Georgina and Honey were holding their Louis Vuitton pet carrier bags containing matching super-cute pet rabbits, Arabesque and Claudine. They'd have hated it if they'd known, but I was always stopping by the pet shed to cuddle their rabbits; particularly Georgina's, Arabesque, who was really adorable and had the sweetest pink eyes and the softest, floppiest ears. Honey's toffee-coloured rabbit, Claudine, was always biting me (no surprises there).

I would have loved a rabbit of my own, but one of the things about being an American freak at an English boarding school is that you don't get to have a pet because of the totally cruel quarantine laws. My parents probably saw this as character building, like everything that depresses me.

My parents are big on character.

Both my parents are writers in Hollywood. I long to write myself – only not the sort of dreary stuff they write. They think of themselves as really hip and liberal because they say I can call them Sarah and Bob (like I'd ever do that!). Besides, they are so *not* cool. For a start, they drive a Volvo and say things like 'swell' (Dad) and 'super' (Mom). My mom is a senior staff writer on a crappy soap that doesn't even air in the UK, so no kudos there. My dad is writing the Big One (that's Hollywood-speak for the script that will finally make a name for him, but currently brings in no money).

They didn't think LA was the place to bring up a teenager. They told all their friends that they were afraid I would become 'too Hollywood'. They sent me to *Le Lycée Français de Los Angeles* when I was a kid, which is where I picked up my fencing problem. But the real reason I was in this hell was because my mom's British and she went to Saint Augustine's, and she ADORED it.

'It'll be super, darling. You'll make friends for life – just wait and see,' she promised me on the flight over three years ago.

All I'd come up with in the friend department so far was Star. She's the daughter of a rock star who was huge in the eighties, and even though he was mega (and is still adored by several million tragic people with bad hair worldwide) and is one of the richest men in Britain, Star was too random and unconventional to be accepted at Saint Augustine's, or to have any kudos like Antoinette did. Antoinette's entire family are famous pop stars. Even though Antoinette was in the year below us, she was considered the trendiest girl in school – unlike Star, who was a total goth with a lot of weird habits: 1) wearing only black, 2) fencing, 3) having a freaky extended family, and 4) being friends with me.

Honey pointed one of her long, French-manicured fingers at the list and said, 'Oh yaah. But, darling, look, it's not *just* the American Freak. Guess who else you've been roomed with? Only her weird friend, Star!'

Georgina's eyes almost popped out of their long-lashed sockets. 'Darling, are you serious? I am so going to get Daddy to complain,' she declared loudly as she looked despairingly down the list and held her own perfectly manicured hand to her brow.

Honestly, I thought, it's a wonder these two don't wear tiaras . . . whoops – they do on occasion!

This was going to be a great term.

My despair at having to share a room with Georgina was somewhat diluted by the thought of Star being in my room too. I had asked to share with Star, but, as Georgina now knew, you don't always get to share with your first choice.

Star's my best friend. As I said earlier, she was my *only* friend on account of us both being the form freaks.

We had bonded the first day of Year Seven (my first year at Saint Augustine's) in fencing. We spent so many hours alone together in the *salle d'armes* practising (i.e. escaping from the other girls and, in Star's case, fancying Professor Sullivan, our fencing master), that we grew pretty close – especially when we both chose sabre as our weapon. The other girls were beginners, so had to start on the foil, but because Star and I had been fencing since we were quite young and were showing so much enthusiasm, Professor Sullivan allowed us to advance to *épée* and then on to sabre.

Sabre is the most aggressive of the three fencing weapons; it has a really cool full-fist guard and a flat cutting blade, with a folded-off end rather than the tragic-looking bobble that you have on foil. Sabreurs have a bit of a reputation for being a swashbuckling, ruthless lot.

In our ignorance, Star and I thought ruthlessness and swashbuckling would be agonisingly chic qualities to foster. But that was before we realised that being sabreurs would make us stand out – something that wasn't done at Saint Augustine's.

Things that make girls stand out (and therefore make them the object of ridicule and derision) at Saint Augustine's School for Ladies:

1) Not being willowy and not having really long hair (preferably blond).

2) Not having a title or at least a double-barrelled surname (although *using* your title was considered tragic).

3) Not owning a massive house in the country and a quite big one in a really smart area of London.

4) Having a spot problem (i.e. any spots whatsoever).

5) Being overweight (i.e. being of average or above-average weight for your height). NB: even bulimia and anorexia were more status-enhancing than being a chubba.

6) Having unusual amounts of body hair (i.e. any).

7) Having a funny accent (i.e. any accent that wasn't madly posh and English).

8) Not being asked to be a debutante (i.e. be presented to the Royal Court). Perversely, actually

agreeing to be a debutante, marked you out as even more uncool than if you hadn't been asked in the first place.

9) Not being attractive enough to pull fit boys (preferably older ones) who then went on to leave messages on your mobile for other girls to listen to.

10) Not being completely obsessive about sweets and fags.

11) Having clothes that no one else would buy (i.e. non-designer, like mine).

Number 9 was the clincher.

Pulling fit, older boys is vital for all girls, but especially for girls who live in an all-girls school, where the ability to pull fit boys confers status like nothing else can.

I knew this because of what happened to Octavia, a girl in the year above me. Octavia had very little social cachet and stood out like a sore thumb with her short, dykey hair. She also had this body hair problem (i.e. she was *covered* in the stuff) that had earned her the nickname Pubes.

Like me, Octavia had been one of the girls who hid in the cupboard at lunch-time to avoid being confronted by her total lack of friends. (Who sits next to whom at lunch says everything about your status at Saint Augustine's.) Then suddenly after the Christmas break, Octavia was transformed into one of the most popular girls in the school and one of Georgina's best mates – all because she pulled a Lower Sixth boy from Eades. Eades College is the madly posh school where the world's grandest boys are educated in privilege and the art of effortless charm (well, that was how Star puts it). One exeat (that's a weekend when you are allowed home) he even came and picked her up on his Ducati motorbike. We never saw her again.

You could fail every other test, but developing a reputation for never pulling boys was the end. Like providing the alcohol at social events, pulling boys was always the girl's responsibility and consequently we talked of little else. When I say 'we', I mean the cool girls – not me, but the girls I wanted to be like.

Failing to share stories about the boys you had pulled was as bad as not sharing your tuck. It was vulgar.

Over Easter, I tried to explain the imperative of pulling a boy by the time I was fifteen, but my parents went totally ballistic about it – as if I'd said I wanted to start having sex. Naïvely imagining that it would calm them down, I explained what pulling actually meant – i.e. kissing and that sort of thing. I mean, *hello*! They work in Hollywood for goodness' sake! Kissing is PG-13 there! But instead of saying something sensible like, 'Oh, yes, darling. Of course we understand. Get on to that pulling business right away! If there's anything we can do to help, just let us know, dear,' they delivered this really long dissertation about how you can get mono (glandular fever) from kissing. Until eventually I nodded off into my carb-free meal.

As an American with parents who have virtually impoverished themselves (in Hollywood terms, not real terms, obviously – I mean, they could still afford to pay for the fees, the flights and the tragic uniform; it just meant they had to do without a pool) in order to send me to boarding school in England, I pretty much flunked all eleven tests. I suppose I am tall and thin and my hair is blondish (if I spray myself stupid with Sun-In). But it's not sleek and straight like the cool girls' hair, it's wavy and has little fluffy bits at the front that stick up like horns no matter how much I try to stick them down.

In Year Seven when we were all eleven, the dorm bedrooms had six or more girls in them, but as the years went on, the number of girls per bedroom was getting smaller and smaller, and it became harder and harder to hide what a freak I was compared to all the other girls who were pulling boys left, right and centre.

Years Nine and Ten were housed in shared bedrooms of three per room in a building called Cleathorpes. It was an ancient house with a gabled roof and mullioned windows. In some ways I guess it looked kind of spooky and Addams Family-ish, but I had always longed to be roomed there. It was away from the main building where all the other dorms were.

Cleathorpes had good points and bad points:

Good points: It was away from the main building and meant we could sneak out at night through the bursar's window, which was conveniently never locked. This meant that IF we could dodge the guard dogs and armed security guards, slip through the electric, barbed-wire fence and sprint through the woods (where it was rumoured flashers and rapists lurked) and take the 23:23 train to London, we could go clubbing at one of the really cool London clubs like Fabric (that is if you knew someone who knew someone who knew the doormen). Not that anyone in my year had done anything as cool as that yet, but all the Lower Sixth girls claimed they had done it all the time when they were in Cleathorpes.

Bad points: The House Mother (or as we referred to her, House Spinster) was the horrible Miss Cribbe. Not only was she bearded and mad and always trying to get all chummy with us like we were her real children or something, but she had a disgusting incontinent springer spaniel called Misty, who was constantly sneaking into the dorms and weeing on our duvets.

All Miss Cribbe ever said was, 'Oh, Misty, you are a naughty little doggins, aren't you?' (Miss Cribbe always spoke to Misty in a baby voice.)

The whole of Cleathorpes smelled of wee, even though we all made a concerted effort to get Misty to run away by spraying her with Febreze.

I lugged my trunk up the narrow, dimly lit, oak-panelled stairwell that wound around the central hall. Each of the cold stone stairs had been hollowed in the centre from about two hundred years of wear. As I struggled alone, behind all the parents, guardians and valets carrying up the other girls' trunks, I took in the smell of bee's wax and floor cleaner.

The stained-glass window depicting Saint Theresa doing something miraculous cast a wintry half-light on the stairwell, even when it was fabulously hot and sunny outside. Bent double under the weight of my trunk, the strap of my fencing kit cutting into my shoulder, I looked up at her peaceful features . . . and wished she'd do something miraculous for *me*, like carry my wretched trunk up these stairs.

My parents lived in LA, so I suppose they couldn't accompany me every time, but also they claimed lugging a five-thousand-tonne trunk on my back was character-building. Clearly the fact that I was going to end up looking like a hunched-up old woman by the time I was eighteen didn't concern them in the least.

TWO

Friends for Life

Georgina's full title is The Honourable Georgina Castle Orpington, but she was far too grand to use it (as I explained, using your title was considered vulgar). So she went by Georgina Castle Orpington. Obviously, though, Georgina was not so grand that she didn't want everyone to *know* that she was titled and grand and should be treated as such.

By far the best bed in the room was the one by the window. It had drawers underneath and a view over the ancient oak woods (known as Puller's Woods) where all the illicit high jinks went on.

We were only a couple of miles away from Eades. Although Eades was too grand to have a formal relationship with any girl's school (especially a Catholic one like Saint Augustine's), because we were the nearest one, we shared loads of activities. We had an *amicabiles concordia*, as our Latin teacher loved to call it.

I totally hate Latin. What am I supposed to do with *amo, amas, amat*? We were always telling Ms Mills, our

Latin teacher, that Latin is a dead language, to which she replied, 'You'll be dead if you don't finish your declensions' – even though, as a Catholic, she shouldn't be threatening the physical manifestation of our souls.

The teachers at Saint Augustine's are such hypocrites – apart from the nuns, who are mostly really cool and devout (or at least old, deaf and indifferent). The dead nuns are all buried in the nuns' graveyard near the apple orchard. When I'm feeling really sorry for myself about being the form freak, I sometimes go and sit there and ponder the strangeness of their existence compared to my own.

You couldn't see the nuns' graveyard from our window, but you could see the most beautiful spread of bluebells, like a carpeted pathway through Puller's Woods.

'Do you want the bed by the window, then, Georgina?' I offered, when all the toff parents and toff valets had left.

I knew Georgina would take whichever bed she wanted anyway, on account of her being head of the Year Ten cool girls, but I was just trying to make conversation.

I've *so* got to stop doing that.

'*Whatever,*' she replied, mimicking my American accent. Nevertheless, she threw Tobias (her ancient teddy bear) on the window bed.

Tobias had his own mini-trunk of designer outfits and his own passport. Whenever Georgina hated something or someone, she'd say, 'Tobias can't bear that/them!' All her friends found Tobias and his temperamental personality hilariously funny.

You can see what I was up against.

I was counting down the seconds until Star's arrival.

It's not like I thought that Georgina, Honey and their kind were fantastic role models or anything tragic like that. It was just that I was sick of being the class freak. I was sick of being mocked about my accent, sick of having nasty Post-it Notes stuck on my back, saying mean stuff about what a tragedy I was.

Also, another part of me wanted to know what it was *like* to be part of the cool pod of girls, whose ingrained sense of entitlement both excluded and intrigued me.

My plan to start fitting in first came about when I was talking to my mom's PA. Once he got over the hurdle of his amazement that I get teased for sounding American ('But you sound sooo British!'), he started to come up with some really cool ideas. Personal assistants can be very wise.

Jay had been assigned the task of looking after me on the studio lot during the Easter break. My mom's PAs were usually Valley Girls who just wandered around the lot talking on their mobiles while I followed them around like an old dog they've been asked to walk. But Jay chatted away to me like I was an actual person and he even let me drive the golf cart around the lot, something my mom would never allow.

I could tell Jay felt really sorry for me when I told him about how I locked myself in cupboards to avoid things like lunch or makeover parties where I knew I'd be excluded. I might have made it all sound worse than it was. I mean, everyone locks themselves in the cupboard sometimes – even Georgina (although she only does it to avoid Mass and lame stuff like that).

I suppose I didn't bother to explain to Jay that my

parents sent me to boarding school because they wanted the best education for me. Also I didn't tell him about the sacrifices that my parents make in order to send me here. Or that we would have lived somewhere nicer than East Hollywood and had a pool and a Mercedes like everyone else in Hollywood if they didn't had to spend what amounted to most of their salaries on flying me to and from my exorbitantly expensive school in England.

But boarding school isn't the 'done thing' in America – especially in the socially liberal world of Los Angeles – and when I told Jay about how unpopular I was on account of being American and having no money and no pulling history, he came up with the idea of turning my social fortunes around by having me pose as a worldly wise *Sex and the City* type, who pulls lots of fit boys.

So this was the term when things were going to change. I was never going to be asked to be a debutante and curtsy to the Queen, I might not own a mansion in the country or a posh house in Chelsea, but I didn't see why I couldn't pull a boy – preferably an older, fit one.

First step, Jay said, was all about creating the illusion that I held a fatal attraction for the opposite sex.

'Hey, isn't this great?' Star squealed dementedly when she finally arrived. Ray, her father's valet (enveloped in his trademark stench of patchouli), was trailing behind her with her trunk. 'After all this time we finally get to share!'

She was referring to me, not to Georgina, who hates Star almost as much as she hates me – and don't worry, the feeling is mutual.

Georgina glared as Star stumbled in and threw her arms around me in a big hug.

I do love Star.

Georgina pretended that she was chucking up at the sight of our cuddle and started filling up the tiny wardrobe we were all meant to share with her numerous expensive designer outfits.

Star pulled away and said, 'Gosh, you've grown again! I wish I was tall and skinny like you, Calypso.'

Oh yes, that's another thing – my name: Calypso Kelly. I have the crappiest name ever. My mom let my dad choose it so he could feel more 'involved' in the parenting process. He clearly thought giving me a freakish name and packing me off to boarding school was all the parenting he needed to do.

Star's the only girl at Saint Augustine's who doesn't make fun of my American accent, which is strongest after breaks.

It totally sucks being an American in the twenty-first century.

It's not as though I was the only American in the school or anything. There were twelve Americans in the Upper Sixth, known at Saint Augustine's as The Manhattan Apostles (because there were twelve of them). As far as I know they never got stick for their accents, but then they didn't really talk to anyone outside their group – not even the other Americans. They all came from the same junior school back in New York. All their school fees were paid for by one girl's father, who didn't want his pampered daughter to feel lonely at school in England.

Which brings me to the ultimate DBI (Daddy-Bought-It) accessory: friends.

My daddy couldn't afford any friends for me.

He couldn't even afford to give me a decent allowance, which meant I had to buy all my clothes secondhand off the girls in the year above who were always dropping by with their hardly worn designer clothes. The saying *'Mi casa es su casa'* (my house is your house) is translated as 'Daddy's plastic is my plastic' at Saint Augustine's. *My* daddy didn't buy into this philosophy – he claims not to believe in plastic!

'You can't not believe in plastic,' I told him. 'It's there, it exists! Like trees and grass – it's out there, everywhere. Face it, Dad, we live in a world of plastic!'

He told me he didn't want me to grow up spoiled. He's always changing the subject like that.

My mom actually applauds the idea of me having to buy secondhand clothes off the other girls because she's so environmentally aware (and not as rich as all the other parents who send their kids here).

Ray dumped the trunk by Star's bed and grunted something incomprehensible before handing Star a bundle of twenty-pound notes.

'Tiger said to give you some readies.' (Tiger is Star's dad, but at least he doesn't ask her to call him that.)

Ray was wearing tight black leather trousers and a black T-shirt with *Roadie* written on the front and back. His long black hair hung in a limp ponytail down his back. He used to tour with Star's dad's band until it had its first bust-up (now a bi-annual event, as apparently it pushes up album sales). After that, Ray and all the rest of the roadies became staff at Star's parents' enormous Derbyshire estate. And even though they still tour every few years, once the tour was over the roadies always returned to their valeting and other duties in Derbyshire.

I sometimes spend exeats with Star, which is cool because no one supervises us – basically because they are all usually stoned.

My dad is a massive fan of Dirge, Tiger's band, and thinks it's 'swell' that I spend time there. I've heard him boasting to his LA friends about it. He would totally freak if he knew what actually goes on in that house. And I'm not just talking about the perilous quad-bike racing Star and I get up to.

Once I saw Star's father fall backwards off his chair at breakfast and all Star's mother said was, 'Tiger, I wish you wouldn't do that.'

I was like, HELLO, your husband is on the floor in a dressing gown with cereal all over his face. Don't you want to *do* something? It was gross – his penis was peeping out of his robe – but everyone just kept munching on their toast like nothing had happened. He was still there on the floor, snoring away, when we came in at lunch and we all had to step over him.

I am so never doing drugs.

'Cheers, Ray,' Star said as she handed him one of the twenties back. He held the note up to the light as if he thought it might be a fake or something, then he gave her head an affectionate pat and told her not to drink or drug too much and loped off.

THREE

My First Fake Boyfriend

'Cute guy, Star,' Georgina said, sarcastically referring to Ray as she flicked through a copy of *Tatler*. (Georgina had appeared in the social pages once and ever since she always had a copy on her.) 'Is that your new boyfriend, then?'

Star sneered. She wasn't intimidated by Georgina the way I was. She was quite happy to get into total screaming bitch fights with Georgina and her mates if they pissed her off – which, of course, they did all the time.

And now we were all going to be sharing the same room! Even more reason to start fitting in, if just for the sake of peace.

So, while Georgina read *Tatler* and Star began to unpack, I nonchalantly started pinning up a large photograph of Jay and me driving around in a golf cart on the Paramount lot.

I could tell Georgina was peering over her *Tatler* as I pinned up a second photograph – a glam headshot of Jay that he had given me for just this purpose.

'So who's that, then?' she asked fake-casually, still flicking through her magazine.

I acted as if I hadn't heard the question and set about pinning up my *pièce de résistance* – a close-up shot of Jay and me, Jay staring into my eyes adoringly. We both fell apart laughing after the shot was taken. Have I mentioned that Jay is gay?

'Oh my God,' Georgina cried out, no longer capable of faking indifference, 'Did you actually pull *him*?'

She scrambled on to my bed and scrutinised his gorgeous face more closely. She was wearing an expression I had never seen on her before . . . I think it was amazement.

I just shrugged. Not being effusive was another part of my makeover. I was determined to stop being an idiot chatterbox and start being more mysterious and enigmatic like the cool girls. That was Jay's idea too. He said that sometimes 'less is more'. I told him that less of Georgina and Honey would definitely be more, but he just laughed and told me to trust him.

Georgina obviously hadn't worked out that I had developed a mysterious side over Easter because she asked me again if that was my boyfriend. By this stage Star had plugged in her electric guitar and was messing about with her own blend of minor chord compositions.

Star utterly worships Morrissey, who was this totally morose musician in the mid-eighties – I mean, she wasn't even born then! As a homage to him, Star writes and performs her own songs about hating her life as a rich rock star's kid and wet, suicidal afternoons at boarding school. Her father thinks she's a total genius and lets her use his recording studio, even though her songs would make the most positive person want to self-destruct.

Georgina gazed at my photo gallery. 'I can't believe you pulled someone so hot, darling!' she announced.

I had to hide my amazement. Georgina and Honey and their friends always called one another darling. But she had certainly never called *me* darling.

I wasn't sure if this meant I should darling her back. What is the etiquette on that, I wondered? So I merely shrugged enigmatically.

Star stopped playing her guitar and peered at the phots. 'Nor can I!' she agreed – somewhat disloyally, I thought.

I disappeared into the en-suite and started unpacking my woeful little selection of toiletries and make-up. I'd managed to decant some vodka into some empty Body Shop bottles when my parents were out. I knew from experience that these were vital components of being part of any dorm party. The cool girls always take Body Shop Specials down to the woods and I wanted to be prepared for my first invite to this exclusive club of dissipation. Georgina had already claimed the entire cupboard with about ten thousand little Body Shop Specials, so I just stuck mine on the wobbly shelf above the sink.

'Calypso!' Star called out to me. 'Is this for real? Like, did you really pull this guy when you were back with your folks in LA?'

Star knows only too well how deeply dull my trips to LA normally are, because I'm always moaning about them.

'Yaah, of course,' I told her breezily, as if fit, older boys falling madly in love with me was an everyday occurrence.

And then Georgina said the words that I had wanted to hear ever since I first arrived at Saint Augustine's. 'He's seriously fit, Calypso. I'm impressed.'

So that was that. I knew then that whatever else happened in my life I would always have this memory to cling to. *I* had impressed *Georgina Castle Orpington* – the most deeply unimpressed girl in our year. First she called me darling and now *this*! A little imaginary slide show started playing in my head:

Georgina, her cool gang and me sitting together at lunch.

Georgina, her cool gang and me climbing out of the bursar's window for late-night dashes through the woods to take the 23:23 train to London to some ultra-cool club like Fabric.

Georgina and me, waxing each other's legs and giving each other facials on Saturday nights.

Georgina and me, spraying Sun-In on each other's hair.

I didn't even really like Georgina, but I couldn't help wanting to be liked by her . . . maybe even be a little bit like her. Because girls like Georgina lived the good life. Girls like Georgina were always at the centre of things and I was so *over* being on the periphery. In just over a year I would be sixteen and I had never been kissed.

I wanted to be respected enough to be accepted by the core of girls at Saint Augustine's who made things happen.

I just hadn't expected it to be this simple. If I'd known,

I would have done it ages ago. I mean, how easy could this be? Three photographs and I had already impressed Georgina Castle Orpington, a girl who had never just randomly spoken to me – apart from when she was trying to flog her clothes for exorbitant sums of money or telling me what a freak I was.

She shook her head. 'I mean it, Calypso. I am seriously impressed.'

I tried to look all nonchalant and casual.

'Are you coming out for a fag, then?' she asked – and she didn't even do a piss-take of my American accent or anything. She spoke in her normal Sloaney voice, just as if she was talking to one of her It-Girl friends.

'Erm, well . . . the thing is, erm, I don't actually smoke,' I replied before I could stop myself, '. . . much,' I added, thinking on my feet. 'That is, I'm trying to give up – 'I mean, cancer and all that – you know how it is.' I gave a little cough.

I can make a total arse of myself when I try. Sometimes even when I don't try.

Georgina looked at me strangely for a moment, but then she just said, 'Yaah, you are so right, darling,' in her drawly way. Then she added that she was thinking of giving up too. I almost fell backwards like Star's dad!

'I've really got to give up trainers,' Star declared from her position on the floor, breaking the spell of my little bonding moment with Georgina. 'They are totally taking over my life.'

Georgina and I watched as Star jammed the last of her six hundred black trainers in her cupboard and slammed the door with her foot.

Georgina looked Star up and down – from her shoes to her hair and then down to her shoes again. She has a lot of dismissive looks like this down pat. All the cool girls have this ability to shrivel your confidence with withering looks.

Star doesn't shrivel easily, though. I guess the fact that her father's way richer than Georgina and her cool pod of friends put together helps her confidence.

Or maybe she really just doesn't care.

Star had a saying which had always helped us survive the slings and arrows of Georgina and her friends' jibes: 'Wear your pain like lip-gloss'. The first thing any girl does when she's in a jam or stuck for words is reach for her lip-gloss. So whenever we're nervous or someone says something bitchy to us, we pull out our lip-gloss and apply.

I pulled out my lip-gloss and applied, but Star didn't notice because she was busy giving Georgina her own withering look, which, as looks go, is like a cross between the gym mistress's pre-menstrual scowl and a tiger growling – i.e. pretty damn frightening.

Then Georgina gave Star another look of *her* own.

I'm telling you, it was a war of looks.

I have always admired Star for standing up to Georgina and the other girls, because I was completely terrified of them. It's not like Star was bursting with confidence either. I mean, she was fully self-conscious about her weight – not that she was a chubba or anything, but like I said, Saint Augustine's had a reputation for producing tall, willowy girls, whereas Star was more your classic ordinary-sized girl with red hair (she calls it Titian, but it doesn't alter the fact that she always got teased for being a ginga).

Star always says that she envies my figure. I keep telling her she has nothing to worry about because she has a love-ly figure and beautiful hair, but she says she'd still rather trade with me. I suppose I *am* tall – although I'm more gangly than willowy. My mom says I've got stunning cheekbones, but the older girls were always coming up to me and pinching my cheeks and saying stuff like, 'You've got the cutest little chubby cheeks.' I hated that.

'God, you're a loser, Star,' Georgina sighed as she put her Gucci sunglasses on (presumably to save her eyes from the glare of our ugly rays).

I wanted to defend Star – not that Star would have wanted me to, and anyway, anything I said would only have made things worse. But then something almost mag-ical happened. Georgina turned to look at me through her sunglasses and smiled. 'Bet he was a great kisser, darling,' referring to Jay. 'You can always tell by the lips.'

'Definitely,' I lied, trying not to puke at the thought of kissing Jay. I mean, yes he's fit and all, but HELLO he is SO gay. He practically walks on tippie-toes.

Georgina lowered her glasses down her nose slightly so she could give me the searchlight look, only without the dismissive sneer that she used on Star. I could tell she was genuinely awestruck by my pulling prowess. Well, maybe not *awestruck* exactly – I mean, Georgina is no beginner in the art of pulling. At the last social she pulled five boys! But she was rattled, I could tell.

I was shaking my duvet into its cover when Honey and Arabella came in and slumped on Georgina's bed. 'Hey, check this out, darlings,' Georgina urged, pointing to my photographs. 'Calypso has pulled an actual hottie.'

The girls clambered over onto my bed and scrutinised the photo. 'Wow! Calypso, he's *really* fit,' Arabella agreed.

'So what's his name?' Honey asked nastily.

'Erm, Jay.'

'*Jay?*' she squealed. A look of undiluted disgust flashed across her flawless It-Girl face. 'How tragically American is that?' Then she started saying 'Jay' with an exaggerated American accent, which set the other girls off.

I went bright red.

Star looked over at me pityingly then she made psycho stabbing motions behind the other girls' backs, which almost made me giggle.

'Did you seduce him on your teen duvet, then, Calypso?' Arabella asked bitchily, referring to the Club'N cover I was trying to shove my duvet into.

It was the cover my mom had bought me when I first came to Saint Augustine's – back when Club'N were cool. I know – tragic. OK, so maybe I had begged her for it at the time, but I was only eleven! The picture of Club'N was fading, but it was still a Club'N cover and way embarrassing. It was also a single bed duvet, made of synthetic fibres, not a goose-down double like all the other girls had.

I should have made my mom to get me a new cover, but I'd hardly seen her the entire break. I should have made up a cooler name for Jay too, but I was so thrilled about the photo gallery success that I hadn't given the matter any thought. Stupid, stupid, stupid, Calypso.

'Actually, Jay is just short for James,' I lied, suddenly

inspired (James being a much posher name than Jay).

The cool girls nodded, clearly satisfied with this explanation.

Star flopped on to my bed with the others. 'I snogged that Rupert guy,' she groaned. 'My tongue got caught in his braces. It was so embarrassing.'

'*You're* embarrassing, Star,' Georgina said with another sneer. 'I can't believe I'm going to be sharing a dorm with someone called Star. What's up with that anyway? Were your parents stoned out of their heads?'

I was shocked. Not about how nasty she was – I was used to that – it was just that usually it was me she said stuff like that to.

Star didn't seem bothered. That's what I love about her. Even with her name and her weird parents she's really chilled about herself. Also, like I said, she thinks Georgina and Honey are the freaks.

Honey did her screechy little fake laugh. She looks like a hyena when she laughs, although it was obvious that she'd had botox (to give her eyebrows 'a lift') in the break. She'd already had collagen injected into her lips at Christmas.

Honey was a total psycho toff; in fact, she made Georgina and the other posh girls seem positively friendly. I always got the impression that even they sometimes find Honey too much. But Georgina's father and Honey's biological father go to the same hunting meets and the two of them used to stay overnight together at a hotel for posh tots in Chelsea called Pippa Pop-Ins. Then when they were four they were packed off to the madly grand Hill House in Knightsbridge which was where Prince Freddie, his father, Prince George, and, well, all the grandest children went. Georgina and Honey even learned to ski together at the school's Swiss annex. So when anyone dared to question Honey's behaviour, Georgina always stuck up for her.

Honey's mother was a way-famous It Girl who presents a programme on celebrity homes for a cable station called E. She had Honey when she was about seventeen, so she still looks incredibly fit.

Georgina might have had a somewhat grander-than-thou way about her, but Honey was a genuine Class-A bitch. She was always giving Georgina a really hard time about her weight and her looks, even though Georgina was really stunning and slim. Also, everyone knew that Georgina's had huge food issues, mostly on account of her parents' divorce.

Just about everyone at Saint Augustine's has issues with food – and not just because they feed us slops that taste like sewage. In fact, the nuns tick your name off at lunch and dinner and check your tray when you stick it in the cart to make sure you've eaten everything because anorexia is so rife. If you miss two meals, you have to speak to Sister Dempster in the infirmary about how anorexia can make your bones brittle and even kill you.

In Year Nine when Georgina's parents separated she became bulimic. Star says that sometimes bulimia and anorexia are ways to control something when you feel everything else is out of control. Star actually tried to be really helpful, pointing out that anorexia and bulimia can cause your hair to go thin and fall out and make your skin go all old and wrinkly looking, but Georgina just told her to piss off. We heard she stopped throwing up her lunch and supper, though, so I think Star might have hit a nerve. Georgina's hair is beautifully long and straight and luxuriously thick and I know she'd hate it to fall out.

'I'm going for a fag. Anyone coming?' Star announced, stuffing her cigarettes in her bra and her Febreze in her bag.

The smokers always sprayed themselves with Febreze to take the smell away after a visit to the tennis courts for a fag. Then they'd come up to non-smokers like me and ask, 'Do I smell?' and I'd have the responsibility of sniffing them. Of course if a teacher later smelled smoke on them, I'd get the blame.

At least Star smokes, I thought enviously. At Saint Augustine's everyone smokes, even the nuns. I tried to smoke once, but I threw up because I'd just come from an interschool fencing tournament and was totally starving. Anyway I actually don't want to smoke because it would affect my health and even though I haven't even told Star this, I really, really love fencing, and I actually dream of fencing in the Olympics one day.

The smokers trailed out of the room leaving me to finish my unpacking. I was just about to take my fencing gear down to the armoury when Clementine Fraser-Marks came running into the room. 'Oh, it's you,' she said, clearly disappointed. 'Erm . . . hi, how was your break?'

'Oh yaah, fine,' I replied, pretending that I believed she actually gave a shit.

'Great. Where's Georgina?'

'Up on Puller's Hill.'

'Fair enough.'

I could tell she was uncomfortable having to be alone in the room with me but was too well brought up to show it.

'You sharing?'

'Uh-huh.'

'Cool. Well, Antoinette is selling listens if you want.'

'Cool.'

'Is that your boyfriend?' She pointed to the photographs.

I shrugged. 'Guess.'

'Fit. He looks like an adult sort of thing.'

I said, 'Yaah, well, that's on account of how he is . . . an adult sort of thing.'

'Wow. Well, it's Blake from Cell anyway, if you're interested. She's only charging fifty p on account of how it's the first day back.'

Cell was the hottest new band of the year. They'd had two number ones already and had also admitted taking coke. Blake, the lead singer, was Antoinette's brother.

It's a Saint Augustine's custom to sell 'listens' of mobile phone messages left by famous family members or really hot brothers or boyfriends. They don't always have to be famous, but you get more money for a famous listen. After the social last term when Georgina pulled five guys and they all left messages she made a small fortune and the queues snaked down the corridors.

Jay had promised to leave a message on my phone.

I was actually starting to believe that he was my boyfriend.

FOUR

The Royal Sport

There were only about twenty girls who fenced at Saint Augustine's and only three were on the sabre team – Star, Portia and myself. None of the willowy cool girls took fencing that seriously, which made the fact that I was the captain a badge of shame. Tennis, lacrosse or riding were the sports that were taken seriously by Saint Augustine girls. The other girls only did it because, aside from drama, it was the only opportunity to have contact with boys during school.

I couldn't help myself, though. I loved fencing. I was fifth in Britain in the under sixteens – and I wasn't even fifteen yet.

It was my mum's idea that I take up fencing when I was a little kid at the Lycée. In those days I didn't realise I could have a say. Now that I was almost fifteen, I could have stand-up screaming matches with her if I wanted, but it was too late for me to chuck it in now and make a fool of myself on the tennis courts.

Actually, forget that. What am I saying? It's never too late for me to make a fool of myself.

In Year Seven, Star had a tragic crush on our fencing master, Professor Arthur Sullivan. Neither of us mentions it any more, although I suspect that Star still carries a torch for him. I mean, he's a nice guy and everything (although there's a rumour that he once wore a cravat), but he's at least thirty-five or something ancient like that. He's extremely grand and only teaches fencing because of his love of the sport. He's absolutely loaded and drives four jaguars (not all at once obviously) – a racing green one, a powder-blue one, a black one and a silver one. I liked the powder-blue one best.

Professor Sullivan always spoke to us in French during fencing training because he thought it made us think harder. 'Fencing is a physical form of chess, an intellectual debate between two bodies.'

He was always telling us stuff like that . . . only in French.

Once he drove Star and me to Star's house on an exeat (in the powder-blue jag) and for a brief nano-moment we were the envy of all (being driven to London by a teacher confers a special status, especially if the teacher is even mildly fit).

As it turned out we had the whole house in Chelsea to ourselves because Star's parents forgot to show up. Star said it was probably because they were too stoned. I guess she was used to it, and anyway it meant we could do anything we wanted!

I'd like to boast that we threw a wild party with fit boys and alcohol, but we were only twelve and largely friendless so we just ate loads of sweets while Star enjoyed the luxury of smoking cigarettes without spraying herself with Febreze.

On the Saturday night we went out to the cinema covered in make-up and managed to talk our way into a 15. Later we wandered down the Kings Road, which is where boarding school kids go to pull on exeats. They do a sort of promenade up and down the street, trying to look cool, checking one another out and trying to get into pubs. All Star and I managed to do was strike up a conversation with a homeless guy and his bedraggled dog, Ralph, whom we patted and fed jelly babies to.

I would have loved to have a dog, or any pet, for that matter. We are allowed to keep rabbits and hamsters and things in the pet shed, but then we have to take them home in the breaks and I can't exactly take a rabbit back with me to LA all the time. Also customs would confiscate the poor little thing and shove it in quarantine.

Star had a pet rat called Hilda and a python called Brian. Even though we weren't officially allowed to keep snakes, they made an exception for Star after her dad donated loads of money to build a new music wing. Georgina and Honey were always threatening to sue if Brian so much as hissed at their rabbits, Arabesque and Claudine.

I wasn't too keen on Hilda and Brian myself, but out of loyalty to Star I always made a huge fuss of them when we went up to see them and asked if I could hold Hilda.

'I'm worried Hilda's got a cold,' Star told me as we were doing our warm-ups in the fencing salle. The salle or rather *salle d'armes* was the latest addition to our sporting complex.

It was like a squash court only far, far bigger. The floor was sprung, there were three pistes and the surrounding walls were flanked with fencing masks, weapons and ancient photographs of Saint Augustine's teams triumphing at tournaments.

'Poor Hilda,' I said, in my best fake sympathy voice.

Star was always paranoid that the rat had picked up an infection even though Hilda was the healthiest pet in the pet shed. She fussed over it all the time, treating her as if she were a gentle, nice animal like a hamster or a bunny instead of a vicious rodent with beady eyes.

We always had to give Hilda vitamin drops in her nasty little mouth and she would sometimes bite me while I tried to part her yellow teeth so Star could squeeze the dropper in.

'Yaah, she had a little sniffle when I went in to visit her at lunch,' she said sadly as she lay on the floor doing her leg raises.

'Oh no. Poor Hilda,' I sympathised as I stood up and moved on to my stretches and my lunging exercises.

The Eades College boys were here for an interschool tournament, but most of the Saint Augustine team girls were too busy flirting to bother with warm-ups, so it was left to Star and me to make fools of ourselves with our sidelong leaps down the fourteen-metre piste while the others looked on sneeringly. Like I said, the other girls mostly only did fencing as another way of meeting boys – also I was pretty sure they weren't immune to the fact the all-white fencing outfits made tall, thin, gorgeous girls look even more stunning.

The Eades boys were mostly there for the girls too

(rugby is the serious sport at Eades), but there were a few who were serious about the sport anyway. Eades is *the* most exclusive boy's boarding school in the country – maybe even the world. Royalty and rich people from all over the world send their sons there for a pukka British education. So do lots of ordinary rich people, some of whom made their money in their own lifetime (slightly tragic by Eades standards), doing not-so-pukka things.

The school has been around for hundreds of years, so they can get away with their mad traditions, and with making the boys wear tailcoats and funny shirts with stiff collars and things called 'ribbons' around their necks.

Loads of the girls at Saint Augustine's have brothers at Eades, which gives them extra status (but only if their brothers are older, obviously).

Honey said that Eades has gone awfully downhill since her father went there. She said it is full of plebs and the sons of East End gangsters – known collectively as kevs. My father asked me why we called these boys kevs and then got all champagne socialistic and hot under the collar when I told him that Kevin was a lower-class name in England and so kev was an alternative word for pleb.

Honestly, I don't know why he thrust me into this elit-ist world if he didn't want me to pick up elitist slang!

Less than three miles apart from each other, Eades and Saint Augustine's tend to share fencing and drama activi-ties, so while not many of the pupils take the activities themselves seriously, they take the inter-gender aspect very seriously indeed.

The Eades fencing team is known to be totally rubbish,

even though they have a huge pool of boys to pick talent from. Most of the team were chatting to girls, but a few of them (mostly the Europeans, and Billy, their sabre captain) were valiantly warming up on the piste beside Star and me.

I was surprised to notice that one of them was Prince Freddie. I mean, everyone knew he fenced, but he'd never struck me as being particularly keen on the sport. I'd figured he, like his mates, was only on the team to meet girls.

Freddie was second in line to the British throne, after his dad, Prince George, so naturally there were girls clustered about watching him. He was clearly loving the attention, even though he pretended not to notice them.

His security men were loitering with intent. They were dressed in polo-shirts and chinos, as if they were just out for a stroll, but they so looked like bodyguards with their squaddie haircuts, massive muscles and little earpieces.

The security guys in the fencing salle weren't all for Prince Freddie, though. There are more international royals at Eades than there are tiaras at a debutante ball. And then there are the regular famous people – a lot of them have scores of bodyguards – Prince Freddie seemed to be able to manage with just two. I quite respected him for that – especially given that he was always being hounded by the media.

Some of the security guys were hired by the kevs just so they could show off how wealthy they were – a bit like sporting a gold bracelet or a sovereign ring, according to Honey. Boys can be just as status-tragic as girls, I suppose.

You get used to seeing bodyguards hanging around

Eades boys. A few girls had them at Saint Augustine's, but they were made to keep a much lower profile. I don't think the nuns are that keen on having them around.

So anyway, once the warm-ups were finished, the president started calling the bouts. I'd seen Prince Freddie fencing *épée* before and he hadn't been very good so I was surprised when our names were called together.

FIVE

Flirting With Princes

The president called Freddie's name first, and as I watched him lope down the piste to the *en garde* line in this really sexy way, I couldn't help but think he was fit. Not just fit, actually, but sooo fit. He'd grown a lot last term and was now a good few inches taller than me. He was also much cooler-looking, as this time he wasn't sporting a gross pimple on his forehead.

Even though I knew I was going to slaughter him on the piste, I started to feel a bit nervous. I was even blushing because he was so utterly . . . well, there's no other word for it – fit. Thank God for the fencing mask covering my burning cheeks.

To fence sabre, you needed a metallic jacket worn over your plastic plastron, to register hits and to avoid serious injury to vital organs, sabre being the only cutting weapon used in fencing. Officially, you are not supposed to hurt your opponent too badly, but in practice sabre is a dirty weapon. Sabre is the most aggressive and impressive type of bout to watch. Most sabreurs like to make the most of their weapon and as a result we were usually all pretty bruised and sore by the end of a few bouts.

Our teammates had helped us hook up the backs of our jackets to the electrical apparatus that was linked to a box on the ceiling and registered our hits with coloured lights and a buzzer.

Freddie and I saluted the president first and then one another, casually lifting our blades to our lips and back down to the fencing position. Whenever I salute my opponent before a bout, I think how strange it is that there is this much etiquette involved before two people try to kill each other. But there we are, or as Sister Regina would say, 'diddlie-dee'.

Then we put our masks on and waited for play to be called. *'Prêts, allez!'*

I advanced down the fourteen-metre piste first, figuring the Prince, being a bit of a wimp, would either retire or parry. But instead he riposted, attacking into my offensive, which took me a bit by surprise. I made my attack swiftly, though, scoring a hit. The buzzer rang and the president called my hit.

There's this thing called a captor inside the sabre guard, which allows hits to be recorded on the electrical apparatus, but only if the blade arrives on the *lamé* by way of a cut or a point – any other hit is invalid in sabre. Sometimes, with everything happening so fast, you don't really know if your hit is valid or not until the buzzer sounds and the president calls *'Halte'* or 'Stop', at which point the clock is stopped until play is called again. A bout lasts for around five minutes of actual combat time, but it seems a lot longer.

Freddie scored the next hit with an obvious attack, provoking me into a parry of quinte (neck) by threatening me with a cut to the head and then disengaging the parry and rotating his blade to cut at my flank. 'An old one but a gold one' as Professor Sullivan likes to say (in French, of course, even though it doesn't rhyme).

Freddie's balance was excellent and his coordination reasonable, but he was no match for my compound attacks and disengagements, moves that require skilful wrist action (which you'd think he'd be brilliant at . . . being a boy). Actually, Professor Sullivan isn't wrong – fencing *is* like chess. But it is so fast that your brain must be completely focused. That can be difficult when your opponent is a totally fit member of the opposite sex. There was a moment when an image of me wilfully committing a *corps-à-corps* (a totally illegal move) flashed through my mind, and Freddie scored another hit.

The rest of the hits were all mine – although, to be fair, Freddie was pretty cunning and his parries and ripostes were totally respectable. But as Star always said, in sabre you can parry and riposte all you like, but you're only putting off the ultimate moment of your slaughter.

Fencing might be chess of the body, but the sword is a weapon and in sabre it is often a case of the most aggressive, fearless player winning – especially at our level. I was totally wired. Hit after hit went to me.

'Cheers,' Freddie said as we shook hands after the bout. He'd taken off his mask to reveal dazzling cornflower-blue eyes and ink-black hair.

I took off my mask, revealing the fluffy bits at the front

of my hairline, which I didn't need a mirror to know were sticking up like horns. 'Yaah, erm . . . thanks, well played.'

'My name's Freddie, by the way.'

Like I wouldn't have known that? *Hello*, second in line to the throne and the constant topic of media speculation. Where does he think I'm from – the Moon?

'Erm, m-mine's Calypso,' I stuttered.

Please don't mention my name, I thought. Please God, don't let him mention my name. Why do I have to have such a stupid name?

We grinned stupidly at each other as they detached us from the electrical recorder.

God must have been listening because Freddie just said, 'You were terrifying out there! You really rinsed me.'

'Gee, erm . . . thanks.'

'Quite cutting, aren't you,' he drawled.

Was that a flirty look in his eyes?

'Thanks,' I said stupidly. 'I didn't know you fenced sabre.'

'I've only taken it up recently. Which probably explains why I'm such bollocks, right?'

'Well, you were pretty fit actually – I mean . . . erm, competent. Like, your flunges weren't horrendous or anything. And your renewal was sort of, erm, impressive.'

My father reckons when I'm in a hole I like to keep digging.

I was saved from further bad dialogue by Honey and Arabella and a few of the fencing girls who'd already fought their bouts and been seeded out from the pools (which meant more time to chat to boys).

'Wow, Calypso, that was so amazing, darling. Well

done,' Arabella squealed as they all clustered around the Prince like atoms.

Yeah right, like they were actually even watching me.

'Thanks,' I muttered as I was squeezed out of the circle.

They were fluttering their eyelashes at the Prince so hard I thought they were going to knock themselves out. I watched him closely as he chatted amicably in that charmingly deferential Eades-ish way and I couldn't help but feel a tiny frisson of something. Probably dehydration, I thought. I decided to leave the It Girls to it and went over to the refreshment stand for a drink.

Star was there, getting into her plastron. 'Cool bout, Calypso. Freddie wasn't bad either. I mean, seriously, at the tournament last year I thought he was totally tragic. I didn't even know he did sabre.'

'Yaah, it was OK. I thought he was pretty good actually.'

'Even though you rinsed him, right?' she laughed. 'Listen, after we've finished our bouts do you want to come to the pet shed with me to check on Hilda? I'm really worried, her eyes looked all sad and bleary this morning.'

'Sure,' I agreed, even though I would have preferred to chat a bit more with Freddie.

When almost all the bouts were over and tea was served, Freddie came over and stood near me – only he was still enveloped in a bubble of Honey's friends so I couldn't get to talk to him. We were watching Star trounce a member of his team. I thought for one second Freddie was looking at me, but then it turned out he had something in his eye.

Honey helped him to get it out.

Star dragged me away before I even had a chance to say goodbye, which was completely irritating because when we got to the pet shed Hilda was running around on her rat wheel like there was no tomorrow.

We still had to give her a cuddle, though.

SIX

Dorm Party Heaven, Duvet Hell

That evening during study period all I could think of was Freddie. I had to stop myself writing his name on my folder. Everyone was weirdly nice to me that night and Clementine, Arabella and Honey invited our room to their room for a makeover party.

It was normal for one room to be invited to another room but in other years Star and I hadn't been included in these invitations and would only go to one another's rooms and hang out, ignoring whoever else was in the room. When Arabella and Honey burst in with their invitation, which clearly included all three of us, Star and I caught each other's eyes. I bit my lower lip, terrified that Star would tell them to piss off, but instead she shrugged her shoulders in a 'why not?' sort of way and off we went.

Georgina called up for a pizza from the Pizza Express in Windsor, which you're not really allowed to do, but everyone does, because you can't survive on the inedible grey slops they feed us. Smuggling the Pizza Express guy in isn't that hard, and as long as you tear the box into a thousand pieces and distribute them in lots of different bins around the school, you never get caught.

Later we pooled our tuck in the middle of the floor. Everyone was really impressed by all the American sweets that I'd brought back this time. Jay had taken me to this really cool candy shop in the Beverly Hills mall and I'd just bought everything that looked different.

Georgina said, 'Wow, Calypso darling, these Hershey's Kisses are so delicious.'

'I like the Pixie Stix,' Star added as she tipped one up and sucked the sugar out of the tube.

I was thinking about saying that Jay had bought them for me, which was kind of true, but for some reason I didn't want to talk about Jay anymore. Maybe I was afraid of jinxing the mileage I'd already got out of him or maybe it was because I couldn't stop thinking about Freddie and how fit he looked in his fencing gear. I especially liked the way he had his hair – all sort of longish on top but not floppy like some of the Eades nerds. It was all bunched up like it was gelled – only it wasn't, because gel is so tragic. His hair was just thick and cut in a really cool way.

We gave one another homemade facials, using porridge and bananas and honey and other goopy stuff we nicked from the kitchen. Georgina even offered to wax my legs! Star rolled her eyes, but I couldn't have been more thrilled. Even though the pain was almost too horrendous to describe I kept my grin fixed on my face.

Star let Clemmie rag her hair so she could have ringlets

and then Star braided Clemmie's hair, which looked really cool.

'You look stunning,' Arabella told Clemmie – and she did. Her long, dark hair braided down her back seemed to bring out her gypsy looks. I felt proud of Star because it was her idea.

Star and Clemmie's family estates were near to each other, so despite their differences, Clemmie often blagged a lift home with Star on exeats.

Looking around the room now, I realised why Star had never really felt like an outsider in the same way I did. She'd grown up in this world, she'd gone to prep school with these girls. They spoke the same language. For her, there was no inside or outside – for her, it was a case of 'choose to refuse'. But for me, that night was like being in an entirely new country – the cool country.

Later we snuck down to the science lab to steal some of the condoms they used for sex education lessons so we could practise putting them on over bananas, the way they taught us.

Ms Argos had come in from a local comprehensive school, as a concession to the curriculum, especially to give the Sex Ed talks, because . . . well, it wouldn't really do to have a nun rolling a condom over a banana, would it? Although it would be quite funny! I suppose a non-nun teacher could have done it, but then the really, really Catholic parents would have thrown hissy-fits.

I'd hardly ever been invited to someone else's dorm party and I'd definitely never had someone as cool as Georgina offer to wax my legs. This was the longest that anyone apart from Star had gone without mocking me and the way I spoke.

Star kept rolling her eyes at me as if to say, 'What are we doing with these freaks anyway?' But I just pretended not to notice.

'I can't wait to do this to Freddie,' Honey announced as she was rolling a condom over a banana.

'Are you serious?' I asked before I could stop myself. Firstly I was horrified at the thought of her with Freddie. And secondly I hadn't realised that anyone had actually gone that far yet in our year – apart from Lucy, who was one of the druggie girls that Georgina *et al* didn't talk to. There was a rumour going around that Lucy had even slept with one of the plebs from the village, which was considered as tragic as it could get at Saint Augustine's.

But obviously not as tragic as being unable to pull anyone!

'Oh yaah,' Honey went on. 'Freddie was totally into me, darlings, as I'm sure you all noticed. He asked me all this really personal stuff about our holiday in Kenya last year. Like, we only know about *everyone* in common. I could tell he wanted to invite me out, but no one would leave him alone. It was like that time we went to that club in the limo and everyone kept asking me if I was a model – remember Georgina?'

'Darling, your hair was out-of-this-world amazing that night that we ragged it,' Georgina said, applying eyelash dye to Clemmie's eyes.

'It would be so cool to pull Prince Frederick, darling,' Clemmie sighed wistfully as a drop of dye rolled down her cheek.

'But would you . . . you know, actually *do* it with him?' Star asked, speaking directly to Honey for the first time that night – or maybe even ever!

All the girls looked at Star as if she were from Year Seven or something. '*Hello*, we *are* talking Prince Frederick – second in line to the throne!' Honey reminded her, rolling her eyes in disbelief.

'So if he asked, you'd actually, well . . . ? Darling, that's quite a big step,' Arabella added and then she giggled as the banana burst through the condom.

'Darling, I heard Lucy's already given a boy a blow job,' Clemmie added.

'She's such a slut, though – she'd give one to Mr Morton if he asked,' Georgina remarked. Mr Morton was the octogenarian groundsman.

'Are you going to pull him at the social then, Honey?' Georgina nudged Honey's leg with her toe.

'I don't see that I have much choice,' she sighed, as if kissing Prince Freddie would be such an effort.

'I thought he fancied Calypso, actually,' Star interjected, giving me a supportive smile.

I went bright red. If I was caught fancying a boy that Honey planned to pull, it could destroy me.

'Pah-lease. As if,' Honey sneered, flicking her perfect blonde tresses over her shoulder. 'Can you honestly envision a member of the royal family with an *American*?' Then she started laughing in a really nasty way and everyone apart from Star joined her. Star looked over at me and pulled out her lip-gloss. I pulled mine out too and applied liberally.

'Well, what about Mrs Simpson, that woman King Edward married?' Star reminded them.

'My point exactly!' Honey said.

Wait, were they comparing me to that prune-faced old woman?

'I'm not being horrible,' Honey said, 'Calypso, you know that. It's just, well, you know how it is.'

Did I? I shrugged. Maybe she was right, though. Princes are probably really restricted in who they are allowed to fancy. I seem to remember that they totally loathe Catholics. I thought of reminding Honey of this, but decided against it.

'Besides, you've got Jay, haven't you, darling?' Georgina reminded me, offering Tobias a Hershey's Kiss.

I'd temporarily forgotten about my tragic fake relationship with gay Jay. 'Yaah, totally,' I agreed.

'Has he called you or anything yet, darling?' she asked kindly, popping the chocolate into her own mouth.

'I haven't actually checked my phone messages, erm, and . . .'

She smiled at me and passed me some of her coconut and passionfruit cream to put on my legs. 'This smells just *so* divine, darling. Try it.'

I looked at my legs. They were still all red and blotchy.

'I know a girl who spent a night in a sleeping bag with Freddie's cousin Alfred,' Arabella remembered.

I rubbed the cream into my legs and wondered what it would be like to share a sleeping bag with Freddie. I wouldn't even mind if he was sweaty.

When we got back to our room, it was clear that Misty

had been there. The stench was horrific. And when I went over to my bed I found out why: She'd weed all over my nerdy Club'N duvet.

'Bugger, Misty,' I cursed, just as Miss Cribbe walked in to say it was time for lights out.

'Language, Calypso!' she trilled.

'Miss Cribbe, it's not fair. My duvet is all wet. Misty's weed on it.'

She put her hand on my soggy duvet to feel if it was wet. 'Don't be silly, you don't know for certain that it was Misty.'

Hello, it smelled of dog wee and Misty was the only dog living in Cleathorpes!

'Now, stop fussing. Give it to me and I'll wash it. It's a warm night and you can sleep with a sheet just for tonight.

Star waded in to my rescue. 'Miss Cribbe, that is so unfair! Poor Calypso will freeze. And anyway, it *was* Misty. You know it was.'

'That's enough cheek from you, young lady. Apologize immediately.'

'I will not,' Star shouted. (She can be very stubborn.) 'Misty's always weeing all over the dorm – it's disgusting.'

'Star, I'm warning you, that's enough,' Miss Cribbe replied with a wobble in her voice. 'Misty is a lovely dog. She adores you girls – why, you're like family to her. She'd be devastated if she heard what you were saying.'

'It's OK, Miss Cribbe. I don't mind sleeping under a sheet,' I assured her. I hated it when Miss Cribbe cried. It meant someone had to cuddle her and she'd completely soak you in tears. I gave her the duvet and she grabbed me for a beardy kiss on the cheek.

'You don't really think Misty did this dreadful thing, do you, dear? It was probably a dog from the village.'

Yes, that would be right. A dog had walked the two miles from the village, managed to get through the electrified, barbed-wire fence, negotiated its way past the hordes of roaming attack dogs and armed security guards, found its way inside our locked building, just in order to pee on the faded faces of Club'N.

'Yes, you're probably right,' I comforted her, patting her back, hoping to escape from her bosomy embrace sooner rather than later. She smelled a bit like dog wee herself.

'Now Miss Cribbe will bring you a nice clean sheet and tuck you in, dear.' She often referred to herself in the third person, as if she were royalty or something. I wondered if Freddie referred to himself in the third person. I didn't think I'd want to pull a boy that did anything to remind me of Miss Cribbe.

'You can use my spare duvet, Calypso,' Georgina offered.

'See what a lovely friend you have in Georgina, dear.' Miss Cribbe wiped away a tear with her sleeve. 'You might take some notes from Georgina, on how to be a good friend yourself, Star.'

'As if,' Star muttered. But Miss Cribbe didn't hear, or pretended not to, anyway.

'Now, I know you don't mean to be unkind, but it's very hurtful when you talk about dear Misty like that. I love you girls as if you were my own – you know that, don't you?'

'Yes, Miss Cribbe,' we all said – anything to shut her up.

'Good girls. Now, say your prayers and go to sleep.'

Georgina and I nodded solemnly. Star turned over to

face the wall and muttered something under her breath that no one could hear.

'As for you, young lady,' she said, referring to Star. 'You can see Sister Constance tomorrow after supper for a suitable punishment for cheeking me.'

'What did I do?' Star yelled.

'I won't have you cheeking me, young lady.'

'Fine,' Star replied, but when Miss Cribbe left the room she blew a big raspberry.

'What a freak,' Georgina said, climbing out of bed to get me her duvet.

'Sorry about getting you in trouble, Star,' I told her.

'You didn't get me in trouble. I hate her stupid old dog. Everyone knows Misty is always weeing everywhere. This whole building stinks. It's foul. Besides, all Sister will do is make me sweep the corridor.'

'And give you a big fat Mars Bar afterwards, darling,' Georgina added and all three of us laughed. It was nice laughing together. Star even gave me a look as if to say, Maybe Georgina's not that bad *really*.

The nuns are never particularly interested in punishing us. Not unless we get caught taking drugs or fighting in the corridor or smashing school property or something heinous like that. We all quite like the nuns, actually, mostly because they are very old and seem to live in their own little nun world, complete with its own sweet little cemetery.

Georgina threw the duvet over me and then pretended to tuck me in like Miss Cribbe. 'Now give my moustache a big sloppy kiss, Calypso dear.' She put loads of saliva on her lips so they glistened, and then puckered them up the way Miss Cribbe did.

After the lights were out I snuggled into the lovely, plain, white Egyptian cotton-covered duvet, said a few silent Hail Marys, and asked Mary if she would petition God on my behalf so that a horrific accident might befall my teen duvet (something more permanently destructive than Misty weeing on it) so that I could have a nice grown-up duvet like this one. Then I fell asleep.

That night, Star walked and talked in her sleep. It wasn't a new thing. As long as I've known Star she's talked in her sleep, although usually she only does it when she's at home. We woke up to find her sitting on Georgina's bed, babbling on about not wanting to die. Georgina helped me get her back into bed.

She was quite sweet about Star's sleepwalking, really, considering she'd been woken up. I would have expected her to go ballistic and scream about what a freak Star was, but all she did was giggle.

Maybe Star and I had got Georgina all wrong before, I mused as I drifted off to sleep.

But then Georgina whispered to me, 'Hey, Calypso. Tomorrow let's tell Star she was going on about pulling Professor Sullivan.'

SEVEN

Food Fight Fiasco

As it turned out, there was no time to tease Star for sleeptalking about Professor Sullivan, because the three of us slept through all six bells and finally Miss Cribbe came into our room bashing away on her wretched copper gong.

'Wakey, wakey, girls! Wakey, wakey!' She cried out in her special morning sing-song voice.

There was a mad scramble to dress, then we all clustered around the sink in our en-suite bathroom to clean our teeth before tearing down the stairs in time to grab a dry croissant each from the canteen. We shoved these in our pockets, planning to eat them surreptitiously during first period, which was English literature with Ms Topler. Yawn.

I swear, Ms Topler is the Antichrist of literature. Theoretically it should have been my favourite subject, given how I love reading and writing. I've had two letters published in *Teen Vogue*, but my dream is to write articles in the witty, satirical vein of Nancy Mitford or Dorothy Parker.

Ms Topler doesn't appreciate my wit or satire, though.

If anything she is ethically opposed to wit and satire. Where there is literary joy she can be relied upon to throw cold water on it through critical analysis, and if she happens to prescribe a classic like Simone de Beauvoir, you can rest assured she will slaughter it with one of her diabolical deconstructions.

She loved giving us tragic books to read, like *Little Women*, and as if this wasn't bad enough, she made us discuss them *ad nauseum* in class.

Every time I was about to put a piece of croissant in my mouth, she'd ask me something lame about the tragic Jo. I told her that 'despite an indefatigable independent streak, Jo was the classic L to the power of three – a Literary Lady Loser'.

I wasn't even trying to be funny, but Star and Georgina and a few other girls laughed – and no, not in a piss-take sort of way. Georgina's crowd were acting like I was actually one of the girls now, and then to top it off, Georgina announced that Tobias couldn't bear *Little Women* and had refused point blank to let her read it.

The class fell into paroxysms of mirth.

Ms Topler gave me a 'blue'.

A 'blue' handed out by a teacher means having to write lines like *I must pay closer attention in class* one hundred times or something annoying like that. It's called a blue because you write the lines on blue paper. Older girls can hand out blues too, but we could usually slack them down – although not when we were in the younger years. Once in Year Seven, Star tried to slack down one of the older girls who gave her a blue for something really minor, and the older girl reported her, then Star ended up having to write lines from six a.m. to seven a.m. (pre-breakfast lines have now been deemed too barbarically cruel, even for boarding school).

When we got lines we could petition Sister Constance and usually get a transmuted sentence – something really easy like sweeping the corridor. As Georgina pointed out, the best part of getting Sister Constance involved was that she always gave you a sweet as a reward afterwards – which sort of defeated the point of giving a punishment, but you don't need to be rational to be a teacher, or a nun.

Having missed breakfast, my mouth was watering at the thought of a Mars Bar.

By the time class was over I was starving and the already-stale croissant was a pile of flakes in my pocket. Our sadistic dorm matron was going to go mental when I put it in for wash if I didn't remember to get every minis-cule crumb out. I would try to remember to flush my pocket out tonight, but deep down I knew I would forget and get one of Matron's lectures about my manifest lack of wash-bag respect and how I would end up being ridiculed by my children – if I ever had the good fortune to have any, which she seriously doubted because what sort of man would want to marry a slattern like me, who eats food from her pocket?

Like I said, a sense of proportion isn't part of the job description for working at Saint Augustine's.

Because of the wretched Ms Topler keeping me back late in order to give me her stupid blue (Star and Georgina had both waited for me), we were late for everything and on the charge to the canteen at lunch, we were all clutching our stomachs with exaggerated hunger pains. Even though it was unprecedented, it just seemed natural to sit with Georgina and her group to eat. Georgina, Arabella and Clementine all seemed fine with that. Clemmie even squeezed over, practically sitting on Arabella's lap, so that we could all fit on the bench. Even Star seemed fine with it, but Honey glared at me when I sat down with my tray.

'Are you sure you have enough there, Calypso?' she asked nastily.

I had encouraged the dinner lady to pile the fish nuggets pretty high, because they were one of the few edible things they served at Saint Augustine's and I was famished.

Star grabbed one of the fish nuggets off my plate and threw it at Honey. She riposted with a chip. And that was it. The food fight was on . . .

Clementine tossed a broad bean from her salad at Arabella, who chucked it across at Star. Georgina wiped a glob of mayonnaise on my nose and I flicked a pile of peas at her with my spoon. Within seconds it was a free-for-all. Food was being pelted around the canteen by everyone.

We were told to report to Sister Constance in her office after supper.

Sister sat in silent prayer under the massive gruesome crucifix that loomed above her desk. Its ivory Christ with an enormous spear jutting out of his bleeding side always made me feel really guilty and a little scared. In this setting, Sister Constance looked quite scary too. Generally, she has a very stiff, formal manner (although sometimes you catch her suppressing a smile).

Her office was lined from floor to ceiling with holy texts. The ancient literary feel was rather spoiled by a nasty, grey metal filing cabinet, supporting an enormous wooden statue of Our Lady of Lourdes. I don't know why, but Sister Constance's office always smelled of an old church bible, that mixture of mustiness, wax, frankincense and furniture polish.

Seconds turned into minutes and I swear I heard Christ groan with the agony of it all as he hung from his cross. Although maybe it was just my tummy – I hadn't actually got to eat any of my fish nuggets, because of our food fight. And at supper they'd served us the grey slops, which I had vowed never to eat after a rumour went around the school that it was made from dead pets from the pet shed.

Eventually Sister broke her meditation. She looked up at the six of us standing in front of her table and told us how disappointed she was. We bowed our heads solemnly striking what we hoped was a remorseful pose.

'How wantonly wasteful to treat food in such a cavalier manner.'

'Yes, Sister,' we all said together.

'Did you even spare the slightest thought for the poor little hungry children of the world who haven't got enough food to fill their distended bellies?'

'Yes, Sister,' we repeated. I was looking out of the window and was slightly distracted by the sight of a group of girls heading off through the bluebells towards Puller's Hill.

But I was brought back to attention by Sister Constance, gasping in shock.

'Well, if you thought of those poor little hungry children and their desperate need for food, what possessed you to throw it about?'

We looked at one another, startled. Star spoke for all of us. 'We meant no, Sister.'

'No what?'

'No, we didn't spare the slightest thought for the poor little hungry children of the world who haven't got enough food to fill their distended bellies.'

'I thought as much,' she said with a sigh, disappointment etched in every line of her face. 'Your mother would be especially sorry to hear of you abusing food, when she does so much good work in her capacity as a senior fundraiser for War Children, Miss Castle Orpington.'

'Yes, Sister.'

'However, I can see you are all deeply ashamed about this affair now.'

'Yes, Sister,' we all agreed.

'Yes, Sister what?'

'Yes, Sister, we are deeply ashamed of ourselves.'

'Well then, let's press on. What do you think your punishment should be on this occasion?'

'We could . . . erm . . . sweep the corridor, or something nasty like that, Sister,' Star suggested.

'Actually, Star, that was going to be your punishment for cheeking Miss Cribbe last night. She was very upset about your suggestion that Misty may have been responsible for wetting Calypso's bed.'

Star didn't even struggle with herself. 'Sister, she wees all over the place.'

'Star!'

'It's true, Sister,' Georgina piped up. 'Mother says it's really unhygienic.'

'I've no doubt it would be if it were true, but then so is throwing food all over the canteen. No, I'm afraid sweeping the floor won't be a suitable penance for this severe wickedness. I've decided to assign you a special task.'

We looked at one another and swallowed. This sounded ominous.

Sister Constance went on. 'I want you to come up with some fundraising ideas for the Children of the World Charity. Last year, the Lower Sixth raised six thousand pounds. We're aiming to improve on that figure this year.'

We all weren't quite sure what to say – or what it meant. Even though six thousand pounds wouldn't even pay for a term's fees at Saint Augustine's, I knew it was a lot of money.

My parents are always going on about money. I am always reminding them that I wasn't the one who came up with the idea of flying across the world to an exorbitantly expensive boarding school – to which they always reply that nothing in life is really free. They say they are more than happy to make sacrifices in order to give me a rounded education, and if that means driving around in a crappy car and foregoing pools and holidays, it is a small price to pay. Parents have a very odd sense of logic.

Just the same, I realised that six thousand pounds was a

drop in the ocean compared to what it would take to help all the suffering children of the world.

'Here are some brochures to inspire you.' She pushed across some pamphlets that depicted sad-eyed children clustered around an empty bowl. I suddenly felt miserable and pointless as I scanned their hungry faces.

'Now, I know it's too soon for you to be thinking about gap years, but later on this week one of Saint Augustine's old girls will be visiting us and giving a talk at assembly about the wonderful inspirational opportunities that Raleigh International offer to girls like yourselves; opportunities to meet girls and boys from different backgrounds; opportunities to give something back.'

My stomach rumbled really loudly, which was desperately embarrassing given how I'd only missed lunch and these kids were like missing their whole lives, basically.

'That will be all, ladies,' said Sister Constance.

'Thank you, Sister,' we replied.

'Star, you will also have the duty of sweeping the Cleathorpes corridor.'

Damn, I thought, I'd forgotten to present my blue and now I'd missed my chance to transmute my lines to floor sweeping.

'Yes, Sister,' Star agreed, her eyes downcast – even though I knew she must be whooping it up inside because she didn't have to do six double sides of lines.

'I'll come and see you shortly, to see how you've got on.' (In other words, to bring you your Mars Bar.)

We backed out of her room, heads still bowed, the way

we'd been taught to when we first arrived at Saint Augustine's. Sometimes we did it to other teachers who weren't nuns, just to wind them up.

'This is so random,' Honey complained, once we were out of earshot.

'I think it could be quite fun,' Star argued. 'Doing something worthwhile.'

'Worthwhile?' said Honey. 'Are you insane? Rattling a tin around like a beggar. You are such a plebeian, Star.'

But Star wasn't backing down – she never does. 'No, think about it. We could do some really cool things, like have parties and stuff. I mean, it would be the perfect cover for all sorts of cool outings. And anyway, it would be for a good cause.'

Clementine had to agree, reluctantly. 'She's right. We could use it as an excuse to hire a minibus to take us to the Feather's Ball. We could raffle places on the bus.' So typical of Clemmie, who was the most boy-mad girl in our year. She rarely spoke unless there were boys around and even then she mostly only ogled and giggled.

'Whatever,' Star said dismissively. 'Personally I think the Feather's Ball is the lamest thing out. The bands they have . . . pah-lease!'

'Didn't stop you pulling that gross boy from Worth Abbey at the Valentine's Ball,' Honey riposted.

Star curled her upper lip and looked Honey up and down. 'I'm surprised you can remember, after all the vodka you drank. As I remember, you were staggering around cutting in on everyone. In fact hang on, I remember you cut in on me, *darling*, and pulled him yourself. But perhaps you were having one of your blackouts and don't recall.'

Honey was about to open her mouth when I heard someone say. 'Oh shut up both of you!' Actually in the brief silence that followed I realised that the words had come out of my mouth, but no one said anything. Instead Clemmie merely continued with her line of thought adding, 'We could charge some random amount like double or triple?'

The discussion went on and no one seemed to notice I was there. I felt completely invisible. Being the school freak and not having parents with a madly grand house in Chelsea, I'd never been to any of the Capital VIP balls. But I knew about them. In the weeks leading up to a ball, it was all anyone spoke of. The balls are usually held at the Hammersmith Palais or some other huge venue and they are a highlight of the boarding school calendar. Although no alcohol is allowed, only the boys are frisked, giving girls like Honey a free hand to smuggle in whatever they wanted. Absolutely everyone who matters goes to at least a few, because it's a great place to pull. There are bands and DJs, and goodie bags at the end. Even Star had been to one, although she said the tongue of the boy she kissed felt like a small fish. But I know she only said that to make me feel better.

'Charging more is a fab idea darling, actually we could charge different prices depending on how rich and important you are,' Arabella threw in. 'Although I do think the VIP balls are getting a little tired,' she added – for once agreeing with Star. By important, Arabella meant how many hyphens you had in your name. Her full name is

Arabella Basingdom-Morgan-Heigbrewer-Tomlinson-Protvost-Smith. But she just refers to herself as Arabella Smith, knowing full well that everyone knows the portentous enormity of her name.

Arabella flicked her mane of carefully highlighted blonde hair, and a strand of it stuck to my lip-gloss. I brushed it away and started applying more lip-gloss.

Georgina said, 'Or we could have pulling competitions!'

'Five-quid fine if you don't pull at least two boys at the Eades social.'

'Make that ten for everyone who doesn't pull a prince,' Honey added cattily, arching one of her professionally styled eyebrows. She was always going on about her Russian eyebrow stylist, as if she were some sort of guru or something.

'See you back at the dorms, I'm going down to check the post,' Arabella told us before dashing down the stairs.

'Grab mine, darling,' everyone called back, apart from Star and me.

Obviously Star didn't expect mail from parents who are perpetually stoned. My parents' excuse is that they are too modern and technologically aware to send 'snail mail', as they call it. They prefer to communicate with me by e-mail, which is so lame.

Honey's mother sent postcards of herself chatting to various celebrities, and Honey had them pinned all over her board. But you can't pin an e-mail to your board when you're homesick – which means that everyone thinks you're a sad loser whose parents don't love you.

EIGHT

The Royal Summons

As soon as we got back to Cleathorpes, Star went off to do her sweeping punishment and the rest of us slumped on Clementine's bed to consider the task Sister had given us.

'I suppose it could be a blessing,' Honey conceded eventually. 'An excuse to slack off on work.'

'Got any of those cool sweets from LA left, Calypso darling?' Georgina asked.

'Sure.'

I think Sister totally overreacted,' she sighed, pulling herself up from the bed. 'I mean, even my parents have food fights!'

I tried to imagine Sarah and Bob having a food fight, but couldn't – they are just way too Californian, and besides, they hate waste. 'Yaah, totally,' I agreed.

'You know, Tobias is growing quite fond of you, darling,' she confided as we walked off arm in arm down the corridor towards our dorm room to fetch the vodka and sweets.

'Yes, well, the affection is a . . . erm . . . a mutual-ish thing. I mean, I adore bears – well, most soft toys, actually.'

I honestly don't know how I let lame things like that escape from my mouth, but Georgina seemed to find this enormously funny and fell about laughing.

'You've got mail,' Arabella announced, in a bad impression of my accent, as she walked into our dorm room and tossed a FedEx package and a letter on to my lap.

Georgina looked up from her magazine. 'Oh fabbie! Is that from Jay, darling?' she asked, jumping on to the bed beside me.

I turned the package over and read the sender's address. It was my mom's office on the Paramount lot. 'Looks like it,' I replied casually.

Everyone clambered on to the bed as I tore into the package. Inside was a DVD of a movie that wasn't even out in the UK yet and a postcard of the Hollywood sign.

Wish you were here, babe!
L.O.L. Jay xxxxx

I wasn't too impressed by the 'babe' bit, but still, it had the required effect. Everyone went totally crazy about it and Clementine rushed off to show Antoinette, who had said she didn't believe I had a real boyfriend.

I didn't open the letter. Actually, I was so swamped with questions about Jay, I forgot all about it and then the study bell went and I had to run, leaving the letter abandoned on Clementine's bed.

Later that night, Georgina had a bubble bath that smelled all lovely and coconutty and we all sat on the edge of the bath or on stools around the bathroom for a confab about our charity fundraising. (The bubbles were very high.) We made a list of possible fundraising ideas. All of them included pulling boys, sweets and fags.

Honey continued to be quite prickly with me, but I decided to rise above it. Now I was at the centre of things, with a fit boyfriend, I could afford to be magnanimous.

When we came out of the bathroom, Star had the pile of sweets she'd received from Sister Constance laid out in front of her on her bed. Unfortunately, our room still stunk of wee so we sprayed everything with Febreze before piling our duvets on the floor for a vodka and sweet feast.

That was when Arabella came back from picking up her fags from her room. She was holding my letter.

'You left this on Clemmie's bed, darling,' she said, tossing it onto my lap.

So with my mouth bulging with chocolate I tore open the envelope. I had no idea who the letter was from, I couldn't place the distinctive, flowing writing. Inside was a single sheet of heavy parchment paper with the royal seal on the bottom.

Hi Calypso,
Great to meet you yesterday. Hope to see you at the social –
without your sabre!
Freddie x

'Who's it from?' Star enquired, passing me her mug for

a sip of vodka. She always mixed hers with warm milk so it didn't taste so yucky. We were allowed to keep milk and biscuits and other snacks in the small kitchen of Cleathorpes. We were even allowed to make ourselves toast, which Georgina did regularly – only not for herself, obviously ('Think of the carbs, darling'). No, she fed the toast and marmalade to Tobias ('He simply adores it, darling, and you know how he can't *bear* the food they feed him in the canteen!')

The milk was an inspired idea, though, because if Miss Cribbe burst in Star would just show her the milk and say something really innocent like, 'I find it really helps me sleep, Miss Cribbe.'

Miss Cribbe just loves us when we act babyish.

I stared at the letter for some time. My mind had gone totally blank. I reread it a few times before it all sank in and then I dropped the letter onto my lap in a daze. Prince Freddie had written to me? A mere mortal?

Star grabbed the letter and read it out loud before I could stop her.

To be fair, she knew what a horrible thing she'd done before she'd read out his name, but it was too late – the damage was done.

'You complete and utter slut,' Honey shouted, pulling her head back in from the window where she'd been blowing out her cigarette smoke. Then she came over and slapped me hard across the face.

Even Georgina looked horrified.

Star screamed at her, 'What the hell do you think you're doing? Get out, you absolute bitch!'

I started to cry. I couldn't help it. It was all just too much. One minute I was the envy of all, with my fake boyfriend, the next minute I was being vilified because an HRH fancied me. Also, my face stung. I'd never been slapped before.

Honey was just standing there, and I was worried she wanted to have an all out fight, so I was glad when Georgina said, 'Look, Honey, I think you should leave.'

Honey flounced out of the room, followed by Georgina, Arabella and Clementine. Clemmie cast me a sympathetic look, but I threw myself onto my bed and sobbed.

Star was really sweet and said I should have been singing from the rooftops, having received a summons from royalty.

She was the best friend ever and suddenly I felt really guilty about ever wanting to be in with the cool girls and making her put up with Honey and the others, just to satisfy my egotistical wishes.

I'd actually started to think that Georgina might not be so bad. And not just because she called me darling, but it seemed like she understood my humour, and she'd helped me out with my bedding when Misty had weed all over it. God, I was so stupid.

'I'm really sorry about reading out the letter,' Star told me.

'It's OK. You weren't to know.'

She passed me some lip-gloss. 'Wear your pain like lip-gloss . . . Besides, you've still got me.' We had a big cuddle. 'And Jay!'

But that just made me start crying again.

'Calypso, it isn't that bad really. Who cares about bloody Honey?'

'It's not that,' I told her, trying not to cry any more. 'It's Jay.'

'What? You're not being paranoid, are you? Seriously, he just wrote to you! He must really like you.'

'I'm not being paranoid,' I told her. And then it all came tumbling out. 'He's my mom's gay PA.'

And then she cuddled me even harder, only it was wobbly sort of cuddle because she was laughing so hard. 'You are so mad! Gay?'

She was laughing so hard now that she fell on the floor. 'Gay Jay, your mum's PA!'

And then even I had to laugh, because I hadn't realised how it all rhymed before. After that, I told her the whole tragic tale of my pathetic attempt to fit in with Georgina and her cool pod of friends. Star didn't get it – well, I didn't expect she would – but I felt better having told her, although I was now petrified that someone would walk in and hear her singing, 'Gay Jay, my *mom's* PA,' which I couldn't get her to stop doing for ages.

Eventually I turned the conversation around to parents generally, and Star did her impression of her parents and their friends when they were stoned. 'You know . . . like, stop crying, man – you're freaking me out.'

It all felt so comfortable, Star and I alone and just being how we'd always been, that I almost forgot about Honey and the trouble I was going to be in. But then Star reminded me by asking what I planned to do. We both knew bad things were about to happen.

It is a law at Saint Augustine's that you don't pull boys that other girls have already declared their territory – especially when that girl is Honey O'Hare. In a school where bitchiness is a currency, Honey was filthy rich. I had seen her destroy girls in the past.

When we were in Year Nine, a girl from Year Seven called Josephine annoyed Honey by being disrespectful towards her. I don't even know what she said, but Honey mounted a relentless campaign against her and pretty soon Josephine was crying herself to sleep every night. By the end of term she was self-mutilating – cutting herself with blades from the art room. The school tried to get her parents to visit her more to reassure her, but they refused, saying, Josephine would just have to deal with the problem, which even the meanest teacher in the school would agree was really mean. Eventually the school suggested to her parents that Josephine might not be suited to boarding school life.

Honey went around the school with a big grin on her face for weeks after that. I was pretty sure I didn't have the guts to self-mutilate, being as grossed out by blood as I am, but I was definitely going to be crying myself to sleep.

It wasn't long before Honey came screaming back into the room, shrieking at the top of her voice, 'You are so dead, bitch!'

Then she grabbed the letter from Freddie and tore it into about a million pieces. OK, maybe not a million – but only because she didn't get the chance. Georgina managed to grab it from her, so she only managed to tear it in half.

Arabella, Star and Clementine pulled her off me,

because by then she had grabbed my head and started pulling my hair out, while spitting obscenities into my face and telling me about the various painful ways I was going to be murdered.

A crowd of girls was gathering outside in the corridor, trying to catch a glimpse of what was going on. I was rubbing my head and trying to gather my thoughts together, when Misty came in and started barking. Shortly after that, Miss Cribbe came in with her knitting and threw everyone out of the room, apart from Star, Georgina and me.

Misty squatted as if about to wee, and Miss Cribbe shooed her out too and went bright red. If Misty hadn't done that, I am pretty sure we would have been in big trouble.

My mobile started ringing, but Miss Cribbe took it from me before I could answer it, saying that it was time for lights out – even though it was only nine-thirty and lights out was officially meant to be ten! None of us argued, though.

I couldn't get to sleep that night.

'Are you awake?' Georgina asked me after the lights had been out for a while.

My head was still hurting from Honey pulling my hair and I could still feel the sting of the slap on my cheek. Georgina was Honey's best friend and I couldn't help being a bit scared of what she might say or do. So I didn't say anything.

Georgina went on. 'Personally, I think Honey is over-reacting, darling.'

Her words seemed to echo in my head. I thought of all the benchmark moments of the term – how she'd called me darling, stood up for me, given me her duvet when Misty weed on mine. Then I recalled all the other benchmark moments of my time at Saint Augustine's and the way Georgina and Honey had isolated me so terribly and made me feel like the school freak.

Star was muttering in her sleep.

'Darling?' Georgina repeated.

I suppose I took it as a good sign that at least she was still deigning to call me darling.

'I didn't ask him to write to me,' I explained. 'It's not my fault. Can't you make Honey see that?'

'Arabella told me about the whole duelling thing you had with him.'

'But I didn't ask him to write!' I repeated.

For a long time she didn't say anything and I was left hanging by a thread, afraid of being back in the freak seat again.

'Honey has a lot of issues,' she said, after what seemed like half an hour – I'd almost fallen asleep. 'Seriously . . . a lot of issues.'

Hello, like I hadn't noticed! The insane bitch had just tried to murder me. 'Oh, I didn't know,' I replied softly.

'Yaah, there's all sorts of stuff going on between her mum and her latest step-dad to be, Lord Aginet.'

Good. A part of me was glad she was having a horrible time of it at home. 'Oh, that's sad,' I said.

'But Arabella and Clementine stood up for you, darling.'

I tried not to make too much of the fact that she hadn't added herself to that list and just said, 'That's sweet of them.' Then I thought, Well, maybe I'm overreacting. Maybe it would be all right. Maybe I wouldn't be totally vilified by everyone in my year and be forced to hide in cupboards for the rest of term. Maybe I would go to the social, pull Freddie and be the envy of everyone. Maybe I would be accepted for who I was and judged by more important things than my accent.

'Obviously, you still can't go to the social, though, darling.'

'Oh.'

'Yaah. Also, darling, if you did go, Honey would so totally kill you.'

The fact that she'd called me darling didn't dilute the poison in her words. 'Oh?'

'My advice is be sick and spend the night in the infirmary.'

Be sick or be dead is what she meant.

NINE

The Fine Line Between Pleasure and Pain

The next morning I woke up with a pounding head and it wasn't just because Miss Cribbe had banged her wretched gong for ten minutes while I tried to hide under my duvet.

I always get the most horrendous headaches before my period's due. Eventually Miss Cribbe decided I wasn't faking it – or maybe her own head had started to ache from her gonging – so she sent me down to the infirmary where the much-hated Sister Dumpster (real name Sister Dempster) was no doubt waiting to torture me or poison me (depending on how sadistic she was feeling).

There are two sisters in charge of the infirmary: Sister Dumpster (not a nun, but an actual professional nurse who specialised in the demeaning and torturing of poorly children), and dear little Sister Regina (an actual nun) who handed out the Co-codamol like there was no tomorrow.

My mom says you shouldn't take more than six pills in a twenty-four hour period and that actually it's not even an over-the-counter medication in the States. But Sister Regina says 'pish' to that, and plies you with them until you feel better again.

Sister Dumpster says 'pish' to the six-a-day rule as well. In fact, she says 'pish' to Co-codamol altogether. She did her nursing training in an era when child cruelty and sadism were in their heyday: 'A temperature of one hundred and fifty degrees? Why, that's nothing. In my day we said 'tish-tosh' to a temperature like that. These days, you girls want it all your own way,' etc, etc, *ad nauseum*.

For some reason Sister Dumpster is *always* on duty when I am sent to the infirmary.

But miracles do happen (as Sister Constance is always reminding us) and it wasn't Sister Dumpster that morning, it was sweet little Sister Regina.

'Poor Miss Kelly, now you just lie down here, and I'll get you a sanitary napkin and some Co-codamol.'

She tucked me up in one of the horrendously uncomfortable infirmary beds, which I'm convinced are all from World War II and still smell of sick soldiers. The springs in them are so ancient, and make so much noise that you can't relax, let alone sleep.

Whenever you go to the infirmary for period pain, the sisters insist on handing out these pads that look like skis. The story is that the nuns were given shed-loads of them in the last century, and they are still trying to get through them all. Seriously though, you could go white-water rafting on them they are so enormous.

In the Easter break I'd finally got the hang of tampons, but I wasn't going to discuss such modern advances in personal hygiene with Sister Regina, who probably wasn't even aware that they'd been invented.

I said thank you and gave her a hug, because she was just trying to be sweet, and nun hugs are so lovely, smelling as nuns do of incense and the flowers that they pick to decorate the chapel and the gazillion statues of Mary and Jesus that are dotted about the school.

After I'd knocked back my pills and my headache had subsided, Sister Regina gave me another one of her little hugs and said I may as well miss the morning classes and rest until lunch break. I think she was feeling a bit bored so together we read the copy of *Teen Vogue* that I'd brought back from LA, and she said how none of the models could touch me for looks and poise.

The nuns love the word 'poise'. Maybe because it is one of the few things they were able to hang on to when they gave up everything – like make-up and cool shoes – when they took their vows. Still, it was very sweet of her to say (even if it wasn't true).

She said she found it perplexing that any girl would want a job like that – standing about all day having her picture taken.

Actually, she's probably right. I don't suppose it would be nice being a model, apart from the money side of it, of course, although apparently lots of models make virtually nothing – just like actresses in LA. Also, I bet you'd always be worried about people saying mean things about your weight, or saying your nose was too big. Though according to Star they airbrush out all your nasty bits –

and Kate Moss might be the size of a house, for all we know.

I eventually left Sister Regina just before the bell rang for lunch, and took a detour via the pet shed so I could have a quick cuddle with Arabesque. I always felt a bit disloyal going to visit Arabesque, because I knew Star would rather my affections lay with Hilda and Brian. But the truth is, I much prefer cuddly rabbits to rats and snakes.

I did check on Hilda, though, who was running along on her little rat wheel in her usual demented fashion. But, honestly, how excited can you get about a rat? Star goes on and on about how intelligent rats are and I'm sure she's right, but I wasn't really looking for witty repartee from a pet, so I moved swiftly on to the rabbit area where Arabesque was softly sleeping. See, that's what so sweet about rabbits – they do everything so softly.

At least I thought he was asleep, until I took him out and held him to me. Instead of his lovely, warm, little body wriggling against me, he was all cold and stiff.

I gasped and put him straight back in the cage, and ran to the canteen, bumping into everyone and knocking over trays in my search for Georgina.

'Georgina,' I panted when I finally found her. 'You have to come. It's Arabesque!'

Honey glared at me. 'You are so dead, Calypso. I've told Poppy what you did. She's going kill you.'

Poppy is Honey's older sister and, if anything, even meaner than Honey. She's stunning-looking and always appears in the social pages under the name of The Honourable Poppy O'Hare – although she always makes a massive fuss over how she told the journalists she didn't want them to use her title. Yeah right, whatever. The boys at Eades went potty for her, but as Star reminded me, it was probably not her personality that they were going potty over.

But I didn't care. I had to tell Georgina about Arabesque, that was all that mattered.

Georgina said, 'Just chill out, will you, Honey?' but she didn't look up at me; she just moved some peas around her plate dismally. I could tell that a decision had been made regarding my standing in the group. I was definitely out. Honey had won. Last night when she'd told me that she thought Honey was overreacting, I'd more or less taken a kind of cold comfort from her words. I'd told myself that although she'd have to stand by Honey because, after all, they'd been friends forever, at least she'd criticised Honey and acknowledged that her behaviour was out of order.

But now, as I looked around the group I'd naïvely imagined I'd become part of, I saw how stupid I'd been. Maybe Georgina did sort of like me. Maybe she'd decided I wasn't really that bad, but at the end of the day Honey was of her world and scored ten out of ten when it came to cool. However nice my American sweets tasted, I was still considered a freak. And besides, I was almost out of Hershey's Kisses.

Then Poppy came over to the table. 'Hey, American Freak,' she said, slapping a Post-it Note on my back. I knew it was a Post-it Note, because I was always getting them slapped on me. Usually they said random stuff like

AMERICAN FREAK or just plain *FREAK*. But when I reached my arm around and pulled this particular one off, it said, *DEAD*.

The word 'dead', combined with the experience of finding poor little Arabesque, made my eyes fill up with tears. I wiped them away with my sleeve. Georgina and Arabella turned away, as if embarrassed.

'Georgina,' I said again, a wobble in my voice now.

'There's nothing I can do, really, Calypso,' she snapped, not even looking up as she twirled her peas.

'Oh, is poor little American Freak girl crying?' Honey asked, in a baby voice.

Georgina looked up at Honey and shook her head as if to say 'that's enough'. I could tell she was in conflict over Honey's behaviour, so I took my chance and asked if maybe I could have a word with her alone, but she said that she was too busy.

Peas can be very demanding.

I couldn't just leave it, though. I couldn't go through the day knowing Arabesque was lying there dead in his cage and not tell Georgina. Whether we were friends or not I had to tell her, and I had to tell her now.

It was awful. I shuffled about for a bit and said 'erm' a few times but in the end, as another Post-it Note was slapped on my back, I just blurted it out: 'Arabesque is dead.' Then I started crying, and then, after looking at me for what seemed like forever, Georgina started crying too and Arabella put her arms around her and gave her a cuddle.

Clemmie arrived with her tray laden down with the usual slops and asked what the matter was.

Honey rolled her eyes and said, 'Georgina's rabbit's dead,' like it was no big deal.

By now our little group had become the lunchtime spectacle. Star arrived and she must have been to the pet shed already because all she said was, 'Oh, I guess you all know, then.'

'Oh Georgie,' Clemmie said and gave her a cuddle.

Georgina was really sobbing now and I think I might have been too, but I was too shocked by what Honey said next to really remember.

'Honestly, I don't know what all the fuss is about. I mean, he was quite old, darling. Actually, I always thought he was a bit manky. Besides, Daddy can buy you a new one. A better one.'

I couldn't believe it – Honey was meant to be Georgina's best friend!

Georgina looked up and for a second I thought she was going to throw herself on Honey and rip her hair out. But Honey had started to file her talons with an emery board. When she eventually looked up and saw the look of thunder on Georgina's face, she seemed genuinely perplexed.

'What?'

'You are such a bitch.' Georgina spat the words out at her best friend.

Everyone looked at Honey who blinked innocently and said, 'What?', as if she had no idea that she was the spawn of Satan. Eventually everyone just shook their heads, like people do over lost causes, and silently filed out of the canteen, leaving their trays on the table.

Even Star went with them.

I was left alone with the bitch from hell.

'God, you're a freak,' she said with a sneer, and picked a chip off her plate and nibbled at it in her special way so that her lips didn't touch it.

I didn't really feel hungry now and I didn't want to spend another second around Honey, so I left the canteen without eating and chased after the others.

When I got to the pet shed, Star was stroking Arabesque's still little body.

'Oh no, Arabie!' Georgina was screaming while the others held her back. Georgina's cry was so sad that I wanted to give her a hug, like Arabella and Clemmie were doing, but I wasn't sure if she'd want to be touched by an American freak, so I just said, 'Oh Georgina, I'm so sorry.' It sounded a bit lame, I know, but Georgina pulled herself away from the others and threw her arms around my neck. She sobbed and sobbed and sobbed until I thought she would die of dehydration.

'I really loved Arabesque,' I said. 'He was by far the sweetest rabbit in the whole shed and I used to come and see her and cuddle him. I knew you would hate me if I told you, but . . .'

'I don't hate you,' Georgina said. 'Oh, Arabie.'

It was only when Sisters Hillary and Veronica passed by and asked us what had happened that I realised I was sobbing just as hard as Georgina.

Star told them how she had come to the pet shed to see Hilda and noticed that Arabesque wasn't moving. Sisters Hillary and Veronica gave us all comforting little nun hugs.

'You poor dear girls,' they clucked, as if we were only five years old. 'Oh poor, poor, poor little things.' Then they said we should all say a special prayer for Arabesque, '. . . even though we know that bunnies don't actually have souls.'

So we all said a Hail Mary and a Glory Be To The Father and somehow that seemed to calm us down a bit.

The rest of the day was pure hell.

The death of Arabesque did nothing to dilute Poppy and Honey's Post-it Note campaign. Between every class my back was plastered with variations of the *YOU ARE SO DEAD, CALYPSO* theme. But all I could really think about was poor Georgina, and how horrible it had been holding Arabesque's still, cold body in my arms.

Georgina didn't eat anything for dinner that night and, because she hadn't been ticked off for leaving her tray at lunchtime, she was sent to the infirmary for a lecture from Sister Dumpster about the dangers of anorexia.

That evening, during study period, Star wrote me a note and slipped it in my English book.

I hope Georgina's eating disorder doesn't come back!

I hadn't thought of that, but it made me a bit worried. I gave her a nod and tore the note into a million pieces and threw it in the bin so no one would see it.

TEN

The Fall-Out

'I think we should bury him as soon as possible,' I suggested, while we sat in our room waiting for Georgina to return from the infirmary. 'I just can't bear to think of him lying dead in her cage.'

'Yaah. It must be really upsetting for the other pets too,' Star added. 'I mean, I got a feeling from Hilda that she was devastated, you know?'

As far as I had noticed Hilda had been frantically racing along on her little wheel, looking as if she didn't have a care in the world, but I said, 'Exactly.'

'Should we go and speak to Sister Constance about having a funeral for him, do you think?' Star suggested. 'I could make a little cross for his grave.'

There was a pet cemetery in Phipp's Forest, but none of us ever went there because it was just too sad.

'That's really kind. I mean, I know Georgina is a bit of a . . .'

'I don't know, she's not that bad, I suppose . . .' Star said. 'She's growing on me. I get the feeling that Honey wields a lot of influence over her . . . Should we ask Sister if we can hold a funeral?'

'Animals don't have souls, remember, girls,' I replied, mimicking the nuns.

Star riposted, 'Oh, bollocks to that,' just as Sister Constance walked in the room with Georgina.

'Thank you, Star. You're right, Calypso, animals don't have souls, so there will be no funeral. But nonetheless, we will be holding the usual burial-blessing ceremony tomorrow at break for Arabesque. We think it would be a nice way for Georgina and her friends to say a final goodbye to her pet. Father Conran will preside over the blessing.'

'Thank you, Sister,' Star and I said.

Georgina didn't say anything. She didn't look very well. Her eyes were puffy and her face was all red. Sister Constance put her arm around her in the stiff, awkward sort of way that she has.

'We'll have to arrange for a coffin,' Georgina said, speaking for the first time.

Honey came in then, and I noticed that Georgina didn't even look at her, even though Honey reached out and held her hand. 'Why don't you bury her in her LVT pet carrier? They're kind of last term anyway, darling. Then we can buy those cute carriers that Prada are doing. We could even get those really cool, pink rabbits that they've bred now. Wouldn't that be fab, darling? I'm quite bored with Claudine anyway, so I'll give her away to one of the younger girls and get one of the pink ones too – or maybe mauve. Mauve is so *now*!' She said all this in the same, over-excited, high-pitched voice she had when she discussed handbags and shoes.

Georgina shook Honey's hand away like it was diseased. 'You just don't get it, do you? Arabesque was my best friend, not a fashion accessory, and now he's dead and you're acting like he was just a pair of bloody shoes! You are such a bitch, Honey. I totally hate you.' Then she started to cry again.

Sister Constance spoke in her Mother Superior voice, which always makes my knees go a bit trembly. 'Now, that is quite enough, girls. I appreciate that this is an emotional time for you, Miss Castle Orpington, dealing with the loss of Arabesque, but screaming at your friends is not going to help.

'As for you, Miss O'Hare, I would like you to go straight to the chapel and pray to the Sacred Heart of Jesus for the mercy you clearly require in order to enable you to empathise more appropriately with your friend's sad loss.'

Honey rolled her eyes and said, 'Whatever', and then stormed off.

I didn't know what to say to Georgina after that, but then I knew saying nothing would be really lame, so I was pleased when Clemmie and Arabella and a whole pile of other girls poured into our room to comfort her.

Honey slunk in later, and I think she realised that we were all really upset and that she wasn't going to be very welcome, but I was still surprised when she said, 'Oh, by the way, Calypso darling, you can borrow my Juicy Couture dress for the Eades social, if you like. I'm guessing you've got nothing cool enough to wear of your own.'

I did my goldfish impression for a bit before saying, 'Erm, yaah, that would be great, thanks.'

But then Star said, 'Oh, piss off, Honey. As if Calypso would want to borrow one of your slutty toff dresses.'

I could have killed Star just then. I mean, I had *no* cool dresses – well, nothing cool enough to wear to the Eades social anyway. Also, the fact that Honey was no longer talking about killing me, but actually offering me a cool outfit to wear to an event she had previously banned me from attending, was nothing short of a miracle.

'Fine,' Honey replied casually. 'I just thought you'd look really cool in it, darling.'

Huh? Did Honey just call me darling? Was I in a parallel universe here? I knew she had to be up to something, but I figured it was her way of getting back into Georgina's good books by not acting like a complete bitch.

'Erm, is it the baby-blue one, with the strappy bits?' I enquired, as nonchalantly as I could.

'That's it. You've got the figure to carry it off, darling.'

I had the figure to carry off one of Honey O'Hare's outfits? I was stunned. I simply couldn't respond.

'Anyway, it's too last term for me,' she added. 'I'm wearing my new Earl jeans with the real diamond-studded Dior top.'

Of course she was.

'Oh, thanks,' I replied, almost relieved by her bitchy comment. It was just too bizarre having Honey being nice to me. It made my skin crawl.

I could feel Star's stare piercing through me, but I

ignored it as Honey flicked her hair back over her shoulder and said, 'Fine, darling, no biggie,' and flounced out of the room without another word.

That evening we were all so emotionally drained that we couldn't even summon the energy to collect our mobiles from Miss Cribbe. I guess she must have felt a bit sorry for us, though, because she bustled in with them in her arms, which was unheard of. Most of the girls had two mobiles; a declared mobile, which they handed in before lights out and picked up after study period, and another one (their really, really cool, madly expensive ones that took photographs and everything) that they kept with them at all times. Sadly, I only had one mobile, more of a brick than a phone but Miss Cribbe returned it to me kindly as if it were a holy relic.

Everyone immediately started dialling friends and checking messages on their microscopic, fourth-generation, trendy phones.

I noticed that Georgina didn't even pick hers up.

I checked my voicemail messages on the brick and the clear tones of Prince Freddie announced, in a jokey, uncannily good New York gangster accent: 'So, Foxy, you don't call, you don't write, you don't come see me no more. Am I not good enough for you? You don't want your old Freddie no more?'

I tried not to laugh, but I couldn't help myself.

'Was that *him*?' Georgina asked, suddenly bright-eyed.

'Yaah,' I admitted, casually.

'Are you really missing him, then?' she asked kindly. I realised then that she meant Jay.

'Actually, it was Freddie.'

Star said, 'You are kidding!' only I could tell she wasn't surprised because she winked at me as she grabbed hold of my mobile and replayed the message before I could stop her. Then she cracked up laughing and suddenly Georgina grabbed the phone and even she laughed. Then it did the rounds of the dorm rooms on our floor, with everyone chipping in the thirty pence it cost to call my mobile phone voicemail messaging service.

It was the first time at Saint Augustine's that anyone had wanted to pay for a listen to one of my messages. Even Star had passed around listens once when her father had Ozzy Osbourne call her up to wish her happy birthday.

Later, when Star and I were cleaning our teeth, I wondered aloud how Prince Freddie had got my number.

Star gave my mirrored-reflection a guilty look.

'What?' I asked.

'Are you annoyed with me?' she asked, as if she actually thought I might be. 'He asked me at fencing,' she explained, 'and, well . . .'

But I didn't let her finish. I wrapped her in a big cuddle and lifted her off the ground with excitement.

Prince Freddie had called me. Oh my God. Oh my God.

When we were tucked up in bed and the lights were out, Georgina said, 'I guess this means you're going to the social after all, darling.'

'I guess,' I agreed, trying to keep the excitement out of my voice.

'Tobias is *so* relieved, darling. He said he simply couldn't bear it if you didn't go.'

Then, just as I was dropping off to sleep, I felt someone sit on my bed, 'Calypso,' Georgina whispered. 'Promise me one thing.'

'What?'

'I know I shouldn't say this, because, well, Honey's been my friend for ever, but darling, promise me you won't trust her.'

'OK,' I agreed, carefully – not that I was ever likely to trust someone like Honey anyway. But I couldn't get to sleep for ages after that. What had compelled Georgina to say that? Was she actually worried about me, or worried that I'd become Honey's friend and that she'd lose her? I decided I'd ask Star what she thought in the morning. But one thing was definite, Georgina clearly wasn't the massive fan of Honey that I'd always taken her for.

ELEVEN

The Burial of Arabesque

The burial ceremony was really lovely, even though it was raining quite hard and we all had to huddle under big black umbrellas that the nuns just seemed able to produce like magic from nowhere.

It took place in Phipp's Forest, near the hockey fields, in a little glade where all the dead pets of Saint Augustine's have been buried over the years. The forest smelled of damp oak trees, which gave the occasion a sort of sacred atmosphere. I think we all felt it.

All the dead pets in the cemetery have little wooden crosses above their graves, and some of the crosses are painted in bright colours. All of them bear the pet's name, and have *RIP* written above.

Star had made a cross for Arabesque, painted it black and written Arabesque's name in white, swirly Arabic sort of writing – only in English obviously because none of us can read Arabic. Most of us have enough trouble with our French and Latin.

Several of the the nuns (or, as we say, a flock of nuns)

were there and we all held hands, umbrellas touching, while Father Conran stood saint-like in the rain in all his vestments and said a few prayers and sprinkled holy water over us.

Mr Morton, the groundsman, wore a black overall for the occasion rather than his standard grey, although his solemn attire was slightly spoiled by his umbrella which was a bright green contraption with *Heineken* written on it in white lettering. However, he had taken the trouble to find black satin ribbons to lower the cardboard box containing Arabesque into a hole he had dug earlier that morning. That's one of the things I love about being a Catholic – we do have a great sense of occasion and ceremony.

As the little coffin disappeared into the freshly dug earth we sang Arabesque's favourite song, which was actually a pop song by Robbie Williams, so not really sad-sounding in the least. None of the nuns knew the words, so they just sang 'la, la, la, diddlie-dee' in their funny little nun-like way, but we all cried, because . . . well, you just do.

Even Honey, who was holding Claudine, looked really upset – although knowing Honey, that could have been eyedrops. Afterwards we all went back to the convent where the nuns live and had a little wake. We're often invited over for tea and it's always fun, mostly because they treat us like we're the most exciting people in the world.

They served us the sort of food you usually see at tiny children's parties – sandwiches, butterfly cakes, fairy bread and lemonade. And they didn't even make a fuss when Claudine threw up a gherkin all over their sofa.

* * *

That afternoon, one of Saint Augustine's Old Girls came to the school chapel to give us a talk on Raleigh International and the gap year possibilities available to Upper Sixth students. She had really long, dark hair, a gorgeous tan and showed us slides of the school she was helping to build in Africa.

It wasn't a bit like the boring talks we usually get, because she had all these really funny stories about the different children and the mad things that had happened while they'd been building the school and how, even though the children were really poor, they were all still into a lot of the same things as we were.

She said that she had shown them pictures of Saint Augustine's and they were really envious, or maybe just incredulous, of our art room facilities. She had even brought a painting they'd done of their class in Gambia.

Sister Hillary and Sister Veronica carried the painting into the hall. It was so bright and funny, done in a cartoon style, with all their names scrawled across the bottom of each of their faces in graffiti-style writing. I couldn't believe how cool it looked. I mean, they didn't even have walls on their school, let alone the luxuries we take for granted – like television, mobile phones and computers.

It made me feel pathetic in comparison, trying to change my life by inventing a fake boyfriend for myself – a gay one at that. When we were filing out of assembly, Star and I discussed what we would do in our gap year. Honey interrupted, bragging that her mother had already arranged for her to do a three month stint at Condé Naste.

'That's what I love about you, Honey,' said Star, 'your incredible desire to look beyond your own tiny little pointless world! Maybe they'll have you research a piece on distributing make-up tips to the starving!'

As ever, I was awed by Star's ability to carve Honey up fearlessly, but most of all I was surprised that Clemmie and Arabella and a few other girls who'd overheard actually giggled.

Honey's face turned puce and I could tell that she wanted to give Star a slap, but Georgina intercepted by reminding us that our gap years were at least three years away whereas we were already late for Latin.

I wrote a chatty letter to Freddie in Latin class when I should have been translating Cicero. I thanked him for his call and told him about how Sister had handed down this mad punishment to raise money after we'd had a food fight. I didn't mention how it started or anything like that. I made it sound as madly amusing, enthralling and exotic as I could. I deliberated forever over whether to sign it *love* Calypso or *from* Calypso and opted for just *Calypso* so I wouldn't sound too desperate.

After study, when Star was off buying sweets at the tuck shop and Georgina was having a shower, I lay on my bed and wondered how I would cope if my parents were killed in a war and I had to rebuild my life with mud bricks and humanitarian aid.

I looked at the photographs I had put up of Jay. I know they had worked in a way, but it was all a lie and it wasn't me. I felt so angry with myself that I tore them down and shoved them in the rubbish bin. I reached under my pillow for my copy of Nancy Mitford's *Love in a Cold Climate* and began to read it for about the hundredth time.

Nancy Mitford survived the war and grew up in an even madder family than Star's. Her father had hunted her and her sisters and brother with hounds. But even while the bombs fell all over London, she had managed to write books. That's what I wanted to do – to *write*.

My other favourite writer, Dorothy Parker, also endured a horrendous childhood – her mother died when she was young, and later her brother died on the *Titanic*, but by the age of twenty-one she was working for *Vanity Fair*.

Then it hit me. Where would I be at twenty-one if all I focused on was fitting in with a cool pod of girls? I should be focusing on what I really wanted. I wanted to write and read and fence, and be accepted for who I actually *was*, rather than making myself fit into the world of posh toffs. But, OK, I thought . . . I *would* quite like to pull a boy or two or three.

I snuggled down under my duvet, but that was when I noticed that as well as the sound of water running in the shower, there was the unmistakable noise of Georgina throwing up her dinner.

I got up and tried to open the door to the en-suite. It was locked so there was nothing I could actually do. I just sat there and waited dismally with my book on my lap, looking out over the oak trees of Puller's Woods while Georgina heaved and heaved and heaved some more.

It sounded horribly painful. Finally she stopped and I heard her flush the loo. She came out with a cheerful look on her face and asked me what I was reading.

I desperately wanted to say something, but I still hadn't thought of the right words. I didn't want to sound like a teacher or a community nurse or something lame like that.

I wished that Star were here because she would definitely know what to say. In the end I asked her if she was OK in a breezy casual sort of way and she said, 'Of course I'm OK – why wouldn't I be?' in a pissed off, back-off-and-how-dare-you-even-speak-to-me? sort of way.

'No reason,' I replied and pretended to be engrossed in my book.

Then suddenly she said, 'Oh, I love Nancy Mitford!' as if the last ten minutes or so hadn't happened. 'Don't you just love *A Talent to Annoy*, darling?'

'Adore it,' I agreed, going along with her denial, and then rambling on in that way I have when I am nervous. Then out of my mouth came the words that would change everything and I heard myself saying, 'I'd love to write . . .' before I could stop.

'Well, why don't we, darling? Start a writing salon, I mean?'

I looked at her, stunned. 'You mean like the Algonquin Round Table? Erm, I don't think we could actually scratch enough girls together to go around a table.'

'No, I mean like the Hons,' she said, referring to a code word in Nancy Mitford's book used to describe a secret society the Mitford children had when they were young. A gathering of the favoured few who would sit in the closet, heated by the boiler, and talk irreverently about everything from life to death and beyond. 'Don't you think it a fabulous idea, darling?'

'Do you really think it would work?' I asked, still amazed at the sudden change in Georgina's mood, not to mention the fact that we seemed to share an interest. I mean, minutes before, I'd been considering speaking to Sister Dumpster about her throwing up and now, here she was, babbling away about a writing salon.

Georgina laughed and sat on the bed beside me. 'Oh darling, we simply must. I need something to cheer me up.'

I definitely agreed with that, anyway.

Miss Cribbe wandered past and said, 'Well, aren't we all the best of friends today then, girls?' and we fell apart laughing – more about the way she said it rather than what she had said. But I suppose that was when it really struck me that Georgina and I were sort of becoming friends. And that even though up until recently, it had been Georgina and her type that had made my life at Saint Augustine's sheer hell, I was seeing another side of her now. Maybe she was seeing another side of me too? Or maybe it was only when she wasn't around Honey that she was the Georgina I liked.

Whatever the reason I wasted no time in agreeing to the salon and insisting we try and find members immediately.

'Well, there's already the six of us,' she pointed out. 'Our dorm room and Honey's dorm room.'

All of a sudden a feeling of doom swept over me. The thought of having anything more to do with Honey filled me with horror. And I could just imagine Star's reaction.

TWELVE

The Lit Chick Salon

We held our first salon later that evening after lights out, by torchlight. As I'd predicted, Star confided in me while we cleaned our teeth that she had her doubts about being stuck in a writing salon with Honey. Actually what she said was, 'Are you dead or just mad? Hell can freeze over and Miss Cribbe can be made Queen but there's no way I am going to be part of a group with that evil bitch.'

I pleaded and did my jokey sad face – the one where I let the toothbrush hang limply from my mouth and make weepy-eye gestures. 'OK, but this is going to take a lot of lip-gloss,' she said, 'A lot!'

Writing has never really been Star's thing; in fact, *books* have never really been Star's thing. I've tried to get her into Nancy Mitford, but it takes her forever to read a book. She just prefers music. Sister Hillary, who simply adores Thomas Hardy (erk), says you can't really push these literary things, you either like something or you don't. Ms Topler should listen a bit more closely to Sister Hillary on that point.

When the girls snuck into our room (Honey wearing her high-heeled Jimmy Choo slippers), Star rolled her eyes and reached for her lip-gloss.

'I don't see the point of all this writing rubbish, darling,' Honey said. 'Can't we just break out the vodka and talk about boys?' Even though it was too dark to see each other properly, I could imagine the pouty face she'd be pulling.

'No, just listen, Calypso and I think it would be a fab way to raise money for Children of The World. You know, for our punishment.'

Had I heard correctly? Had Georgina just united our names in the same sentence?

Honey groaned.

'When did this happen?' Star asked.

'Erm, while . . .' For a moment I was about to say, 'Right after Georgina finished making herself vomit,' but stopped myself in time. 'You were, erm . . .'

'Look, think about it,' Georgina interjected. We've got to make this money somehow and Calypso came up with this fantastic idea that we could ask everyone in our House Block to write something satirical which they would then have to read out loud at a literary party.'

My head was spinning, but Georgina didn't so much as draw breath. 'We could fine non-contributors five pounds.'

'Oh, I like that,' Honey added. She would make a great traffic warden. She's always trying to introduce fines for things. During our first term she had tried (almost successfully) to introduce a fine for girls who didn't have long, straight hair.

Star said, 'Er, maybe I'm just being stupid, but will

everyone know what we mean by satirical?' She was looking pointedly at Honey as she said this.

'Correct, you're just being stupid,' Honey replied with
a sneer.

'OK, so what does it mean, brain drain?' Star challenged.

Honey holding her torch to her face, rolled her eyes.
Obviously she had no idea what it meant herself.

'Erm, well, actually, I don't know what it means,'
offered Clemmie.

'It's sort of a piss-take, isn't it?' Arabella asked, looking
to me for comfirmation.

'Exactly,' I agreed. 'A tease, really.'

'There, so it doesn't really matter whether people know
what it means – we can simply ask them to do a tease,'
Georgina suggested. 'Only cleverly done and fun, not
nasty,' she added, looking at Honey as she spoke.

'Yes, funny rather than viscious,' I added, thinking of
Honey although I didn't dare look at her.

Honey groaned again and flopped back on my bed, her
feet on my pillow.

I rose above her – not literally, because I was lying on
the floor – and suggested that we start with a reading
from Nancy Mitford, the greatest literary tease of all
time.

I read out the part of the book where her father hunts
the children with hounds and how all the locals thought
him a total sadist. (Of course, all the hounds did was lick
the children, but perhaps they imagined they tore them to
pieces and ate them.)

We muffled our laughter with our dressing-gowns and

then Georgina read a Dorothy Parker poem about being misunderstood.

'It is awful to be misunderstood,' Georgina said with a loud sigh at the end of the piece, as if she knew first-hand what being misunderstood was all about.

Star was looking fidgety, so I asked her what was up.

'Well, I just don't think it's fair to fine people who can't write,' she announced firmly.

Everyone raised their professionally-sculptured eyebrows (apart from me, of course, because I pluck my own). Fines, after all, were a part of life at Saint Augustine's – like betting, smoking and selling listens.

'Why, can't you afford it?' Honey asked cattily.

Star curled her lip. 'No – because we're meant to be raising money for charity. I don't think fining people is really the best way to go about that – do you?'

'Why not? We could raise the money in an evening if we went down and terrorised the Year Sevens.' She laughed her hyena laugh so loudly that I don't think she noticed that no one else was laughing with her.

Star shook her head in disgust. 'God, you're loathsome, Honey. Maybe we could raise money hunting *you* with hounds!' She was looking at Honey with such undisguised hatred that even I felt afraid.

'Better still, we could have your wretched rat put down!' Honey giggled. 'I'm sure the whole school would chip in for that, wouldn't they, darlings?' She looked around at everyone (apart from Star and me because . . . well, we didn't actually exist as far as she was concerned).

But Georgina started to cry. Clemmie and Arabella

tried to calm things down by offering her a cigarette.

Star, Arabella and Clemmie joined her on her bed so they could blow the smoke out of the window. I sprayed the room with Febreze, just in case. Then just as I finished spraying, Honey lit one up in the middle of the room.

I wondered if I sprayed her with Febreze whether she'd explode or self-immolate.

'We could always call the fine a donation so as not to upset anyone,' Clemmie offered, poking her head in from the window.

Honey tipped the ash from her cigarette into the slipper by my bed – my pink Hello Kitty ones that I love to pieces. I was really annoyed, but I didn't know what to say.

Georgina, coming in from the window, said, 'Hey, that was Calypso's slipper you just used!'

Honey shrugged. 'Oh, sorry, darling, I didn't notice.' Only she didn't say it to me.

Star emptied my slipper out of the window and sprayed it with Febreze. Then she squirted Honey's back with Febreze. 'I can see it's a good idea for fundraising, but all my writing is morbid and gloom-laden. Witty writing isn't exactly my strong point.'

'Funny, I wasn't aware you *had* a strong point, Star,' Honey began.

But Georgina turned to Star and said, 'Gosh darling, don't worry about not being a literary genius.' Then she whispered, 'Tobias can't read a word, he's completely illiterate, actually.' As she spoke she held her hands over his ears to save him from the shame of it all.

Honey groaned. 'Well, I think the whole thing is a waste of time anyway. It's just a stupid punishment for heaven's sake. Let's just have our fathers donate big fat cheques – charities love those. Let's leave it at that.'

I could see my writing salon dream dissipating before my eyes. 'That's *not* what all this is about, though,' I explained.

'Oh? I forgot, your father can't afford it, can he, Calypso?' she remarked in a syrupy voice as she stood up and smiled down on me like a cat that's just licked the cream. 'I suppose the rest of us can always chip in for your share.'

I was shocked out of my embarrassment by Georgina. 'Better still,' she said. 'Honey, why don't you just fuck off!'

I couldn't believe it. I was totally stunned.

Actually, everyone was. Honey included. Honey *especially*. She stood there for a few moments, staring blankly at Georgina, wondering if it was all a joke, or if she'd heard correctly.

Everyone stared at her and said nothing, which in a way, said everything. Honey had made a fool of herself. She had gone too far and you could actually watch the realisation hit her as it sank in. But in true Honey fashion, she pulled herself together and declared, 'I don't want anything to do with your stupid salon anyway.' She flounced off, slamming the door really loudly as she went.

We stayed silent as her Jimmy Choo slippers clipped down the corridor.

'She's losing it,' Clemmie said, looking at Star as if they'd discussed Honey together, maybe on one of their long drives back to their country piles in Star's dad's limo.

'Mummy thinks it's because her mother's still waiting on an invitation from Lord Aginet to propose and blames Honey and Poppy for his hesitation.'

'Vodka, anyone?' I asked, trying to change the mood. Even though I loathed Honey with every fibre of my body I wanted to get the writing salon going and not waste the evening bitching about Honey.

'Yes, let's toast our salon,' Georgina agreed. 'You know, I think this is going to be the start of something really good.'

I nipped into the en-suite and grabbed my humble vodka stash. Once I had passed around the five Body Shop Specials, we held them up in a torch-lit toast. Georgina put her arm around Star and told her that she'd better not bottle out, and I think Star was about to collapse at the shock of it all, but then we heard the heavy footfall of Miss Cribbe's Hush Puppies squelching towards our dorm room.

There was a mad scramble as we screwed the tops back on our vodka bottles, switched off our torches and dived under the duvets.

Clemmie and I were clutching each other and trying not to giggle as we waited for Miss Cribbe to wave her torch around the room and listened to her wheezy breathing as she moved our bin and used it to prop our door open.

None of us dared breathe.

When we finally heard her Hush Puppies shuffling back down the corridor we turned on our torches and pulled the bin away and used pillows to muffle our laughter.

Later on, Star said, 'Actually, I might have a bit of an idea. Instead of fining girls, why don't we start a school magazine, you know, like a satirical sort of thing with teases about the teachers and prefects? We could even do illustrations – and charge money for it. If it were funny, I'm sure everyone would want to buy it?'

Star's father was right. She was a genius.

'That is a great idea!' Arabella agreed, almost squealing with excitement.

'We'd need a really cool title,' Clemmie added.

'What if the teachers won't let us do it, though? Ms Topler for example?' I reminded them. 'She'd probably think it was going against the laws of her literary snore curriculum to have fun with writing.'

'Well, then she can bugger off,' Georgina giggled.

'*Nun of Your Business*?' Star suggested.

'What?'

'*Nun* – as in N-U-N – *of Your Business*! For the name?'

Georgina held her teddy to her ear. 'Tobias just said he totally adores that!' she squealed and threw her bear in the air.

THIRTEEN

Countdown to the Eades Social

he Eades social was only a day away, but we were
almost too pre-occupied with our salon to care.
Just joking. I had received seventeen – *seventeen* –
messages from Freddie. But I had only told the others
about a few of them – apart from Star, obviously. It wasn't
just because I was trying to be cool. It was just that I was
bursting with excitement and worried that if I started talking too much about Freddie I wouldn't stop, which would
be too tragic for words.

My phone's memory was now full, so I had to start deleting the messages, which was very dispiriting as I wanted to
keep every one forever – like Georgian and Victorian ladies
who kept their letters tied up in pink ribbons (only I'd use
blue because blue is my favourite colour).

Every time he left a message he used a different accent,
which was really funny and made me feel special. His last
one was a Russian accent: 'Darlink, I can't vait to share my
matzo ball soup with you.'

I replied to his messages with my own accented replies –

although not all of them, because I didn't want him to think I didn't have a life. Georgina said his messages were suggestive and that I was definitely going to pull him.

'Yaah – it's as bad as text sex!' Star teased.

After the incident at the writing salon, Poppy and a few of her friends from the year above came down to Cleathorpes, looking for Georgina. Poppy actually slapped Georgina across the face and called her a bitch for telling her sister to F-off. After that Honey started to hang out with her sister's crowd.

Clemmie said, 'I wouldn't be surprised if it wasn't Honey who woke Miss Cribbe and complained about us keeping her awake that night.'

We all agreed.

And so did Tobias.

There hadn't been a repeat of Georgina's bulimic episode as far as I knew, but she was smoking herself stupid every night and I was worried that I was going to die of Febreze poisoning. We were all immersed in the writing salon, even Star. Only Honey had returned to her poisonous ways, which meant my days were spent pealing Post-it Notes off my back. But even that didn't bug me the way it once had. I didn't feel like a freak any more.

Honey had issues way bigger than mine.

Star was making me keep all the Post-it Notes. She said we might be able to do something artistic with them in the magazine. Arabella agreed, and said she'd write satirical pieces on us all. Clemmie said, 'I can't wait to read what you write about Honey!'

Georgina giggled and started taking the piss out of Honey. 'Yaah, darlings, why don't we simply have our daddies chip in a few thou?'

Star was busy doing little drawings of us all. She did one of me in my fencing kit with arrows pointing to my fluffy sticky-out bits of hair which she'd drawn to look like horns. Then she did a drawing of Honey with arrows pointing to Honey's Botox, collagen and other surgical enhancements.

I was having to pinch myself at how well my life was going. Instead of being the school freak, I was part of an actual writing salon and getting a school magazine off the ground. I know it had only really come about as a result of a punishment for our canteen food fight, but still it was the first time at Saint Augustine's that I had ever really been part of something. And as well as all that I was being pursued by phone by a real, live prince.

So why did I still feel like an impostor in an exclusive member's club . . . especially around Honey? I tried to bring it up with Star during our warm-up exercises in the fencing salle, but it came out sounding like a whine and Star lost patience.

'What is it with you and this outside/inside rubbish anyway?' she responded almost in anger as we finished our supermans. 'Being accepted for who you are doesn't come down to where you're from, like you seem to think, Calypso. Maybe you need to accept yourself for who you are before blaming your isolation on everyone else.'

My head was in a mess. Star seemed really annoyed with me as if I had accused her of a heinous crime – the crime of being one of Them, presumably. The crime of being of

Their world, at least. I put my mask on and saluted, know-ing I was in too much of an emotional mess to distinguish myself on the piste. The sensible thing to do would have been to retire, to say I felt sick or had a cramp. But the only thing I had a cramp in was my brain.

It was only a friendly bout, with Professor Sullivan pre-siding, but in my attack *au fer*, Star gained priority by par-rying and I put my whole body into the counter-attack, lost my balance and landed sprawling at her feet. It was so embarrassing.

'*Halte!*' declared Professor Sullivan. I gathered myself together and we went back to the *en garde* line. I was dying under my mask – *dying*. Star's words were echoing in my head: 'Maybe you need to accept yourself for who you are.' For once not even 'a physical game of chess' could grab my focus. I thought of Freddie and tried to imagine it was him I was fencing but that only made matters worse.

After she'd totally slaughtered me, when we were changing back into our uniforms, I think Star could tell I was still in a mess because she put her arm around me and said, 'Listen, I've been going to school with them all my life. Do you think that makes *me* one of them?'

'No,' I told her, laughing at the absurdity of it all and giving her a hug.

Yes, I was thinking as I grabbed my gear and left the salle.

The day before the social, the five of us – Star, Georgina, Arabella, Clementine and I were in Ms Topler's class (yawn), reading her latest offering of Literary Realism, as she called it.

I knew it was very worthy to know all about how hard life was for women in a previous age, but honestly didn't these people have any sense of humour?

Then Miss Topler called me up to the front and I was afraid that she was going to give me a blue for my eyebrow-raising every time we were told to bring our latest yawn-till-you-drop book out.

'So, Miss Kelly, I hear that you and your friends have organised an *exclusive* writing salon.'

I glared at Honey, who looked up at the ceiling.

'I wouldn't call it exclusive exactly, Ms Topler.'

'No?'

'No . . . well, you see the thing is, it's more or less part of our punishment.'

'Explain.'

'Yes, well . . . erm, six of us were given the task of coming up with ways to raise money for this charity called Children of The World. They raise money for kids, like the class who –'

'Yes, yes, yes. I am perfectly aware of the nature of this charity and the good works they do for children in areas of distress.'

'Well, we have to find ways to raise money, so the writing salon was one of the ideas we had.'

'An idea – one that you didn't wish to share with others?'

Georgina, clutching Tobias to her chest, stood up. 'Ms Topler, this is so random. Why are you hectoring poor Calypso about it? It's not like we're having carnal relations with Satan or anything. Besides, the whole idea is to share the group. We're putting together a literary magazine which is open to the whole school to contribute to.'

'I am perfectly aware of this clandestine magazine, thank you, Miss Castle Orpington. Now kindly sit down and please put that ridiculous bear in your bag. I merely wished to put to you that perhaps it might have been more Christian of you to discuss your magazine in the forum of the English Literature class . . . i.e., *my* class! The one you are presently sitting in.'

OK, so this was it. Once again, I could see my dream tumbling down around me. Honestly, who was I kidding thinking this idea would work? I said a Hail Mary without much hope, but I said it with a fervour never before applied to my prayers so that I missed what Ms Topler said next. All I heard was, 'Thank you, class dismissed. In the name of the Father, the Son and the Holy Ghost, amen.'

I trudged along behind the others towards the canteen, listening to no one, saying nothing. Even the discovery that we had fish nuggets and chips wasn't enough to raise my spirits. I was only dragged from my well of misery by the occasional thump on the back as a Post-it Note landed.

Everyone else seemed on top of the world, proving what I always knew – that I was a freak who placed far too much emphasis on amusing writing. I couldn't even get excited about the Eades social while everyone else was chattering on about it. I sat with the others and picked disconsolately at my fish nuggets while Star peeled the Post-it Notes off my shirt.

'OK, this is weird,' she said, showing me one of the pile. It read:

Enjoy your dinner, Shit Face

'Whatever,' I replied. I couldn't be bothered any more.

'Maybe it's time to show these to Sister Constance,' Arabella suggested, flicking back her blonde-streaked locks. 'Seriously, Calypso, this is harassment. Daddy's done all sorts of famous litigation cases and I'm sure he'd do you a good rate if you wanted to sue.'

I munched on a chip, too miserable to even smile at the irony of someone like Arabella (who could trace her family back to the fourth century) suggesting that I, Calypso Kelly, mount a legal suit in the High Courts against Honey O'Hare, daughter of England's most famous It Girl.

After supper, when Star and I were alone, I complained, more to myself than to anyone else, 'I just can't believe what's happened . . .'

'What?'

'The magazine.'

'Why? It's great,' Star said. 'Didn't you hear what Ms Topler was saying?'

'Banned us from doing the magazine and probably showered us in blues.'

'Are you mad in the head or just deaf? The school is going to let us off study time to work on the magazine *and* they are going to organise the printing.'

FOURTEEN

The Night of the
Eades Social

While everyone else was getting dressed up in their finery, I was in the infirmary with diarrhoea. My money was on Honey slipping a laxette in my dinner. So was everyone else's – even Tobias had his suspicions.

What was worse, the horrible Sister Dumpster was being really nasty, telling me how in her day, diarrhoea took fifty percent of the population and they didn't complain.

She was only about sixty years old so I seriously doubted it, but I said nothing.

I tried to cry myself to sleep but it wasn't working. It must have been the dehydration.

Honestly, as if being kept away from the man of my dreams wasn't bad enough, I had to put up with Sister Dumpster knitting away at the end of my bed like old Madame Guillotine of the French Revolution who had knitted away in the front row while the bourgeoisie were beheaded.

I was too sick to even ask for my mobile phone to call

Freddie – not that I had any credit left on it. I'd probably have to sell my mobile to survive the term – not that anyone would want to buy a brick like mine.

Having friends was lovely, but it was costing me a fortune in sweets and pizzas alone.

So I told God that I'd give up all the sweets in the world to be sitting next to Freddie at the social.

Then I ran to the loo.

Sister Dumpster looked at the little watch pinned to her chest and wrote down the time of my motion on her pad. She would make a fantastic prison warden.

'Sister, maybe I need another Lomotil?' I suggested when I came back. 'I mean, I'm going every three minutes and I feel awful.'

'You've gone from five to seven minutes actually, Miss Kelly. That's perfectly good progress, medically speaking. Keep up your fluids and I'll reassess you in an hour.'

The social started in an hour.

There was a knock at the door. 'Oh, darling, are we poorly?' It was Honey, dressed in the baby-blue dress with the strappy bits that she had promised to me.

'You will look after her, won't you, Sister Dempster?'

'Thank you, Miss O'Hare, all is in hand. The best thing for your friend is to keep up her fluids and wait for the squitters to pass.'

'Hmm, lovely. Well, enjoy your evening, Calypso. Chance for you to catch up on your reading. I know how you love that! Toodle-pip.'

I didn't even have time for a spiteful riposte. I was off to the loo again. This was definitely not easing up.

I came out of the toilet weak as a kitten and tearful. Self-pity was now engulfing me. Earlier I had half hoped I would be over the worst and still make the social, but seeing Honey looking sublimely divine in her/my baby-blue strappy number had destroyed all hope.

Now all I felt was despair.

'Oh, will you just look at yourself, you poor baby.'

It was Sister Regina. As large as life (in a four-foot-nine sort of way) sitting in the nurses station.

'Oh, Sister,' I moaned. 'I feel so poorly.'

'I'm not at all surprised. You take these tablets *tout de suite* and drink that jug of water with mineral salts that I've placed by your bed. I've read your chart and if this nasty business hasn't passed in an hour's time I'll be calling the doctor before you flush yourself clean away.'

An hour later we were both sitting in the horribly uncomfortable infirmary bed, flicking though *Teen Vogue*. I suppose I would survive not going to the Eades Social.

More or less.

Star had popped in to say goodbye and brought a mock-up of the *Nun of Your Business* magazine to cheer me up. Sister Regina thought it was hilarious and asked if we couldn't include some of the nuns. 'We do love a giggle,' she confided. 'Especially now that the telly is on the blink. They've only gone and taken us off Sky.'

Sky television had hundreds of channels and the Sixth Formers were allowed televisions with Sky. 'Why?' I asked.

'The governors didn't think we needed it. Costs too much.' She folded her little arms across her chest and shook her head grimly. 'It's all about money these days.'

'That is so mean. How are you meant to stay up to date with life?' I asked.

'You tell me. They'd have us drawing water from the well like monks if it wasn't for the fearsome grief they'd get from Mother Superior.'

I can't really explain why, but I started to cry. I knew that I didn't have to draw my water from a well, but everything had been going so well and now, here I was, spending the night of the Eades Social in the infirmary with a nun, discussing school governors, when I should have been pulling my handsome prince. And no doubt Honey was dancing her heart away in my dress. OK, so it was her dress, but whatever.

Sister Regina made me pour my heart out and, ten minutes later, I was sitting in the passenger seat of her old Citroën 2CV, with a stash of special tablets to 'keep the cork in', wearing a little black dress made by some Sixth Former for her textile's exam.

She must have been a funny shape, and that's all I have to say on the matter . . . it was miles too short and too baggy. Sister Regina insisted on using safety-pins (the really big ones like they use on babies nappies) to pin it up at the back.

'Just keep your back to the wall,' she warned, 'and no one will even notice.'

It was all very Shakespearean, with a bit of Wagner thrown in for good measure. Wagner's 'Ring Cycle' was blasting out on the cassette-player as we skidded around hairpin bends, through the woods and down the unlit fern-clad lanes that led to Eades. Sister Regina was singing along in her thin little high-pitched voice.

At four-foot-nine, she could barely see over the steering wheel and I had to tell her when to turn. Occasionally, I even had to resort to grabbing the wheel.

'It's been very difficult driving since the governors took away our cushions,' she commented at one point.

I told Sister Regina I would write to them and complain.

We screeched into Eades and I dashed across the floodlit quad where men with sniffer dogs were patrolling for drugs and bombs.

Sister Regina tooted her horn and called out to me in her thin little voice. 'You just mind you keep your back to the wall so no one sees your safety pins, luvvie. I'll say a decade of the Rosary and you shall be the belle of the ball.'

Thank God only the security guards and the sniffer dogs heard.

FIFTEEN

The Brat of the Ball

I felt like a Lilliputian in a land of giants as I entered the enormity of the Eades dining hall, with its grand chandeliers and mahogany wall-panelling. The first face I saw – the only face I searched for – was Prince Freddie. He was sitting next to psycho toff Honey. My heart thudded to the floor – I even thought I could hear it echo throughout the hall. I felt like such a fool for even coming.

The brat of the ball was nibbling away on her main course and Freddie didn't even look up. A costumed usher led me to the table where I was to be seated. As I made my way through the lines of long dining tables I saw Freddie craning his head to hear something hilarious that Honey was saying between nibbles.

I scanned the packed room for Star, but there was no sign of her anywhere.

I felt like backing out of the room and running back to Saint Augustine's. This night was doomed, and it wasn't just because I was The Queen of Doomsday Prophesies that I knew it. For a start there was no way I was going to be able to conceal my safety-pinned dress. I would have to sit down all night which meant that I couldn't dance.

Nor could I eat, due to the state of my stomach.

All I could do was sit and watch in silence while Honey pulled Freddie.

Fabbo.

Oh, bloody hell, where was Star?

The costumed usher led me to a seat at the table parallel to Freddie's. In fact, I was seated directly behind him, so, in effect, the only thing my back was going to be against was him. The boy sitting next to me was spotty and clearly keener on his trout than he was on chatting. I watched – my empty stomach rumbling – as he dissected his fish and removed its bones, placing them clinically one by one on his side plate.

On my other side, the chair was empty. I smiled bravely at the huge portraits of whiskered men on the wall – because they were the only faces in the room prepared to make eye contact with me.

'Good evening,' the male teacher at the end of the table eventually announced. He looked a bit like Lurch in the Addam's family. I shrank further into my high-backed, elaborately carved Victorian chair as he raised one single eyebrow at me.

I've always been intrigued by people who had the ability to do that. I had practised raising one eyebrow a lot when I was younger, but eventually I'd realised I just wasn't the type. Still, I gave it my best shot – only I think it made me look a bit drunk.

Lurch looked down his nose at me and frowned, so I

flapped my napkin on to my lap and tried to stop my face turning bright red – a nasty habit my face picked up when I was quite young.

I still couldn't see Star anywhere. What had I been thinking – letting myself be talked into coming to the Eades social, wearing a dress fastened with large safety-pins at the back by a nun who couldn't even see over a steering wheel?

A voice behind me drifted over – it seemed to come from a long way away.

'My darlink, at last. You finally decided to grace me with your beauty.'

It was Freddie, leaning back in his chair. I could smell an intoxicating mix of limes, oranges and lemons, but that turned out to be the sorbet and I finally began to relax and even managed to ignore Honey's nasty looks.

I leaned back. 'Vy of course, darlink,' I replied, mimicking his Russian accent as best I could – at least I think it was Russian. It could just as easily have been Polish or Romanian, or even Glaswegian for that matter. I can only really do an LA Valley Girl accent with any conviction.

For the duration of the meal we tried out every accent we could think of, finally settling on Cockney – although I had to give up when it came to the rhyming slang. It turned out that the empty chair on the other side of me belonged to a boy called Kevin, and he actually was from the East End of London and one of Freddie's best mates.

'Oh, so you're the sabre champion everyone's been going on about!' Kev announced as he returned to his seat, which made me go so red that my head almost exploded.

Then the band started up and I finally had to stand and face Freddie – I put my hands behind my back to hide my safety-pins, but the main thing on my mind was the anticipation that he would invite me to dance.

But that privilege went to Honey, who asked him first.

Kevin was really sweet and asked me if I would do him the honours, in a piss-take of an OTT posh accent – even though, like all of the Eades boys, his accent is madly posh anyway. I think the school probably offers that assurance to all prospective parents: 'Eades will guarantee that your son will leave this hallowed institution sounding like an upper-class prat' – or words to that effect.

On the dance floor, I tried to keep my back to the speakers to hide my safety-pins and decided to be philosophical about things – although, to be honest, philosophy was my worst subject. What sort of madness was I thinking of anyway, imagining I could pull the heir to the throne of England?

Still, he was fit. The fittest boy in the hall, in fact.

Georgina sidled up to me just as the philosophical thing was starting to work and Kevin and I were getting on really well.

'We're just going on a mercy run with Honey – coming?'

Mercy? Honey? I don't think so.

I thought I was just thinking it to myself, but apparently I actually said it. Even Kevin, who must have overheard, looked startled at how mean I sounded.

'She drank too much vodka before we came. She's busted if one of the teachers sees her swaying on the dance floor like that,' said Georgina.

I looked around and sure enough there was Honey, totally bladdered and moments away from a suspension.

Just then, Freddie came up to us and said to Kevin, 'So, can I cut in on your trouble, mate?'

'You keep your pork pies off my trouble's bacon, if you know what's good for you,' Kevin replied.

I didn't have a clue what they were on about and my blank look must have given me away.

Freddie explained as Kevin went off. '"Pork pies" is eyes. Trouble is "trouble and strife" – wife. And bacon is "bacon and eggs" – legs.'

'Obvious, really,' I said, as Freddie clasped me to his chest for a slow dance.

He asked me what LA was like. 'I've never actually been there,' he said, 'but I understand it's quite spread out.'

'Yaah, that's why it's called the city that never walks!' I told him, which made him laugh.

I rested my head on his shoulder. This was so cool.

'Hang on, what's going on back here?' he asked, feeling my safety-pins.

'Erm, well, yes. Bit embarrassing, but I didn't have a dress for tonight so Sister Regina sort of gave me someone else's from the textile's class, only it was too loose and –'

'Enough,' he said, holding up his hand. 'Don't spoil the Elizabeth Hurley-ness of the moment,' then he moaned in a really turned-on sort of way. I couldn't believe that a girl like me could create an Elizabeth Hurley moment! HELLO, the dress *she* wore (the one with all the safety pins that exposed most of her body – and made her famous) was made by Versace . . . not the oddly-shaped Charlotte Chapman of the

Lower Sixth at Saint Augustine's. I was also quite pleased about him stopping me mid-ramble or I might have mentioned my diarrhoea – in fact, I definitely *would* have, predisposed as I am to verbally digging my own grave when nervous or embarrassed, or madly keen on a prince.

I said a silent prayer of thanks to Mary for sending an angel like Sister Regina, whose large dose of Lomotil had done the trick. My tummy wasn't even rumbling.

'Would you like to go outside for some air?' he asked, when the music stopped. Well, I almost swooned – if swoon's the right word. Anyway, I felt all light and giddy. I think the Horsey Girls call it skittish.

Freddie led me down a series of dark passages so we could lose his security guards. None of the musky, dark-panelled windowless corridors looked very promising. Finally, we stopped and he tapped on a heavy old mahogany door. When no one answered we entered the most magical room I had ever seen.

The entire room was lined from floor to ceiling with books. There was even a wooden ladder that slid along the shelves so you could reach the high books, and above that there was a balcony with still more books which you could examine, strolling along a little walkway. We have a fabulous library at Saint Augustine's, but it is manned (or rather, woman-ed) by the horrendous anti-bookist, Ms Parkes, who wears old men's suits that smell like men died in them.

Ms Parkes always followed you around the library and if you reached for a book she would grab it before you could, and then pass it to you suspiciously as if you might be a book burner. She also stood over you while you read it (muttering things about how defacing books is a criminal offence) and if you asked to borrow it, she'd remark, 'I shall bring it to your dormitory room after lights out', which meant we could only read it by torchlight.

It didn't make for a very comfortable reading atmosphere.

This library, on the other hand, seemed like heaven, and I would have liked to check out the books more thoroughly, but I thought it might spoil the moment, and besides, Freddie was holding my hand and pulling me along.

I wanted to ask him lots of things about what it was like being a prince, but I didn't want to seem tragic, so I relaxed into the silence that seemed to spread over us like the darkness.

He pulled off his tailcoat and asked me to hold it while he drew back the purple velvet drapes and lifted one of the large sash windows so we could climb out into a darkened . . .

Erm . . . bush, actually. A big prickly bush. But I didn't mind in the slightest because Freddie put his jacket around my shoulders and guided me gently through the bush and into a tiny clearing where he kissed me.

Sister Regina had given me a couple of Curiously Strong Mints before she dropped me off, so I wasn't worried about my breath being gross, but I wasn't absolutely positive about my kissing technique either. Of course I knew that when the other girls asked what it was like I was going to say 'amazing'. But as it was my first time, I was not quite sure what to do with my tongue and lips and the other bits and pieces of my mouth. My brain was not helping. All I could think about was kissing, and how I'd never done it. Freddie's tongue, meanwhile, was gently fencing mine. It was quite nice, actually, so I tried to concentrate on Freddie, and on his lovely boyish smell, and his soft, warm lips. Suddenly he moved his hand up my back along the safety-pins and slipped his hand under my hair and rested it supportively at the back of my neck. My stomach went *whoosh*, my heart started thumping and my brain stopped and it was the loveliest feeling ever.

'Excuse me, sir, but perhaps you should step back inside.'

It was one of his security guards, reeking of CK1. 'I'm bringing His Majesty back in now, sir,' he spoke into his little ear-to-mouth piece.

It was all so unbelievably and maddeningly annoying.

'Sorry about that,' Freddie apologised, as we stumbled through the bushes and out into the brightly lit quad.

We passed Honey on the way. She smelled of spew, but I didn't say anything – although Freddie gave me a look that spoke volumes about what he really thought of her.

'Freddie, Freddie!' she called after us, 'Sorry to leave you like that earlier. Only I had to do a bit of a favour for a friend. I hope you'll forgive me, darling?'

'Absolutely fine,' he said, giving my hand a squeeze.

It took more than a squeeze to get rid of the sick feeling I always had when faced with Honey. She slithered up close to us and ran her arms up both our backs.

'Oh, what are these, Calypso?' Then she did her hyena laugh.

Freddie and I smiled stiffly – well, I smiled stiffly. Freddie looked right through her.

'I forgot you two knew each other, darling. All those funny messages. "You don't call, you don't text . . .",' she mimicked the first message he had sent me – the one that had done the rounds of Cleathorpes. 'God, Calypso, you must have made an absolute fortune from those messages. Although I guess you're used to that, Freddie – having the plebs trading on your royal status. Still a girl has to make a dime,' she joked, nudging me in the ribs. Then she wandered off, laughing insanely to herself.

Only it wasn't funny.

I really needed Freddie to give my hand one of his big manly squeezes just then, but instead he pulled it away. 'What's this all about?' he asked tersely.

'What's what?' I replied, playing for time.

'You sold *listens* of my messages?'

It was like being slapped across the face. 'I so did not!'

'Calypso, I'm not a fool and I didn't think you were. I don't particularly like your friend, but she's right on one point. I *am* used to people attempting to trade on my royal status. I just didn't imagine you would be one of those people.' Then he turned on his heel and crunched his way across the freshly cut grass of the quad, back towards the hall.

I stood there for a bit, with his tailcoat wrapped around my shoulders – until Kev came out to retrieve it.

'Sorry, but you know how it is. He's none too pleased.'

I knew if I said anything I would start crying, so I just passed him the coat. It felt like I was Cinderella and it was time to go back to my pots and pans.

SIXTEEN

Crying for Britain

After Kevin retrieved Freddie's jacket, I ran crying into the loos where Star was trying to help Clemmie pull the zip of her top up. Apparently on their mercy run, Honey threw up on poor Clemmie, so they left Honey with a hose and told her to stay in the shadows until she sobered up. Then they had washed Clemmie's spewie top under the tap and dried it under the hand drier.

Once I'd finished garbling out my sorry story, Star immediately offered to go and give His Royal Bloody Stuck-Up Highness a smack. She was furious. Clemmie was keener on getting back into the social and wrapping her lips around someone with the unlikely name of Razzle.

I felt ill again and with the smell of spew in the air I vomited. The others filed off back into the hall while Star arranged for us to go back early on the minibus.

I couldn't stop sobbing and feeling ashamed. I suppose I shouldn't have let anyone else hear his messages, but then I hadn't really had any choice in the matter. Star had grabbed my phone, then Georgina and after that . . . oh, it was all such a mess.

When we got back, Sister Regina insisted I spend the night in the infirmary. She said she blamed herself for making me go in the first place and started crying as well.

I woke up late in the morning to find her still sleeping, slumped in an uncomfortable chair at the foot of my bed. As I watched her I replayed every horrendous moment of the night before in my head.

Star walked in with the newspapers. Every paper you can name had a photo of Freddie and me tongue-fencing in the bushes. The photograph showed my hair covered in leaves and the papers all had clever head-lines. My favourite (not) was, *The Prince and His Bit of Rough-and-Tumble*.

'I just can't believe the audacity of the guy!' Star ranted. 'A girl stinking of spew, whom he's virtually told you he despises, tells him that you've been trading on his royal status and he believes her? Now his own bloody security guy, or one of his other mates, sells a photo to the press! Talk about Prince Bloody Charming.'

Sister Regina, who had woken up and was reading one of the papers, shook her head. 'What a bounder. What a bounder. You are well out of it, luvvie.'

Star said, 'Well I've got a mind to bound right over to Eades and tell him exactly what I think of him.'

Georgina flew into the room next. 'This is so random, darling,' she cried out. 'I can't believe it – what a bastard!' Then, seeing my puffy eyes, she dispatched Sister Regina for cucumber slices. 'I've never seen such puffy eyes in my life, darling. Now that you are a national icon you have to look your best.'

Then she sat on the bed and gave me a cuddle.

'National icon?'

'Darling, you are the first girl that Freddie, heir to the British throne, has kissed! You will go down in history. This is huge, sweetie. *Huger* than huge.'

'Oh yes,' I replied in my drollest droll voice, 'this is what my parents have invested their swimming pool, holiday and car fund money into – my place in history as Prince Freddie's bit of rough and tumble.' I couldn't believe that Georgina was so shallow, as if being made out to be an utter slapper was the loveliest thing in the world. All because Freddie was a prince!

'Oh, darling, don't dwell. No one believes what they read in those trashy papers. Believe me, you will be the envy of every girl in this country.'

My next visitor was Sister Constance. Her mood was a little more circumspect, to say the least. She had her hands tucked up inside the sleeves of her robe. 'Your parents will be arriving the day after tomorrow, Miss Kelly. I have given them permission to take you to their hotel for the weekend and filled out the necessary exeat form.'

'I don't understand, Sister.'

She gestured with her chin towards the fan of newspapers on the floor. 'It would seem that news of your liaison with His Royal Highness has crossed the Atlantic. Your parents, quite understandably, feel you may need them. I shall discuss the details with you after you've been signed out of the infirmary. Needless to say, both Eades and Saint

Augustine's will mount a full and thorough investigation into how this sordid story manifested itself.'

'Thank you, Sister,' I replied, in the most humble voice I could muster, which was pretty humble, quite frankly, after all I'd endured recently.

She made the sign of the cross, told me she would pray for my soul and swept out of the room imperiously.

'"News of your liaison has crossed the Atlantic",' Star and Georgina mimicked, once they were sure she was out of earshot.

I couldn't see anything funny about it, though. All I could think of was Freddie and what he must be feeling. Or rather what I hoped he must be feeling. Was he having second thoughts? Was he missing me?

Basically, was he even thinking of me?

At all . . . ?

He probably hated me. His own parents must be furious. I must be the most hated girl in Britain where the royal family were concerned.

I was so obsessed with Freddie, in fact, I hardly gave a thought to my parents' impending arrival and what that would mean . . .

SEVENTEEN

Wear Your Pain
Like Lip-Gloss

After the Prince and His Bit of Rough-and-Tumble episode, the school swarmed with paparazzi. Sister Constance immediately doubled the number of security men and guard dogs patrolling the grounds. They could be seen everywhere – behind trees, the stone crosses along the driveway, next to sheds and bushes, talking in that strange language they use when they communicate on walkie-talkies – 'Ten-four', 'That's a copy', and that sort of thing.

The sight of terrified cameramen being chased by dogs, security men and nuns through the grounds became routine. Sister Hillary and Sister Veronica caught one photographer hiding in the chapel when he'd 'popped in for a quick prayer', and wasted no time in pressing the fire bell, then whipping him with gladioli from the altar. He was finally rescued, cowering in the confessional, by security guards. Later that day, Sisters Veronica and Hillary regaled us with stories of the episode, embellishing their bravery and righteous fury with each telling, until the tale sounded very much like that bit in the Bible where Jesus chases the money-lenders from the temple.

The press were desperate to speak to someone in the school who actually knew me, but no one would say a word. Apart from anything else, we were collectively threatened with expulsion if we so much as made eye contact with the press.

Sister Constance broke her own rule when she had Mr Morton move the umpire's stand from the tennis court on to the playing fields where she broadcast a scathing message to the press on a megaphone, suggesting they pray for mercy and forgiveness and describing them as emissaries for Satan and the servants of Beelzebub.

We were all in our classrooms at the time, but the teachers let us peer through the mullioned windows for a glimpse of our Mother Superior in all her superiorness. We were very proud of her, but we had no idea who Beelzebub was.

My parents' arrival had all the fanfare and status of a Hollywood premier. Even though they drove up in a taxi, everyone had lined up in the driveway as if expecting royalty to climb out. Instead, Bob and Sarah clambered out in their trackie bums and hoodies, trying to look all young and hip and 'street'.

God, it was embarrassing. Why they couldn't just wear Laura Ashley and Saville Row suits like everyone else's parents, I'll never know.

I hadn't really given myself time to think about how I would feel about their arrival, which I suppose sounds very self-centred and un-daughterly. I know it was very sweet and parentally responsible of them to take that horrible flight across the world to be with me in my hour of need, but all I could think of was Freddie.

He hadn't called and he hadn't responded to my text messages. I'd sent him three. The first one asked for a chance to explain. The second asked if he'd received my first text. The third text was a repeat of the first. Tragic, I know.

Clemmie's brother, who was in a lower year at Eades had said that although I was the talk of the school, Freddie was being very tight-lipped over the situation. When she'd told me this, all I could think of was how soft and loose his lips were when we'd kissed.

'He probably thinks you orchestrated the whole thing, darling,' Honey had remarked, sitting on my bed smoking a fag.

Star had grabbed the cigarette and flung it out of the window.

'What do you think you're doing,' Honey had shrieked.

'You'll set the fire alarm off and only get us all suspended, you idiot.'

Honey had sighed heavily. 'OK, *whatever*, Star!'

Honey had been hanging around in our room again as if nothing had happened.

As if her sister, Poppy, hadn't slapped Georgina across the face.

As if she hadn't mounted a campaign of Post-it Note harassment against me.

As if she hadn't spiked my lunch with laxatives.

As if she wasn't the total psycho toff who had ruined my life.

Instead, it was all 'darling' this, and 'sweetie' that, and we were sort of playing along with it because, well, it was just so random and none of us really knew *how* to deal with it.

It was only Georgina and Star who hardly spoke to her, and when they did, they were polite, but left her in no doubt that they loathed her. I wondered how it made Honey feel that Georgina, after all their years of friendship, now hated her. And not just hated her, but was now friends with Star and me – the two girls they had had so much fun taking the piss out of over the past three years.

'So, as I was saying before Star went berserk,' Honey continued, staring pointedly at Star, 'Freddie is probably worried that you are still trying to trade on his royalty, darling. Princes do tend to get the teeniest bit worried about these things.'

Star snapped, 'Funny that, Honey, given that *you* were the one who told him that Calypso was doing just that.'

Honey raised her eyes towards the ceiling, and stood with her hands on her hips, her puffy, pouty lips bursting with indignation. 'That is so untrue, darling. I was just mucking about. I thought that he might have a sense of humour. If being amusing is a crime now, fine, shoot me.'

I really would have liked to shoot her.

Honey was the first to introduce herself to my parents too, charging down the stairs, clutching her ghastly new pink rabbit, Duchess. '*Sooo* thrilled to meet you, Mr and Mrs

Kelly,' she smarmed. 'My name's Honey O'Hare. I'm a very close friend of Calypso's. We're more like sisters, really.'

What? Why on earth was Honey sucking up to *my* parents, my 'nobody' parents – untitled, without so much as a helicopter or a pile in the country to make them worth wasting her breath on.

'Swell,' Bob said.

'Super,' agreed Sarah.

'Any friend of Calypso's is a friend of ours. Call us Bob and Sarah, Honey,' Bob told her vaguely, looking about the crowd for me.

I was standing on the steps, but Star pushed me forward so that I sort of fell into their arms and they cuddled me really hard. Then Dad picked me up and swung me around like I was five or something. He had tears in his eyes. 'Oh, Calypso,' he sobbed.

Could he make more of a spectacle of me? I wondered as I applied more lip-gloss.

Yes. He could.

Sister Constance swooped down in an attempt to restrain the atmosphere. She extended her hand stiffly, speaking in her most imperious voice. 'Mr and Mrs Kelly, welcome to England. Perhaps you'd like to come into my office. As I said, you are free to take your daughter for the weekend, although as you will appreciate her workload . . .'

Bob, being Bob, was having none of her imperiousness, though. 'This is just swell, Sister. Just swell. Sarah and I can't thank you enough.' With that, he grabbed her in a bear hug and gave her a little spin, which caused the entire school, teachers included, to smirk.

I just kept reapplying my lip-gloss.

'Quite,' was Sister's response.

She smoothed her habit down and rearranged the large wooden crucifix that hung around her neck, and without further lapses into the strange realm of my parents' Californian informality she bustled them through the doors and down the corridor into her office.

I waited for the onslaught. At least when I was just the class freak I was largely ignored. I would gladly swap those good old days of invisibility for this new hell of being the subject of an international news scoop and having my parents turn up and swinging my nuns around.

'Your parents are so cool,' Clemmie cooed.

'Wow,' was all Star could say. And this from a girl whose father thought nothing of falling backwards off his chair at breakfast and spending the entire day on the floor with cereal all over his face.

'They certainly have a lot of energy, don't they? I mean for parents, that is?' Georgina said.

'They do yoga,' I explained.

I didn't really know what else to say. I was running out of lip-gloss.

EIGHTEEN

Hollywood Hits Windsor

My parents had booked a room in a chintzy hotel near Heathrow. It was quite strange being on my own with them after everything that had happened this term. I suddenly realised how much I'd changed. I mean, *hello*, I'd pulled the Prince and become a media sensation.

We ordered dinner from the room service menu. I had the most enormous burger with chips and my parents didn't so much as mention the word carbs or the dangers of eating gluten products. I kept waiting for them to start on me about being a slapper, and complain about how they'd had to drop everything and spend exorbitant amounts of money on flights across the Atlantic, etc, but all they did was ask me to take them step by step through the evening of the Eades social.

They wanted every detail.

Especially my dad, who kept asking questions like, so where was Star when this was happening? Or where was this Honey girl when you were dancing, and how much did I trust Georgina. It was like an interview, but not a threatening one. I got the impression they were really keen for me to realise that I was the victim and not the criminal.

They didn't once tut or sigh but made sympathetic noises, and when I told them about Freddie accusing me of trading on his royalty I noticed a knowing look pass between them. At the end of the story my dad declared that I'd been framed, and Mom agreed. Dad said he was going to get to the bottom of it.

Later, we watched an in-house movie. Actually it was all really cool. It was weird, though, sharing a room with my folks. My parents were in the same bed together. I mean, they always sleep together, but not when I'm in the room, if you know what I mean. They had offered to get me my own room, but I would have felt too lonely. Actually it was kind of nice. Apart from when my mom started snoring. I swear I don't know how my father puts up with it.

Saturday was great. We went for a ride on the London Eye and Dad kept telling lame jokes the way he does when he thinks I'm down, but I didn't mind. On the Eye I even snuggled close to them and told them I was really pleased they'd come.

And I was.

On the Saturday night my parents – or rather, Bob and Sarah, as everyone was now calling them on their insistence – took Clemmie, Arabella, Georgina, Star, Honey and me to dinner at Pizza Express in Windsor. I'd tried to convince them that I didn't want Honey there, but Sarah (even I had been reduced to calling my parents by their first names now) said, 'Nonsense, she's one of your closest friends, Calypso. It will be super.'

Honey brought the horrible pink Duchess in her new matching pink Prada bag and my mother made the most awful fuss of it, and asked me why I didn't have a rabbit.

I was gobsmacked. HELLO, *you* were one who said being deprived of a pet was character building!

But I didn't get a chance to say it because Honey said, 'I know. Isn't it a shame, Sarah? I offered her my old rabbit, Claudine, but she refused.' Honey looked at Sarah sadly and sighed heavily.

I glared at her, as did the other girls, but my parents were completely taken in. So I said, 'You don't just give pets away because you're sick of their colour.'

Honey made her ridiculously puffy lips wobble as if she were about to cry. 'I just thought it would be really sweet if our rabbits could be as close as we are, darling,' she explained – only she was looking at Sarah when she said it.

My mother was such a softie. She reached out and took Honey's hand and my hand. 'Come on, you two. I suppose in a way, Calypso, Honey was just, well . . . maybe it's a bit like recycling?' she suggested, trying to smooth things over.

Surely, though, even *she* could see what an utter psycho toff Honey was for giving away her pet because it wasn't this season's colour?

'It's a pet,' I reminded my mother. 'Not an empty milk carton, Sarah!'

'Calypso. Don't be churlish,' Bob chastised.

'Oh, whatever,' I said churlishly.

Sarah explained to Honey that the whole tabloid fiasco had been really hard on me.

I couldn't believe my parents were being so taken in by Honey. I know I'd never told them about her horribleness, but wasn't it blatantly obvious in her every mannerism that she was evil incarnate?

'Swell,' Bob said, trying to change the subject. 'Let's order.' Then he called over a waiter and asked which pizzas were gluten and carb-free which made all the girls giggle. Apart from me. I was still feeling extremely churlish.

Star gave my hand a supportive squeeze under the table, which helped a bit, and then my father asked about her father's band and that cheered me up even more because it meant Honey was left out of the conversation entirely.

The pizzas (loaded to the rafters with carbs and gluten) arrived and we all tucked in. Arabella asked Sarah about her work and my mother was surprisingly funny, regaling us with stories of the latest melodramatic plot lines and the hissy-fits the stars were always throwing – especially the men.

I started to relax. I even started to look at my parents in a different light. I mean, it was quite sweet of them to drop everything and come all this way to see me in my hour of need, and they seemed to be making a surprisingly good impression on my friends. I was glad they'd come. It hadn't occurred to me that I wanted them to come, but now they were here I realised how much safer I felt. And their visit had helped to take my mind off Freddie . . . for a while.

My parents had been really kind about the Rough-

and-Tumble photographs. Bob had told Sister Constance that we shouldn't be too hasty in blaming the paparazzi for the photograph. 'From what I understand, Sister, there were an awful lot of security guards patrolling the grounds that night, what with the Prince there and all. More often than not, you find these things turn out to be inside jobs.'

Inside jobs? Honestly, where does my father come up with these lines . . . oh yeah, I forgot, he's a Hollywood writer.

'By the way Calypso,' Sarah suddenly said. 'Jay sends his love. Asked if you got his package.'

'Jay as in James?' Honey asked, all ears.

Sarah went, 'No, Jay as in Jay, my assistant. Why? Has Calypso mentioned him?' She looked at me questioningly.

I shook my head at her in a pleading, please-don't-go-there sort of way.

Sarah tilted her head, trying to grasp what was going on.

Honey screeched, '*Told* us about him, Sarah? She had his pictures pinned all over the board. She was so mad keen on him. Well, at least she was until she pulled Prince Freddie.'

So this was it. I was going to be exposed as even more tragic than Honey and the others had always imagined. Just when I thought it couldn't get any worse.

I reapplied my lip-gloss.

I closed my eyes and resigned myself to my fate. Fine. Bring it on, I decided, as I kept running the lip-gloss over and over my lips. Let's just have it all out . . .

Sarah laughed. Well, I couldn't blame her, she had no idea what she was about to do to me. No idea that she was about to turn me into an object of ridicule. I could already feel the slap of Post-it Notes landing on my back.

Then she said, 'I was exactly the same at your age,' and giggled like a teenager.

I opened my eyes and looked up at her and she gave me a wink.

Oh, thank you, Sarah. Thank you for being weird, and Californian, and liberal, and understanding. I love you!

'One boy after another,' she went on, looking at me conspiratorially. 'Every one of them was The One, the love of my life. I used to write all their names on my pencil case.'

I have never loved my mother as much as I did at that moment. I wanted to run out and graffiti a bus stop shelter. *Sarah is the coolest mother in the world.*

'So tell us about what it was like at Saint Augustine's when you were there, Sarah,' Georgina urged.

So she did – only she made it all sound so funny and mad, and not a bit boring like she did on the plane when she first brought me out here nearly four years ago and promised me it would be 'super'.

I could tell that Honey was peeved that she was no longer centre stage, because she'd started sending text messages on her phone.

Bob leaned towards her and said, 'Is this one of those third-generation phones, Honey?'

Honey looked up. 'Sorry, darling? What was that?'

'I just wondered if your phone there took photographs?'

'*Absolutely*, darling,' she said, beaming, thrilled to be in the spotlight again. 'Shall we take one of all of us? Star, you take it,' she ordered, handing her the phone.

Typical of Honey to want Star excluded from the photograph.

'Oh no, I'm sure the guy that served us wouldn't mind,' Bob insisted. 'That way we can all be in it.' He summoned the waiter back.

After the waiter had taken a few shots, my father asked if he could have a look at the camera-phone and Honey eagerly swapped places with Sarah so she could show him all the phone's various features. Then Honey lost interest and left Bob to play around with it on his own.

'Hell of a lot of scandal these camera-phones are causing in Los Angeles,' he remarked after a while. 'Now anyone can snap a photo of a star in a restaurant or at a premier – *anywhere*, really.' He smiled at Honey.

She smiled back, only it was a wobbly, weird smile.

I didn't understand what was going at first, but then Bob casually passed the phone over to me, and there on the screen was the photo of Freddie and me, kissing in the bushes.

NINETEEN

Coventry

Word that Honey was the culprit of the Rough-and-Tumble photographs spread through Saint Augustine's and Eades like spilled nail varnish.

I didn't even get time to miss my parents. I had been sad to see them go, even though they had invited all my friends to LA for a couple of weeks in the summer. I had almost melted into the ground with embarrassment.

'We'd love to have you visit. Calypso gets a bit bored during the vacation don't you, sweetheart?' Bob had declared.

'Thanks, Bob, that sounds really cool,' Georgina replied. 'I'd love to come to LA, check out all the stars and do the shopping malls. Wouldn't that be fab, darling?' she trilled, grabbing my shoulders as if she really meant it. Clemmie and Arabella jumped about excitedly.

'I'd definitely come,' Star agreed in a more subdued sort of way . . . no doubt casting her mind back to all the stories I'd told her of my life in Los Angeles – the unglamorous version.

She looked at me sympathetically while Georgina,

Clemmie and Arabella danced about. I could just imagine what Georgina *et al* would make of my tragic LA house, with its new furniture and lack of pool and helipads and horse. What would they say when they saw my bedroom with its tragic single bed? And then there was Jay, my fake boyfriend to discover . . . It was all just too horrendous for words. Also, even though darling Bob hadn't realised it, I knew that from the girls' perspective, his invitation meant that he had actually offered to pay to fly my friends out – first class, of course. As Georgina and Honey always said, 'Never turn right, darling – only plebs do that!' (Only people who fly First Class turn left when boarding a plane.)

My only hope was that they'd forget all about it before term ended.

Before Sarah and Bob went home they took me to a pet shop in Windsor and bought me a baby rabbit – a tiny black one, with the softest, biggest ears and the sweetest, little golden eyes.

When Georgina saw it she kissed its little nose. 'Oh darling, she's so sweet. What are you going to call her?'

'I thought, maybe, Dorothy Parker . . . ?' I replied.

'Oh darling, I love it – and I'm sure Tobias will too!' She kissed little Dorothy on the nose again.

'That's brilliant,' I told her, 'because I was hoping we could share her . . . I mean, that she could be *our* rabbit. I mean, well, I can't exactly take her back to Los Angeles with me, can I?'

'Are you serious, darling?'

'Yaah!'

And then she wrapped Dorothy Parker and me in the

biggest cuddle. 'I'm so glad we ended up sharing a room together this term.'

'Me too,' I agreed. And I was.

Star came round the corner and gave little Dorothy a pat. 'I still think you should have got Bob and Sarah to get you a rat. They are *soooo* intelligent. Also, that way I could have taken her home with me in the holidays.'

'I've asked Georgina to share her with me.'

Star nodded. 'I hope you're not planning on carrying her about in one of those sad LVT carrier bags,' she warned Georgina in a mocking way.

But I was secretly hoping she would.

'No,' Georgina agreed. 'But we should get something cool, though?'

'Or you could decorate one in art class so that it looks cool,' Star suggested.

'We are not having a black pet bag for a black rabbit,' Georgina insisted – to which we all laughed.

For a second, my thoughts flashed back to the first day of term, to our initial mutual dread of sharing a room with Georgina. But after everything we'd been through it seemed like ages ago. Underneath all her grandeur and away from Honey, Georgina was actually really kind. I suppose Ms Topler was right – she was always babbling about there being 'more things in heaven and earth than dreamt of in your philosophy, Horatio'.

Or, as Sister Regina would say, 'diddley-dee'.

Even the excitement of having my own pet was over-shadowed by the school's reaction to Honey. Every dorm room – including Honey's – was burning with gossip.

Everyone in the entire school wanted her sent to Coventry. I'd first heard the term used by some girls in the Upper Sixth. There was a rumour that one of them had stolen another girl's boyfriend, and everyone had voted to send her to Coventry.

It was when no one looked at you or spoke to you at all: not in class, not in dorms, not walking down the corridor, not in canteen, not in sports and not even during that part of mass where you shook people's hands as you offered them the sign of peace.

And at boarding school, where there was no respite, being sent to Coventry was a million times worse than having Post-it Notes slammed on your back.

Even Poppy – her own sister – wasn't speaking to her. Which was how I came to find myself in the unlikely situation of being Honey's only ally. I use the term in the *loosest* sense.

I did actually feel genuinely sorry for her, though.

Her parents had been summoned and were informed that if Honey was given so much as a blue they would have to find alternative schooling for their daughter. As it was, she had been suspended for a week and gated for the rest of the term. A gating meant you couldn't go home on exeat weekends – sort of like boarding school in the old-fashioned days. Sort of like boarding school for me.

And then I received a letter from Freddie. It was a formal letter, written on palace paper, apologising in the grandest way for his inappropriate behaviour! I read it, and reread it, and my stomach turned with the formality of it all. The tone of it left me feeling worse about Freddie than I did before, so I didn't show it to anyone, not even Star. Just the same, I carried the letter around in my pocket.

We had other things to discuss. Star and I were in the fencing salle having a practice bout when I first explained to her why I thought it was too mean to send even the horrible Honey to Coventry.

Star said she sort of agreed, too. 'I know Georgina and the others are cool with us now, but they did put us through absolute hell for ages!'

'I suppose,' I agreed, as we lugged our gear back to the armoury.

'Don't you remember how evil they were to us?' Star said. 'I didn't really give a shit, personally, but I think you did . . . although you never said anything.'

'But that's what I'm saying. Even though she is the most horrible, meanest, nastiest, psycho toff at Saint Augustine's . . .'

'Honey will bounce back. She always does,' Star said.

'Maybe you're right, but still . . .'

'Well, I hope you're not suggesting that either of us should become a Honey friend?' she gasped.

'No!' I laughed. 'I just think that we shouldn't be part of the Coventry thing.'

'Mmmm. Not convinced. I think it might do her a bit of good, actually. Maybe she'll become all saintly and won-derful like us,' Star teased, nudging me in the hope of breaking my serious mood. 'And let's face it, she basically ruined your night with Freddie.'

While we were hanging our kit back in the armoury, I showed her the letter.

'Well, obviously someone at the palace wrote it for him.' She passed it back.

'But he signed it.'

'I told you I thought he was a jerk for believing all those evil things Honey said about you. Forget him.'

I shrugged. 'Yaah, besides, I'm totally over him,' I replied brightly, even though I so totally wasn't.

After that we rounded up the rest of our writing salon and went along to Sister Constance's office to discuss the launch party for *Nun of Your Business*.

We had to wait for her to finish her conversation with Father Conway and it wasn't long before our talk turned to Honey and sending her to Coventry.

'I don't know why you're so bothered about it. Honey's always hated you!' Georgina reasoned.

Star gave me a meaningful look, as if to remind me that it wasn't so long ago that Georgina had hated me too.

Clemmie and Arabella agreed. The irony of it all didn't escape me.

Clemmie added, 'It's true, she deserves Coventry.'

'No one deserves anything,' I snapped irritably, which made everyone shut up.

We sat in silence after that and my thoughts turned to Freddie and his royal apology for inappropriate behaviour. Did he mean kissing me? Did he think that kissing a common girl like me was inappropriate. Was that what he was saying? He'd signed off, wishing me well. Wishing me well! What was I – a leper?

Star's fury with him over his behaviour the night of the social now seemed spot on. How could he have believed a girl like Honey over a girl he'd just shared his mouth with for ten minutes? Still, I couldn't help wanting to relive that kiss in my mind, and I did, over and over, and over again. Only I didn't share this with any of the others.

'So what do you think Sister will say?' Arabella asked.

'What, about sending Honey to Coventry?'

'No, about *Nun of Your Business*!'

'Piss off?' Georgina replied. 'Let's face it darlings, after the fiasco of the Eades social, she's hardly going to allow us to use the hall and invite the Eades boys from our year.' I slumped down in my seat . . . I was the "fiasco of the Eades social".

'I suppose not,' Clemmie agreed dismally.

'On the other hand, it is for charity,' Star pointed out, as Father Conway walked out of Sister's office.

'Oh well, here goes nothing,' Georgina whispered, smoothing her uniform as she knocked softly on the gothic old oak door.

Sister's voice was clear and neutral as ever. 'Enter.'

Sitting behind her desk, straight-backed, her arms resting in her lap she looked imposing enough, but with Christ looming over her on his cross, the effect was just plain scary.

'Good afternoon, Sister,' we trilled.

'Girls.' She nodded to indicate we could proceed.

I nudged Georgina. We'd elected her as our spokesperson earlier.

Georgina nudged me back. Obviously she'd decided to back out. So I nudged Star. One of us had to step forward and it wasn't going to be me. Or Star, apparently, who then nudged Clemmie.

'Stand still, girls. This is not the appropriate setting for a vaudevillian tumbling act,' she warned. 'You have something to say. Speak.'

So I spoke. 'Erm, well, you see the thing is, Sister. Well, you know we're hoping to have the launch for our, erm, magazine thingamy and that sort of thing. Well, we were thinking. That is, if you say it's OK with you, we'd quite like to hold it in the hall,' I stuttered.

'And invite loads of boys,' added Clemmie.

'Or not,' I added hastily. 'I mean we appreciate that you might not feel that was appropriate.'

Sister Constance had a special fondness for the word 'appropriate,' so I was hoping the mere use of it might soften her.

'On the contrary. I feel it is extremely appropriate, if not imperative that we open up the hall to as many paying guests as possible. I've discussed the matter with Mr Raymond, the Head Master of Eades, and he feels as I do that this magazine launch party is the perfect opportunity to put last week's unpleasantness behind us.

'Quite separately, but no less important, is the cause for which we are raising money. I've suggested a ticket fee of twenty pounds. Initially Mr Raymond felt this was a little steep, but, as I reminded him, all proceeds of the launch will be going to the Children of the World.'

Star interrupted, 'You're kidding, Sister?'

But we all knew Sister Constance wasn't much of a one for kidding.

Georgina said, 'I need a fag,' and started fanning herself.

Not even that could wipe the smug smile off Sister's face.

I remembered that when Bob and Sarah had dropped me off on their way to the airport, Bob had remarked, 'She's a swell gal, your Sister Constance.'

Thinking of that made me smile and realise something. I missed Bob.

Actually, Bob was a bit swell himself.

TWENTY

Moonwalking

That night the Lit Chick Salon (Clemmie, Arabella, Star, Georgina and I) decided to go for a moon-walk.

Moonwalking was a Saint Augustine's tradition that went back further than anyone remembered – even Sister Francis, who was a hundred-and-two years old, couldn't remember how far back the girls of Saint Augustine's had been moonwalking. But then I suppose the nuns weren't really meant to know about it, otherwise everyone would have been rusticated (suspended).

Now that the security men and the guard dog numbers had been cut back to normal, we'd decided that a party in the woods under the light of the full moon was the perfect way to celebrate our victory over Sister Constance – or was it her victory over us?

Armed with torches, blankets, fags, Febreze, tuck and, of course Body Shop Specials, we snuck downstairs and out through the sash window of the bursar's room, which for some reason was never locked.

Our dash through the bluebells of Puller's Woods went smoothly, without any of us being devoured by guard dogs.

As we entered the woods, we looked back at the gabled roof of Cleathorpes illuminated by the moon. In a little bluebell glade, enclosed by the ancient woods, we lay out our blankets and booty and looked up at the ceiling of stars above us. The early June air was still and smelled of spring. I have always loved springtime at Saint Augustine's; there was electricity in the air, a sense that anything could happen.

Time, the seasons, everything seemed suspended in the hush of the starlit night. Well, at least it did before we heard a fox doing something horrendously cruel to some small animal.

'What do you think will happen with Freddie and you now?' Arabella asked as we began to open up our tuck.

I watched a shooting star flash across the sky and suddenly I felt tears spring to my eyes. I didn't know what I could wish for. I didn't even know what I wanted to happen with Freddie any more.

I was saved from replying by Star. 'What a jerk,' she went. 'I mean, what was that formal crappy letter begging forgiveness all about?'

Georgina sat bolt upright. 'He sent you a letter?'

'The palace did,' I replied bleakly.

'Cool. But don't you find it weird he hasn't called and left a message, though?' she added.

I did find it quite strange. I mean before the social he was a text and voicemail message demon.

'You know what?' she went on, 'I reckon he's still paranoid that what Honey said was true.'

Arabella added, 'Portia said that her brother, who's in his year, said that Freddie's totally gone on you. It's just that he has to lie low while the gossip dies down. Apparently the palace has given him a talking-to.'

I wondered why Portia hadn't told *me* this. After all, she was the only other girl on the sabre team, and I fenced with her three times a week. But then I supposed Portia hardly ever spoke to me. I'd always thought she was just quiet, the sort of girl who kept herself to herself, but clearly she had been chatting away to Arabella.

Star snorted in disbelief.

Clemmie snorted in agreement which caused her vodka to go down the wrong way and she started choking. When she recovered, she said, 'I heard pretty much the same from Antoinette. Her brother says Freddie never stops talking about you, darling.'

'Remember Kevin, Freddie's, mate?' Georgina said.

'Yaah. He was so fit,' Clemmie gushed, having long since turned her affections from the Razzle guy she'd met at the social to Kevin.

'Well, his brother is only Poppy's boyfriend.'

'You mean Poppy would deign to date someone from the East End? I doubt it,' I said.

I watched another star shoot across the sky as Arabella offered me a crisp – well, actually, she tickled my nose with it until I opened my mouth and she shoved it in.

'Got any matches, Georgie?' Star asked.

Georgina took the cigarette from Star's mouth and

stuck it in her own where three other cigarettes were already arranged. 'We only brought three matches down with us,' she explained, speaking out of the side of her mouth as she lit all four with the one match and distributed them.

'So Freddie's best friend's brother is Poppy's boyfriend,' I repeated, trying to get my head around what that might mean – if anything.

'Yup,' Georgina replied.

'So he must know if it's true or not?' I went on.

'Or he might have been convinced by Poppy that it *is* true.'

'As if anyone in their right mind would believe Honey or Poppy? According to Mummy, Lady O'Hare – and by the way, she's not married to a Lord any more, so she shouldn't even have a title – will appear at the opening of an envelope! Do you know she was even on some sordid Sky television channel last week showing off their house in Knightsbridge? I mean, how tragic do you have to be to do that?'

'What was it like?' Clemmie asked, her blue saucer eyes popping with curiosity.

'Darling, what do you think it was like? A five-star luxury hotel – so absolutely ghastly. No personal touches. Nothing eclectic, and all their furniture was bought new – well, it was riddled with antiques of course, but all of it was bought this generation, if you know what I mean! Mummy was like, "*Hello*, do you not have any ancestors?"'

This is where not being part of the English class system really gets to me. 'Well, erm, actually, Georgina, all my parents' stuff is new too.' I didn't add that our house doesn't even look like a five-star hotel, although I suppose it is madly eclectic.

'Yes, but that's different, darling. You're not trying to be all pretentious and pretending that your great-great-great-grandfather was best mates with the King. It's just fake and false and, well, tacky. I love modernism. When I get to buy my first house it's going to be madly Space Odyssey. I hate old stuff. It's all dusty. I bet your parents' place in LA is like super cool. Is it in Malibu, darling?'

'No.'

'I think it's really cool that we might be coming over to see you,' she added.

I watched another star shooting across the sky and wished like mad that Georgina would forget about Bob's offer.

'Honey's always been pretentious,' Arabella sneered a little later.

I didn't really give a toss about how tacky or pretentious Honey was. All I could think of was that if Freddie's best friend's brother was going out with Honey's sister, he'd be getting a whole different angle on everything.

Star took a deep drag on her fag and said, 'I mean, the mere fact that his best friend's brother would go out with a girl like Poppy means he's tragic. And if he's tragic, his brother's probably equally tragic and *ipso facto*, so is Freddie. You can tell a lot about a person by their friends.'

Georgina took a slug of her vodka. 'Oh, don't *ipso* bloody *facto* me. I'm only going to fail Latin, darling, and Daddy says if I fail Latin he's going to choose all my subjects in Lower Sixth.'

'Oh, look, there's a shooting star!' Arabella pointed up at the sky. 'Let's all make a wish.'

'To *Nun of Your Business* being a huge success,' Star declared.

'For raising thousands and thousands of pounds for Children of the World,' Clemmie added.

The girls all held their cigarettes against one another in the air in a toast. Georgina, realising I was left out, handed me one of the last of the two precious matches and I held it against their embers where it exploded in a whoosh.

'I told you this was going to be a great term,' Georgina reminded me, taking my hand in hers. I reached out and took Star's hand and all five of us held hands and looked up at the sky, silent in our own thoughts.

'And anyway,' Georgina remarked later as we took another swig of vodka, 'you've still got Jay back in LA,' which made us all howl with laughter for some reason.

'Actually, I haven't,' I told her when the laughter stopped and we were all just lying there silently again.

'Darling, you didn't drop him when you pulled Freddie, did you?'

'I didn't have to,' I told her as a shiver went through me at what I was about to do. 'He was never really my boyfriend, see. I made him up.'

I felt Star's hand squeeze mine and that gave me the courage to say what I knew I had to say if I was going to be honest.

'But the photographs?' Clemmie asked.

'He's my mom's PA. You know Sarah . . . Jay is her gay PA.'

Georgina spat out her vodka. 'Your mum's gay PA?'

'Uh-huh. Look, I'm not particularly proud of it,' I told them, praying that Georgina wouldn't pull her hand away from mine. I could take it if Clemmie and Arabella did, but not Georgina.

Georgina laughed. 'Darling, you are the end.'

'Delusional, you mean?'

'Delusional women and the boys they fall for. Let's do a piece on it for the next edition of *Nun of Your Business*,' Clemmie suggested.

'Or not,' I told them.

That was when I realised that I'd just fessed up to my greatest shame and here we still were, still holding hands, and the moon was still full and the stars were still shooting in the sky, and even though I'd pulled my prince and even though he'd dumped me, I was going to be OK. And suddenly all the things Star had been trying to explain to me, about friendship not being based on being an insider or an outsider, or pulling princes, but on moments like these, rang true.

People aren't always what they seem. All my time at Saint Augustine's I'd been so wrapped up in my preconceptions about Georgina and their kind. What was it Star had said, that I'd have to accept who I was before I could expect other people to accept me?

Arabella interrupted my epiphany. 'Anyhow, you'll see him tomorrow.'

'Who? Gay Jay?' Star giggled.

'No, darling – Freddie. You've got fencing at Eades, remember? You might even be up against him again!'

Star nudged me. 'Possibly even a bit of tongue-fencing, if you can lose the security guys.'

God, how could I have forgotten about fencing? Especially when it meant I'd be face-to-face with Freddie again.

'Tongue-fencing? You are totally gross sometimes, Star,' Georgina declared happily as she lit another bundle of cigarettes.

TWENTY-ONE

En Garde,
Your Royal Highness

I was unusually quiet on the minibus ride to Eades. It was almost like I was having one of those out-of-body experiences. My head was whizzing about and my heart was doing funny fluttery things, and it wasn't funny in a nice way.

Georgina said it was despair poisoned by hope (she'd been getting very literary in her language since we started up the writing salon). She had a point in a way, I suppose – only I think it was more a case of love poisoned by pissed-offedness.

Our moonwalk discussion about Freddie actually believing that I was trading on his royalty was now ringing true to me. I felt very confused about it all, because:

a) I was really pissed off with that wretched letter he'd sent me.

and

b) I really, really wanted to kiss him again.

I still remembered the kiss vividly. It was on some kind of loop in my brain. On and on it played, always accompanied by the tingly feeling I'd had as he'd handed me his jacket to hold while he held open the window in the library.

Followed by the warm feeling as he placed his jacket over my shoulders and guided me through the bushes as if I, me, Calypso Kelly, were the princess.

Followed by the way his mouth felt pressed on mine.

Followed by the crescendo as my heart went *whoosh* as he ran his hand up my safety-pinned back and supported my neck as he kissed me.

It had all been so lovely and then within minutes it had all gone so sordidly wrong with the 'trading on my royalty thing' and the Rough-and-Tumble photographs. And if anything, it was made even worse after his stupid formal letter begging for forgiveness.

None of it felt sorted.

Of course he was the first and only guy I saw when we entered the fencing salle at Eades. He was looking even more fit than I remembered. He was doing warm-ups on one of the pistes. His hair was all tussled . . . oh no – I wanted to rough-and-tumble him again.

When he saw me he smiled, but I couldn't tell if it was an it's-all-OK smile or merely one of those false how-charming-am-I? smiles, which he'd no doubt been trained to do since birth.

Star, sensing my pain, whispered wickedly in my ear, 'Excuse *me*, but do you know who I think I am?' which did actually make me laugh.

Star, Portia and I were on the first team – which didn't mean much as there was only one sabre team at Saint Augustine's. The thing was Portia also did *épée*, so she was called to a bout almost as soon as she'd finished her stretches.

Star and I were sitting around on the benches watching the other three bouts going on around us when Star nudged me. 'I think that's Kevin's brother, Billy, over there, fencing Portia.'

'God, he's really going for her, isn't he?' I marvelled.

He was good. Some boys have a very different approach to their game when they fence girls – actually, make that *most* boys. They didn't like to hit you anywhere above or below the stomach. There was nothing worse than a guy letting you win – it was like being lied to, or being made to feel you weren't worth the trouble.

Star agreed with me, but Clemmie thought we were mean. She thought they just let us win because they were being nice. But then Clemmie thought it was mean to eat Jelly Babies because they looked like her little brother Sebastian.

But Billy was ruthless. He was throwing everything he had at Portia.

I liked that.

When my first bout was called, I guess I had imagined it would be against Freddie, but instead it was against his captain Billy, who was not only one of the best sabreurs in the country, he was probably going to be on the Olympic team.

As I waited to be hooked up to the electrical point recorder, I looked him up and down. Suddenly I wasn't

thinking about Freddie at all. I was thinking of winning
. . . and of Billy.

He looked like Kevin in a sort of older, better-looking
way – short, blond hair, and eyes that seemed to be laughing at you even when he wasn't smiling. I figured he'd
probably be tired, having just been fencing Portia.

The president, in this instance the Eades fencing
master called, 'On guard, ready, fence!' He wasn't as mad
keen on French as Professor Sullivan.

Billy lunged at me first, which sort of shocked me, so I
parried and riposted with a hit to the back of his neck.
This didn't actually register as a point and wasn't really the
done thing, but it really, really hurt. (I knew this from first-
hand experience!)

Billy cried, 'Ow!' and the president called, 'Stop.'

We began again – only this time Billy waited for me to
make the first attack, probably because he was still in pain
and a bit unsure of what I might do. Like Professor
Sullivan was always reminding us, fencing was a physical
form of chess.

I decided to unnerve him further by not moving from the
en garde line for ages. When I did move, I scored a straight
hit to the torso. After that, the bout was mine, five hits to nil.

After the game was called, Billy took off his mask and
shook my hand. 'You're everything I'd heard you were and
more.' He was laughing as he said it.

I was going really red, but I took off my mask, revealing my fluffy horns in all their embarrassing glory.

We shook hands again. 'Billy,' he said. 'I think you
know my brother, Kevin?'

'Calypso,' I said, smiling. A fuzzy warm feeling started tingling through my body. I don't know how much time passed before I realised we were still shaking hands and everyone around us who wasn't fencing was looking at us.

The best thing was, it wasn't just me that couldn't stop shaking hands and staring. He was staring at me too, not letting go, and smiling.

Eventually, we both got a grip. I even rescued a slight chink of dignity by pulling my hand away first.

'Calypso,' he repeated.

'Uh-huh.' Here we go, I thought . . . my name again.

'She who causes men to be diverted from their goals?' he teased, referring to Calypso in Homer's *Odyssey*, who held Odysseus captive on her island until the gods petitioned her to let him go.

Normally I would have started digging a verbal hole to bury myself in, but something about Billy made me feel . . . well . . . like *me*, really, and instead I teased him back. 'Some men need a good diversion.'

To which he replied, '*Touché*,' and bowed in this mad, regal sort of way.

That was when Freddie came up to us.

'Hey man, how's it going?' Billy said.

'I think I'm up against Portia next,' Freddie replied – only he was looking at me as he said it, and he was looking sad.

I surprised myself by acting really cool. 'Hi, Freddie. Portia's quite good actually.'

Freddie said, 'Only not as good as you,' in a meaningful sort of way, which made me blush.

Billy said, 'If she is as good as Calypso, all I can say is watch the back of your neck, man.'

Freddie looked confused, having not seen our bout.

'Anyway, I'd better get going,' Billy said. 'My next bout's with Star. But listen, Calypso, great to have the shit sabreured out of me by you.'

I must have grimaced with embarrassment because he winked.

'Kidding – the pleasure was all mine. Catch you later, I hope,' he added pointedly.

'What's up with you guys?' Freddie enquired, obviously jealous.

Even though one part of me wanted to kiss him, another part of me was still too humiliated by the way he'd treated me. Either way, something inside me just snapped and I let out a heavy sigh.

Then he said, 'We need to talk. That is . . . I have some explaining to do, I think.'

Suddenly all my pent-up confusion, my anger over his letter, and my longing for more of his kisses just sort of exploded out of me.

'I don't think we have anything to say to one another.'

Then I turned to leave, aware that now *everyone* in the salle who was not in a bout was watching us.

'Wait, Calypso,' he said, grabbing my arm.

I looked at his hand gripping my elbow and my mind flashed back to the night of the social as he'd helped me climb out of the library window. I looked up into his ink-blue eyes and he let go, which was probably for the best because a part me suddenly wanted to kiss him again and we know how that ended up last time, don't we?

'You don't understand, actually,' he said.

'Actually,' I said, moving into motor-mouth mode. 'I understand just perfectly . . . you and your wretched royalty and all the ghastly people like me you're so paranoid are trading on it!'

'It's not like that.'

But I wasn't to be swayed. 'Who do you think you are?' I demanded, my hands on my hips. 'I mean, apart from heir to the throne and master of the nation or whatever other fancy titles you have, and . . . well, erm, that sort of thing?'

He looked shocked, so I really went for it. 'And anyway, another thing – even if I *had* sold all your bloody messages for like a thousand pounds a listen, it still wouldn't have been worth all the trouble you've caused me! Well, would it?'

He shook his head. He tried to say something, but I didn't give him a chance.

'To hell with your royal status. What about me? Do you think it's some sort of royal privilege for me to be labelled as the Prince's Rough-and-Tumble?'

He opened and closed his mouth for a bit so I told him he could shove his wretched royalty and elitist behaviour anywhere it would fit, as long as it wasn't anywhere near my life.

I think I said a lot of other things too, because I was quite red-faced and croaky by the time I finished.

'I think you were just called,' was all he said in the end.

'What?'

'You've got a bout – they just called your name.'

'Oh, right. OK then, well, goodbye.' I turned on my heels and walked towards the piste, trying to gather myself together in the manner befitting the Captain of the Saint Augustine's sabreurs.

Then I heard him calling out my name again.

I turned around. 'Good luck!' he called and gave me a little wave.

'I don't need luck,' I replied haughtily, because I felt wrong-footed by his unexpected kindness. Still, I was sounding almost like Honey and I wished I could take it back.

I won all my bouts, but I was still shaking over my exchange with Freddie when we finally clambered into the minibus for the journey back to Saint Augustine's.

Everyone immediately started going on about me giving Freddie a Right Royal Dressing Down, but I felt sick inside and didn't rise to the bait. I hardly said a word. I couldn't quite believe the things I'd said. I had been like a mad erupting, volcano and I hadn't even given him a chance.

Should I have given him a chance?

I didn't ask any of my friends because I knew what they'd say. 'No way. You were brilliant, Calypso . . . blah, blah, blah.'

Thank God it was an exeat weekend and we all got straight off the minibus with only half an hour to get ready for the coach that took us to London.

Star had invited me to spend the weekend at her place in Chelsea. This time her parents were there. That is, her parents and their roadies and their rock-star friends and their hangers-on – and, of course, their drugs.

That night there was a big party with loads of models and It Girls and really ancient rock stars, all of them acting like they thought they were sixteen or something. What is it with adults who can't grow up? They reminded me of Sarah and Bob.

Star and I wandered through the party, sipping on our Jack Daniels and Coke, which tasted ghastly, but Star insisted it was the only drink one could drink at a rock-star party.

I suppose it was quite cool – not the yucky drink, but seeing all these famous people being really happy to see Star and talking to us like we were real adults, even though we were about a hundred years younger than they were.

The best part was when Elsa, a really famous supermodel-turned-writer hung out with us in the cupboard under the stairs and we talked about school and friends and make-up. We told her about our magazine. She was really impressed and asked if she could come to the launch. She said she was writing a book, which made me worship her even more.

The party went on all through the night and when we went downstairs for breakfast the next morning there were loads of sleeping bodies everywhere. Mostly they were Tiger's roadies, but as Star said, even really famous people look totally gross when they are sleeping and there is no one to airbrush them.

They were sprawled on sofas and the floor, and Star and I were quite wicked and put Coco Pops in their mouths and then ran off and hid.

All in all it was a weekend free of worry. Feeding sleeping rock stars Coco Pops turned out to be the perfect antidote to all my dilemmas, but on the coach back to Saint Augustine's they all came flooding back. I discovered a text on my phone, which had been sent on Friday.

I hadn't even looked at my phone all weekend.

PLEASE DON'T H8 ME. I DON'T H8 U. ACTUALLY . . .
QUITE THE OPPOSITE. CAN I CALL YOU TO XPLAIN? F

I immediately texted him back.

I DON'T HATE YOU. C X

Then I immediately regretted the X.

Nun of Your Business

A week later, on the morning of the launch party for *Nun of Your Business*, I woke up pre-gong, which put Miss Cribbe into a bit of a mood. Honey was back at school, no longer in Coventry, ensconced in her role as Queen B (that's B for Bitch), but in a weird sort of way, it was actually quite fun having her back. There was too much going on for me to be bothered holding a grudge.

Honey had had a complete makeover. She'd had ringlets put into her hair, which was now blonder than ever, and Rystaline injected into her smile lines (even though she didn't have any). She'd also had her navel pierced and as a punishment/reward her mother had given her a diamond navel ring for it. Duchess had a real Tiffany diamond collar, with a white gold bell, so she could drive the other pets bananas.

'It's barbaric. Hilda is terrified!' Star had complained. 'She's so stressed out by that bell, she's constantly on her wheel now. I'm scared she's going to have a heart attack if she keeps this up.'

On this occasion even I felt quite sorry for Hilda (and all the other pets in the pet shed – especially Dorothy Parker). I mean, imagine having a bell sounding every time the horrible Duchess moved! It would be like Miss Cribbe banging on her gong all the time.

'I'm actually quite bored with her anyway,' Honey yawned when Star complained about her rabbit's bell. 'I'm thinking that the diamond collar would look so much more stylish on a white rabbit. Perhaps I'll give Duchess to Poppy.'

None of us said anything. I guess the makeover hadn't been that complete.

We had far more important things on our minds – making sure everything was in place for the launch. All day long, girls kept coming up to us and saying, Is Jono (famous rock star) really coming to the launch? and stuff like that. No one could pay attention in classes that day.

The nuns had volunteered to supervise everything (i.e. to wander around the hall oppressively, making sure no one had an iota of a chance of pulling any of the boys).

We had a plan, though.

My plan went like this. After sending Freddie the X on my text, I decided to go for gold i.e. march straight up to him, grab him by the hand, and lead him to the secret passage under the stage and, while Star and Georgina diverted any nuns nearby, we would nip in the secret door and tongue-fence like mad. All the complications between us – whether to 'X' or not – had made me think that some things are better said with tongues than words.

It was Clemmie's idea, actually. All term it had been

clear that she'd been heading this way, but since the Eades social she had officially gone Boy Crazy. All she could talk about was who she was going to pull at the launch – she had a list with five names on it:

Kevin.
Kevin.
Kevin.
Kevin.
Kevin.

Georgina had a list too. Her list had thirty-six names on it (all different) but only twenty-four of the names on the list attended Eades. But Georgina could pull boys effortlessly (eighteen was her record so far), whereas Clemmie was a bit more like me – single-minded (or as Georgina called us, dramatic).

Star was back on with Rupert who'd had his braces taken off and was now a realistic pulling option. She was hoping to pull a few older, fit boys as well, just in case Rupert was as hopeless a kisser without braces as with.

Arabella was keeping her pulling list open, but she had sworn that she was determined to pull at least six boys before the night was out.

Thank goodness our nuns were so old and innocent.

The painting that the kids from the village in Africa had sent us was hanging above the stage, next to the DJ's station. The nuns had really gone to town with decorations. The main hall was lit with multicoloured flashing lights and the standard disco ball hanging in the centre.

Sisters Hillary and Veronica were manning the *Nun of*

Your Business desk at the entrance. Everyone who had bought a ticket to the launch was given a free copy as they came in, but we were also selling a limited edition of two hundred copies signed by the editors, that is us, the five Lit Chick Salon girls (Arabella, Clemmie, Georgina, Star and me) for ten pounds each.

All the Eades boys were arriving by coaches, and I tried to loiter nonchalantly around the entrance, looking out for Freddie as coach after coach arrived. Our hall was already at capacity by the time Kevin ambled in, laughing and chatting away with a few of his mates. I sidled up to him very casually/desperately and said, 'Hiya.'

He looked genuinely pleased to see me. But then that's how Eades boys are brought up to look.

'Hey, Calypso. How's it going? I heard you trounced my bro at sabre last week. Well done.'

I giggled like . . . well, a schoolgirl, I suppose.

'So, erm, how's Freddie, then?' I asked, craning a look over his shoulder for my prince.

'Down with some stomach bug, unfortunately. He said to say hi.'

Clemmie skipped over and my window of interrogation had closed. So I stood there at the entrance, clinging to my pathetic message.

Freddie said to say hi.

What could I read into that? Answer: A LOT.

I mean, did he say, 'God, I'm gutted that this stomach bug has prevented me from resting my eyes on the beautiful, intoxicating sight of Calypso Kelly, but say hi for me, will you, Kev?' Or did he say, 'If you see what's-her-name, the fencer girl – Calypso, is it? – tell her hi.'

Or worse still, did he say nothing at all, and Kevin, not wanting to make me realise how irrelevant I truly was, had made up the 'hi' to save my feelings?

I watched as Kevin and Clementine disappeared through the secret stage door.

Sister Veronica was polishing her spectacles.

Sister Hillary was eating a scone.

Clemmie was hotly followed by Star with Rupert, and Georgina with an Eades Sixth Former.

'So, Calypso, can you talk to mere mortals, or do I need to petition Zeus?'

I spun around. 'What?'

'Billy. We met at . . .'

'I know. Hi, how's it going?' I got that funny wiggly feeling again. Maybe I was coming down with Freddie's stomach bug? Wouldn't that be romantic, sharing a gastric flu . . . or not! The thing was, my wiggly feeling didn't feel gastric, it felt sort of . . . nice, really.

'It's going fine. Cool magazine, by the way. I love the satires, especially the one on Honey.'

And then I remembered. 'Oh, that's right, you go out with Poppy, don't you?'

He looked embarrassed and did that funny I'm-going-to-look-at-my-feet-now thing that boys tend to do. 'No . . .'

'Oh, OK. It's just that, erm . . .'

He still looked embarrassed and he didn't take his eyes off his shoes. He sort of shuffled them a bit, burying his hands in his pockets, and he looked so cute.

'We went out a few times over the Easter break,' he

explained. 'You know, down the Kings Road – that sort of thing. Nothing major. But we're not like *going out*, going out.'

'Darling! I wondered where you'd got to.' It was Poppy, looking divine in a breathtakingly short, pink, wispy number with matching Jimmy Choo sling-backs. She threw her arm around Billy in a proprietorial sort of fashion. 'Quick, darling, this way. I've got some vodka in my bag.'

With that, she took him by the hand and led him towards the stage passage. He looked back at me like a man being led off to a firing squad.

With a wardrobe like hers, it was no wonder Poppy could pull a boy like Billy. I looked down at my carefully constructed outfit, bought the night before for a fiver from one of the Lower Sixth girls. It was last year's cut, last year's colour and the shoes I was wearing were a label no one in England had ever heard of, which I'd bought in LA in the sale at Bloomingdale's. Honey had declared them 'Don't-Fuck-Me Shoes!' But then I didn't really give a toss what Honey said, did or thought any more.

Besides, it wasn't all doom and gloom. In fact, it was really cool especially when Jono, famous for his views on world debt, arrived. He looked quite cute standing on the stage next to Sister Veronica – they were about the same height – especially when he put his arm around her and she started to giggle.

Hello, was Sister Veronica flirting?

He gave a stirring speech about why the rich countries of the world should cancel the debt of really poor ones, and everyone cheered.

He said it was really cool that we'd put so much effort

into raising all this money. Then Star's dad, Tiger, got on stage with Elsa, the supermodel Star and I had chatted with at the party, which was just totally random and unscripted.

Tiger was wobbling a bit when he grabbed the mike off of Jono and asked us if we were having a 'rocking good time'.

Everyone screamed back, 'Yes!'

Then he said, 'That's cool, but just remember, if all the rich arsehole countries in the world cancelled world debt, ninety million girls in Africa could have an education.'

Everyone clapped and I looked over at Star to give her a supportive smile about her dad being dead embarrassing, but she didn't look in the least bit embarrassed. In fact, she looked proud. And once I thought about it, I could see why. It was a very good point.

Then Elsa took the mike and she very sweetly reminded everyone that the magazine wouldn't have got off the ground if it wasn't for Star, Calypso, Arabella, Clementine and Georgina and their friends, and everyone clapped.

Then the party really kicked in.

I ended up dancing with a few random boys, but I didn't even really look at their faces – apart from Rupert's (he must have got the thumbs down after his no-braces kiss with Star).

It was a fantastic party, but the only thing I pulled that night was a good laugh when we arrived back at our dorms.

Misty had weed all over Honey's duvet.

You could hear her scream throughout Cleathorpes.

TWENTY-THREE

The Glory and the Embarrassment

The week after the launch no one could talk about anything other than the party – or rather, who'd pulled whom.

Even though I'd pulled a grand total of nil, I was still caught up in the excitement. Also, both Freddie and Billy had sent me text messages and voicemails afterwards – but, to tell the truth, pulling boys was the last thing on my mind. I was more excited about the next meeting of the Lit Chick Writing Salon.

We'd decided to wait until Friday to discuss our strategy for the next issue of the magazine because we wanted to find out exactly how much money we'd raised altogether.

Sister Constance made the announcement at Thursday's assembly and it was unbelievable. With the twenty-pound tickets all sold out, and with roughly eight hundred boys from Eades and four hundred girls, from Saint Augustine's we'd made loads of money. Also people like Tiger and Jono had made extra donations.

Sister Constance had stood on the hall stage flanked by

two ancient statues of the Virgin Mary. There were enormous vases of lilies surrounding them. The other nuns were all gathered on the stage with her. The elderly ones (all those over ninety) were sitting on chairs. It was like a conceptual girl-power exhibit – in a nun-ish sort of way.

She announced how much we raised, unable to suppress a smile. It was much more than the Lower Sixth girls had managed the year before.

No one even clapped at first. I think we were all too shocked. After a moment's silence the nuns all clapped for us and Sister Constance congratulated Star, Clemmie, Arabella, Georgina and me. Suddenly everyone burst into applause and throwing their ties in the air, as is the tradition at Saint Augustine's. (Any excuse to rid ourselves of the revolting bows. We would have thrown them in the air if we'd raised five quid to be honest.)

When the deafening noise had died down a little, a girl from the Saint Augustine's Old Girls Society took the microphone and talked to us about how much that money would mean to The Children of the World charity.

It was one of the most fantastic days of my life . . . well, it was up until the point when Camilla (the Old Girl) asked Georgina, Star, Clementine, Arabella and me to come up on to the stage.

Talk about catastrophically random; no one had even hinted that we might be called upon to embarrass ourselves in front of the entire school. We all immediately started applying lip-gloss as we made our way through the aisles. The whole school started stamping their feet (even the nuns – apart from Sister Constance who never lets her austere demeanour drop for a moment) and demanding, 'Speech, speech, speech!'

Sister Constance took the microphone and asked for hush. Everyone fell silent immediately.

'Now, I'm sure you'd all like to hear from one of the girls responsible for raising all this money,' she said, handing the mike over to me.

The school responded in the affirmative. 'Erm, well thanks,' I mumbled. 'I mean yaah . . . brilliant. This is so random and totally unexpected,' I stuttered. My mouth went all-dry and so I applied a dab more lip-gloss.

Here I was, on stage in front of the entire school, a sea of girls all looking up at me, expecting me to say something profound or at least comprehensible.

How could this happen? So I tried to pretend I was Nancy Mitford or Dorothy Parker (the writer, not the rabbit) and say something poignant and witty, something inspirational – and not to mention how our writing salon, from which the magazine had sprung, all started with a food fight in the canteen. I had quickly decided that wouldn't sound very inspirational.

I did one of those little cough thingamies Oscar winners do in the hope that it would add some glamour to the occasion, and then I just let my subconscious do the rambling for me, figuring it couldn't do a worse job than my conscious self – which couldn't think of much apart from whether my hair was sticking up and if it was possible to apply lip-gloss while holding a microphone and speaking. I must have said something vaguely reasonable, though, because I heard the applause. Also no one teased me afterwards.

When it was over I went to the technology room and sent Sarah and Bob an e-mail about it. I thought about texting Freddie, but couldn't think of an excuse that wouldn't seem tragic, so I joined the celebratory dorm party.

TWENTY-FOUR

The Myth of the Midnight Dash

Georgina invited Clemmie, Star, Arabella and me (and Dorothy Parker of course) to spend half-term break at her massive stucco house on Eton Square.

We spent our mornings lying in the late-spring sun of her vast garden square, sipping on various health drinks dreamed up by her housekeeper after which we would head off to Sloane Street and do a bit of shopping.

Sarah and Bob had finally upped my allowance to a reasonable level – not to the heady heights of Georgina, Star and the others, but at least I could afford to chip in for a pizza now. Sarah and Bob said it was because next school year I was going to be turning fifteen, but I suspect they also felt that after the Rough-and-Tumble episode, my character had been built up as much as it was ever going to be.

The best part, though, was in the evenings, when we dressed up in all our finery (even Tobias put on his best suit) and set off for the Kings Road to pull boys.

The Kings Road Promanade. It was a tradition. A tradition that up until now I had never properly felt a part of.

Girls and boys from boarding schools from all over England came in droves, like homing pigeons, to march up and down the Kings Road in Chelsea. American teenagers went to malls, we strolled up and down the road every evening, checking one another out and trying to pull.

The boys tried to look all cool and wasted, like they didn't give a toss and the girls, having spent hours trying to make themselves look effortlessly stunning, pretended not to look at the boys while arguing the fitness and pullability rating of each.

Clemmie and Kevin were an official item now. Star and Georgina both found her fascination with him immature, and teased her mercilessly about stuff like when were they going to set the date for their marriage, etc.

My pulling rate that half-term was pretty low, mainly because I had Freddie on my mind. Although I did kiss Hugo, this totally fit boy from Downside (a posh Catholic boarding school), who was writing a novel.

A novel! Imagine that. An actual book. And it sounded really cool and witty too. I could have listened to him talk about it all night, but I had kissing on my mind and we had an eleven o'clock curfew, so I just flung myself at him.

Shame he was such a crap kisser – well, compared to Freddie anyway.

I'd heard/read that Freddie was away with his family in Scotland so I didn't expect to hear from him . . . well, I tried not to expect to hear from him – although I did see him on television one evening, looking all gorgeous and charming. He was standing outside one of the royal retreats with the Queen and King, and his mother and father, but just the same, I was disappointed he hadn't called.

I bumped into Kevin on the Kings Road a few times and he said that I wasn't to worry as it was game on with Freddie and me, as far as he knew. I didn't dare mention his brother – although Kevin did say Billy was studying. I know that as he was in Year Eleven he probably was – but I still couldn't help imagining him with Poppy.

On the last day of half-term, while we were sipping lattés on the Kings Road, Georgina brought up Bob's mad invitation to visit LA in the summer.

I stared into my milky drink.

'The thing is, darling, Star and I have asked our parents and we're coming.'

'Oh,' I said, trying not to make it sound like a groan of pain. It wasn't that I wouldn't have loved spending the summer with them, it was just that I knew Sarah and Bob could never afford the first class travel and entertainment they'd expect. 'That is, are you sure? I mean LA's pretty dull in the summertime.'

Star pitched in. 'Well, my dad spoke to your dad last night and it's all arranged. My whole family's going and I've invited Georgina because she was only going to spend the summer with her family in the south of France –'

'Which would be boring beyond belief,' Georgina added. 'All we do is go out on the *bâteau* and lie in the sun and eat loads and loads of really fattening food. I'd much rather be on the Atkins diet with you in Malibu.'

'I don't live in Malibu!' I insisted, looking up from my drink for the first time to see Georgina and Star grinning at each other.

'Darling, don't be so mad. You really are the most awful snob,' Georgina declared. 'As if we mind where you live. Besides Sarah told us she had a new PA, and he's not gay!'

Clemmie and Arabella admitted that they were madly jealous and wished they could come to LA too, but that they were already booked to go on a safari in Kenya with Arabella's family.

So that was that. Georgina's parents sent us all back to school in the family Rolls Royce and then Georgina gave Miles, the chauffeur, a fifty-pound note to carry all our bags up to Cleathorpes and unpack for us so that we could race off and settle Dorothy Parker back in the pet shed.

It was a far cry from my inauspicious arrival at the start of term.

The second half of the term was crammed with study. Our teachers must have held a heinous meeting over the half-term break about not being cruel enough to us because they were really putting the pressure on us now. They said we needed to start adopting a more serious attitude to our work and went on and on about how important the next school year was going to be because we'd be starting our GCSE coursework and 'defining our futures'.

Yawn.

'Your lives depend on the grit and determination with which you apply yourself to your studies, girls!' they trilled every moment of the day.

But finally the day came when our last piece of work for the term was handed in and we were able to put into action the dream of every self-respecting Saint Augustine girl. The legendary midnight dash into London to Fabric, where Georgina's brother knew someone who knew someone who could get us all in.

We went to bed in our trackie bums and hoodies; our party dresses and shoes and make-up in our gym bags by our beds. Miss Cribbe turned our lights off at ten and we even let her give us big beardy kisses on our cheeks. In fact, we even let Misty lick us to keep Miss Cribbe sweet.

'Aren't you lovely little girlsies? Misty loves her wittle girlsie-whirlsies, doesn't she, Misty?'

Misty showed her love with a big smelly fart and Miss Cribbe bustled her out of the room as if nothing had happened.

Actually, none of us hated Misty nearly as much now since she'd weed on Honey's duvet.

As soon as the clock hit half-past ten, we all snuck downstairs and climbed out of the bursar's window. Honey (we had to include her or she would have told on us), Clemmie and Arabella were already outside waiting for us.

We dashed into Puller's Woods and changed into our party gear, hiding our gym bags under leaves and fallen branches.

The plan – perfect in all its details – was to dash to the train station and catch the 23:23 to London (having successfully dodged guard dogs, security men and climbed through the electric barbed-wire fencing that surrounded the school grounds).

Once in London we would dance ourselves stupid at Fabric and pull older fit boys before catching the 6:03 back to the station.

It was the perfect plan. Next year we would regale the Year Ten girls with tales of *our* Midnight Raving.

When we got back from London, we'd dig our bags back out from their hiding places and change back into our trackie bums and hoodies and stick our clubbing gear back in our bags, hide them back under the leaves and jog off to breakfast. If anyone saw us dashing back to our rooms, we'd simply say we'd been for a run. How athletic and disciplined were we?

We'd then collect our gym bags from the woods at lunch, giving the smokers a chance for a quick fag.

Like I said, the perfect plan . . .

Unfortunately, the guard dogs discovered us just as we finished changing – which meant I only got as far as up an oak tree while a vicious, blood-thirsty Alsatian barked and bared its fearsome teeth at me from below.

The other girls, who didn't share my fear of dogs, tried to persuade me to leg it with them, but my dog didn't look like the type to let me escape with my legs.

Honey didn't even bother with me or anyone else. She just ran off back to the dorm and eventually the other girls followed, although they at least promised that they would come back and save me later.

I watched them disappear through the woods hotly pursued, by the dogs (not mine). I guess all our cross-country running hadn't been for nothing, as none of them were dragged down and mauled.

Half an hour later my dog was still growling and salivating at the thought of tearing me limb from limb. I started to cry, imagining myself being discovered by a security guy and reported to Sister Constance and being excluded from the trip to the village school in Gambia.

'Talk about random,' I whimpered to myself and then it happened

A torch illuminated my face. The security guys had finally found me. I began to cry harder, not that I thought tears would in anyway get me out of this . . .

'Calypso?'

I looked down. Instead of the burly, mean security guy I was expecting, there was Billy, standing at the foot of my tree and grinning from ear to ear. He had the dog by the collar.

'I've often dreamed of what you girls get up to at Saint Augustine's after lights out, but I have to admit this particular fantasy hasn't featured.'

'Oh, shut up,' I said. I couldn't help smiling, even though I tried my best to look cool, collected and unamused.

'Nice dress.'

'Thanks.'

The dog was whimpering and licking Billy's hand now.

'Do you usually dress up for midnight tree-climbing?' he asked.

'Always. A girl can never be too stylish.'

I couldn't believe I was being so fabulously collected. I mean, the quality of my repartee was phenomenal. Dorothy Parker – the writer not the rabbit – would be proud.

'The grey knickers being the *pièce de résistance*, of course,' he added.

I was wearing my big grey knickers – well they'd started off white, but matron had managed to turn them grey in the wash along with all my bras and gym skirts. Unlike the other girls' parents, Sarah and Bob wouldn't allow me to wear sexy Calvin Klein knickers. 'Not at your age, sweetheart!' Bob had ruled, and at thirty pounds a pair I simply didn't have the resources – not even with my increased allowance.

'So, are you coming down, then?' he asked. 'Or do you usually wait for dawn to break?'

Ha, ha, very amusing. But see, here was the thing. Climbing up the tree had been a breeze; I'd been driven by pure adrenalin. But clambering down without looking graceless, destroying my dress and scratching myself to pieces was another matter.

'Shall I catch you?' he asked, sensing my hesitation.

I know it sounds like a nice offer, but if you'd seen the smirk on his face you would have wanted to slap it.

'Well . . . ?'

God, I so wanted to say no.

'It's fine – just sort of throw yourself backwards and fall and I'll be here to catch you. That way you won't scratch yourself.'

Yaah, right.

But I did it anyway. OK, so it wasn't my most graceful moment – plopping backwards out of a tree into the arms of a gorgeous boy who made me feel all wobbly inside. But it was nice. Especially the part where he held me in his arms for a bit, before placing me on the ground. (NB: He smelled delish.) The Alsatian even gave me a little lick.

For a minute I thought Billy was going to kiss me – or rather, that I was going to kiss him, but then I remembered Poppy and started brushing the bark off my dress dementedly.

'You're seeing Freddie, aren't you?' he went.

'Erm, well, I'm not actually sure.'

Billy laughed.

'You're seeing Poppy, though,' I reminded him.

'I so am not. That's what I've just been doing at Saint Augustine's. I told her in the break we weren't an item, but she kept texting me and pretending we were. I figured I'd better have a face-to-face with her.'

'Just now?'

He nodded. 'Yaah, just now. What, do you think I just escaped from Eades and struggled with the electric barbed-wire fencing for a stroll in the woods?'

'So it's all over with Poppy?' I pretended to be all casual and cool about it – and not turning bright red.

'Yes, but that's enough about me. Tell me about you and Freddie. What's the deal?'

I wished I had a simple answer. Even more importantly, I wished I knew what I wanted the simple answer to be.

Then suddenly Billy whispered, 'Shit, I've got to leg it – so do you. Here comes a security man. I'll text you.'

I didn't have time to ruminate on our encounter as I sprinted back to the dorm.

I told Georgina and Star about Billy in a whispered voice. It all sounded very nice and romantic, but how was he going to get my mobile number?

'Is it possible to fancy two boys at the same time?' I asked Star as we were lying in bed, too exhilarated by the evening's events to sleep.

'Absolutely, darling,' Georgina pitched in. 'In fact, it's normal.'

I wasn't so sure, though. The thing with Freddie was very troubling, what with all his security men and the paparazzi, but then he is a prince, so maybe that's all part of the royal package?

On the other hand, Billy was sooo fit and hadn't given me the least bit of trouble. In fact, he'd saved me from a ferocious dog and a tree.

Then again, I couldn't stop thinking of the night I'd pulled Freddie and how lovely kissing him had been . . .

I could see I was going to have a lot on my mind over the summer holidays.

Acknowledgements

Enormous amounts of praise and gratitude must go to my gorgeous children for entertaining me with their stories of boarding school life, especially my eldest son Zad for his advice and tales about sabre. Thanks also to the old girls and boys of Saint Mary's School Ascot, Eton, Benenden and other boarding schools around England, where clearly a good time was had by all. Also to Eric Hewitson for his map, my agent Laura Dail for her vision, and the team at Piccadilly – Brenda, Yasemin, Lea *et al* – whose fab support and encouragement made this story complete.

Stealing Princes

THE CALYPSO CHRONICLES

by Tyne O'Connell

Piccadilly Press • London

Having pulled your boy
and found him to be a prince,
you might want to kiss him twice . . .
just to be sure!

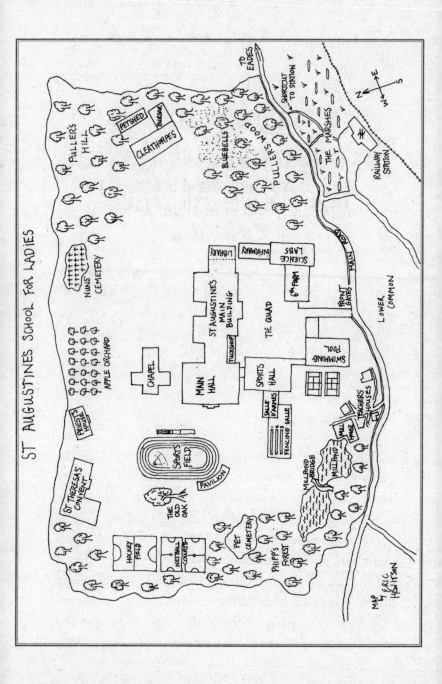

ONE

The Agony and the Text-acy of Flirt-texting Two Boys At Once!

I was standing in the en garde line, wired to the electrical recording device which would register hits (should I be lucky enough to get any). I saluted my opponent casually and focused. Well, I focused as best as a girl can when she's about to fence one of the fittest boys in all the word.

Eades is the grandest of grand boys' schools in England and they know it. Royalty, the good, the great and the madly wealthy of the world all send their sons to Eades to be educated in the art of effortless charm and entitlement. I suppose they teach them hard sums, Latin, and a bit of Greek too but then so do other schools. It's the effortless charm and sense of entitlement bit that sets them apart – and the fact that each and every Eades boy is distressingly fit. I suspect that their entrance exam includes a fitness test.

Billy Pyke, captain of the Eades sabre team, and the boy I was about to fence, isn't a bit grand, though. Well, his family is ridiculously rich and he speaks in the grand way all Eades boys do but he's actually from the East End of London. His father runs the country's largest limo sale and hire business, but being ridiculously rich doesn't necessarily make you grand. In fact, it can work against you and earn you the term *nouveau* which is worse than being a pleb. Most boys from Eades can point to their name in *Debrett's Peerage and Baronetage* or, if European, the *Amanach De Gotha*. At the very least your people's money has to go back hundreds of generations for it to be respectable in the high-stakes world of English boarding schools. Billy's family money only goes back one.

'Better to be as poor as a church mouse, than rich and common,' as they say here. Which is especially tragic for me because my parents aren't titled and they aren't rich, even new-money rich. They struggle to send me to Saint Augustine's because they are obsessed with giving me the best education money can buy, which according to my mum isn't available in LA. Also she's English and went to Saint Augustine's, and she thought it was 'super'.

Apart from the new-money thing, Billy is distressingly fit and cool, and tall, blond, blue-eyed and dashing. And did I mention older? He's seventeen. Older is always a plus. So clearly it was pretty tricky to focus the mind on combat, knowing of the gorgeousness that lurked beneath the tight white fencing gear and the electrically conductive metal mesh mask he was encased in.

The fencing master called 'Play,' and I advanced swiftly down the piste, preparing for an attack. Usually boys are a bit hesitant to hit girls on the chest. When I say hesitant,

I'm speaking in nano-milliseconds. Obviously they still hit you, and just as hard! Nonetheless, their hesitation often gives a girl an advantage, because that's all you need in sabre to grab the point.

Billy was renowned for not being in the least bit hesitant when it came to hitting girls. Actually, he was the most aggressive fencer I've had the privilege to be rinsed by. Sabre is all about speed and concentration and the attacker always has priority, as long as the opponent's target (anywhere above the leg) is continually threatened. I won my first point and after that I made sure that Billy's target area was continually threatened for the rest of the bout.

If I say so myself, I was unbelievable. My mother, Sarah, often says that false modestly is artless, so all modesty aside, my footwork was absurdly faultless. Honestly, I was shocked by my own talent as each lunge sent the electrical recorder lights flashing and buzzing. I was a veritable Olympian. I was indestructible and what's more, I didn't even feel the few hits Billy *did* manage. And in sabre that is something because it's not like the graceful fencing you've probably seen in the Zorro films or the fencing you see on ads for hair products. It's brutal and you get bruised and sore and seriously sweaty.

At the end of the bout, I triumphantly tore off my mask but instead of the usual spray of sweat and mucky hair, my unruly blond mane came out like . . . well like, hair-commercial hair. *Incroyable,* as my French teacher would say.

The applause was deafening as a victorious V was chalked on to the board, but all I cared about as I strode towards Billy to shake his hand was snogging him. Not that I would be allowed to obviously. Single-sex boarding schools like to keep inter-gender activities strictly lips-off. 'There must always be a balloon distance between boys and girls,' as Sister Constance likes to chant.

Time moved into slow motion as I stretched out my hand to shake his. I watched his hand begin to remove his mask, tugging the chin guard upwards, revealing inch by inch, not the features of Billy, but Freddie, as in HRH – you know Prince Freddie, heir to the British throne.

'You have to put your seat belt on now,' the flight attendant warned as she woke me. 'We'll be landing at Heathrow in a moment.'

OK, it was only a dream, but it was kind of spooky, actually, because all summer I'd been text-flirting with Freddie and Billy. I know it sounds bad but you can't blame me. We are talking about two wildly fit boys here – even by Eades standards – and after taking so long to pull a single boy (fourteen years) I now had two boys text-flirting me. What girl is going to resist that? How was I ever going to choose between Freddie – heir to the British throne – and Billy, captain of the Eades sabre team who had rescued me from the jaws of a girl-eating attack dog before we broke up for summer?

My two best friends, Georgina and Star, have both found the text relationships of my summer hugely enter-taining. I forwarded them every text, even though a part of me wanted to keep some of them a secret all to myself. Like the one where Freddie said his parents wanted to meet me.

Me, Calypso Kelly, a complete nobody from America! No title, no money – not even new money – and yet the King and Queen of the United Kingdom and all its territories wanted to meet *me*. I could have swooned with the excitement of it all, only then he went on to say how of course he'd never put me through that, because apparently it would mean spending a weekend at Bardington with his gran's Labradors who are elderly and yet quite nippy.

I sent a text back telling him that I wouldn't mind being nipped to bits by royal Labradors. I was madly restrained in fact – deleting the bit about how I'd be prepared to be mauled by them if it meant staying a weekend in one of his family's castles.

Freddie sent back a text saying:

HA, HA, HA! X FREDS

You see, my fear of dogs is legendary at Eades ever since news got out about my attempted escape from school to go clubbing one night last term. I was chased up a tree by one of the school's attack dogs. That's how I first became friendly with Billy. He had helped me down while the girl-eating dog happily licked his hand.

Freddie knows all about my shameful stuck-up-a-tree experience, though he doesn't know about the wobbly feeling I felt in my tummy as Billy helped me down and held me in his arms. And he definitely doesn't know I've been text-flirting Billy all summer.

I'd already pulled Freddie, but everything between us got complicated because Honey O'Hare, the most toxic psycho toff ever, sold a camera-phone snap of us kissing in the bushes to the tabloids. It all ended in a bit of a messy misunderstanding which is why I got mixed up and started flirt-texting Billy.

Only now Billy's texts are getting progressively steamier and I know I can't go on text-flirting two boys from the same school without it all blowing up in my face. So while my furious text-flirting with two boys may have made my holidays in LA and the prospect of returning to Saint Augustine's exciting, I was going to have to sort my feelings out by the end of the week when I faced them both on the fencing piste. It was that or – *quelle horreur* – risk having no boy texting me at all! Just like the old days.

Even as my taxi dropped me at school the thrill of having two fit Eades boys texting me was beginning to feel like a pressure more than a flattering thrill. And guess what? Mental telepathy really does work because no sooner did this thought flash through my mind than my text alert sounded:

CAN'T WAIT TO SEE YOUR NAVEL PIERCING. X FREDDIE

I texted him back immediately.

CAN'T WAIT TO RINSE YOU AT SABRE. X CALYPSO

I didn't really feel like confessing that I'd been forced by my parents, Sarah and Bob, to remove my navel ring. I quite fancied the idea of Freddie thinking of me as this madly cool wild-child American girl who did her own thing and made her own rules. Sadly, nothing could be further from the truth.

TWO

It's Hard Teaching Your Parents Where Their Dreams End and Yours Begin

I will turn fifteen on 15th December. Just ten days before Christmas. This explains a lot about me. Firstly it means my parents are Catholic and didn't practise birth control. They've never admitted this (the lack of birth control thing), but I ask you, what sort of unfeeling parents would purposefully elect to bring their child into the world at Christmas? Who do they think they are, Mary and Joseph?

Secondly, it explains why I am quite cynical. By the age of ten, I knew that when people say, 'I just opted for One Big Present for Christmas rather than two small presents,' they are *definitely* lying. What they really opt for is the economy of one regular-sized gift.

That's where my third skill comes in handy – my precocious gift for being able to keep my disappointments to myself – because you can't really challenge people about the One Big Present Lie without sounding ungrateful, can you?

But that's OK because cynicism and the ability to suppress disappointment help you survive the single-sex boarding school system of England. And those two aspects of my character are what I relied on the first day back at school as I scanned the dormitory list to discover with whom I'd be rooming.

My cynicism prevented me from hoping that I would be sharing with someone lovely and fun. And cynicism soon gave way to suppressing the disappointment that I didn't have a valet to lug my seven-thousand-ton trunk up the ancient, narrow, dimly-lit, winding stone staircase that leads to the dormitory rooms.

My parents, who insist I call them Sarah and Bob (what can I say, they still listen to Bob Dylan and eat tragic brown food), live in LA and had long since given up accompanying me back to school each term. Now that I was about to turn fifteen, they thought they were off the hook.

That was the other thing, because I'd come to England from the American education system and having feverishly pushy parents, I was almost a full year younger than anyone else in my year – Year Eleven. My parents are always bragging to their friends about me, as if being the youngest, most physically immature girl in my year is something to boast about. They weren't the ones having to stuff their bra with toilet paper throughout Year Nine. By the end of that year I was even lying about having my periods so that when I finally started to menstruate and discovered that I had blood on my white fencing breeches, I was so relieved I forgot to be embarrassed.

This summer I sat my parents down and said, 'Look, Sarah, Bob, I know you love me and you know I love you but you have got to stop living vicariously through me!' Star put me up to it, although she suggested I just say 'get a life' because Sarah and Bob still think I should have the same aspirations I had when I was six and wanted to be the next Marie Curie. Actually, let me put that more accurately; *they* wanted me to be the next Marie Curie and I went along with it so they'd make a fuss of me.

My best friend Star always says, 'It's hard teaching your parents where their dreams end and yours begin.' Although, as far as I can see, her parents – Tiger of Dirge and Tracey the commensurate Rock Star Wife – are perfect parents. Mostly because they're always stoned, I guess.

There was no sign of Star's or Georgina's friendly faces in the mad scrum of toff parents, toff valets, guardians and girls (all dressed in the tragic Saint Augustine's uniform of maroon pleated skirt and green ruffled shirt) clustered around the notice board. I scanned the lists of dorm rooms, hoping I'd be sharing with Arabella or Clementine, two of my other friends. But instead a cold band of fear tightened around my heart as I read one of the names on the list with mine for the Saint Ursula room: Honey O'Hare.

I was literally shaking as I edged my way back out of the braying adults and girls squealing with delight or groaning with disappointment. As I turned around, I slammed straight into the devil herself – or rather, the devil's new manservant.

'Watch out, you American Freak!' Honey shrieked in her special shrill way as she stepped out from behind the man. The poor fellow stumbled a bit under the weight of her heavy Louis Vuitton trunk and other assorted designer luggage including a mauve Prada pet carrier no doubt containing her designer pet of the term.

'I'm sorry,' I apologised, trying in vain to make eye contact with the poor guy I'd bumped into. He was two hundred and ninety if he was a day.

Then Honey added darkly, 'If you damage my manservant, your parents can buy me a bloody new one and pay to have him shipped out and processed through immigration.'

Honey is your *classic* psycho toff. In other words she has all the characteristics you might imagine spoilt aristo-girls – also known as Daddy's Plastic Girls – to have, only thank goodness for me they usually don't. But Honey does. Unbridled, unrestrained horribleness exudes from the tips of her platinum card-breaking, Nicky Clarke-personally-coloured hair to her designer French Soles. And mostly her horribleness is turned on me, who as an untitled, ordinary American, is a classic sitting duck.

Last term she laced my dinner with laxatives and, as I mentioned, sold a photograph of me kissing Prince Freddie to the press, which almost destroyed my life. It created such an international brouhaha that my parents flew over from LA to be by my side. Actually it was Sarah and Bob who discovered that Honey was the culprit and Sister Constance had her rusticated for a week.

Even when she returned to school and realised how evil

everyone thought she was, she was totally unrepentant. All she said was 'Soz', which is Sloane for 'sorry' and translated in Honey's case to 'So sorry your misery has impacted on my life'. Because you see, horribleness comes naturally to Honey, a bit like photosynthesis comes naturally to plants.

The other name on my room list was Lady Portia Herrington Briggs. Of course she didn't go about referring to herself as *Lady Herrington Briggs*. That would be considered vulgar at Saint Augustine's. Naturally all the girls and teachers were fully aware she was the daughter of an Earl and treated her accordingly – apart from the nuns that is, because they think the only title of merit is Saint.

I *sort* of know Portia, but not as well as I should, given that she is on the sabre team and I am the captain. I suppose 'enigmatic' would be the word for Portia. I love the word 'enigmatic'. I've tried to be enigmatic all my life but I can't seem to stop this awful habit I have of blurting things out. Portia would never blurt something, in fact the word 'blurt' probably isn't even in her vocabulary.

In the past I'd been more interested in her talent on the piste than her grand ancestors and to be fair she'd never pointed those out to me. But I could well imagine with Honey in our room, my American-ness and own lack of grand antecedents would go against me.

Honey isn't titled – well she is an Hon., thanks to her new stepfather, but not a real one. It really grates with her that of all the men her Society It Girl mother has married, none of them has done his duty in bringing a truly grand title to the marriage table. Her latest stepfather is a lord but he's only a life peer so while she gets to be an Hon. she'll never assume the title she *really* covets, that of Lady. However, on the plus side, her new father gave her Oopa, a manservant to fetch and carry after her.

At Saint Augustine's School for Ladies you get to request the girls you want to share a room with. I'd opted for Clemmie and Arabella. But as our head nun, Sister Constance, is always remarking, 'There are no guarantees in life, girls!' I'm cynical about that too because there is one guarantee; if you share with someone one term you won't be sharing with them the next. This policy is meant to tackle bitchiness but all it really does is stick you with people who have the capacity to make your life miserable. I wished I was sharing with *exactly* the same girls as last term, my best friends Georgina and Star.

The people you share a room with at boarding school define your term. Popular, fun people = popular, fun term. Anything else is *merde*, as our ghoulish French teacher would say. If she hears us say how *merde* her French class is though, she showers us in blues.

Most of my terms at Saint Augustine's have been *merde* but last term was the exception and I honestly thought my popularity had turned a corner. I was finally out of the cul-de-sac of loneliness and isolation that had marred my previous years in England.

The reason my school life got so much better during that term of Year Ten was because I'd been roomed with my best friend, Star, who is rock royalty and the Honourable Georgina Castle Orpington and her opinionated teddy bear, Tobias. Yes, we are talking about a teddy with his own custom-made miniature Louis Vuitton trunk in which he stores his designer teddy bear wardrobe. Even madder, Georgina's father actually pays full fees for Tobias to attend Saint Augustine's! I used to think it was just a rumour but it soon became clear that it was true which is probably why the school adores Georgina so much.

Despite being friends with Honey, Georgina turned out to be far less grand than I'd always imagined. Star and Georgina and Tobias had even come to Los Angeles and spent two weeks of the summer holidays with me – although Tobias couldn't go out in the sun because he burns easily.

My parents were horrified when Georgina told them about Tobias being a full fee paying student. My mother declared it tantamount to a bribe. Georgina told her not to be so mad and explained that Tobias happened to be exceedingly bright and what's more did *all* his coursework *and* hers. She said it with such conviction that Bob and Sarah didn't know how to respond. Living in LA, they'd never met anyone as self-possessed and truly grand as Georgina.

'Besides, Sarah,' Georgina had added sweetly. 'You've been lovely enough to set a place for Tobias at dinner every evening during our stay so you must see how special he is.' This was true and Sarah and Bob were forced to acknowledge that Tobias was no ordinary bear.

Sarah and Bob were completely different people when Star and Georgina came to stay. Despite threatening to wear love beads and show my nudie baby photographs, they behaved themselves beautifully. Well, as beautifully as parents can be expected to behave.

Basically, they let us hang out at the mall just like real teenagers, and drive ourselves recklessly about the film studio lot where my mum works; you know on those little golf cart thingamees.

They even agreed to allow me to go to my very first ball, the La Fiesta Ball this term. La Fiesta is one of the Capital VIP balls that the posh schools all attend. Capital VIP run several balls and parties a year, including the Mistletoe Ball and the Valentines Ball. They have really cool bands and famous DJs and pop stars perform. All the boys go in black tie (Americans call them tuxes), which makes them look even *more* distressingly fit, and girls get to wear achingly cool clothes.

Previously, Bob and Sarah had barred me from attending any of the balls despite the fact that *Tatler* has declared them, 'the most exclusive teenage parties in the world'. I had even smugly directed them to the parent section of the website where it states: 'For forty pounds we promise you that your daughter will be followed by security all night, besides which, we hardly let any boys in anyway unless they're royalty or arrive by helicopter. Also, we totally guarantee to shoot on sight anyone caught with alcohol or drugs or attempting lip-attachment-manoeuvres.'

I'm paraphrasing, but you get the idea.

Bob and Sarah said they thought these balls sounded, 'a bit too risky'. Then again, brightly-coloured cereal is 'a bit too risky' for my parents. It's granola all the way with Bob and Sarah. But even that all changed when Star and

Georgina were staying. We had Oreo O's Cereal (miniature chocolate biscuits) and Lucky Charms. The Lucky Charms were a favourite with Georgina and Star who thought the cereal shapes were madly rude – actually, comparisons with testicles were made, and even then all Bob and Sarah did was laugh.

So there it was, in two weeks Georgina and Star triumphed with my parents where I had failed for the past fourteen years. Everything they spoke of or suggested was met with delight. 'What super fun these VIP balls all sound!' Sarah announced one evening as we were drinking wine in the courtyard. Yes, even alcohol (in moderation), was given the green light by S and B while my friends were staying.

'But you always said . . .' I began.

But Sarah dismissed my interruption. 'Of course you must go Calypso, don't be such a stick in the mud!'

My eyes almost sprung out of their sockets. They even gave me extra money so we could all buy our outfits together at a trendy shop on Robertson Boulevard. We were all going to wear sleeveless cashmere tops with beading and sequins, tiny, tiny mini-skirts and pointy-toed kitten heels – in different colours, of course.

I was sooooooo excited, though obviously I acted madly blasé about attending my first ball. Prince Freddie often attends them. I'd already texted Freddie and Billy to say I would be there, which meant I would have to choose which of them I fancied the most because I didn't want them to think I was a slut. Which I am not.

I was certain that as soon as I laid eyes on them at

fencing I'd instantly know which of them I fancied properly, but at the time all I could think of was the excitement of it all. I'd been listening enviously to the other girls going on and on about these balls and all the fit boys they've pulled for the past three years. This time I would be going to the ball myself! Thanks to the influence of my two best friends on my parents.

Star and Georgina kept saying, 'Your parents are sooo cool, Calypso,' and by the time we waved my friends off at LAX I had even started to believe it myself. Maybe my parents really *were* cool?

THREE

OK, So Maybe it Did Get a Little Bit Septic . . .

Thank goodness I am cynical because my parents went back to their draconian ways. As soon as Star and Georgina's plane was out of LA airspace they noticed that I'd had my navel pierced. Being cynical and capable of harbouring secret disappointment doesn't help you avoid crop-tops in the heat.

The three of us had decided to have it done in a shop near the Beverly Center in Beverly Hills. Star said it was like having friendship rings, only more painful. But actually it was all madly hygienic and the guy who did it was like so fit, we were all swooning so much we didn't even feel the pain.

It's true that mine *had* gone slightly septic and pus-y, which admittedly was fairly nasty, but Bob and Sarah *totally* overreacted the way only Liberal Parents can. First, they made me take it out and then they marched me, yes marched (I blame all the Save Our Environment marches they went on before I was born) me to the shop where I'd had it done.

Everyone in Los Angeles – give or take a few million people – was staring at us as we entered the shop, which also did a bit of tattooing. I hadn't noticed that on the sign, but Bob and Sarah had. Initially I refused to get out of the car but of course that failed and S and B made this hugely embarrassing scene which I am so ashamed about that I haven't even told Star.

Star has no idea what parents are like because her dad is usually so stoned he doesn't even remember who she is. She claims the reason he calls her 'darling' all the time is because he forgot her name in the early Nineties.

Anyhow, Sarah and Bob kept asking the poor guy (who'd been really, really, really, really nice to us and was so fit it was untrue) questions that they'd then answer themselves.

Bob asked, 'Do you know how old she is?'

The guy went to open his mouth, but Sarah replied for him, 'A minor!'

To which Bob added, 'Do you know what would happen to you if we were to get the police involved?'

I went bright red and tried to shrink so I could hide behind Sarah's skirt as she answered, 'You'd be closed down, and very possibly incarcerated, that's what.'

For a couple of old hippies, Sarah and Bob can be quite quick to call in the forces of law and order. All in all it was possibly the most embarrassing scene in their long history of embarrassing scenes.

But that's OK because I had my outfit. I was going to the ball.

FOUR

The Fine Line Between Honey and Hell

I came across Oopa a second time as I was lugging my trunk up the damp, narrow, winding, dimly-lit stone stairwell of the main building. The main building is the oldest building at Saint Augustine's, apart from the chapel and the convent of course. I'm not big on manservants myself but I felt sorry for Oopa as I heard one of the vertebrae in my own spine cracking as I struggled under the strain of the steamer trunk on my back. I was also carrying my wheelie hand luggage and sabre kits aren't exactly light.

The main building is so ancient, there is always a renovation programme in progress which means the place is always covered in scaffolding. This provides a handy escape route at night, according to the Upper Sixth girls who'd been housed here the year before, but it also makes it very dark and dingy. The only guiding light in this narrow winding stone stairwell is filtered through a stained glass window depicting our Lady of Perpetual Succour.

Oopa looked like he needed some succour. He was buckling under the weight of Honey's heavy trunks and bags, and my American sense of fraternity couldn't help exerting itself, even though the English call it wading in where I'm not wanted.

I was worried he was going to have a seizure and collapse – because seriously, he was gasping for breath and swaying about dangerously.

Honey was skipping ahead of him, totally oblivious to his struggle and chatting away loudly on her mobile about how she was sharing with a freak that term and how she was *so* going to have Mummy's PA speak to Lord Aginet about speaking to his lawyers. 'Honestly darling, it's outrageous that I should have to share with an American Freak. You should hear what she does to her vowels. My ears ache every time she opens her mouth. It's beyond plebbie even. It's disgusting.'

'Erm, excuse me, but do you need a hand?' I asked Oopa, about to reach out the hand holding my sabre kit to help support the enormous LVT trunk on his back. It was a really cool old steamer that Honey's grandmother had owned – you know the ones that open up with drawers and hanging space? Cool as they are, they must be really heavy.

Oopa was not impressed by my offer to help. At first I thought he must still be bearing a grudge about my bumping into him earlier because he went totally bonkers and started yelling at me. All the other guardians, parents, valets and girls stopped and stared at me too, like I'd just set fire to someone or something.

I realised in that moment how blatantly stupid I'd been

to offer assistance to anyone associated with Honey. My French teacher has always told me that I do a great line in *faux pas*.

I didn't have a clue what he was babbling about because he was shouting at me in his native tongue which I think might have been something Asian, but I couldn't be sure. He was definitely quite cross with me, though.

Honey turned and looked me up and down in that clever nasty way she has. 'Honestly, you Americans are sooo insensitive. How *dare* you question Oopa's ability to carry multiple heavy objects up a dimly lit stone staircase!'

Well, she didn't actually say that, but her dismal look said it all, and what's more the mood of the crowd seemed to be with her.

Predictably, halfway up the stairs, Oopa did eventually tumble down, but this time I wasn't insensitive enough to look, let alone comment or help. I decided just to carry on towards my room while Honey yelled at Oopa to stop embarrassing her or she'd report him to immigration.

Finally I arrived at my prettily decorated room to find Portia lounged cat-like on one of the three beds, reading *Tatler*. She'd already smothered her pin board with magazine pages and photographs. I noticed a really fit boy in the magazine pages had his arm around her in a society photograph. On her bedside table there was a photograph of her family. There was also one of the school's ancient oil paintings above her bed. It was of Saint Ursula, the patron saint of virgins. Above another bed was an oil painting of Saint Augustine, the patron saint of our school.

My focus was on the best bed though, the one against

the window overlooking the chapel with a view across to Puller's Wood where the leaves were already beginning to turn various shades of orange and gold. There was no painting above it, but there was a radiator running along the side.

I watched Portia's very English valet as he quietly, yet purposefully, unpacked his mistress's trunk. All I could think was, how very odd that Portia hadn't grabbed the best bed, the one by the window with the radiator.

'Hi, Portia, do you mind if I take this bed?' I asked cautiously. Every girl at Saint Augustine's dreams of having the bed against the radiator in the winter term and it was beyond me why anyone would pass it up.

For a second, a paranoid thought that a practical joke was being played on me flashed through my mind, but then Portia looked up from her copy of *Tatler* and smiled what seemed to be an actual genuine smile. 'Oh, hi, Calypso. Take whatever bed you want, darling, I don't give a toss frankly. As far as I'm concerned dorm rooms are all an endurance test any way you look at it.'

How cool is that? I was thinking as I dumped my trunk beside it and tossed my fencing kit on top of the coveted bed. I was still rubbing my arm to try and get my circulation going when things got even better! Lady Portia tossed her *Tatler* on the floor, climbed off her bed, walked over to me and embraced me, saying, 'Darling, I'm so pleased we're sharing, especially with the British National Fencing Trials coming up this term! I was worried I'd have no one to stress out with!'

'I know, me too. It's erm, nice isn't it,' I agreed. Why do

I say these things? *Nice?*

'But anyway,' she continued, 'how was *your* summer break? I want hear all about it. Did Star and Georgina really go out to LA? Has Freddie been texting you? I'm sooo jealous.'

Portia, the quintessential Saint Augustine It Girl was jealous of *me*? I mean, I know pulling an HRH might be the height of cool to some, but for the girls of Saint Augustine's the world of royals was their natural pulling ground. 'Yaah, totally cool,' I replied, automatically falling into the use of 'yaah' rather than my Californian 'yeah' which I knew from experience would result in a piss-take of my American-ness.

I was just about to tell her about my fantastic summer and how Star and Georgina and I had spent the whole time shopping and how Freddie and Billy had *both* been texting me, but then Honey strode in with Oopa limping behind her.

FIVE

My Favourite Mad House Spinster Ever!

I'd always hated Honey and she had always hated me, but at least in the past I'd had the buffer of a wall. Now she would be sleeping in the same room, sharing the same air, the same bathroom and there would be no respite.

I watched her snapping her tinier and cuter-than-thou bejewelled mobile shut with a sharp *clack*. I watched as she flicked her long, artistically streaked blond locks over her skinny golden shoulders. I watched her violet contact-lens covered eyes as they surveyed the prettily decorated room with its breathtaking view of the old oak woods.

Last year my Year had been housed in rickety, run down Cleathorpes but this year we were in the main building which had been newly decorated and now had lovely marble bathrooms. I'd had a peek when I'd deposited my Body Shop specials in the bathroom cabinet. We all decant vodka into empty shampoo and conditioner bottles. That's how we disguise alcohol so House Mothers don't catch us. Getting sprung with alcohol usually means a gating – not being allowed out on weekends – but it can even lead to expulsion if you're discovered revoltingly drunk. Anyway, the marble bathrooms were divine and even included a separate shower and a bath!

'Oh, isn't it dismal darling,' Honey groaned, pressing her French-manicured hand against her botoxed brow. 'Isn't it all just sooo *evil*.'

I accidentally responded, blurting something tragic, like, 'At least we have new mattresses this year.' As I said, I am marvellously gifted when it comes to the art of the blurt.

She glared at me. 'Excuse me? Was I speaking to *you*, American Freak?'

I looked over at Portia but she was immersed in her *Tatler* again. Honey pointed at my fencing kit, grimaced, and instructed Oopa to remove it from the window bed. Predictably enough, she ignored me when I muttered something ridiculously pointless about how I'd grabbed that bed already.

'Oopa will you stop panting,' she scolded as he wheezed and limped his way about the room. 'It really gets on my nerves,' she warned, pressing her fingers against her temples as if warding off a migraine. 'I don't want to have to call Daddy and have you sent back,' she warned.

I cringed as I witnessed the fear that flashed across Oopa's face. I might not know precisely where Oopa was from, but if it was worse than working for Honey it must be grim. I looked over at Portia hoping she'd concur with a raised brow but she remained immersed in her *Tatler*.

'You are sooo NQOC,' she whispered in an aside to me

before turning away and leaning down to Portia for an air kiss. 'But darling,' she drawled in her OTT toff voice, 'at least I'm rooming with *you*.'

'Yaah darling, really looking forward to it,' agreed Portia mildly as she flicked a page of her magazine, which slightly annoyed me because if it were my friend Star, she'd say something pointedly cutting like, 'I'd rather chew through my own cheek than share a night in the same room as you.'

Rock stars' daughters don't take crap from the likes of Honey, you see. Then again, Honey would never even *pretend* to be glad to share with Star. She hates her almost as much as she hates me. In fact, if Star's father wasn't Rock Royalty and the richest father in our year, I suspect Honey would hate Star *more* than me.

I watched with horror as Honey roughly threw her mauve Prada pet carrier on her bed (the one by the window that had briefly been mine). Her rabbit was still inside and I was wondering if I could get away with rescuing the poor thing. But Portia put my mind at rest by asking, 'Oh Honey, is your rabbit in there, can I hold it?'

I really wished Georgina would get here so I could cuddle little Dorothy Parker, the black rabbit we shared. Georgina looked after Dorothy on her grand country estate during half-terms and holidays. Star was always the last to arrive but surely Georgina would be here by now and she'd want to find where I was roomed . . . wouldn't she?

Honey picked up her dyed-mauve rabbit, which was wearing a blue Tiffany collar and large diamond hoop earrings. They might well have been real diamond, as she boasted, but I was more worried about how very big they were. The poor rabbit's ears were dragged down by their weight. She passed Absinthe, as she referred to the poor little thing, over to Portia with disinterest. Then she started calling people on her phone again to tell them about the hell of her journey, the shoddiness of her manservant and the evil American freak she'd been landed with.

'Bless,' said Portia as she stroked the rabbit. 'Do you want me to take her down to the pet shed for you, Honey?'

'No, I'll sort out my packing first,' replied Honey as if she was doing it herself.

I set about unpacking my own trunk, fighting for what little space I could find in the wardrobe allocated to my inferior bed. As I swung open the door I noticed a few designer jackets already hanging.

'So sorry, darling, I simply didn't have room in mine, hope you don't mind?' Portia asked, making a face of what looked like genuine shame and regret.

Portia was very beautiful, with long hair – albeit raven than the more typical blond of Saint Augustine girls – a willowy figure and the peach coloured skin of the English aristo. Her most significant feature was her aloofness. I don't mean aloof in a madly superior way because that would have been unbearable and marked her out for secret-hatred. No, Portia was aloof in a quiet, self-contained way that you couldn't really challenge. Nothing ever fazed her. Her hair was never mussed or sweaty, even after games. When I took off my fencing mask I had fluffy little bits that crowned my face like wet horns, but when

Portia took off her mask and shook out her mane of long dark hair, she looked like she'd just come from the salon.

I was about to tell Portia that it was fine to steal my precious wardrobe space – which it was really, because quite honestly my clothing allowance is pretty meagre compared to the other girls – when I was distracted by the sound of clapping.

We all turned towards the direction of the clapping. A four-foot-nine hunchbacked woman stood leaning on a cane in the doorway of our room as she announced in a loud, screechy Essex whine, "Ello girls, my name's Miss Bibsmore. I'm your new 'ouse mother. Now, I don't want any trouble 'ere, so don't you go getting ideas! Just because I'm short and hunched doesn't mean I'm ignorant, understand?'

'Yes, Miss Bibsmore,' Portia and I replied in the Saint Augustine chant of perceived obedience. That's the rule with House Mothers, you just let them rant on and hope they don't try to hug you and eventually leave you be. House Spinsters, as we call them, love to wield their power so you definitely never cheek them, which was effectively what Honey was doing as she totally ignored Miss Bibsmore and loudly bossed Oopa about, telling him where to put her designer outfits and shoes while she sat on the bed and stroked the poor shivering Absinthe.

That was another thing. Pets weren't allowed in rooms, and if she'd been anyone other than Honey she'd be trying to conceal Absinthe from Miss Bibsmore, not openly stroking her!

Miss Bibsmore entered the room in a series of awkward

little steps and shuffles, her eyes glinting with the suspicion of a woman who can see inside a girl's soul. Finally she was looming over Honey's bed. Honey looked up at Miss Bibsmore as if she were a mad witch – which of course she must be, because all house mothers are mad, although perhaps Miss Bibsmore took mad to a new level. She had a jutting out chin and messily-arranged teeth. Her grey hair had been loosely gathered together in a bun that was doomed not to hold despite the net around it. Last year's house mother, Miss Cribbe, seemed virtually normal by comparison. And Miss Cribbe had a beard!

'I'm not here to pick up after you nor nothing neither, so don't you go giving me none of your airy graces, madam, because I won't 'ave it, 'ear?'

Honey sneered at her. Honey is the queen of the sneer. Actually she's sneered so much that she's upset the balance of collagen in her lips so that the sneer side has a permanent nasty swelling on it.

'Did you hear me, madam?'

Honey ignored her. 'Oopa, I said in the top drawer! Are you deaf, because if you are I'll complain to Daddy,' she screeched.

'I mean it, madam. I'm not like the likes of 'im, that fellow there. I'm not 'ere to doff my cap to no one,' she warned, making to prod poor Oopa with her cane.

But Oopa, like his mistress, sneered as he avoided Miss Bibsmore's prod. Honey snapped, 'Oh shut up and leave my manservant alone, you mad old witch.'

Portia and I looked at one another, and her look seemed to suggest she was as concerned as I was and equally uncertain as to whether we should do or say something to diffuse the tension between Honey and Miss Bibsmore. Arousing the wrath of a House Spinster at this early stage of the term would mean misery for all of us. Then Portia raised an eyebrow in Honey's direction so I knew that she was as appalled as I was at the way Honey had just slacked Miss Bibsmore down. And that made me feel better, like maybe Portia was on my side and actually quite cool. Even her valet with his impeccable manners raised a brow. Portia nodded at him and he made a slight bow and departed.

Miss Bibsmore glared at Honey. Her eyes actually flashed. 'Right, that's it. Off 'e goes. Go on, git out!' she shrieked, hussling a confused Oopa out the door with her stick. The poor fellow looked terrified, but soon he was gone and Miss Bibsmore had Honey in her sights again. 'There'll be no bowing and scraping 'ere, madam. Grandee or not, I'm warning you now, I don't like the cut of your jib. You'll be treated like anyone else while you're in my dormitory, understood?'

'Don't be ridiculous,' Honey shrieked back at her. 'Do you know who I am? Daddy sued the last person who threatened to treat me like anyone else, and he won't think twice about doing it again.'

I looked over at Portia again and our eyes met in a look of shared disbelief but the rest of her face was concealed behind the magazine. I suspect she was hiding her suppressed giggles – the ones I was trying to suppress by applying my lip-gloss.

Miss Bibsmore grinned. 'He can sue 'imself sick far as

I'm concerned. I is what I is. I spent the first nine years of my life in a pram! If I wanted to see the light I 'ad to peer out from under the canopy. No footman, no butler, no servant for me, just a pram and an old tartan rug that kept falling off. Then, when I was well enough to get out of the pram, they put my legs in these braces.' With that, Miss Bibsmore hiked up her skirt and stuck one of her metal encased shins athletically up in the air. 'So if you think I'm afraid of your father setting a pack of nancy, fancy lawyers on me, you'll be disappointed.'

'Well, perhaps the school will feel differently,' Honey responded mildly but there was blatantly an obvious threat there.

Portia and I were struggling to stop our eyebrows riding up our foreheads by this point. Neither of us knew what to say.

Honey, on the other hand, was far from stuck for words. '. . . when my lawyers shower them in litigation suits for allowing an insane old witch like you to care for me.'

Miss Bibsmore's eyes were glinting gleefully as she asked, 'Insane, am I? Well then, you had better watch out all the more, 'adn't you?'

Portia rose imperiously from her bed, clearly deciding enough was enough. 'Thank you, Miss Bibsmore. I think we're all clear now and we wouldn't want to keep you from your rounds,' She spoke with a calmness of one who's family traced their roots back to the Domesday Book and had survived the Catholic purgings of England with their title and lands intact.

Miss Bibsmore seemed to concede Portia's suggestion.

That is, she stuck her lower lip out and humphed. One thing was certain, though: she was on the warpath and Honey had been marked down as Enemy Number One.

'I am *so* complaining,' Honey muttered under her breath. Then she turned to Portia. 'I'm calling Daddy *now*.' She began to punch numbers into her phone but Miss Bibsmore snatched the tiny little gem of a mobile from her, popped it in the pocket of her long skirt and shuffled out of the room. 'And you can take that poor creature down to the pet shed an' all. No pets in rooms or I'll have you rusticated.'

Miss Bibsmore didn't officially have the power to rusticate girls, but the fact that she even used the word proved she wasn't to be messed with. I was definitely going to regret the thought running through my mind, but as I watched Honey's mouth open and close in uncharacteristic helpless shock; but I couldn't help admiring Miss Bibsmore's style. I was beginning to think I liked the cut of her jib. And as I caught Portia's eye I got the feeling she might even be feeling the same way.

SIX

God's Law versus Sod's Law

Within seconds of Miss Bibsmore's departure, Star and Georgina burst into our room in a tumble of long limbs, long hair and laughter. They tripped over my fencing kit, which had been dumped on the floor by Oopa, and landed on the floor in a giggling heap.

'Guess what!' asked Star, untangling herself from Georgina and dive-bombing on to Honey's bed by the window. I looked at Honey, anticipating fireworks, but before she could formulate her put-down, Georgina declared, 'It's the best news ever!'

'Please tell me, Star's finally being sanctioned?' Honey hazarded sarcastically.

'We're sharing!' cried Georgina, throwing her arm over Star's shoulder. The two of them started bouncing up and down on the bed, punching the air with their fists.

'Wow, that's sooo cool,' I told them enthusiastically, although really I couldn't help feeling a bit disappointed. I remembered a time when Star and I were considered the school freaks – not that I enjoyed being the school freak, obviously, but it meant we were closer than close. Besides, as far as Star was concerned, Georgina and Honey et al were the school freaks. She didn't even want to be friends with Georgina initially – that was my idea. Now they were finishing each other's sentences.

Georgina went, 'Calypso! You have *got* to meet Indiamaca . . .'

Pulling a stray lock of her strawberry blond hair from her mouth, Star added, 'Yaah, she's a new girl, an *actual* princess from Nigeria. Only she calls herself Indie.'

They were still jumping up and down on Honey's bed. I guess Honey probably felt she wasn't in a position to say anything as Georgina was the closest thing she had to a real friend. Even though she knows how toxic Honey is, the two of them have known each other since they were four, when they were packed off to school at Hill House in Knightsbridge. They learned to ride together, ski together, use Daddy's plastic together and pull together. Plus their biological fathers still attend the same hunt meet so I guess that gives them a bond that won't ever totally be broken.

Watching Georgina's exuberant bed-jumping I was quite glad it *wasn't* my bed now. The mattresses at Saint Augustine's are about as comfortable as lying on lumpy porridge because we all jump up and down on them.

'Calypso, she's sooo nice you have to love her and also, she's got this amazingly cool limited edition Hermès bag. They covered it in a purple Nigerian fabric just for her. So individual,' Star enthused.

'And loads of vintage clothes, all purple because that's her favourite colour,' Georgina added.

'Oh, how cool,' I said, trying to get into the swing of their enthusiasm for this new girl.

'And she plays guitar! I showed her one of my songs Calypso and she *totally* got it,' Star said.

I should explain that Star writes these Gothic anthems about the despair and pointlessness of being a successful rock star's daughter and the miserable privilege of her life in an all-girls boarding school. Love Star though as I do, even *I* want to eat my own tongue when she starts playing her minor chord compositions.

'She said she loved my angst. Isn't that gorgeous?'

'I love your angst too!' I blurted for want of something more ridiculous to say.

Thankfully though Star didn't hear my pathetic suck-up attempt because Georgina had cut in breathlessly. 'She used to go to Cheltenham Ladies', only she said it was too plebbie. She's already pulled loads of Harrow boys.' Harrow on the Hill, also known as the Dump on the Hump, was another toffer-than-thou school for boys. There was always a lot of debate amongst the girls of Saint Augustine's about whether it was cooler to pull Eades boys or Harrow boys. Eades was a lot closer to us, which made Harrow seem more exotic, although that was mainly because we didn't pull as many of them and they didn't get to break our hearts as much.

Star went, 'I told her about you and Freddie, Calypso and she can't wait to meet *you*. We both love her don't we, George? She's our new best friend.'

'I can't wait to meet her either, she sounds really cool,' I sort of lied. I say 'sort of' because while I was thrilled that my friends were in a great room together, I couldn't help feeling a bit jealous. OK, make that hugely jealous. Especially about Indiamaca, because if she was their New Best Friend that made me . . . the *old* best friend! And when did Georgina become George anyway?

I looked out over the lawns that trailed into the oak woods with their flaming leaves and wondered how long before the trees would be bare and we'd have snow. I love snow. Star and I used to sneak off up into the woods on our own in winter to do snow angels.

It's a Saint Augustine's tradition to have snowball fights with the new Year Seven girls. Once a year, someone has to throw a snowball at Sister Constance as she steps out for her morning perambulations (that's what she calls her meditative wanders though the school grounds and woods). Sister just laughs these attacks off and throws snowballs back at us – unlike the lay teachers who, if you hit them with a snowball, shower you in blues.

Once Star was gated for hitting Ms Topler, our evil English teacher. It was not only an overreaction but resulted in Star's parents and every member of Dirge turning up at the school to complain. Star's mad extended family is like a pack of wild things when they're on a mission. All the members of Dirge and their roadies and friends think of Star as a surrogate daughter. It's so sweet when they all turn up for Parent Teacher Day, and the school is infiltrated with long-haired, tattooed men and their wildly dressed rock chick girlfriends.

Star says parents don't pay the equivalent of twice the average annual wage in order to have their daughters taught by teachers who have no sense of fun. I think Sister Constance agrees because she overruled the gating and Ms Topler got a telling off.

But now as I sat listening to my friends' excited chatter about their new exotic *friend*, I wondered if maybe Star would prefer to do snow angels with 'George' now, or purple star angels with Indie! So much for Sister Constance's rule about not sharing with the same girl two terms in a row, I thought to myself bitterly.

'So much for Sister Constance and her rule about not sharing with the same girl two terms running,' Honey said with a sneer, eerily echoing my own thoughts.

'Sod's Law, darling.' Georgina shrugged as she air-kissed Honey. 'But anyway, tell me about your summer in Kenya, darling,' Georgina asked airily. I noted the way she pronounced Kenya *Keenyah*. 'Star and I had the *best* time in LA with Calypso,' she told her, grinning at me fondly.

I was always very aware of the way the other girls spoke when I came back from LA. The way you speak defines you, and after four years here, I pretty much sound like them. Even so, my accent still lets me down when I spend too long in LA which leaves me open to very bad piss-takes of the way I speak. Ironic, given that in LA everyone does very bad piss-takes of my English accent.

'Absolutely terrific,' Honey replied, stroking Absinthe's mauve fur with her mauve-coloured nails.

I was looking over at Portia, who had barely said a word. I wondered if, like me, she was feeling left out or whether she was really as absorbed by the magazine she was reading and rereading.

Suddenly Honey dropped Absinthe like a bag of sugar on to the bed and started posing in front of the mirror. 'Goffy – that's what we call Mummy's latest husband, Lord Aginet – bought me Oopa, *the* most adorable manservant ever.'

Star and I rolled our eyes at one another but Honey didn't notice the mood as she played with her expensive hair. 'Portia met him,' she continued. 'Darling, didn't you think him adorable?' she asked rhetorically, not even looking at Portia for confirmation. 'He was a refugee. The luckiest refugee in the world as it turns out. Goffy discovered him in Nairobi and said I could have him.'

'He's a man, not a discovery, Honey,' I blurted, before I could stop myself.

'Yes, you really should pay more attention in biology, darling.' Star added, dragging out the word daaaahrling in the OTT way Honey did.

'Oh, what would you know with all your father's plebbie hangers-on,' Honey snapped back, referring to the roadies who hung around Star's family's estate in Derbyshire, where they did a spot of valeting (between spliffs) when the band wasn't touring.

'They're roadies and friends, actually. At least I don't go round referring to people as manservants or exploiting refugees. What century are you from, anyway?'

'Yes, darling, how old are you really – underneath all that surgery of yours?' Georgina teased. The smile on her face didn't do anything to break the chill in the air, though.

I had never heard Georgina openly tease Honey. She and Honey, well, apart from the odd falling out, they were always civil to one another.

Honey ignored the remark, or at least she appeared to as she began brushing her hair. 'Honestly, Oopa would lay down his life for me and little Absinthe,' she said with a sigh, as if relishing the idea of poor Oopa lying dead in a ditch for the sake of her and her rabbit. 'But enough of me,' she said, speaking directly to Georgina. 'How's *your padre*, darling? Daddy said he had a drink with him at his club recently and invited Koo-Koo and him to join us for Christmas in Saint Moritz.'

No one ever mentions Georgina's father unless she does. Sure enough, I noticed her eyes welling up with tears. Her father divorced her mother a couple of years ago after his second bypass operation. After her mother had nursed him back to health he had announced that he felt 'suffocated' by her and that if he was going to die in the near future – which looked highly probable – he'd rather do it in the arms of a younger, less intelligent (he actually used the words 'supportive' and 'less demanding', but Star says it amounts to the same thing) woman than Georgina's mother.

Georgina had a bit of a scary brush with bulimia over it and she's still really cut up about it. Catholics aren't meant to get divorced, although Honey's mother does it all the time. Not that all the girls at Saint Augustine's are Catholic, their parents merely send their daughters here because it's conveniently close to Eades where their sons and heirs go.

Georgina's father had married Koo-Koo over the

summer at what was once Georgina's family home in Gloucestershire. Georgina was with me in LA as her excuse not to attend the wedding and we all took our cue from her and didn't mention it. Koo-Koo is a twenty-nine-year-old and refuses to let Georgina stay overnight anymore. Koo-Koo says, 'It's better for everyone this way'. As a consequence, Georgina barely sees her father now.

Honey knows about all this, of course. She was just mentioning him to get back at Georgina, to be cruel in the way small boys pull legs off bugs or older boys say they'll text you and never do.

Honey definitely hit her mark. Georgina looked miserable. I tossed her my lip-gloss but she didn't even attempt to catch it, and it just landed on the floor, near her feet.

'Oh my god, what's that, darling?' Star asked, breaking the toxic tension. Picking up a piece of dusty fluff from the top of the radiator, she held it up, pretending to examine it carefully.

'Don't worry,' she announced in mock relief, 'it's just a piece of dust. For a minute there I thought it might be your brain, Honey.'

Georgina bent down and picked up the lip-gloss. She smiled at me as she applied it. Honey sneered, probably to give herself time to think up a sarcastic response, but Star pressed her advantage. 'I always forget, *darling*, you don't actually have a brain though, do you, Honey? They sucked it out during the lipo.'

Georgina chucked me my lip-gloss and I started applying like mad. Who knew where this confrontation would end? OK, so Honey was a walking advertisement for teen cosmetic surgery but suggesting that she may have had liposuction was suggesting she may have once been fat, a taboo topic at Saint Augustine's where Eating Disorder specialists were on tap if any girl showed the slightest sign of developing an eating disorder. But as everyone knows, Saint Augustine girls are slim – mostly because they feed us inedible grey slops here.

Honey smiled evilly. 'Star, you are too, too hilarious. How fortunate your parents are giving you their full support to break into vaudeville.'

Star's response was to pull the lip-gloss out of her pocket and apply it ostentatiously close to Honey's face. It was one of our secret mottos, 'Wear your pain like lip-gloss.' Lip-gloss is a girl's biggest asset when dealing with difficult situations. When Star and I were out of the cool-loop, we used to use it as a secret sign to show we weren't dealing with something. It made me feel a bit better seeing Star use our special sign language.

And then out of blue, Portia remarked, 'Oh yes, lip-gloss. What a good idea,' and although she didn't apply any she smiled at me warmly. It seemed significant.

SEVEN

Aloof Demeanours versus the Scent of Eau de Parbitch

Georgina doesn't like to get involved in Honey's issues with other girls. None of us does, really, and so, keen to change the subject, Georgina grabbed the *Tatler* Portia was reading and asked her, 'So darling, what about you, good summer?' Calypso, Star and I had our navels pierced, see!' She and Star both lifted their shirts to expose their rings.

I was about to come clean and 'fess up, when Portia looked Georgina straight in the eye and replied, 'Hardly,' her voice laced in pain.

I suddenly felt really guilty and self obsessed. I hadn't even bothered to ask about her summer when she'd asked about mine.

'Mummy was killed in a car accident,' she explained flatly and then picked up her magazine and adopted an absorbed look. None of us knew what to say to that, apart from Honey of course.

'Darling, how absolutely devastating,' she remarked breezily, gathering up her rabbit and popping her into her matching mauve Prada pet bag. 'I'm so sorry, but these things do happen.' Her lower lip dropped in a look of regret as she gave the room a little wave. 'I'm just going to take Absinthe down to the pet shed before the hideous Miss Bibsmore returns.' She rolled her big violet eyes at the thought. 'Do you want to come, darling?' she asked Georgina.

Georgina looked up at her but not with the sort of look you could interpret. Star claims that one of the major reasons parents pay exorbitant sums of money to send their girls to Saint Augustine's is so they can develop a poker face – known to the toff parents as an Aloof Demeanour, a sort of non-look. Honestly, if you could buy an Aloof Demeanour, effortless charm and a sense of entitlement on Bond Street, England's boarding schools would be out of business in a day. Nuns are very good at poker faces. They're very good at poker too. Sometimes when they invite us around for tea they cut us in on a game. They always beat us, but we only play for sweets, which they then insist we eat or take with us afterwards, so that's OK.

Honey chose to take the look as a no. 'Well, *ciao, ciao!*' she called as she swept out of the room on a cloud of *eau de parbitch*.

We all turned our attention back to Portia. 'Darling, what happened?' Georgina asked gently, sitting down on the bed and rubbing poor Portia's back. Star was sitting beside her and so I sat beside Star.

The thought of Portia's loss distressed me. The tears were banking up behind my eyes as I tried to think what I might want someone to say to me if anything happened to Sarah.

Portia put down her magazine and replied calmly. 'It was the first day of the holidays. We were shopping, she was walking across Sloane Street, only not at the pedestrian crossing and this Range Rover ran over her. It was all so fast. I was right there . . .' Her voice faded, and Georgina took her in her arms and kissed the crown of her glossy raven head.

If it had been me, I would have cried. As it was I was wiping back a tear at the horrible sadness of it all. I was too paralysed by the shame of my own awkwardness though to join Star and Georgina in hugging her. I knew I was being inept and I wanted to say something more . . . I don't know . . . ept, I guess, so I got off the bed and sat on my haunches in front of Portia and passed her my lip-gloss.

'Do you want some lip-gloss?' I asked, attempting a smile.

Portia took the lip-gloss, smiled bravely at me and applied liberally as I added, 'I'm really sorry I didn't ask about your break before, Portia. Actually, I mean I'm sorry about your mother and everything else too obviously, it's so sad . . .'

Portia gave me another brave smile as she passed me back my lip-gloss. I told her to keep it as I had loads, which was true. 'Honestly, it's so sweet of you, but I've dealt with it now,' she said. 'Honey's right; it's devastating, but these things happen. It's Daddy I'm worried about, rattling about all alone in that big house.'

By all alone, of course there would still be gamekeepers, butlers, valets and staff galore, but her sadness and concern were real and my heart went out to her. Suddenly my text alert sounded and without thinking I dug my phone out of my pocket and read:

CAN'T GET YOU OUT OF MY HEAD. X FREDS

I smiled, mostly because I had invented the nickname Freds. How cool was that; I had invented a nickname for the heir to the throne who couldn't get me out of his head? No one seemed to notice me reading the text but the inappropriateness of my joy wasn't lost on me though and I shoved the phone straight back into my pocket.

'I met your mother loads of times,' I told Portia. 'She was always lovely to me. She was so tall and beautiful and I loved the way she would always kick her shoes off and fall asleep at the back of the chapel on your father's shoulder during Mass.'

A half-smile broke across Portia's face. 'And snored,' she added. 'She always snored.'

'Well, Father Conran *can* go on,' Star said, which made Portia laugh, even though I noticed a solitary tear running down her cheek, and then we all laughed in the way you do when crying is the only other option and you know tears won't help.

'Thanks,' Portia said, wiping her tear away. 'Since the funeral I've been so miserable and pathetically wrapped up in my own self-pity. I've just stayed in my room and tried not to think about Mummy, but I can't help it. Daddy's lost loads of weight.'

'What about Tarkie?' Georgina asked, referring to

Portia's older brother Tarquin, the Marquess of Eaglemere, who attends Eades in the year above Freddie.

'Tarkie's dealt with it by throwing himself into partying,' she replied. I sensed she was being economical with her feelings about Tarquin's partying in that upper-class way of the English which had taken me so long to adapt to. Actually let me amend that, I am still getting used to it. 'He went to Rock with friends straight after the funeral.'

'What? Surfing?' I blurted, shocked at what I saw as Tarquin's callous abandonment of his sister and father.

'Yes, well it was pretty gloomy in Eaglemere and we've always spent that fortnight in our house in Rock . . .' She trailed off as if remembering past summers with her family when it was complete.

'But what about you? What about your father?' I asked, frustrated by my own inability to say anything useful and annoyed that I was saying anything at all, because it was pretty obvious by the way Portia's head was bowed and her demeanour in general that she didn't want to answer questions, didn't want to discuss her mother's death any more than she had to.

'Daddy locked himself away,' she answered politely, as if I'd asked about the weather, but she was looking at her hands which were folded neatly in her lap. 'He told me to go with Tarkie. My ghastly grandmother came to stay.'

'Oh,' I replied as if I genuinely thought the arrival of a ghastly relative made everything OK.

Then Portia looked up at me. 'And she told me I should have gone with Tarkie to Rock too and so I locked myself away from her.'

I could see she was about to tear up again and I felt bad. 'Boys are different,' Star said, then pinched me in the ribs, which made me squeal, and Georgina pinched me too.

Portia smiled as I beat off Georgina and Star. She was clearly relieved that my probing was over.

'Honestly, Tarquin's been brilliant. He sent Daddy and me a postcard every day. Daddy said he wasn't even sure Tarquin could write before that.' Then a real smile broke across her beautiful features as if she was remembering the brightly-coloured postcards as they were placed on the table at breakfast by the butler. 'Actually, do you mind if I *don't* talk about it?' she asked, looking at me almost pleadingly. 'I mean I can't stop missing Mummy but it did feel good to laugh again just then.'

'In that case,' Star urged, pulling Portia to her feet, 'you have *got* to come to the pet shed and see Hilda. She's learned this really cool new trick.'

'You've taught her to talk?' Portia asked teasingly.

Star's always trying to teach her rat, Hilda, and her snake, Brian, to do clever tricks, but all Brian does is slither about and all Hilda does is run herself stupid on her little rat wheel. If you ask me, those two are a lost cause as far as tricks go.

'Almost. She can beg for her little rat pellets now.'

'Ooooh, bless,' Portia said. 'Let's go.'

'Just one sec,' Star said as she rushed off to her dorm room, returning with a can of Febreze concealed inside her blazer so she'd be able to have a fag at the pet shed and spray the smell away.

We all traipsed downstairs and outside across the

school grounds. As we passed our old dorm, Cleathorpes, I remembered our last term there when Star and I had first become friends with Georgina. Soon I was straggling behind, musing about what sharing with Portia and Honey was going to be like this term.

My parents had big hopes for me this year they'd told me as they waved me off at LAX. This year we'd be sitting our GCSEs, which meant the work would be piled on us; but far more important to me were the National Fencing Trials in December. As one of the top sabreurs in the Under Sixteens, Portia was probably focusing on the trials as well, which could bond us on one hand and make us competitors on another. I had to rate in the trials if my big dream to fence in the Olympics was going to come to anything. Freddie's message couldn't have been further from my mind until my text alert sounded again.

SO GOING TO SLAY YOU ON THE PISTE NEXT WEEK! BILLY XXX

Three kisses from Billy, one from Freddie . . .

EIGHT

House Spinster Alert

It was a very quiet dorm that first night. Hardly a word was spoken as we each took our turn in the pristine luxury of the marble en suite bathroom; showering, brushing our teeth and changing into our winter pyjamas.

Portia appeared gorgeously cool in a pair of black tight jersey shorts with a pink lace frill and a matching long-sleeved, tight-fitting top that showed her athletic figure to greatest advantage.

Honey sashayed out later as if trotting down a catwalk in a flesh-coloured, slinky, lace La Perla nightie that was very grown up, sexy and see-through. I came out of the bathroom last so that they could witness together my madly un-posh, un-sexy, Hello Kitty flannelette pyjamas.

'Oh bless,' said Honey sarcastically.

I had thought them adorable when I bought them with Star and Georgina at the Beverly Center over the summer, but now realised how tragically babyish they were. My parents might be proud as punch that I was almost a full year younger than everyone else in my year, but they weren't the ones who had to endure the feelings of immaturity that went with it.

I dived into bed and pulled my lovely new goose-down double duvet up against my chin, trying to ignore the look Honey was giving me. A nasty look, pregnant with derision and loathing. I thought she was about to say something else, but she merely pulled her mauve silk eye mask over her eyes. I suppose she decided I wasn't worth it.

Portia was reading another magazine: *The Fencer*, this time. I was exhausted from the flight, and I could feel my eyelids getting heavier and heavier as I read Edith Sitwell's *English Eccentrics*. Eventually I turned my light off and began to float off, thinking how different the atmosphere of this dorm room was compared to last term, when most nights held the excitement of a pyjama party. Eventually Portia said 'Good night', to which I responded, 'Sweet dreams.' Honey just ignored us even though I suspect she was still awake.

Lying in the quiet, I almost welcomed the *tap, tap, tap* sound of Miss Bibsmore's stick as she made her way down the corridor in an odd series of little steps and shuffles. I could hear her giving warnings about 'chatting after lights out' to other rooms. And I listened to her dragging bins across bedroom floors to wedge the doors open so that she would hear any late-night chatting that wicked girls might try to engage in.

At ten-thirty, her odd little shape was silhouetted in our doorway. We already had our lights out which must have been a first at Saint Augustine's because *everyone* always waits for the lights out rule to be enforced by the House Spinster. And let's be honest, what room of girls would voluntarily turn their own lights out at fifteen years of age? Apart from when it was exam time maybe.

'Lights out now, girls,' announced Miss Bibsmore in her shrieky voice as she perversely turned our evil fluorescent strip lights back on.

I peeked out from under my duvet and watched her as she cast a suspicious eye over our room.

'Wot's that then on the floor by your bed, Miss Kelly?' she demanded.

I leaned over and scanned the floor, but there was nothing on it. For once, my area was spotless. 'I don't know,' I told her honestly.

'Don't know!' she screeched, using her stick to lift one of my Hello Kitty slippers into the air with a circus performer's agility, then dangling the offending slipper in my face. It was definitely time to get over my Hello Kitty stage. In three months, I would be fifteen and looking at my little pink slipper as Miss Bibsmore wobbled it on her stick made me feel like it was high time I grew up and got some cool nightwear like Portia.

'It's by *your* bed, madam, so I suggest you acquaint yourself with the item and identify it quick smart!'

'It's a . . . well, it's a . . . a slipper. Isn't it, Miss Bibsmore?' I asked uncertainly. I could hear Portia struggling under her duvet to suppress laughter.

'No, it's not a "slipper", Miss Kelly and well you know it.'

At which point, Portia pretended to have a coughing fit to disguise her giggles. Honey was silent, no doubt waiting for a chance to stick the knife in.

I was genuinely stumped. Maybe there *was* another term for slipper that I was yet to learn. As an American, I was always discovering new words for everyday objects. It had taken me all the first term of Year Seven to work out what vests were, and jumpers had me stumped me for a further year. So I asked cautiously. 'Sorry, Miss Bibsmore, we call it a slipper in America.'

'Well *I* call it your classic death trap. I can smell the stench of a dead girl just looking at it. Wot if there was a fire, an' all? Wot if you had to evacuate at a moment's notice? You'd dive out of bed, blind as a bat, and trip over this so-called "slipper", and knock your 'ead on a bed or the floor. You'd be out cold while the flames licked about your body. A slipper indeed! I've never heard such nonsense.'

This time I heard Honey suppress a laugh – only I think she was laughing at the tantalising thought of me burning to death rather than the absurdity of Miss Bibsmore's rant.

'Sorry, Miss Bibsmore,' I replied.

'Now in the future, I want all so-called "slippers" under the bed. Do I make myself clear?'

'Crystal, Miss Bibsmore,' I agreed obediently.

Miss Bibsmore patted me on the head. 'Right you are then, sweetie. Off to the land of Nod with you now, little love. Say your prayers.' I stuck my head deeper into my duvet, secretly delighted by her comforting words. 'And sweet dreams to you too, Briggsie,' she added gently.

Using an affectionate abbreviation of Portia's surname and calling me 'sweetie' was a privilege I suspected Honey wasn't going to enjoy.

'Thank you, Miss Bibsmore,' Portia replied.

She patted Portia's head again. 'I'm sorry to hear about your mum too. Sister Constance told me what happened an' all. It can't have been easy for you. I understand she was a proper angel with an 'eart of gold and it's a curse on those like me wot didn't get to meet her.'

'Thank you, Miss Bibsmore,' Portia answered quietly.

'I won't mention her again, mind, but I felt I should say something. It's only proper. I might be stern but I'm not made of stone, Briggsie. As for you, Miss O'Hare,' she added, her voice changing tone as she shuffled back toward the door, 'don't think I'm not on to you, pretending to be asleep indeed. As if butter wouldn't melt in your mouth. I've 'ad a good look at your record, madam, not to mention your sister Poppy 'oo I had up 'ere two years past, so may the Good Lord Jesus Christ and the saints in 'eaven protect you if I ever catch you up to anything.'

'Whatever,' Honey muttered.

'Hail Mary, full of grace . . .' Miss Bibsmore began and Portia, Honey and I joined her in a decade of the rosary.

By the time our lights actually did get turned out, it was eleven o'clock and the jetlag was seriously kicking in.

NINE

Secret Disappointments and Less than Secret Hatred

After Miss Bibsmore left, Portia expressed what I'd been thinking. 'She's *really* gunning for you, Honey.'

Honey turned on her torch and tore off her eye mask, 'Oh, don't worry, darling. I've already called Daddy on one of my other mobiles and his solicitor is writing a letter as we speak. Her days are numbered and Daddy said he'll make sure she'll never get a reference.'

Suddenly the florescent strip lights flickered on again and framed in the doorway was the ghostly figure of Miss Bibsmore. 'I warned you, Miss O'Hare. I might not be bright but I'm blessed with a nose for trouble, I am, and I'll not have your kind having one over on me. Do you understand?'

With that the florescent lights flickered off again.

'Would you kindly allow us to sleep you mad old witch. It's against the Geneva Convention to wander in and wake us up you know!' Honey spat, but the *tap, tap, tap* of Miss

Bibsmore's stick was already fading away down the corridor.

'Did you get much fencing practice in during the break?' Portia whispered to me about ten minutes later once we heard Miss Bibsmore descending the stone staircase. I could see that the stone staircase was going to be a great advantage if our dorm *did* ever become fun. We'd hear Miss Bibsmore coming easily.

'Yaah, a fair bit but it's hard finding decent opponents over there. The standard just isn't as high. Fewer people do sabre in LA so the competition isn't great. I worked on my lunges and footwork though. What about you?'

'Daddy hired me my own fencing master. We've got a piste in the gym at home so I was planning to be practising all the time, but then, after Mummy . . .'

'We'll be back on the piste tomorrow,' I reassured her, not wanting to torture her further over the loss of her mother. She'd made it quite clear she didn't want to talk about it and I was going to respect her wishes.

'We'll both need to push ourselves with the BNFTs coming up in December. It's such a ghastly time for Professor Sullivan to take a sabbatical.' She sighed.

'Has he left?' I asked.

'For a term at least.'

This was an enormous blow to me. Professor Sullivan had been my fencing master since I first came to Saint Augustine's. I hadn't counted on this turn of events at all. 'You mean we have a new fencing master?'

'Mr Wellend. I doubt he's a Mr Sullivan but he sounds the business. Olympic silver, quite old apparently but madly accomplished, apparently,' she explained.

'Oh, I'm just surprised Professor Sullivan didn't mention anything.'

'He probably thought we'd make a fuss of him. Besides he's not gone for ever. This Wellend chap used to coach the Eades team so I'm sure he's the business. I'll go down tomorrow in the break to speak to him to see if he's willing to give us extra lunchtime tuition.'

'Do you think he's unlikely to?'

'If you don't mind, some of us are trying to get to sleep,' Honey hissed.

Portia ignored her. 'Hardly. He's not obliged but now's the time to ask. Plus it is in his interest for us to distinguish ourselves.'

'Our success being his success, you mean.'

Honey groaned and moved about noisily in her bed.

I ignored her. 'Well, if you don't mind going alone I'd really like to check on how Dorothy's doing back at the pet shed during break. I really missed her over the summer,' I explained.

Honey switched her lamp on, pulled off her eye mask – which was embroidered with the word HEIRESS – and scowled. Portia smiled conspiratorially at me, blew me a teasing kiss and said, 'Not at all, darling. You check on Dorothy and I'll report back.'

'Deal,' I replied almost delirious with hope that Portia and I were going to be friends or at least get along despite Honey's poisonous presence. I'd thought that Honey would devote her time to putting me down while Portia immersed herself in magazines or pretend to be absorbed by the view.

'You two are really annoying me,' she said as she switched her lamp off and groaned again.

A few minutes later, Georgina, Star and a third girl I took to be Indie crept into our room on all fours with their torches in their mouths which made them look like a pack of pyjama clad dogs on the prowl. Silently moving the bin and shutting the door, they climbed into our beds. I was pleased that Star climbed in with me.

'My feet are *frozen*, I need socks,' she told me.

'Drawer underneath the bed,' I told her.

She stayed under the covers as she opened the drawer and riffled round for socks.

I watched with mixed feelings as Georgina climbed in with Honey and started tickling her and the two of them started giggling together. Just like old times – until a voice piped up from the shadows.

'Hi, I'm Indie,' the new best friend whispered as she stood up and shone her torch around our room, finally shining it under her own face so we could see her properly. She was smiling. She was so stunning I was shocked. She looked like Naomi Campbell and she was almost as tall. 'I've heard so much about you all. Especially you, Calypso,' she said in the sweetest, poshest voice I'd ever heard.

'Same,' I replied brightly, determined in that moment to like her and stop being such a jealous bitch.

Portia invited her to jump in under her duvet. Even though it was only September the nights were already quite chilly, especially as they didn't turn on the central heating in the dorm rooms until November – even if it snowed before that!

'Isn't Miss Bibsmore the weirdest?' Georgina asked rhetorically.

I wanted to say I actually quite liked her but I knew it would only set Honey off.

'Oh, she'll be gone in a week, darling, I've got Daddy on the case. Do you know she even had the audacity to confiscate one of my phones! The pikey way she speaks, ugh! Fag, darling, fag?' Honey suggested.

'I've given up cigarettes,' Georgina told her. 'How about a spliff?'

Even Honey seemed surprised and Honey doesn't do surprised. It's quite hard to do surprise when you've had as much Botox as she's had, I guess. Still, even in the torchlight I was pretty certain it was a look of surprise I saw attempt to flash across her feline features.

A moment later, Georgina and Honey opened up the window to the cold night air, stuck their heads out and fired up their joint companionably.

'Should you be doing that?' I asked Georgina when she pulled in after blowing out some smoke and asked if anyone else fancied a puff.

Star pinched me, leaving me in no doubt I'd said the wrong thing.

'Gee, are you sure you should be doing that?' Georgina parroted in a bad piss-take of a Hillbilly accent.

Honey stuck her head in, blew some funny smelling smoke towards me and drawled, 'Oh go back to LA will you, Calypso! All you Americans are sooo sanctimonious.'

Georgina giggled, just a tiny little bit, but it was a defining giggle.

Honey seized her advantage and carried on. 'Or maybe you could set up an NA group for us, Calypso? You just love setting up little groups and salons, don't you? Would you make Georgina and I confess our wickedness to a counselling group? Would you, darling?'

I declined to reply, consumed by embarrassment and squirming with all the old familiar feelings of being an outsider in their exclusive world with its maddeningly tricky English in-jokes which were so much a fabric of their lives. Here I was again, a foreigner in another world where despite the deceptive similarities, I didn't really speak the language.

Not that any of that mattered because Honey was on a roll and anything I said would have only been used as more ammunition against me. This time she sent herself up as a clever way of sending me up. 'Darlings, my name is the Honourable Honey O'Hare and this is my friend, the Honourable Georgina Castle Orpington and we're the most ghastly spliff-a-holics.'

I descended deeper into my spiral of dread. What was happening here? Why was Star giving Honey free reign to go on like this? Why had Georgina suddenly done an about-turn and cosied up with Honey again? I waited for the inevitable paroxysms of smothered giggles, but instead Indie's voice came out of the semi-darkness. 'This is getting soooo boring.'

Honey shone her torch into Indie's eyes. 'Oh, go back to fruuping Cheltenham, will you?'

Indie shone her own torch straight back into Honey's face, as the room fell silent in this war of torches. 'Hardly!'

she said in a madly grand way. 'I left because of a bitch like you.'

Honey looked around the room for support. Portia had her back to everyone, Georgina merely giggled and Star and I weren't even on her radar. Resigned to the mood change, Honey announced, 'I've got the munchies, anyone have sweets on them?'

I smiled at Indie gratefully and she smiled back. Between Miss Bibsmore and Indie, Honey was going to be facing some stiff opposition this term. I definitely wouldn't want to get on the bad side of Indie, as beautiful as she was, when she'd gone for Honey just now, she'd looked terrifying.

Star stuck her tongue out at me to reveal the new stud in her tongue. She was only doing it to tease in a nice way. I knew that Star would never want to make me feel bad. She winked at me and gave me a cuddle as well but something had changed between us. Once she would have sent me a text to announce a step like tongue piercing. It had always been just the two of us, and while I was pleased that Indie had slapped Honey down, I couldn't help wishing it had been Star.

The spliff was finally spliffed out and Star sprayed Febreze around the room and things went back to normal as if a tidal wave had receded. We chatted amongst ourselves, catching up on things generally, and Indie joined in as if she'd always been part of our group. It turned out she knew loads of the boys we knew and shared lots of the same opinions as us about them.

'So, Calypso,' she said to me. 'I'm *really* looking forward to watching you fence. I wish I'd taken it up now; it looks so achingly cool in all those movies and ads on television. I adore the outfits and all the fit boys seem to fence now.'

'Actually, it's more aching than cool,' I told her, and Portia agreed.

Honey made a sarcastic remark but everyone ignored her. She was sitting alone on the floor now wrapped up in her duvet devouring our room's tuck stash with ridiculous abandon; stuffing herself with M&Ms and jelly babies like there was no tomorrow. I was really glad that Clemmie wasn't here to witness it. She cries when people eat jelly babies because she thinks they look like her little brother Sebastian. I watched in disbelief as Honey consumed a term's worth of tuck, while giggling dementedly to herself and talking drivel. I suppose it was the spliff, although all Star's father does when he's stoned is fall into unconscious stupors. As for Georgina, she didn't seem stoned at all.

When Georgina suggested I bring out my Hershey's Kisses, as Honey might still be hungry, I directed her to where she'd find them in my cupboard.

Georgina ate a few – well we all did – but Honey demolished most of the bag. Normally she's really careful when it comes to sweets, being obsessed as she is with her figure and complexion. I'm sure Honey would have grazed on tuck all night if it we hadn't heard the *tap, tap, tap* of Miss Bibsmore stick on the stone stairwell.

'We'd better scarper,' Star hissed. And then she did it again. Poked her tongue out at me and grinned. If a nun or even a non-nun teacher saw her stud, she would be gated if not suspended. But as I mentioned, the school was far from keen to damage relations with such a generous donor to school funds as Tiger from Dirge, so they were just as likely to turn a blind eye, I guess.

Georgina air-kissed me and Indie gave me a cuddle before she left.

'It was really cool to meet you, Calypso,' Indie said sweetly.

'Same,' I agreed.

'Good luck with *that*,' she said, pointing to Honey as if she was an unpleasant problem rather than a girl. Honey was still on the floor, wrapped in her duvet giggling to herself. 'Please tell me she's a one off?' Indie begged.

'Oh, she's definitely special,' I assured her.

Indie and Portia both giggled.

Then Indie carefully pushed the bin back and slipped quietly out the door.

TEN

The Political Subjugation of Youth

In the large refectory hall at breakfast the next morning the sounds of clattering plates, chatting girls, and squawking kitchen staff was deafening. There was no noise on God's earth that could drown out Sandra though. Sandra, the head of kitchen staff, wields her power ferociously. Everything about her is fake – from her peroxide platinum hair to her St. Tropez tan and everything in between; Louis Vuitton belt, Versace T-shirt, Chanel sunglasses – you name the label, she owns the fake. The only real thing about her is her Essex screech.

Every morning she stands by the milk dispenser, pointlessly screaming, 'No *cups* of milk, always jugs, girls, remember! No *cups* of milk, always jugs, girls, remember! No *cups* of milk, always jugs, girls, remember!'

Not even the Year Sevens ever heeded her, of course. Between teachers, older girls and our workload, there was enough to heed without listening to mad dinner ladies gabbling on about milk.

I grabbed a couple of croissants and stood in the queue by the milk dispenser with my cup and watched the teachers at wretched high table. High table is an ancient, long, dark oak table around which high-backed, ornately-carved Jacobean style chairs are arranged. The whole affair looms over the refectory on a platform under an ancient portrait of the school's founder, Sister Angelo Meed.

The teachers were all chattering away, hatching their plans about how horrible they would be making our lives this term. The nun teachers were with them but every year there were fewer and fewer teaching nuns as they were getting older and older. The three sitting at high table now were all napping. Mostly you just saw the nuns wandering about the school grounds hand in hand, saying things like 'Isn't it a lovely day, girls?' even if a blizzard was blowing their black robes in the air. We all adored the nuns, who always ignored us if we went up to Puller's Wood for a fag – not that I smoked, but Star did. Also, they were always telling us they'd pray for us and we loved knowing someone existed just to say little prayers for us.

The non-nun teachers lived in lovely old houses scattered around the school grounds and ate special food – cooked to be edible. The worst part of it all came when they wandered past us during Sunday lunch (having polished off their delicious roasts) and watched over us sadistically as we ate our grey-slop-roasts. They always say things like, 'Doesn't that look scrumptious, girls?' I'm not even sure scrumptious is a real word. Teachers are pure evil.

Finally it was my turn to shove my cup under the milk dispenser. After snatching a couple of sachets of chocolate,

I joined Star, Georgina and Indie who were still eating their breakfasts. I noted a couple of madly butch female security guards sitting nearby at a discreet but obvious distance. I figured they were with Indie.

Star and Georgina had their hair identically corn braided like Indie's and were deep in conversation about the pet shed renovation next year and speculating on what that might mean for Brian, Hilda and Dorothy.

I was about to join in when Star asked Indie about the animals in the zoo in her palace in Scotland. I dunked a piece of croissant in my hot chocolate and tried to follow what she was saying. I was concentrating on not feeling jealous of Indie when Star nudged me so hard the croissant fell into my hot chocolate.

'By the way, that wasn't a real spliff that George was smoking with Honey last night, darling,' she whispered. 'It was just a trick.'

'What?' I enquired, as if I was wildly cool and not the least bit fazed by the spliff. Then I began scooping croissant out of my hot chocolate trying not to let my mind dwell on thoughts as to why she hadn't bothered to tell me of the trick beforehand, which would have saved me making a fool of myself.

'It was all Star's idea,' Georgina cut in. 'Remember how we were making up ways to get back at her for all the fat remarks she makes about us?' she reminded me.

'Yes, but . . .'

'Star made a roll up using these herbs her father's been using.'

'He's trying to wean himself off weed,' Star interjected.

'Oh, that's good,' I agreed, spooning some soggy croissant out of my drink.

'It's not been any help though,' she added. 'He just mixes the herbs with weed.'

'That's rock stars for you,' I said with a sigh, as if rock stars and me were always in detox together.

'I thought I'd get her to smoke it as pay back for the way she's always having a go at Star for her father's plebbie drug use.'

'And how fat we are,' Star added.

'I knew she'd share it if *I* offered it to her,' Georgina told me confidently. 'And you won't believe this! She's already approached me this morning for *more*.'

We all laughed, even though a part of me was still put out that they hadn't included me on the plan earlier.

'So it was just herbs?' I confirmed, still slightly unconvinced. 'But she had the munchies even! Honey never eats sweets; she just uses them to bribe Year Sevens to do her blues!'

'I know, wasn't that incredible? I've never seen anyone gobble down calories so fast,' agreed Indie looking at me. She threw back her head and laughed long and loud, completely unembarrassed by all the looks she was receiving from other tables.

'We wanted to let you in but we couldn't in case you started giggling,' Star explained sweetly giving my hand a squeeze.

'I wouldn't have giggled!' I exclaimed indignantly.

'Yes, you would. You even giggled when you had your navel pierced. And that hurt.'

'The thing I loved the most was the way she even started talking like she was stoned,' Georgina marvelled. 'You know in that slow, "Hey man, where's my brain" way.'

I brooded on how they'd voted not to share the joke with me as I fished out the rest of the croissant.

'Are you still going to do Latin this term, darling?' Star suddenly asked, changing the subject as Honey approached our table and nestled herself neatly beside Georgina.

I tried to get the sloppy croissant into my mouth. 'Yaah, we both are,' I reminded her, deciding to abandon the croissant as a lump fell on my tie.

We'd both signed up for Latin, Ancient Greek and French in Year Ten for our GCSE subjects because they'll all be quite easy As and so we'd have more time to focus on our fencing. Star looked at me now as if I were mad. 'I *loathe* Latin with every fibre of my being, Calypso.'

'So do I,' I replied defensively.

'So Daddy told me I can chuck it. Besides, I need the extra time to concentrate on my music,' she said.

'Can you do that?' I asked, pretty certain that you couldn't.

'If your father built the music wing you can do pretty much anything, Calypso,' Star joked. Actually though, it was probably true.

'Yes, why don't you get *your* father to build us something,' Honey asked me faux kindly as she joined our table, before quickly adding, 'Oh, that's right, I always forget, he's got no money, has he?'

'Shut up!' Star and Indie said in unison, only Star added the word 'bitch' at the end.

'Darling, that spliff gave me the best night's sleep since Mummy gave me that Valium,' Honey ruptured.

Georgina almost burst into giggles as she leaned over to tell me, 'I'm chucking Latin too.'

'What?' asked Clemmie, joining our table as I took a bite of my dry croissant.

'Calypso's still doing Latin,' Georgina explained, making it sound like I was electing to do voluntary lunch clearing.

'God, what for, darling?' Clemmie asked, looking at me as if I was insane.

'They said it would be quite an easy A for me. We were all doing Latin last year, remember?' Was I the only one who saw this new turn of events as perplexing, I wondered, as I looked at the girls munching their breakfasts around me. 'Have you dropped it too, Clemmie?' I asked, trying not to sound as confused as I was.

Star snorted as if we hadn't *always* chosen our subjects together. 'Calypso, if you really find it *that* easy why not chuck the lessons and sit the exam anyway?' she asked.

'Yaah, I guess I could?' I shrugged, feeling the colour rush to my face. 'When did you decide this though?'

'It's not a big deal. Georgina and I spoke about it on the flight back and then I asked Daddy before Ray drove me back to school.'

'I didn't ask anyone,' Georgina added.

Clemmie shrugged. 'Nor did I.'

Georgina, Star and Clemmie all rolled their eyes at

how seriously I was taking it all but Star knew that Bob and Sarah would never allow me to drop subjects without a big brouhaha.

'I should have told you but I didn't realise you cared,' said Star.

'I don't mind,' I lied.

'Maybe if you spoke to Bob,' Star suggested. 'You know, explain to him how useless GCSEs are. Eight subjects are plenty after all.'

'And besides, the best public schools are dropping them now, it's such a pointless exam. Eades have dropped GCSEs all together,' Clemmie added.

'As Daddy would say, "Structured exams are just a political subjugation of youth, man",' Star added.

Everyone giggled. Tiger had become a bit of cult figure amongst the girls since his appearance last term at the launch of our satirical magazine *Nun of Your Business.*

'Is that really how your father talks?' Indie asked, giggling at Star's mimicking of her perpetually stoned-sounding father. Because even when he wasn't stoned he still sounded stoned.

'There's no way I'd let *my* parents choose *my* GCSEs,' Arabella added as she climbed on to the table with a bowl of cereal. 'It's my life. My parents wouldn't dare imagine they had the remotest right to ask what subjects I'd chosen. I'd cut them off, totally cut them off' – she imitated a pair of scissors cutting – 'if they tried to influence my life in any way whatsoever.'

'Off that table right now,' ordered one of Sandra's henchwomen walking by. 'Tables is for sitting at, not on. I don't know what your parents is teaching you, I don't.'

'Grammar, mostly,' Honey sneered and everyone laughed. Clemmie still sat down on the bench though. 'My parents couldn't care less what I study or what grades I get. They haven't ever read one of my reports.'

'Nor have mine,' Georgina agreed.

'Sophisticated people realise that life is for living, not working,' Honey remarked pointedly, knowing I didn't have a trust fund to rely on like everyone else in the school. 'Besides, I'm probably going to fail everything anyway, what with all the time I'll be taking off this term. Darcy Greggs wants me in his show at London Fashion Week,' she explained. 'Mummy says it's the opportunity of a lifetime.'

'Wow, that's so cool, can you get us seats? I adore his cashmere.' Georgina, Clemmie and Arabella cooed as Honey gave them one of her self-satisfied, pouty-lipped looks.

'More of an opportunity than Latin, that's for sure,' agreed Star, necking her juice.

I felt like I'd been slapped. After all our years of mutual loathing of Honey, it was as if Star were siding with her against me – even if it was over something as dismal as Latin. I looked around the group of girls as they nodded their heads in agreement and spooned their cereal or dipped their croissants. I felt like I was in a play without a script.

'It's not as if I don't loathe Latin too,' I explained helplessly, 'but I do think that I'll be able to do quite well without putting in much work and my main objective is to do as little work as I have to so I can focus on my fencing.'

I looked to Star for support on this as we'd been fencing from the first day we started at Saint Augustine's.

Star avoided my gaze in a guilty-ish sort of way and began playing with her braids. I carried on gamely. 'Maybe you should reconsider because we're going to need all the easy subjects we can get with the Nationals coming up, Star.'

Everyone blinked at me disinterestedly as if I'd been talking about the variety of school jumpers on offer this season. Honey took this opportunity to inform Georgina that she had already secured front row seats at the show for her and her mother. But I barely heard her because suddenly Star, still playing with her braids, remarked casually, 'Actually Calypso, I've decided to drop fencing.'

'No!' I blurted, before I could stop myself. 'You can't drop fencing!'

Star and I had first bonded on the piste. Fencing was how we had distinguished ourselves from the ghastly Sloaney girls she'd always professed to hate. It was the cornerstone of our relationship. She couldn't drop fencing. It would be like dropping . . . well, it would be like dropping me. 'Why?'

She avoided my gaze by looking deeply into one of the corn braids in her hand. 'Yaah, see, Calypso, I'm going to focus on my music.'

I watched as Indie and Star smiled excitedly at one another. 'Indie and I have already spoken to Sister Constance and we're going to lay down some tracks for a demo CD,' she added.

'Isn't that cool?' Indie finished, her eyes brimming with enthusiasm.

I felt like I was hovering outside my body as I watched Star and Indie look at me as if I should be thrilled. As if I should be jumping up and down with glee that my best friend was walking away from our greatest bond. Instead, I looked at her like she was someone I didn't know any more.

What had happened to Star and Calypso – the sabreurs, the girls who wore their pain like lip-gloss, the Star and Calypso who rinsed boys on the piste? Besides, Star had a massive crush on Mr Sullivan our fencing master so I didn't know how she was going to cope without a daily shot of him. And then I remembered we had a new fencing master this year.

Portia joined us then, sitting down in her quiet, long-legged, elegant way and touched my arm. 'Guess that leaves just you and me on the sabre team, darling.'

'I guess it does,' I agreed, only I was looking at Star as I said it. 'The thing is you need three people on three people on the sabre team in order to fence.'

And then suddenly, Indie turned to me and remarked, 'I'm doing Latin, actually, I'll come by your room after inspection. We can share the joy of verb declensions together.' She turned back to the others. 'I'm following Calypso's plan to go for the easy A-star. I'm doing French, Italian and Ancient Greek as well.'

'Ancient Greek!' Honey shrieked in her hyena squeal. 'No one does Ancient Greek, apart from miserable train wrecks like our American Freak here of course. But no one that *matters* does Ancient Greek. It's a dead language.'

'I wish you were dead,' I almost said and then I realised Star had said it for me. She looked at me and I saw she was miming lip-gloss application and looking at me as if wanting my forgiveness. Honey continued to laugh, though. Most girls look far lovelier when they smile and laugh but because of all her cosmetic enhancements, Honey looked hideous. The Botox meant all the wrong parts of her face moved. When she finally stopped her giggles the table was silent and we stared, as Indie slowly and contemptuously raised one eyebrow to her.

'See, that's where you're wrong, Honey. I'm as far from being a "nobody" as you are ever likely to meet in your dismal little world of wind-ups, put-downs, bad piss-takes and designer nastiness.' With that, Indie stood up in the composed manner only Portia had, and gave Honey the most withering look I'd ever seen – and believe me at Saint Augustine's I've seen plenty of withering looks.

Everyone's eyes flicked between Indie and Honey. Honey seemed to shrivel with each passing nanosecond of the look Indie gave her. I was right, between Miss Bibsmore and Indie, Honey was going to have a rough term. I almost felt sorry for her.

Indie smiled gaily at the rest of us, reminded me she'd drop by my room before Latin, before excusing herself with a sweet little wave and walking out of the ref imperiously, trailed by her bodyguards. The effect was slightly spoilt when one of the guards attempted to put Indie's tray in the tray trolley and was ticked off by Sandra and told to fetch 'the little madam' back to do it for herself.

Star and Georgina, their corn braids as stiff and hard as the lump forming in my throat, giggled at the poor bodyguard humiliated in front of a school of girls for being a lap dog. 'Perhaps Cheltenham Ladies let bodyguards fetch and carry?' Star joked.

'Imagine if they allowed that here! We'd all make our parents assign us bodyguards if that were the case!' Georgina laughed.

Honey didn't join in, she just stared evilly after the disappearing figure of Indie.

ELEVEN

Old Enemies,
New Friends

'I'll see you in the salle before French then? Mr Wellend is expecting us,' said Portia.

'Mr Wellend?' I repeated, confused.

'The new fencing master?'

'Oh yaah,' I agreed, remembering that not even fencing was going to be the same this term.

Portia added, 'Think of it this way: now that Star's chucked it, he'll have more time to focus on us, darling. We can be his star pupils.'

I smiled, knowing she was reaching out at me but the truth was I felt like the ground beneath my feet was shifting and that it was only a matter of time before I lost Star and Georgina to Indie for good.

After breakfast, we went to chapel and then back to our rooms to make our beds and clean our teeth before Miss Bibsmore's daily room inspection. Any fantasy I had briefly clung to that Honey's newfound enemy, Miss Bibsmore, would dilute Honey's horribleness evaporated as soon as the first bell went and Honey accidentally-on-purpose spilled a full glass of water on my bed, seriously drenching my mattress.

Portia was in the bathroom brushing her teeth at the time and without a witness it was pointless to dream Honey would ever apologise. All I could do was pull the covers off and hope the mattress would dry out before I had to sleep on it that night. But I wasn't counting on any miracles.

Out of misery more than anything I turned my mobile on to check for messages and Honey's meanness was suddenly the furtherest thing from my mind. I had two new text messages:

SEE YOU IN WINDSOR ON SATURDAY? X FREDS

To which I faux-casually replied,

YOU READ MY MIND! X C

The next one was from Billy, sent early this morning.

WOTS UP? BILLY XX

HONEY'S JUST WET MY BED. CALYPSO XX

He sent me a text straight back.

INCONTINENT LITTLE BITCH! SEE YOU IN WINDSOR ON SATURDAY. B

Honey was in the en suite so I showed Billy's text to Portia. As she scrolled down through the texts she pointed out that my battery was low. Then her face broke into a smile, and as she read the last message she began to laugh.

She was laughing when Honey came out of the bathroom.

'What's so interesting about the text, then?' Honey asked in an I-couldn't-be-less-interested sort of way.

'Oh nothing, darling,' Portia assured her, handing me

back my mobile and I took her advice and plugged it into my charger.

I was feeling so happy that I didn't even feel pissed off when Miss Bibsmore came in and asked who wet my mattress.

'Just an accident,' I told her, no longer bothered by the soggy mattress I'd have to sleep on that night. Boys are brilliantly distracting like that.

Miss Bibsmore didn't look convinced.

Honey laughed. 'Americans are so clumsy.'

'I've warned you, madam, I'm on to you' was all Miss Bibsmore said as she eyed Honey up and down. 'Now don't forget, girls, you've been asked to report to the infirmary after lunch for your flu jabs an' all.'

After Miss Bibsmore was out of earshot, I said, 'Oh needles, just what I need to make this day *perfecto*!'

It was the sort of joke I would make for Star usually, but Portia laughed and, weirdly, so did Honey. Then she said, 'So, are you going to share that text with me then?'

I was saved from replying though because the bell to class suddenly went off and Indie stuck her head into our room, 'Coming?' she asked.

'Enjoy your Latin, girls,' Honey called out after us but we were already in the throng of charging girls rushing down the corridor.

Latin was in one of the older buildings and consequently freezing cold. I was so regretting taking Latin and not just because Star had dropped it. We filed into the empty class and chose a table – I grabbed one by the radiator which gave off a sort of mild warmth. Portia sat beside me and Indie sat in front.

Even though Ms Mills was always threatening the physical manifestations of our souls, at least she knew her stuff. Now we were in Year Eleven we'd been lumped with a Mrs Obar whose only qualification for the job as our Latin teacher we soon realised was 'I've been a teacher for thirty-seven years! Thirty-seven years, so there's nothing you can tell me!'

Indie turned around to me. 'As if there is the remotest chance she'll ever draw breath long enough to let anyone tell her anything.'

Mrs Obar threw some chalk at her as if it was the most normal behaviour in the world, then she ordered us to open our books, sit up straight and pay attention. I noticed Indie bend down and retrieve the chalk from the floor a little later when Mrs Obar wasn't looking.

After Mrs Obar struggled for a while with pronunci-ation, Portia put her hand up to question Mrs Obar's specific qualifications to teach us Latin. Her response was to throw a piece of chalk at her as well, which Portia deflected with her Cicero translation book. Like Indie, I retrieved the piece of chalk from the floor, and later when Mrs Obar's back was to us, I threw it at her, which set all of us off giggling. Of course at our exclusive school no class had more than five in it and in this case there were only the three of us, so our laughter didn't create much of a noise and, to preserve her dignity perhaps, Mrs Obar pretended she hadn't felt the chalk and continued writing on the board.

Indie turned round and passed me a note in her neat handwriting: *Next time throw the book!!*

Mrs Obar didn't pretend to ignore the note though. She swooped down on us like a witch in her black serge gown and snatched it up.

'And what might this note mean, Miss Kelly?'

'We were sharing a translation,' Portia told her swiftly. 'See?' Relying on Mrs Obar's ignorance, Portia pointed to a passage in her book.

'Oh, I see,' Mrs Obar conceded. 'Very good, Lady Harrington Briggs but Miss Kelly will eventually have to come to grips with her translations herself if she's to distinguish herself to the examiners.'

I struggled to turn my barely suppressed smile into a look of humble acknowledgement but failed when Indie burst out laughing in her distinctive fulsome way for which she was given a blue.

By Year Eleven you just hand over your blues to a Year Seven to do for you in exchange for sweets or some other privilege. But as I was already starting to realise, Indie wasn't like most girls.

She refused the blue that Mrs Obar passed to her, and merely looked at it as if it was a pair of dirty knickers. 'I'm not accepting *that*, Mrs Obar!'

Mrs Obar raised her voice. 'Excuse me madam but you will accept this blue or you'll be getting another.'

Indie stood up. 'Hardly!' she exclaimed in a voice of shock, her hand over her heart in mortification. Then she continued calmly, 'With all due respect, Mrs Obar, how can I possibly excuse you for wasting my time when I'm sitting eleven GCSEs and I've learned absolutely nothing in your class so far. I'm sorry, but if I were to accept your blue, in all conscience I'd be obliged to make a complaint to my father about the inadequacy of my tuition.' And then she played her trump card as she held out a clenched fist and opened her hand to reveal the piece of chalk Mrs Obar had thrown at her earlier. 'Also, I doubt he'll be thrilled to hear that my teacher has been hurling chalk missiles at me.'

I was as awed as Mrs Obar, who was blatantly humiliated, was stuck for words. She stood there for a full minute clutching her blue impotently but eventually she gathered herself together, shoved the blue into her desk drawer and returned to the board where she proceeded to write down the pages in our work books that we needed to cover in prep that evening.

Portia, Indie and I all exchanged looks. I mouthed the words 'sooo cool' but by the end of class Mrs Obar was even letting us chat amongst ourselves. She'd been rumbled and she knew it.

Next class was English Literature with Ms Topler. I want to be a writer, but Ms Topler would make the most enthusiastic novelist stick pins in their eyes. We were doing Shakespeare's *King Lear* which is my favourite play of all. You'd think given how much I love the play and how it was Shakespeare it would be hard to ruin. But I trusted that in Ms Topler's capable hands she would dissect and deconstruct my beloved *King Lear* into something we could nod off to. I love Cordelia's honesty. I love that she dares to stick up for the truth even though she knows her father is a total grown-up and ipso facto an egotistical hypocrite on a power trip. A bit like Ms Topler, I was thinking as she droned on and on about *hubris*. There's nothing Ms Topler loves more than a good drone.

After lunch, I trudged off to Ancient Greek. Portia was already there and I sat at the desk beside her. Our teacher, Doctor Buffner told us that we'd be doing *Oedipus Rex* and for a special treat we were going to Cambridge after half-term to see it performed.

'I hope they have a good DVD on the coach ride there,' I whispered to Portia, because that's usually the only fun part about school trips.

'I know, can you imagine listening to an *entire* play in Ancient Greek?' she whispered back.

We both simultaneously slumped on our desks at the very thought of enduring a whole play listening to incoherent piffle.

Indie arrived late and while she had a quiet word with Doctor Buffner, Portia asked me about Billy and Freddie and who I liked the most.

'Well, that's what I don't know,' I confided. 'But I keep telling myself, as soon as I see them it will all work out.'

'I think Billy's seriously fit,' Portia said. 'I mean, as a fencer, on the piste. You know, he is the captain and well . . .'

I looked at her quizzically. 'Fitter than Freddie?' I asked, suddenly feeling an acute need to start getting some perspective on the decision awaiting me, because like I said, as much as having a text romance with two boys at once was fun, it couldn't go on indefinitely.

Portia didn't get a chance to answer, though, as Indie joined us and class resumed.

After lunch, I made a quick detour to the pet shed to check on Dorothy but my head was full of what Portia had said about Billy being fit. Even though she'd qualified it by explaining she was referring to his fencing ability, I felt a bit uneasy. Not jealous exactly; in fact, it sort of tipped my affections in favour of Freddie. Poor Freddie, I thought, feeling fiercely protective of his looks. The truth was, though, they were pretty evenly matched in the fit stakes. Billy was older, which gave him added kudos, but then Freddie was heir to the throne. It was like I had both boys on a set of weighing scales and I couldn't bear to imagine the balance being tipped in one boy's favour.

I picked up Dorothy. She'd put on weight, I decided, as I carried her over to the pet run for a little hop. The only other girls there were Year Sevens and Eights so when they offered to look after her for me, I agreed, as I had to rush to the infirmary for the hated flu shot. The queue was already snaking down the corridor and because everyone was waiting to be jabbed in the arm with a needle, conversation was sparse. It was going to be a long wait. The sadistic Sister Dumpster (real name, Dempster) – who is not a nun at all and quite possibly once worked for the Inquisition, she's so old and nasty – liked to take her time torturing us. Flu jab day was her favourite day of the year.

I found Star and waited with her and we fell back into our familiar line of chat – ripping it out of our teachers and the disgusting lunch we'd just consumed. We both studiously avoided conversations about her giving up fencing, Latin and Ancient Greek although actually I didn't really mind about the Latin and Ancient Greek because Portia and Indie seemed really fun. The fencing was another matter entirely, though.

'Sister Constance said the food was going to be more imaginative this term too,' Star moaned.

'I think she meant more imaginatively evil,' I told her.

'What I want to know is how they make all the meat look identical? How can you make beef, pork, chicken and lamb look exactly the same? It's scary.'

'Well, we do have a salad bar that includes rocket leaves,' I teased, knowing how much Star loathes green things.

Finally, it was my turn to have my arm jabbed.

'It's just a prick,' Sister Dumpster told me menacingly, her eyes dancing with happiness as she shoved in the needle, hard and deep.

Star told her she'd do it herself but Sister Dumpster was resolute. 'It's my special fun and you're not going to spoil it,' she insisted. Well, what she actually said was, 'I'm fully trained' but everyone who overheard, knew what she *really* meant.

Afterwards I headed off to join Portia at the fencing salle. 'Say hi to Professor Sullivan for me,' Star called out.

'He's not our fencing master any more,' I informed her and there it was, back again: the gulf between us. I saw it in Star's guilty expression and I'd heard it in my tone. I almost blurted out something childish like 'What's happened to us?' but thankfully I stopped myself just in the nick of time. Perhaps Portia's aloof demeanour was starting to rub off on me . . .

'Well, have a good one anyway, Calypso,' Star said as we parted company.

I was going to miss fencing practice with Star, although she did allow herself to be distracted a bit much. Mostly by her pet rat Hilda or her snake Brian, who by the way are quite possibly the happiest healthiest pets in the pet shed. In Star's mind however they are more sensitive than all the other pets. She's convinced the rabbits and hamsters say mean things to them when she's not around and give them beady-eyed looks, which really upsets me because Dorothy hasn't got a mean fibre in her soft little body.

And although I can't speak for Honey's rabbit, Absinthe, in my opinion if any of the pets give beady-eyed looks, it's Brian himself. I swear, Star's snake, given half the chance, would eat Dorothy and the others. I've seen him eyeing them up – he practically licks his nonexistent lips as we take the rabbits on to the run. Not that I'd say that to Star. I always say things like, poor Brian, or, poor little darling Hilda. I even cuddle Hilda like cuddling a rat is what I live for. Indie no doubt genuinely adores both Brian and Hilda and doesn't even have to pretend.

But I have decided to stop thinking mean jealous things like that. Just like I have decided to stop being annoyed with Star for dropping fencing. Over that morning, I had worked out that developing an aloof demeanour like Portia could easily be the answer to all my problems. It was sad that Star and I would no longer be the swashbuckling sabreurs of old but as Portia had put it, now

Mr Wellend only had two senior sabreurs, he'd be able to give us more specialist attention. Yes, an aloof demeanour would be the making of me. I would pay more attention to what I said, drop the whole blurting thingamee and work on floating through life like Portia in a dignified way.

Perhaps this aloof demeanour, which by the way I could already feel creeping into my character, would even help me with my Freddie/Billy choice.

TWELVE

Mr Bell End

Portia and I were in the salle d'armes changing into the numerous items of fencing kit and armour when she said, 'Was it Honey who wet your bed?'

'What do you think?' I replied, as I pulled on my new breeches. Like most girls in my year, I'd had another growth spurt over the summer and had to buy new fencing gear online from Leon Paul. I have just about reached the end of my tether with this growth spurt business. I am now five foot eight and if I keep going like this I'll be taller than Freddie and Billy. I was madly taking back all the petitions I had made to Our Lady in Year Seven to make me tall and slim, explaining that when I said, *tall and slim* I actually meant stunning and leggy not a stick-like, freakish, giant.

'Why didn't you say anything to her, darling?' Portia asked.

'It's pointless challenging her. You know what Honey's like,' I reminded Portia.

Star and I could have had a great deal of fun out of the 'What Honey's Like?' conversation, but Portia was as silent as a throne. She simply went back to changing into her fencing gear as if that were the end of the matter. The next time she spoke was as we were heading out to the piste. 'Oh I forgot, I spoke to Mr Wellend.'

'What's he like?' I asked, whispering because I could already hear him out there and I didn't want him to hear our conversation.

Portia began rearranging her plastic breast guard, which is a horrible, nasty piece of armour that is roughly shaped like breasts and is always impossible to get entirely comfortable. 'He said that Emille – you know, she does *épée*; long, straight, blond hair, year below . . .?'

I shook my head. Almost all the girls at Saint Augustine's had long straight blond hair, and while Portia had once been captain of the *épée* team, I had barely noted the girls that fenced foil or *épée*.

'Well, anyway she's moving on to sabre, so she can make up team, which is brilliant.'

'Not as brilliant as Star,' I pointed out.

'No, but at least we can put up a team at interschool matches now, and also he was totally fine about the extra tuition thing. I think he's as keen as us really, just a bit . . .'

'What?' I asked, starting to worry.

'Well, put it this way, he's no Professor Sullivan,' she said.

'You mean he's not going to speak to us in French?'

She laughed as she shook her head.

'Is he really old and horrible and wrinkly and mean?'

'I can't swear to his meanness,' she replied enigmatically as she retied her breast guard, 'but he is sort of odd. I mean old,' she corrected herself quickly. 'Old for a fencing master, that is.'

Quite old is a euphemism for ancient and in my experience most ancient men are pretty odd but Portia obviously wanted to leave it at that and so I dropped it.

Mr Wellend was waiting for us on the piste, practising his theatrical lunges. He looked to be pushing fifty or something woeful like that. And talk about odd, this fellow took the biscuit. He had a beard and I've never understood beards. Even when I was seriously young I was terrified of them. I always think that men with beards smell like soup. And this beard was one of those really neatly clipped ones that pointed at the end like one of the Three Musketeers'. Far worse than the beard thing, though, he was actually wearing a silver medal – an Olympic silver medal *outside* his fencing gear.

'Right girlies, let's start with some warm ups shall we?' was his opening gambit. He had a South African accent and spoke to us in a sneering, creepy sort of way. As Portia and I looked at one another, I could tell we were thinking the same thing. We had a madman on our hands.

I shoved my mask over my head to smother my giggles.

'No masks for warm-ups, girlies, no one's going to get hurt.' His voice was so slimy I couldn't bear it and then he rubbed his hands together. Talk about oily.

I'm sure I must have been mistaken but I was almost certain I heard Portia whisper the word 'creep' under her breath.

I soon decided it was going to be quite good having Portia as my sabre partner. Like me, she was totally focused even in practice sessions. You can always lose yourself in fencing because you *have* to forget everything else and concentrate on the game.

Professor Sullivan was always going on about how fencing is a physical game of chess and incredibly enough for a teacher, he's actually right! You have to anticipate your opponent's moves as much as plan your own, all the while staying in the moment, attacking and counterattacking your combatant. Mr Wellend put it slightly differently . . .

'Think with your brain, girlies, move with your body, slam 'em with your blade.'

I don't know whether it was Portia or me who came up with the nickname, Bell End, but it wasn't long into our session before we were whispering asides to one another, doing piss-takes of Bell End's accent. Which is an achievement in itself because as you can imagine, it's not easy saying the word 'bell end' (which is the name for the end of a boy's . . . well, you know what) while keeping a straight face.

After fencing, I told Portia I needed to go back to my room for a tampon, as I'd just discovered I'd started my period. I was relieved in a way because I decided that was why I'd been so emotional about everything over the past twenty four hours.

'Actually, I think I'll come with you,' she told me. 'I have to sort something out myself.'

We hurried back, anxious not to be late for our next class, which was French. I dashed straight into the en suite. I heard a bit of stomping about going on in the bedroom but thought nothing of it until I came out and discovered Portia struggling with a mattress.

'Can you help me get this on to Honey's bed?' she panted.

'Sure, what happened?' I asked, as I supported the other end of the heavy mattress and helped her manoeuvre it on to Honey's bed.

'Just swapping mattresses,' she explained blithely as she smiled serenely at me. 'You don't want to sleep on a wet mattress, do you?'

I laughed and then hesitated for a moment, imagining what Honey's retaliation might be. 'She'll murder me!'

'Well, we'll murder her back then.' Portia shrugged. 'Besides, she'll probably blame Miss Bibsmore.'

This was a very different Portia Herrington Briggs than the girl I thought I knew, that was for sure. She was as serene as ever but there was a warmth about her as well.

'Good idea,' I agreed. 'Besides, I'm sure Miss Bibsmore wouldn't mind.'

'She might even give us a trophy,' Portia added.

'Oh, my Sarah and Bob would adore that. They've always wanted me to bring home a cup.'

After we finished our war with the wet mattress and remade the bed, I checked my phone for messages from Billy and Freddie.

'Oh *merde*!' I cried, as I saw I'd left my phone on.

'What?' asked Portia.

'I left my phone on.'

'Ten to one Honey snuck a look,' Portia said, echoing my own thoughts.

'Now we'll definitely have to murder her,' I told her in mock solemnity.

'No other option,' Portia said, shrugging, and we burst into peals of belly laughter.

There were no new messages from the boys but I didn't mind. I was feeling a million times better about everything right up until we walked into the French classroom and I had a perfect view of Star, Georgina and Indie chatting and giggling together. Normally, Star would have saved me a seat.

Portia scribbled away, taking notes conscientiously, while I watched my friends enjoy the royal company of their New Best Friend. I gathered myself together and began taking notes because I was working madly at developing my aloof demeanour and girls with aloof demeanours don't behave like green-eyed monsters.

The problem was, though, I was still only a novice at this aloof demeanour business and I found my eyes and attention constantly drawn to the line up of Star, Georgina and Indie. They appeared to be passing notes. I was vaguely aware of Miss Devante droning on and on and on about the importance of the article and I was scribbling away furiously to keep up the pretence of attention but that's all it was really, a pretence. My page was covered in a scrawl of hearts and arrows.

'*Mademoiselle* Kelly?' she suddenly snapped.

'*Qu'est ce que c'est?*' I asked, as I realised I was the focus of her beady-eyed French attention.

'Tell us about your vacation, *en Français.*'

'Oh bugger,' I blurted, before my aloof demeanour could stop me, which earned me a blasted blue.

Portia sidled up to me after class and said, 'My cousin's

in Year Seven, darling and she's fluent in French. Give the blue to me and I'll take care of it.'

'Are you sure, I could speak to Sister Constance? She might be persuaded to transmute it into a chore like floor sweeping?'

'Sister doesn't transmute punishments for Year Elevens,' she reminded me. 'But my cousin's cool. For a bag of Hershey's Kisses she'll do anything.'

I remembered being in Year Seven fondly now. Apart from being teased about my stupid accent, I'd had hardly any work to occupy me, and that, coupled with an insatiable appetite for sweets and a worship of older, worldly-wise girls, made doing their blues an absolute joy. It was so lovely and innocent back then. We didn't even know boys existed.

On top of that, back in Year Seven, Star would always have saved me a seat.

THIRTEEN

The Night Of The Soggy Boggies

Apart from our daily fencing practice with Mr Bell End, I found myself slipping into what Ms Topler referred to as a malaise.

'Miss Kelly, you aren't yourself,' she announced to me – and the rest of the class – during English.

'Oh really, who am I?' I replied and everyone laughed.

'Don't be droll, girl. You know what happens to droll girls!'

'Actually, not really,' I challenged.

'Blues!' she threatened, before softening slightly. 'No dear, I fear you are slipping into a malaise, just like those poor Brontë girls.'

I hate the wretched Brontë girls I wanted to tell her, but then I realised it would just prove her point, so instead I replied, 'Yes, Miss.'

Because she was right; I *was* slipping into a malaise. Brought on, I expect, by lack of text messages from boys – not one text since Monday! I know four days isn't a long time and there were loads of reasons they might not have had the time to text me. But I had begun to panic and started a nasty habit of shaking my phone. Of course it didn't help that every time I so much as looked at my mobile, Honey would pipe up, 'New message from Freddie or Billy, is it?'

And then when I'd say, 'No, they must be busy,' Honey would smile her *Apis Regina* smile (that's Latin for Queen Bee) and say. 'Yes, that's a positive way to deal with rejection, darling.'

Even with Portia around I never felt comfortable in the dorm with Honey and so after these exchanges I'd usually wander off to Star's dorm where she'd invariably be chatting to Indie and Georgina. Or laughing at some new joke of Tobias's, who's always got an amusing story up his sleeve.

Of course I pretended everything was as it always was because after all there's nothing wrong with discovering new friends. That's what I kept reminding myself. It's not as if Star was being mean to me, or cutting me out even, it was just that she wasn't favouring me. Now that she had found someone to share her minor chord compositions with, she was as happy as her rat Hilda. And as much as I was enjoying my unexpected friendship with Portia, and as much as I couldn't help liking Indie, I still wanted my old spiky Star back; the one who made sarcastic remarks about all the other girls and their conformism. The one who got my odd sense of humour, the one who didn't look at me like a freak when I went on one of my rambling blurts.

This new happy, friendly Star was either wandering around the school laughing with everyone or closeted with

Indie in the studio, recording their miserable songs about the sorrows of being Rich, Spoilt and Disillusioned. Also there was something even worse than Star's friendship with Indie playing on my mind. Something I couldn't admit to anyone (and no, I don't mean the fact that I'd taken out my navel piercing because I told Star the whole horrible tale of Sarah and Bob marching me into the shop and humiliating me in front of the entire population of Los Angeles and she'd laughed so hard, she was almost sick).

No, the real problem was that neither Freddie nor Billy had texted me recently and I was beginning to wonder if I'd finally been rumbled for double text-flirting. Or maybe they'd found a new girl to text. Maybe Honey was right, maybe I'd been rejected.

Maybe they were texting Indie?

Don't worry, even I knew I was being irrational. My aloof demeanour practice was definitely starting to pay off. I was feeling much less conflicted – as Bob and Sarah would say – over Star and Indie's friendship. In fact, one evening in our dorm room, when Honey started winding me up about Freddie and Billy, Indie turned to her and asked, 'What about you, Honey, we never seem to hear you talk about any particular boy. Have you ever pulled?' She said it in a pitying way which implied she already knew the answer was no.

Honey almost imploded with shock at the suggestion that she'd never pulled. Before she could respond though, Indie began admiring my wristband. It was just one of those plastic charity bands that cost a pound, like the LIVE

STRONG yellow ones, only mine was a blue BEAT BULLYING one.

'They're the only jewellery she can afford.' Honey sighed heavily, as if this was of great sadness to her.

Indie went, 'That's probably because she spends all her money on patience putting up with you.'

Portia and Star, who were in the room at the time, laughed, so they didn't actually see what I saw. Honey's face twisted into a look of pure hatred, only oddly it wasn't Indie she was looking at, it was Portia.

The big drama of our first week back came on the Friday night – a night which would be known for evermore as *The Night of the Soggy Boggies*. We'd often lie on our beds and shoot soggy wads of paper up on the ceiling or on to the mirror using the plastic casing of our Bic pens, but on this particular Friday night, things got a little out of hand.

One minute we were practising our cool dance moves in front of the mirror – well, Honey was, anyway, and I think I speak for the world at large when I say she looked absurd - doing a sort of slinky tango with herself. Portia was reading an American *Vogue* I'd brought back from LA. I was pretending to read text messages from boys who weren't sending them because there was absolutely no way I'd practise my dance moves with Honey. Of course I practised my dance moves, but I'd slip down to Star's dorm these days for that sort of thing. Everyone looks a bit mad practising dance moves in front of a mirror but, as sorry a business as it is, there's no escaping it.

It's like Star says, 'English boys can't dance for toast so

we girls have an obligation to hold up their side as well as our own.' Naturally Indie was immediately voted the most phenomenal dancer in our school – after Tobias who has been taking special lessons all his life.

(Aloof demeanour note to self: Stop focusing on how marvellous Indie is!)

Anyway, there we were, having a typical Friday night, when Clemmie, Arabella and Georgina came storming into our room and Arabella propelled a sodden loo roll at us.

Splat!

The noise was enormous, like the sound of a wet bag of sand hitting a wall. It landed on the pin board above Honey's bed (the one where she keeps all the paparazzi shots of herself with famous people). We all watched in stunned silence as the loo roll virtually crawled – like it was alive – slowly down the wall, eventually flopping life-lessly in a soggy mass on Honey's pillow.

Predictably, this was enough to escalate the soggy, boggy prank into a full on dorm war, with sodden loo rolls being hurled through dorms by everyone at everyone. We were behaving 'proper mad' as the shop keepers in the village would say.

Miss Bibsmore hobbled up the stairs, just in time to catch Honey who had filled our bin with water and loo rolls and was dragging it up the wet corridor for an apoca-lyptic onslaught on Clemmie's dorm.

Miss Bibsmore raised her walking stick and then she raised her voice to a level that could shatter glass as she screamed, 'Stop right where you are Miss O'Hare, you spawn of Satan you.'

Everyone froze, apart from Honey, obviously.

'Don't. Move. A. Muscle,' Miss Bibsmore repeated.

We all giggled because she was speaking the way super heroes speak when they are heavily armed with superstrength weapons and powers. All Miss Bibsmore had in the way of superpowers was a limited ability to distribute blues, a history of childhood illnesses and a walking stick.

It surprised no one that Honey still totally ignored her. I can't think that even Miss Bibsmore, scary as she is, actually imagines that Satan's spawn are in the least bit receptive to obeying orders squawked by mad House Spinsters who need a stick to walk, but still she persisted. 'I'm warning you, Miss O'Hare, my temper is on a very short fuse.'

Honey flicked her gorgeously long, blond expensively streaked locks across her shoulder and replied calmly, 'Might I remind you who pays your wages, Miss Bibsmore?'

Miss Bibsmore had her bottom lip out. She raised her cane and waved it about menacingly to show she *really* meant business. 'No, Miss O'Hare, you may not remind me of any such thing. However, you might well find yourself gated, or worse, if you don't stand stock-still this minute.'

Honey turned, and for a moment I thought she was about to hurl a soggy boggy at Miss Bibsmore. Instead she mildly remarked, 'We're in the middle of a soggy boggy war here and the battle has reached a crucial stage, if you don't mind!' Which implied that soggy boggies were on par with hard sums or letters home to parents.

Portia, Star, Georgina and all the rest of the girls who were watching the spectacle from the doorways of their respective rooms giggled. Hate Honey though I do, I couldn't help admiring her total lack of fear. Even Georgina was awed. 'Bless,' she said as Honey turned and continued imperiously up the corridor to Clemmie's room and, slightly less imperiously, commenced propelling her wet missiles at the shrieking girls inside.

I think we were all secretly impressed by Honey's audacity at that moment. Even Indie was giggling at her mettle as the shrieks and laughter of the girls inside being splattered with soggy boggies filled the corridor.

Miss Bibsmore wasn't so in awe, though. Not even slightly. In fact she used her stick to smash the fire alarm glass, setting off the sprinkler system and we all ran shrieking into our rooms to rescue our bedding.

Although hitting the fire alarm and setting off the sprinkler system is an age old favourite with House Spinsters, they usually only resorted to it in times of imminent disaster, because as effective as the deluge is, it means calling up the local fire brigade, waking up the whole dorm and setting in motion the fire emergency procedures where we all storm off to the tennis courts for registration and then a report is filed with Sister, who would be less than impressed.

But Miss Bibsmore is no ordinary House Spinster.

Portia sensibly ignored the procedure as we knew there was no fire and started rolling up her duvet, pillow and sheets. I followed suit. Then we helped one another to squeeze our duvets and mattresses out the window of our room on to the hedges below. We weren't the only ones either. Everyone was on the same page as to what needed to be done. There were mattresses, pillows, duvets and clothing flying from all the bedrooms on the second floor. By the time we got to Honey's bedding it was already pretty soggy and heavy but after a hefty struggle we eventually managed to hurl it out the window as well. Then we all charged off to the tennis courts for registration where an explanation of the dud emergency was given to Sister.

Our dorm was all totally drenched and freezing by the time we returned, escorted by Miss Bibsmore, but that didn't stop Honey screaming her head off about Miss Bibsmore being an insane witch and how her father was going to shower her in litigation suits.

Everyone took their place back in the doorways to watch the spectacle. In the silence that followed Honey's rambling rant, Miss Bibsmore calmly and quietly informed Honey that she was officially gated and then, turning the corridor lights off, she hobbled off. We listened to the tap, tap, tapping of her stick on the stone stairs as we all stood in the soggy darkness, contemplating our behaviour and the possible repercussions to come.

Amazingly enough though, apart from Honey, we all got off scot-free. Well, free-ish. We spent most of the night mopping up the mess and struggling up the stairs with our duvets, mattresses and pillows. Honey's mattress was too wet to sleep on though so she went and slept with Georgina in her bed.

'Honey's having a rough ride with wet mattresses this

term,' Portia remarked as we lay in the dark. Even though we were exhausted from all the excitement, it was hard to get sleep.

'Perhaps we won't have to murder her after all, darling,' I replied, referring to our joke when we'd swapped mattresses.

'Bob and Sarah will be disappointed.' Portia sighed.

'I know, they would have loved that silver cup.'

'Perhaps we'll have a cup made up anyway and award it to you for your work with mattresses in the dormitory community.'

'You deserve that cup more than me,' I teased.

'No, but you can keep it darling. Eaglemere is choking on generations of trophies already.'

I fell asleep soon after that. It was the best night's sleep I'd had since coming back. I never would have imagined that sharing a room with a girl like Lady Portia Herrington Briggs could turn out to be the blessing of a lifetime.

FOURTEEN

Just One Of Those Annual Euro-Royal-Bash Thingamees

The next morning was Saturday, so after breakfast, cleaning our rooms, going down for registration, attending chapel and two long hours of study followed by lunch, we all decided to take taxis into Windsor for an afternoon of Eades boy spotting. All of us, apart from Honey, that is, because she was gated.

This was the first year that we could actually go off on our own into Windsor, so we took quite a lot of time dressing in our most casually stunning outfits and applying and reapplying lip-glosses. I almost felt sorry for Honey when we left her sitting on her bed, her arms folded, a pouty expression on her face.

When Portia asked her if she wanted anything from town she replied archly, 'Why, are you offering to bring me back a fit boy?'

I didn't say anything apart from muttering goodbye.

Sister Constance and her agents (also known as the

teachers and House Spinsters) were always reminding us
of the school rule for trips into town – 'Go out in threes,
stay in threes and return in threes' – so I can't say I was
surprised when Star, Georgina and Indie came tumbling
into our room and breathlessly announced that they'd
meet us in town. I mean, they shared a dorm together, so
it was natural that they'd all go into town in a group; and
even though local taxis *can* take four passengers, no one
wants to sit next to the driver. So it would be childish to
take something like that personally, but I did.

This meant that Portia and I had to find some random
horsy girl called Anastasia, who we really didn't know that
well, to go to Windsor with us. The whole two miles were
spent listening to her endless tales of how many polo
players she'd pulled that summer. 'I am such a slut,
darlings,' she told us, as if being a slut was a talent. 'But
honestly,' she said with a sigh. 'I can't help myself, they are
just so gorgeous in their tight jodhpurs. I think I like the
Argentineans best, but some of the Australians were rather
nice this year. I really am the most dreadful slut, aren't I,
darlings?'

Portia and I muttered agreeably and as non-
judgementally as we could. Star would have pressed her
elbow into my rib to try and make me laugh but Portia was
too aloof for that sort of thing. And I was trying to be.

We had the taxi drop us off at the stone bridge that
curves over the River Thames and leads to the castle walls.
As Sod's Law would have it, as we walked over the bridge
into Windsor, the first Eades boys we spotted were Billy
and a bunch of his fit friends. I was determined to be aloof

– as serene as a throne – but my face was going to betray me. I knew it as we approached them and the blood started travelling up my feet towards my head. Then Billy's posse peeled off, and it was just Billy walking towards Portia, Anastasia and me, like one of those cowboy showdowns.

Portia offered to leave too, but I begged her not to. I needed her aloof demeanour as backup, in case my own fell flat on its face. Also, Anastasia was still with us. I think she was still babbling on about her polo pulling score over the summer and groaning about what a slut she was.

All thoughts as to why Billy hadn't sent me a text since Monday flew right out of my head, replaced by all the steamy texts he *had* sent me. As my legs grew weak from lack of blood, I envisioned myself swooning into a faint like a Victorian heroine, and Billy sweeping me into his arms and snog-aging me into a blissful reality.

My heart was pounding and my pulse was racing as I introduced Anastasia, but once she'd established that Billy wasn't a polo player she strode off on her own to find her polo buddies.

Billy was as fit looking as ever and wearing really cool trousers and trainers. He was also wearing a charity band like mine, but in green. Maybe that was a sign?

'Haven't heard from you in a bit,' he muttered, shoving his hands in his pockets, seemingly unable to make eye contact with me. This was bad. The blood was rushing round my head but I kept my cool(-ish).

'Funny that,' I remarked idly, as if I didn't care in the slightest about his recent lack of texts. I wasn't going to give him the pleasure. Also, looking at him, as a light drizzle started to fall, I realised something else. Now that my initial nerves had subsided, I couldn't help noticing that while my blood may have been displaced from one part of my body to another, my tummy wasn't doing funny tumbly things and my palms weren't sweaty. Could it be possible that I had only *imagined* that I fancied him all this time?

I suppose when a boy saves you from the jaws of a girl-eating dog, it's more or less inevitable that you'll feel a certain amount of emotion, I told myself, as he looked up at Portia and asked her about her sabre form. He and Portia knew one another through fencing, and also her brother Tarquin was in his year; so while they chatted away like old friends, I began to feel like a bit of a spare leg. I bet Billy was just doing it out of his shame at not texting me, but still, it wasn't very cordial of him and they were virtually cutting me out.

'Busy week?' I interjected, in a tragic attempt to turn attention on to myself.

Billy stared at me like I'd interrupted an important board meeting. 'What?'

I looked to Portia for support but she looked out across the Thames.

'Busy week?' I repeated, as my aloof demeanour deserted me and dived into the Thames – perhaps that was what had caught Portia's notice.

'Pretty much,' he replied, in an almost irritated tone. 'You?'

'Seriously busy.' I rolled my eyes in what I hoped looked

like a sexy way but I'm pretty sure just look looked freakish.

He still wasn't looking at me. He stuffed his hands in his pockets and rocked back and forth on his feet, which annoyed me. I know that Portia was there so he was probably not in a position to explain things, but still, he was really making me feel rotten.

Portia muttered something about heading off to find Tarkie, but I wasn't going to make it so easy for Billy.

'I've got something to do, actually,' I said importantly. 'Why don't you help Portia find Tarquin, Billy?' I suggested bossily, half expecting that he'd fall on his knees and beg me not to leave.

But he didn't. Instead he said, 'Absolutely,' with a bloody annoying degree of enthusiasm.

'Right then,' I muttered, adding, 'off I go,' just to make my seriously cringing embarrassing exit complete.

I wandered off sulkily on my own looking for the others. Star had suggested we all convene in a tea shop past the castle walls, so I made my way along the cobbled streets, weaving my way through the throngs of tourists and students. I regretted not bringing an umbrella as a light drizzle began to fall, but not as much as I regretted a lot of other things. Bloody boys.

And that was when it happened. I walked slap bang into Freddie and Billy's younger brother, Kevin, as I was turning down a narrow cobbled lane. And not only was my face red but my tummy was doing back flips and tumbles as Freddie smiled at me and said . . .

Well, I don't know what he said actually, my heart was pounding so loudly I couldn't hear a thing. Also my palms were sweating and all I could think of was how fit he looked with his wet hair plastered on his forehead, and then all I could think of was how hideous I must look with my wet hair plastered down my forehead. So instead of saying 'Hi' or something sensible like that, I just stood there like an idiot, watching his lips move and only barely controlling an urge to kiss him.

Kevin asked where Star was, so I told him that I was on my way to meet her in a tea shop further down the main road. I could tell he wanted more detailed directions, but Freddie took me by the elbow and led me around the corner and Kevin peeled off, as if some secret signal had been exchanged.

I couldn't see Freddie's security men but they must have been about somewhere, probably disguised as tourists. I didn't get a chance to have a look around for them, because once we were out of the rain in the shelter of an awning, Freddie took my face in his hands and kissed me long and slowly.

It was so lovely, just like the last time we'd kissed, only without Honey taking a photograph of us with her mobile and selling it to the tabloids. As his hands wove their way through my hair, I closed my eyes and allowed myself to relax, when suddenly Kevin was back again and coughing awkwardly in my ear.

Freddie ignored him and carried on kissing me but I opened my eyes.

'Sorry, Calypso, sorry, Freddie, but which tea shop did you say Star was in?'

Not only did Freddie not open his eyes or take his lips

off mine, he made 'piss off' signals at his friend and kept on kissing me. Which is the most marvellously cool thing that has ever happened to me.

'Sorry,' repeated the now-sodden Kevin, who shuffled off back into the rain which had picked up force during our kissing. The awning wasn't offering us much respite any more.

'Let's make a dash for it,' Freddie suggested and we ran into a pizza place nearby that was popular with both Eades and Saint Augustine's students.

Freddie ordered a pizza, half pepperoni (him) and half Hawaiian (me), but the best thing was, even while choosing and ordering, he didn't take his hand away from mine.

'It's so great to see you,' he told me earnestly. 'Why haven't you been responding to my text messages, Miss Calypso Kelly?' he asked, opening my palm and running his deeply tanned fingers along my life line and up to my wrist.

Mesmerised as I was by his touch, I couldn't help being a bit cross about his accusation that *I* was the one not texting *him*! Boys are always doing that.

'Me?' I asked indignantly. 'You haven't sent me so much as one text since Monday.' I didn't mention that Billy was guilty of the same crime.

'Rubbish, I've sent several. Dozens. Hundreds possibly.'

He said it so confidently that I couldn't really argue. Probably he'd thought he had and been really busy at school, I told myself and changed the subject. 'Anyway, Sarah and Bob have said I can go to La Fiesta. Star, Georgina and me all bought our outfits in LA. I'm wearing *the* most adorably short little...' I hesitated, hoping his imagination would take over. 'Well, anyway I won't describe it completely and ruin the surprise, but let's just say that it's more on trend than the tragic dress I wore to the Eades social.'

'That's the best dress I've ever seen on a girl,' he teased, referring to the last dress he'd seen me in which was several sizes too big and safety-pinned up the back by Sister Regina.

'But anyway, this particular dress is sooo seriously phenomenal.'

Instead of laughing or showing any curiosity, he didn't even look up. He just kept tracing his hand along my wrist and up my arm. I felt all tingly and excited because here I was, an ordinary regular American girl – a commoner – sitting in a pizza shop in Windsor having my hand stroked by Prince Freddie outside one of his very own family castles. It was just so madly cool I was blushing, and even though sometimes the best things are expressed without words, after a while I became desperate for him to respond to my news about being able to go to the ball and say something like how excited he was that he was going to see me at the ball.

But he didn't.

So eventually I pushed the issue myself. 'You *are* going to La Fiesta, aren't you?' I asked, looking deeply into his ink-blue eyes.

He looked away as if wondering where the pizzas were and ran one of his long-fingered hands through his jet black locks.

'No, actually, I've got a prior engagement.'

'A prior engagement?' I repeated, just because, well just because I was floored and I say dumb things when I'm floored.

He started holding my hand again, which was nice but then he said, 'The pizza's taking a while,' as if he wanted to change the subject or maybe he thought eating pizza was more interesting than my tiny skirt and cashmere top with jewels on it, or the ball.

'What sort of prior engagement?' I probed lightly, looking around as if I was really desperate to get to the bottom of the slow pizza mystery as well.

He looked distracted although still managing to look distressingly fit. When I'm distracted I look mildly insane and addled. 'Sorry, what do you mean?' he asked, smiling his easy I'm-the-heir-to-the-throne-and-nothing-bothers-me smile.

'You said you had a prior engagement on the night of the La Fiesta ball?' I reminded him, but all he said was, 'Oh, at last, here comes our pizza.'

As they placed our pizza in the middle of our little table, I wondered how on earth he could even contemplate eating after dropping a bombshell like that on me. All my school life at Saint Augustine's I had longed to attend one these balls and now that I was actually going to one, my prince charming (I'm being sarcastic) was off on a 'prior engagement', whatever that means.

He was already chewing on a piece of pizza but sort of grinning at me at the same time. So I took a slice of the Hawaiian side and pretended I was just as hungry and not churned up inside in the least.

As we ate, he spoke of his holiday and asked about mine. I fell into the trap of pretending nothing was wrong and the afternoon slipped by in companionable fake conversations. All I really wanted to discuss was this wretched prior engagement.

So why didn't I press him?

Why were we acting like I wasn't gutted?

Was I actually becoming English?

After the pizza we ordered tea, and as I was squeezing the lemon into mine (I normally take milk but I was enjoying the symmetry of drinking my Earl Grey just like Freddie) he said, 'My prior engagement. . . It's a sort of Annual Euro-Royal-Bash thing we hold every year. Hellish, but it goes with the job.'

Bloody royals, I thought to myself grumpily as I looked outside at the rain.

Freddie laughed.

'What's so funny?'

'Bloody royals,' he mimicked and I suddenly realised I'd actually thought out loud. I sooooo had to stop doing that.

'Sorry.'

'Don't be, I say it all the time,' he teased.

As much as I wanted to stay with him, I was beginning to get seriously worried about the time and about getting back to school. Our curfew was four thirty, and if we were late we'd get a gating, which would mean no more kisses and pizzas with Freddie. I began to panic about where the others were and whether I should call them. It's amazing how quickly time flies when you're with a prince downplaying a topic that's practically burning an ulcer into your stomach.

I didn't get a chance to probe further because just then, Kevin, Star and Georgina burst in on us. 'Calypso, quick,' Star insisted crossly. 'We've ordered a taxi and it's picking us up at the tea shop where you were *meant* to be meeting us! Indie is waiting there *on her own*.'

Star didn't even look at Freddie. She's never really forgiven him for the way he treated me over the tabloid photograph Honey took. At the time he actually believed Honey's story that I was some sort of Mata Hari-type girl, just dying to get my fifteen minutes of fame.

'What about Portia?' I asked. The rain was bucketing down now.

'She's probably spending some time with her brother,' Georgina replied.

'I can call Tarkie and check,' Freddie offered, pulling his BlackBerry out.

'I think we should,' I pressed. So Freddie made a quick call on his mobile and confirmed that Tarkie and Portia were together and that Tarkie was dropping his sister off at school in a bit.

So that was that. I said an awkward goodbye to Freddie, no kiss, not even an air kiss. More importantly, he made no promise to text or call. I know we were with a whole pile of friends but still . . .

Georgina, Star and I flew out the door, into the rain and legged it to the tea shop.

I understood that Freddie had a prior engagement and that as heir to the throne, that went with the job, but I couldn't help wondering how Billy would have behaved in the same situation. Maybe I'd been a bit too hasty in dismissing Billy? Maybe he'd been awkward with me on the bridge out of guilt? He *was* in the Lower Sixth studying for his A-Levels so it was hardly surprising *he* was busy. Freddie, on the other hand, wasn't even doing GCSEs, because Eades was too grand to even pretend to follow the National Curriculum so he had no excuse at all. Bloody boys.

Indie was already sitting in the back of the local taxi and I ended up being the one in the seat beside the driver, so I had to keep turning around to speak to the others. Georgina pressed me for details about my afternoon with Freddie, so I told her how he wasn't going to *La Fiesta* due to a prior engagement.

I made the words 'prior engagement' sound like some sort of weird, sordid activity, when Indie piped up, 'He'll be going to the ball at Windsor Castle. It's a sort of Annual Euro-Royal-Bash Thingamee. Daddy *always* makes me go.' She groaned, as if it was the most taxing evening imaginable. Only I bet it wasn't.

I looked at her stunning face framed by the long corn braided hair and wondered how long I could go on pretending that I wasn't sick with jealousy.

'Poor you,' I told her as if I really, really meant it and then the taxi driver let out a little windy pop.

FIFTEEN

The Familiar Sound of My Dreams Crashing Around My Feet

The light drizzle had become heavy rain, but we had the taxi drop us off outside the school in the hope we could still sneak in unnoticed and avoid a gating. We crept through the gates and snuck along the edges of Puller's Wood which smelled so woodsy and beautiful in the rain. Finally we filed past the library, bent low so we wouldn't be spotted. We were an hour past curfew and it was starting to get dark. If we were sprung now, it would mean a definite gating.

Our adrenalin was pumping at the possible repercussions, so we were trying to keep utterly silent, muffling even our panting breaths as we raced into the main building. My clothes were clinging to me and I had only one thing on my mind – a hot shower – so I was a bit irritated when Star slowed me down as we were entering the main building and started whispering to me. 'Why are you wasting your time on a royal snob like Freddie

Calypso? Billy is nicer, fitter and a better fencer.'

I didn't respond. Partly because I was too desperate to get indoors to get embroiled in an argument in a cold corridor and partly because I was starting to agree that Billy would be a lot less trouble. And then my text-alert rang.

SO HOW SHORT IS THIS LITTLE SKIRT PRECISELY? X FREDS

I showed the text to Star. 'Don't you think that's weird that after not texting me all week and accusing me of not texting him, he suddenly sends this?' I asked which was another way of saying my life isn't worth living now Freddie's not going to the ball.

'How pervy! Let me have that,' she demanded.

I waited impatiently as she turned her back and typed in a message and then she held out the mobile to show me what she'd written.

BUGGER OFF X C.

Before I could stop her, she pressed 'send'.

'Why did you do that?' I asked in horror.

She kissed me on my wet cheek. 'Because you're worth it,' she teased in a piss-take of a famous hair commercial.

I understood that she's never forgiven Freddie for believing Honey over me during the whole tabloid debacle, but he *was* in a really difficult position, and he had apologised grovellingly. As far as I was concerned it was water under the bridge (along with my aloof demeanour), and to quote Star, he was worth it!

I quickly sent a counter text.

THAT WAS STAR. SERIOUSLY SHORT INDEED. X C

As soon as we got to the dorms, the other girls charged

straight off to their room while I crept into mine, hoping against hope that Miss Bibsmore hadn't done her rounds. I was incredulous when Honey greeted me looking freakishly chirpy and pleased to see me. She was posing in front of the mirror as if Mario Testino was in the room with his camera.

I was a little surprised to see Portia's phone lying on her bed. I had presumed I would have made it back before her as Freddie told me that Tarkie was bringing her back in a bit.

'Hello, darling, how was it?' Honey squeaked with over-friendliness. She was even smiling at me – well, smiling as best she could through her collagen-enhanced bauble-shaped lips.

'Yaah, fine,' I lied as I started to peel off my wet clothes and dry my hair. 'How was your day?'

'Terrific, actually. I went down to the pet shed and gave Absinthe and Dorothy a run. I hope you don't mind; they just looked so sweet together. Here, look at this,' she insisted as she grabbed her mobile, the same one she'd used to take the fateful shot she'd sold to the tabloids. The screen showed me a picture of Absinthe and Dorothy in the pet run together, looking like the best of friends.

I had just pulled on a dry pair of jeans and a T-shirt when we heard the now familiar *tap, tap, tap* of Miss Bibsmore's stick on the stone stairwell and I gave one another one of those 'Aaaaghhh! Here she comes!' looks. As Miss Bibsmore surveyed our room from the doorway, Portia's message alarm went.

'And where might Miss Briggs be?' she asked, looking at the vibrating phone. 'Curfew was over an hour ago.'

'She's in the loo,' Honey told her without even turning around, brushing her hair nonchalantly. 'Slight case of the runs,' she added, elaborating unnecessarily as she wrinkled up her nose job.

Seemingly satisfied, Miss Bibsmore hobbled out and continued her rounds.

I flopped on my bed still dazed and confused. On the one hand Freddie had seemed really pleased to see me but on the other I hated the thought of going to my very first ball without him. And there was still the issue of Billy. So much for my gut feeling that I'd know which one I fancied the most after seeing them. If anything I was more in the dark than anything. What did I feel for Billy? I looked at my mobile willing him to text.

Portia's message alarm kept going off, but just as I was about to ask Honey how long she'd been in the loo, Honey spoke to me. Not in a piss-take of my accent or a spiteful way, just in a normal friendly voice. When I say 'friendly', of course I mean friendly in that special menacing feline way that Honey has.

'So, darling, did you manage to catch up with your two paramours, Billy and Freddie?'

Before I could answer and explain that actually I didn't, strictly speaking, have *two* paramours (and who calls boys paramours anyway?), Portia came panting through the door, drenched to the skin. 'Has Miss Bibsmore done her rounds yet?' she asked anxiously.

'Ages ago, but don't worry, I covered for you. Said you

were in the lav, darling – with the runs,' Honey smarmed.

'Oh, thanks,' Portia replied. Then she spotted her phone. 'Oh, thank goodness, my phone. I've been running around Windsor looking everywhere for it. I had Freddie ringing and ringing it for me.'

What? I screamed, although thankfully the word didn't actually make it out of my voice box, which had fallen to my stomach along with my heart. I watched her open the back of her mobile. 'Odd I could have sworn I'd left it on.'

Honey said, 'Perhaps your mind was on other things, darling.'

All I was thinking was, Why was Portia with Freddie? How did they meet up?

He'd given me the impression that he was heading back to Eades. Well, maybe he didn't actually suggest it, but I'd presumed that he'd leave Windsor when I did.

'I thought you were with your brother?' I said, trying to keep the jealousy I was starting to feel out of my tone.

She answered lightly, 'Oh I was, but he had to go off and so I had some pizza with Freddie. I was absolutely famished.' She smiled at me.

How much pizza can one boy eat? I thought to myself – only I must have said it out loud because Portia replied, 'An infinite amount, believe me. Tarquin frequently eats two large pizzas on his own in one sitting.'

'Oh, so Tarquin was there as well,' I said with relief.

'No, just Freddie and me,' she replied, turning to face the mirror as she rubbed at her long hair with a towel.

'Just you and Freddie!' Honey repeated only she said it

suggestively, looking at me pointedly while raising one perfectly sculptured eyebrow.

'That's right, Honey. Freddie and I, me and Freddie, we ate some pizza.'

Honey looked stung by Portia's tone, which, while not nasty, was definitely warning in its tone, especially for Portia, who was always so calm and regal in her demeanour.

'I was just saying . . .'

Portia turned around and faced Honey directly. 'I'd much rather you didn't trouble yourself in my affairs, Honey.'

'Whatever,' Honey replied sulkily.

'Oh, and by the way, Freddie asked me to give you a message,' Portia said to me.

'What, are you his carrier pigeon now?' Honey said in a bad attempt at sarcasm.

Portia didn't deign to acknowledge her rudeness with a response.

I sat there mute, desperate to hear what message Freddie had sent me through Portia, but Honey added, 'She might be American but she does own a mobile, Portia. I'm sure Freddie is perfectly capable of sending her his own messages.'

My cheeks burned with embarrassment. Portia looked at me meaningfully but then the dinner bell rang, and Star and the others came in on their way to the refectory. Star surprised me by throwing her arms around me and crying out melodramatically. 'My best friend, Calypso! Navel buddies for ever!' Georgina and Indie giggled, but I didn't know what to think. Had she told Indie that I'd had to take mine out and made me sound tragically under the thumb of Sarah and Bob? Indie and Georgina joined the group hug. Oh how I wished I was alone with Portia so she could give me Freddie's message.

'So did you get away with it, then?' Star asked as we walked arm in arm down the narrow stairs.

'Completely fine. Miss Bibsmore came in after I'd already changed. And you?'

'Same. The old dear hadn't a clue.'

'By the way, thanks for covering for me, Calypso,' Portia added.

'Thank Honey. I actually thought you were back,' I replied, still feeling mixed up about her chumming around with Freddie in Windsor, and more importantly wanting to know what my message was.

Star snorted. 'Saint Honey, covering for her dear room mate. Who would have thought?'

Honey, who was walking behind her on the narrow stairs, gave Star a little shove. Not hard enough to make her fall or anything, just enough to take the wind out of her sails. Probably because she couldn't think of a cutting enough retort.

'You're not still upset about Freddie not going to the La Fiesta Ball are you, darling?' Star asked me as we waited for our plates to be piled with grey slops.

Yes! Of course I'm upset; I've waited for this ball all my boarding school life, and now Freddie isn't even going to be there! And Billy doesn't seem to fancy me any more and Freddie's sent me a message and I still don't know what it is and you've dropped fencing and have become inseparable from Indie and . . . well, the list of my vexation was endless.

'No, I'm totally fine,' I told her with faux-insouciance.

When we sat down, Star sat beside me on one side and Georgina on the other. Star was even making sarcastic remarks to Honey again. All was just as it should be. Maybe I'd been reading too much into everything, I tried to tell myself. Princes have commitments, and he had sent me a text and a message via Portia. I still had to find out what Freddie had said. I took a deep breath and attempted to tap back into my aloof demeanour but it didn't work. It didn't feel normal at all, really. Things *had* changed between Star and me now that Indie was here and I know it wasn't Indie's fault. In fact she was actually really, really nice.

I looked across at Portia, who was sitting too far away to talk to directly. Bugger.

Georgina reminded me kindly that Indie wasn't going to the La Fiesta ball either, as if *that* might make me feel better and then Star announced that perhaps none of us should go to the ball.

'Think about it,' Star enthused, swirling her slops. 'We could have a house party at my estate. My parents are always so stoned they'd probably think it was *their* party.'

'Oh my god, darling, you're a genius. That sounds sooo perfect!' Georgina gushed.

'Oh my god, a proper party with champagne and caviar, you mean?' Clemmie chimed. Clemmie has taken to reading *House and Garden* and other domestic design magazines. She'd decided she wanted to be an events co-ordinator which is a fancy way of saying party planner.

'Vintage all the way at chez Dirge, darling,' Star joked. 'Well, Jim Beam and Coke anyway,' she added. 'Actually, guess what! Daddy's installed a Jim Beam water feature in the chill room.'

'Oh my god, how cool! Is it actually a fountain that spurts out Jim Beam?' Georgina asked.

'Better. It's this amazing statue of the Black Angel of Death that pees out Jim Beam into this Japanese black rock pool. Sooo typically Daddy.' She shook her head at her mad father the way most fathers shake their heads over their mad daughters.

'Oh, I adore Jim Beam,' Georgina moaned rapturously. 'It's so rock and roll. Like caviar.'

'Jim Beam, caviar, and boys on ice,' Arabella sang in a sultry accent.

Star added, 'We could even invite some fit boys from the local village. It could be really wild, actually. Maybe Daddy will buy some more quad bikes – think how cool that would be! We could have an all-week-long mad party screaming about in the mud.'

Everyone looked so thrilled at the prospect of not going to the ball that I wanted to be sick. Then there was an almighty crash of pots and pans in the kitchen and for minute I thought it was the sound of my dreams crashing around my feet.

'But what about our outfits?' I asked, trying not to sound hysterical. 'Our cashmere tops?' I reminded the girls. 'Our shoes!' My voice was beginning to screech.

Star threw a pea at me. 'What about them, silly? We can wear them at our house party. Actually I'm kind of

bored by the whole ball thing anyway, it's soo Year Nine –
even the Year Eights go now.'

So Year Nine? Her words seemed to sum up my life. It
was all right for Star and Georgina to be blasé about the
ball; they'd been to squillions of them. And Indie had her
own royal ball to go to, so of course she wasn't fussed. But
I'd been waiting all my school life for this.

As I looked around the table at the excited faces of my
friends, the only person who looked as underwhelmed by
the whole idea of Star's party as me was Honey, who
definitely wouldn't be invited as Star unashamedly loathed
her.

I never imagined the day would come when Honey and
I would feel as one about anything, but then again she had
covered for Portia. And more importantly, she had taken
Dorothy out for a little run. Maybe Honey had changed?

'Of course you're invited too, Portia,' Star called down
to her end of the table.

'Thanks so much, Star, but unfortunately I have a prior
engagement,' Portia called back.

'A prior engagement,' I repeated. She had used the
exact same phrase as Freddie had used, in the exact same
casual, it's-so-not-a-big-deal tone.

'You too? Indie asked. 'The Annual Euro-Royal-Bash
Thingamee?'

Portia groaned as she nodded. 'Don't you just loathe
them?'

'What can you do, though?' Indie agreed. 'I've got to go
too. Daddy said there's no way I can get out of it.'

'At least Freddie will be there,' Portia added, looking at

me as she said it. And I decided then what his message must have been, I bet he was taking Portia to the ball I told myself as I listened to these girls chat about the horrors of attending balls I would never in my wildest dreams get a chance to go to.

'What about your brother?' I asked Portia.

'Of course Tarkie will be there, but he'll never dance with me.'

Then the image of Portia and Freddie dancing together royal-cheek to royal-cheek flashed into my head and I couldn't even bring myself to look at her.

SIXTEEN

A Game of
Emotional Chess

Saint Augustine's fencing salle was pretty impressive for a girls' school – especially given that loads of the girls only took fencing as a way to meet the boys at Eades. We had three pistes, all with the latest electrical point scoring systems installed and a salle d'armes covered in old photographs and fencing memorabilia along the walls. We had once also been fortunate enough to have one of Britain's top fencing masters, Professor Sullivan.

But those days were gone.

I was really missing Professor Sullivan. I liked to think I was his favourite pupil, based mainly on the fact that he once gave Star and me a lift to Star's place in London one exeat. That, and the fact that he said he thought I'd 'go far'. I quite liked the idea that someone thought me capable of going far, as opposed to 'going *too* far!' which is what Bob is always telling me.

There were plenty of younger girls coming up in sabre but Portia and I were the only two really actual sabreurs left in the school now that Star had dropped out. That meant we'd have to rely on someone from the épée team to fence sabre in interschool matches. It wasn't ideal. We'd had a few practice bouts over the past weeks, and Mr Wellend warned us that he'd be stepping up the pressure in earnest this week. I was quite happy for him to step up the pressure. The BNFTs were coming up after half-term and if I wanted to be included on the US Olympic team I was going to have to make a big impact.

I'd had to force myself to be civil to Portia ever since she'd told me she was going to the ball with Freddie. OK, I know she hadn't actually said she was going *with* Freddie but I was uneasy about the situation just the same. She'd passed on Freddie's message eventually and while it wasn't the bombshell I'd imagined, it was a massive let down. 'Tell Calypso I'll text her.'

I'd had plenty of time to brood about everything and my brooding, coupled with the fact that the only text message I had received from him in the last few days was the one in which I had told him to bugger off (or rather Star had told him on my phone) made me desperately worried.

As I attached Portia's back to the electrical cord that ran up to the recording device, I was fully aware that I didn't have the cool head, the *sang-froid* that Professor Sullivan was always on about.

We have to check that all parts of our electric kit are working before play begins, which you do by tapping your sabre on your sword guard, glove, the lame metal jacket and the mask before the salute. Even as Portia and I tapped our weapons, I felt the rawness of my emotions begin to take over, which manifested when I 'tapped' her blade, clean out of her hand.

While sabre is a combat sport, it's also highly intellectual and requires a great deal of balance. Emotion has no place on the piste, and I was one big ball of emotion as Bell End called the words, 'En Garde! Ready! Play!'

The attacker in sabre is at an advantage because they can vary their footwork and their method of delivering an attack. Whereas defending at sabre is more difficult as right of way is initially given to the attacker. Although the arm starts moving first, it doesn't straighten quite as fast as with a thrusting weapon, so even with the electrical recording stuff, it is difficult for the referee/president overseeing the bout to decide who has the right of way. Basically, he'll be looking for the first person to straighten her arm, which in a nutshell means that you *can* play dirty.

The object is to make cuts with a hit which registers on the recorder, but not hard enough to hurt your opponent. But if you deliver strong cuts from the elbow, say, you can inflict a lot bruising. Most sabreurs deliver actual cuts from the wrist because, quite apart from hurting your opponent, it gives you more control and accuracy with your weapon.

I could feel my anger towards Portia taking total control of me. I did try and get a grip as I advanced with crossovers down the piste towards Lady Herrington Briggs with her aloof demeanour and her royal ball and possibly Freddie. As much as I knew I needed to clear my head of these thoughts, my heart just wouldn't let me. What I couldn't say to her in words, I was going to explain with my blade.

I knew the way Portia thought on the piste. I knew her inclination for speed and accuracy, and she knew my skill for aggressive cuts and my well known talent for elegant *prise de fer*. We had joked only last week in fact that we could play one another's game as actors to perfection because we knew each other's form so well.

I think she knew what was coming when our swords were in line and she first threatened my target area. I stepped forward rapidly without straightening my arm, engaged her blade and as I took it with a classic circular parry of *tierce*, we were so close it might have looked to an onlooker like a lovers' embrace. But all the wrong emotions were in that embrace — I was feeling and not paying attention to my footwork. As I made another attack, I lost my footing and fell.

Bell End went ballistic. 'I told you, think with your brain, move with your body, slam 'em with your blade, Kelly. That's slam your opponent, not the bloody floor, ya idiot.'

Bell End may not have been as grand as Professor Sullivan, but he was bang-on in his assessment. I acknowledged this and tried to regain my lost *sang-froid*. I wasn't successful though, my humiliation after the stumble had only served to rattle me further. My form didn't improve and after the bout, Portia and I took off our masks and shook hands formally, but neither of us spoke to the other. She knew what I knew now. I had it in for her.

Bell End was furious. 'Never seen such a waste of electricity in me life. And you're meant to be the captain of the bloody team, Kelly. One more performance like that and you can wave goodbye to your captaincy.'

'Yes, Bell End – I mean, Mr Wellend,' I agreed, as the tears welled in my eyes. I knew I was out of line . . . and worse, so did Portia. While we were showering and changing back into our uniforms, she didn't so much as look at me. She wasn't the sort of girl to have an argument. She was too regal and well brought up for that, and I didn't have the mettle to engage with her *off* the piste.

So there it was. Thanks to my own jealousy, I was now living in a dorm with two girls who hated me. I suspect Bell End was starting to think along the same lines as Bob – I was going *too* far.

As I lay in bed that night I realised I had behaved badly and I wanted to apologise, but I couldn't in front of Honey. And later when Honey started snoring and Portia was turning her light out, my shame only served to render me mute.

She wished me good night, though.

'Good night, Portia,' I replied in a tone that suggested we were as close as we had been the first week of term.

With Honey's evil on one side of me and Portia's disdain on the other, a sense of isolation engulfed me.

SEVENTEEN

Nothing Changes, Everything Changes

In the first week of term, Portia and I had shared seditious asides about Mrs Obar and her lack of qualifications to teach Latin. We even told her we'd be complaining to our parents. But the truth was, Portia didn't want to trouble her grieving father, and I didn't want to trouble Bob and Sarah, who were always very busy trying to make the money to send me here. While they didn't really understand what GCSEs even were, they were always madly impressed by my teachers whenever they met them.

Of course the lay teachers behave wildly different with parents than they do with students – I call it the Hypocritical Oath. The female teachers are the worst. It's really sick the way they fawn over parents and flirt with fathers – even Sarah agrees, although she'd probably adore Mrs Obar because she's so old, not to mention married. Not that marriage would stop Mrs Obar from flirting with Bob. Portia and I even caught her flirting with Bell End! 'Oh, Mr Bell End, stop, you're making me laugh!' she cried. Only she called him Mr Wellend, and while her words said 'stop' as we peeped from behind the wall, she was stroking his muscles, yuk!

'Slut,' I'd whispered in Portia's ear which made her giggle.

'Tart,' she'd agreed which made me snort with laughter – and then we got caught by Bell End who'd chased us out of the salle and called us all manner of horrible names.

But that was then.

Ever since that practice bout we were unofficially not on speakers, as Nancy Mitford would say. That is to say, we still spoke, but only to maintain the barest of civilities.

Now I sat alone in Latin, leaving Portia to sit next to Indie.

'Thirty-seven long years teaching girls like you the why fors and whereabouts of this and that,' Mrs Obar rambled on, 'Well, it's taken its toll on me it has,' she complained – which isn't even proper English, let alone Latin. All she ever wrote on the board were things that were in our textbook, but she never worked through any of the exercises we'd be questioned on in our exams at the end of the year, or anything useful like that.

Just the same, because she was a teacher, we had to pretend to be madly awed. Otherwise she'd shower us in blues, and there are only so many times you can slack down a teacher and only so many times you can trail on down to the Year Seven dorms – which were in another building – and talk them into doing your lines for you. Also this year's bunch of Year Sevens were incredibly mature and hardly worshiped us at all, bless them.

Portia, true to her word, had persuaded her young

cousin to do my French lines for me, but I obviously couldn't count on her goodwill a second time.

At the end of each class, Mrs Obar would pile us with work from the exercise book, which we'd then have to struggle with unaided as well as doing our basic coursework which formed part of our overall GCSE mark. It was a no-win situation.

It was like being on a treadmill.

Wake up.

Get dressed.

Clean our rooms.

Registration (so the school could check that none of us had escaped in the night).

Go to chapel for prayers and school news.

Attend classes.

Fence.

Eat grey slops.

Attend more classes.

Feed our pets and take them for a run.

Clean out the pet shed.

Do prep.

Go to study.

Go to the ref for more inedible grey slops.

Do still more study.

Shower.

Go to bed.

Read until lights out.

Sleep – and in my case brood over my lack of texts from Freddie and Billy.

We were all exhausted by the time exeat weekend came

along, and because things had been so different between us, I was delighted that Star still wanted me to stay at her place in Derbyshire.

In the limo on the way up I admitted that I was pleased she'd invited me. 'Don't be mad, of course you have to stay. You always have to stay. You're my best friend idiot.'

'Well, we hardly spend time together any more, and . . .'

'We spend loads of time together; it's just that we don't spend all our time alone together any more, thanks to you,' she said, pinching me in the side to make me laugh.

'Thanks to me?' I exclaimed fighting her off.

'Yes, you're the one who ruined our status as the school freaks, remember?'

I pinched her back and dropped the topic. I didn't want to mention Indie or her dropping fencing because then I'd have to mention Portia and I was too embarrassed to go there.

We were in the limo on the way up to Derbyshire when my text alert sounded.

IS THERE LIFE ON PLANET GIRL? X FREDS

This time I didn't show the text to Star for fear that she might tell him to bugger off again. I waited until we were at her estate and she'd gone off to the kitchen to steal some sweets to reply.

WHERE R U? X C

WINDSOR. & U? X FREDS

I imagined him in his castle with his parents the King and Queen and thought carefully about how I should reply. In the end I opted for something more exotic than the total truth.

ABOUT TO GO QUAD BIKE RIDING. X C

ALL RIGHT 4 SOME! X FREDS

I was so pleased that he was impressed. Even though we didn't actually *go* quad bike riding, it wasn't a total lie. We did *talk* about riding the quads, and Star's father, Tiger, was quad bike riding with friends all weekend.

The truth was we were so tired from three weeks of hard work all we could do was laze about in her enormous, king-sized, black-patent four poster bed, with its heavy maroon drapery, eating sweets and watching DVDs. Star is so laidback she even told me I could keep Dorothy in the room. Even though rabbits aren't house trained, Star was positive Dorothy would do her wee and poos in the en suite, but of course she didn't, so the whole room had to be sprayed with Febreze.

Star even tried to train her by rushing her off to the loo and rubbing her paws in the wood shavings like you do when you train a cat, but it wasn't wildly effective. Hilda and Brian stayed with us too, and all three seemed to get on surprisingly well, apart from when Brian slithered over me in the night and I woke up screaming and had to pretend I'd had a nightmare. Star would be mortified if she thought I'd screamed because of Brian.

We kept talking about doing stuff, but neither of us pressed the issue. Even on Saturday night when a few bands and their flunkies turned up for a party, neither of us felt like going down or even playing our traditional pranks.

I was just happy to be alone with Star, hanging out just like we used to. Neither of us touched on any subject other than sweets, movies and our pets. We had a pet trick competition but as we were the only two judges it always ended up in a tie. But we liked that.

Star was trying to give up fags and I was helping her by remembering to slap the nicotine patches on her.

'Oh, Sister Nicotene, you're such a good nurse,' she said as I stuck one on her that evening.

I had developed a special make-believe voice and old-dear walk for my part. 'Come on, luvvie, take your medicine like a good little dear.' Then, out of the blue, Star confronted me about Portia.

'So what's up with you and Portia?' she said as I smoothed the patch on her shoulder.

'What do you mean, what's up? We share a dorm; we're perfectly civil.'

'Aaah yes, civil. Civility can cover a multitude of sins, darling, we both know that.'

'Well, she started it.'

'Started what?'

'I don't know what.'

'Well, then why don't *you* stop it. Talk to her.'

'But that's just it. You can't talk to *her*, she's seriously . . .' I struggled to find the phrase I needed – something other than stuck-up.

Star helped me out by suggesting words like 'nice', 'decent', 'respectful' and 'loyal'. 'Look, Calypso, I saw you fencing with Portia the other day, going for her like you were Zorro or something. What were you thinking?'

'You were there! In the salle? Why didn't you tell me?' I shouted angrily.

'Calm down. Look, I came to see you, OK? If you want to know the truth I felt bad about everything. Dropping fencing, not spending enough time with you, everything. And then when I saw you going at Portia like that I couldn't believe it was you!'

I dropped my head. 'I know,' I replied quietly.

'Why, then?'

'Everything's changed, Star,' I told her and as I heard the words came out of my mouth I felt like Pandora opening up the box that would change the world forever.

Star ignored me for a bit so I pushed the point. 'Come on, Star, you know it has. You're always with Indie now.'

She looked annoyed, and Star can look wildly scary when she's cross. 'Nothing's changed Calypso,' she insisted in a voice that brooked no argument. 'Nothing, apart from your attitude.'

I made a decision not to push the point, but the gulf between us was palpable in that moment. I knew both of us could feel it, just as much as we could feel our own hearts beating. And then Star said, 'Shall we have another pet trick competition then?'

And the gulf closed as quickly as it had opened. At least for the time being.

'You do realise,' she said on Sunday as we prepared to head back to school, 'that we haven't left this room other than to go to the kitchen to steal food, all weekend?'

Our small weekend bags were already packed, Brian was wrapped around Star's neck and Hilda was peeping out of her blazer pocket. I was cuddling Dorothy as I looked around the bomb site of the room. It wasn't a pretty sight with all our sweet wrappers and pizza boxes and DVD cases strewn about the bed and floor, not to mention the animal droppings.

'I think it's called growing old,' I said, cuddling Dorothy into my chest and kissing her wriggly little nose.

'No wonder my parents take drugs! Look at what we've become, Calypso!' She marched over to her bed and left a fifty pound note on the pillow for the cleaner.

'We are disgustingly lazy,' I agreed, as we headed out of the house.

'Even Daddy's been quad bike riding most of the weekend,' she pointed out.

'True,' I agreed. 'Also your mother's been having her charity meetings.'

'So, basically at the tender age of fifteen we're already worse than drug-taking rock and rollers! We didn't even drink any Jim Beam from the Jim Beam feature in the chill room! We're boring slobs and now I don't even smoke any more,' she said as we clambered into one of her father's Range Rovers, where Ray was waiting to drive us back.

Just then, Tiger and one of his friends pulled up beside us on their quad bikes.

'Coming for a quick rage round the ranch, babes?' Tiger called out to us over the roar of the engines.

We looked at one another, left our bags with Ray and jumped on the back of the bikes. I got on with Tiger and held on to his leather jacket tightly as we pelted at breathtaking speed out into the fields across the streams and trout-filled river, through the woods and rocky crags.

The wheels churning up mud splattered our clothes, our faces and our hair. Tiger's friend rode beside us with Star. Even though we'd ridden the quad bikes on our own at the same breathtaking speed we screamed and screamed and screamed like terrified children.

An hour later, caked in wet mud, we climbed into the Range Rover. I felt sooo deliriously happy, like a child coming off a fair ground ride. I looked at Star, but instead of saying something relatable like 'Wow!' she said, 'Why don't you like Indie?' in the tone of voice you might use if you were asking why someone didn't like Brussels sprouts. Ray shut our door and Star fumbled around to find the seatbelt.

'I don't *hate* Indie,' I said, with a little too much force. After all, I didn't hate Indie. How could anyone hate Indie? It was just that unlike me, she was so much like Star. They both loved their minor chord compositions, they were both brave and fearless, they were both self possessed and cool.

'Good,' she agreed with an edge of warning to her voice. 'It would really piss me off if you did.' Then she gave my hand a squeeze as if everything was OK.

EIGHTEEN

A New Kind Of Enemy

Back at school, the teachers ratcheted up the pressure another notch. But that was cool because with all the GSCE coursework I didn't even have the time to monitor my lack of text messages. My parents relied on e-mails to communicate, and the rest of my friends were here with me at school, so apart from Billy and Freddie there was no one left to text me. Still, it was dispiriting especially when Portia's message alert was going off incessantly.

The longer I left it to patch things up with her the worse it became. I knew that, but I avoided the issue by hanging out in Star, Georgina and Indie's room.

I didn't want to make an enemy out of Portia, I really didn't. I'd never had an enemy like Portia before. Honey, now *she* was my idea of an enemy. Lady Portia Herrington Briggs, though, was far too magisterial to express her feelings about someone as lowly as me.

The most powerful weapon Portia had in her arsenal was my own guilt, and that guilt included the photo of her family by her bed which included her dead mother. Every time I looked at that photograph I wanted to make up. Even without the reminder of her loss, I actually liked Portia and

I desperately wanted to sort things out with her. Before finding out that she was going to the ball with Freddie, we'd become close friends. But like I said, that was then.

Her wariness hovered over me like a cloud, darkening my every waking hour. The worst thing about it was that she wasn't even a bitch towards me. She remained civil and decent to a fault, which was much harder to bear than Honey's open nastiness. I'd never done anything mean to Honey, but I was totally responsible for Portia's wariness of me. I could have sorted it all out with a simple apology, but I was too jealous and bent out of shape over Freddie to do even that. Especially as day after day, my mobile remained silent and hers merrily rang and beeped with messages.

Indie and Portia barely mentioned the ball again – only insomuch as it meant they couldn't attend Star's house party and what a bore it all was, but how at least they'd have each other. But as far as I was concerned, the Annual Royal-Euro-Bash Thingamee was still there, just like Portia's title, just like her dislike of me, a constant niggling reminder that I would and could never be like her or part of her world, which, when it came down to it, was Freddie's world too.

Freddie might like me, and I really think he did, but he was a prince and I was an American nobody. Unlike Indie, I was as close to being a nobody as he was ever likely to meet. I was in his world but not of it. I was like a random stranger trying on the glass slipper. 'Close, but not close enough,' the Prince's equerries would say.

As I lay in my bed, night after night with Honey smoking herself stupid with the fake weed on one side of me, and Portia serenely reading on the other, I waited for my text alert to sound. Checking I had a signal every few minutes, I finally convinced myself that Freddie probably only liked me for my wild-child Hollywood credentials – and even they were fake. I was about as wild as my pet rabbit Dorothy whose most reckless act to date was dropping her lettuce in her water.

'Many texts from Freddie and Billy today, darling?' Honey kept asking, sometimes even adding, 'It must be hard for Billy.'

'What?'

'Well, I expect you are going to the Royal Bore with Freddie, darling,' she said breezily even though she knew as well as anyone else that I wasn't.

'Oh that's right, I keep forgetting, he's going with *Portia*, isn't he,' she'd add. 'Silly Honey.'

Then one evening when Honey and I were alone and I was reading the school magazine I'd helped to set up, Honey remarked, 'Portia and Freddie seem pretty tight now.'

I flicked a page of *Nun of Your Business* as if I was actually reading it, and replied nonchalantly, 'Really? Why do you say that?' Then I flicked another page just to punctuate the point that I wasn't in the least bit interested in Freddie and Portia. The magazine, now run by the Year Tens, had gone downhill and I was considering speaking to Sister Constance about it. It was meant to be a satirical look at Saint Augustine's school life but had become a boring gossip rag. Oh my god, was I turning into Ms Topler, our English teacher, complaining about the state of modern-day writing?

Honey turned to face me, blew a billowing stream of smoke rings and smiled. 'Well, they're texting one another like mad. I imagined you would have noticed?'

Then, as if set off by satanic forces, Portia's text message alert went off. She was still in the en suite, and Honey wasted no time in grabbing the mobile. I didn't even bother to stop her. For one, Honey isn't the sort of girl you rein in, and secondly, I was madly curious as she opened the message and shrieked, 'Oh look, Calypso, it's from Freddie.'

She passed it over to me to read for myself in case I didn't believe her. I didn't want to believe her, and there were a thousand reasons why I shouldn't. It's not as if Honey has a close relationship with the truth, after all. So I ignored her offer and turned another page of the *Nun*. I began scanning an article I had written about fencing in a transparent attempt to suck up to Bell End, forcing myself to ignore the prickling sensation in my hand, which was itching to grab the phone and read the text for myself.

'Oh my god, darling, you have to read it now, it mentions *you*!' she urged.

I looked her in the eye as she sucked hard on the last of her faux weed fag. She must have sensed my weakening conscience because the next thing I knew, the phone was thrust in my hand and my magazine was cast to the floor. Honey was right, if it was about me. I had every right to read it!

CAN YOU TELL CALYPSO . . .

But before I could scroll down further to read the rest of it, the phone was snatched from my hand.

I looked up and saw the look of hatred on Portia's face.

She didn't say anything. She wouldn't. She merely placed her mobile on her bedside table beside the photograph of her family, plugged in her hairdryer and started drying the wet tentacles of her long black hair.

My face was burning. No, not with shame, not with guilt at reading another girl's text message, but with fury, because all the half-formed suspicions I'd been harbouring about Portia and Freddie now seemed fully warranted.

'I believe you have a message for me from Freddie,' I told her, raising my voice above her turbo dryer.

Portia carried on drying her hair in front of the mirror as she replied quietly, 'As you appeared to have read it yourself, I've deleted it.'

Honey was lying on the bed flicking through the social pages of the latest *Tatler*, looking for photographs of herself.

I winced. 'I didn't actually get a chance to read the whole thing,' I admitted, as I began to acknowledge how wrong my behaviour actually was. *Say sorry, say sorry, say sorry*, my better self pleaded with wicked self. But I didn't apologise. I folded my arms and gave her a filthy look.

Portia eventually turned to me and smiling serenely, told me, 'Perhaps it would be better if you spoke to Freddie yourself, Calypso?'

I flopped on my bed. That was the whole point, though. I couldn't call Freddie to whine about only half reading a text he had decided not to even send to me. Portia knew that. I guess it was the toff equivalent to telling me to lock myself up in the tower of London and throw away the key.

NINETEEN

When Your Obsessions Become Obsessive, a Nemesis Can Prove Very Handy!

I didn't tell Star I'd peeped at Portia's message when she dumped her books in the booth beside mine during study period later the next evening. Star's jaundiced feelings about Freddie were one thing; her feelings about me sneaking a look at Portia's private messages from him would be another matter entirely.

At boarding school, you might share make-up, sweets, fags, phone lists and messages but you didn't just help yourself to other people's phones without asking. I was in the wrong and I knew it and I didn't need anyone else to point it out to me – especially my best friend. So I sat in my study booth, poring over my Latin books as if I cared deeply about conjugations of the verb.

Honey felt differently about sharing my shame. I reddened as I heard her telling Georgina, 'Did Calypso tell you, she stole Portia's phone and read a message from Freddie telling Portia to tell her . . .'

That was the end of my focus. The examiners may as well fail me now, I decided, as my face went through every shade of red before finally settling on a nasty shade of heliotrope.

'It wasn't like that,' I protested.

Star looked disgusted. 'Calypso?'

'Look, Honey showed me a message which was about me, anyway and then Portia walked in and . . .' That was as far as I got because Portia actually did walk in at that moment and heard herself being discussed.

I fled the scene and went into the computer room because I was about to burst into tears. I was struggling with my coursework, at war with my closest fencing partner, and had no idea if I had a boyfriend or not. I decided a bit of self pity was in order but the teacher in the computer room didn't agree. She told me to get back and do my study, so I did, only this time I sat amongst another group of girls from my year and logged on to my laptop to see if I had any e-mails from my parents.

Unlike the other parents, who send postcards and letters, Bob and Sarah don't *believe* in snail mail, so I have to settle for e-mails. Essentially this means I have nothing from my family to pin on my pin board which makes me look like an unloved child.

I was feeling very unloved at that moment.

But there wasn't an e-mail from Bob or Sarah – well, there was, but I didn't look at it, because right underneath there was an e-mail from Freddie.

Dear Calypso,
Given your resolute refusal to respond to my text messages, voice mails and phone calls this week, I am giving you the opportunity to communicate with me by e-mail.
F

This set my mind racing. Freddie was trying to contact me. Maybe the problem wasn't him? Maybe it wasn't even me? Maybe it was my bloody ancient brick of a phone? I started typing rapidly.

I'm sorry but I didn't get any messages, I began to type, before immediately deleting it, deeming the message too seriously tragic. I tried again, but Soz darling . . . was also deleted. It sounded soooo Honey. In the end I settled on:

Sorry, I am a wicked girl also I think my phone might be fruuped. C x

He e-mailed me back immediately. He was online, I was online. If this wasn't fate, I don't know what it is.

Sorry about my previous engagement, I really would have rather gone to the La Fiesta ball with you, but there is no way I can get out of this. I promise, I would if I could.
Best, Freds

And I know it was cheeky, but I immediately e-mailed back:

In that case, any chance you can take a date to this Euro-Royal-Bash thingamee? C xx

I pressed 'Enter' before I could reconsider and an answer came straight back:

Can I come back to you on that? It's not that simple. I'll see you at fencing Monday anyway, we can talk then.
Freds.

Two things stood out.
1) He hadn't sent me a kiss in either e-mail (note: I had sent him two!).
2) He *had* used the special nickname I had given him.

There was no way I was going to be able to concentrate on my coursework now. I logged off without even reading Sarah and Bob's e-mail.

I was half expecting what happened next. After lights out, when Portia and Honey were both asleep – actually even I was fast asleep – Star snuck into my room all alone without Indie or Georgina and woke me up.

'I'm really worried about you, Calypso,' she said as I made room for her under the covers. 'Don't you think this problem you've got with Portia is becoming, well . . . a bit insane?'

Even though I thought she was right, I replied, 'Not at all,' I assured her lightly. And then to change the subject I added, 'Freddie e-mailed me tonight.'

'Look, Calypso, maybe he does like you, maybe he doesn't, the point is you do have other things in your life.'

'I don't understand what happened that day in Windsor. Freddie and I were really getting on well,' I told her.

'You mean you shared a pizza with him?' Star reasoned, her tone dripping with cynicism. I hadn't told her about our kiss when we were on exeat in Derbyshire.

'The point is, as soon as I left, he met up with Portia and shared a pizza with *her*.'

'*Quelle horreur!*' she cried out silently, throwing her hands to her cheeks in mock shock. 'That a boy might share two pizzas in one day!'

'Seriously, Star! Is he just mucking about with me or does he think of me as a mate? And this sending messages about me to Portia – it's all so demeaning. If he wants to give me a message why doesn't he give it to me himself?'

'You just told me that he e-mailed you?'

'Yaah, but there were no kisses on the end.'

'Mmmm. It's a tough one. The only person who can help you though is Freddie, so unless you're prepared to confront him personally, you've got to drop this thing with Portia. It's not her fault and she's got enough to deal with, don't you think?'

'I know, I want to, but I just keep . . .'

'Blurting?'

'Yaah.'

'Why don't you do this to start with? Forget Freddie and his pathetic Royal Bore because that's what it is, darling, a lot of old royals showing off their jewels and titles to each other. Forget the La Fiesta Ball. If I'm not in London you can't stay in our London house alone, which means you don't have anywhere to stay because everyone's coming to Derbyshire. So here's the plan. Come up to my house party.' She nudged me. 'Come on, darling, it'll be a laugh. And without you I'll only pine.'

I smiled in the darkness at my friend's concern. The gulf didn't seem so huge now – and then I remembered. 'I've already bought my ticket though . . . we all did.' She didn't reply but we had a cuddle, and she scuttled back to her own room, leaving me in the dark as it slowly began to dawn on me that she was right. Without Star's London house, I had nowhere to stay during the half-term break. I was going to have to let go of my long-held dream of attending a Capital VIP ball. Like so many of my dreams.

'You can always stay at my house,' Honey's voice piped up out of the darkness, and for a bit I though she must be talking in her sleep. 'It'll only be you, me and the servants. Poppy and Mummy are going to LA for the Dulson première,' she whispered.

The Dulson film was *the* most hotly awaited film in the world.

I told her I'd think about it in an out-of-body-ish sort of way, still wondering if I'd heard properly. I could see the flame of her lighter as she lit a cigarette. She opened the window up an inch and blew out a puff of smoke.

Could it be true that Honey, my nemesis, the girl who had made my life hell all these years was offering to have me as a house guest in her famous Chelsea mansion?

I didn't get time to dwell on this as we heard the *tap, tap, tap* of Miss Bibsmore coming up the steps. Any sensible girl would have put out her cigarette and sprayed the air liberally with Febreze. Honey continued to lay there in the dark though and smoke.

The fluorescent lights flickered on.

'I thought I smelled smoke, Miss O'Hare,'

'Oh bugger off, I can't sleep without a cigarette. It's not my fault they make cigarettes addictive, speak to the tobacco giants, Miss Bibsmore. I'm just a victim of their corporate might.'

'Hah. You're about to become a victim of my might, Miss O'Hare an' all. Twenty pounds, please.' She stuck her hand out for the cash.

Honey pulled her duvet up around her chin and looked at Miss Bibsmore like she was a crazed lunatic. 'Leave me alone.'

'Come on, open up your tight little fist and hand over the readies. Twenty pounds on the spot fine, that's school rules an' all. You knows it, I knows it, so if you have a problem with it, you can speak to your corporate giants.'

Honey put her cigarette out ostentatiously and pulled twenty quid out of her top drawer. 'There, you miserable old witch. Take the money I was saving up for my cancer treatment.' She threw the note at Miss Bibsmore and watched as it fluttered to the floor.

Miss Bibsmore creaked and groaned as she bent to pick it up.

'You really need to exercise more, Miss B. Your joints are creaking,' Honey told her in a voice of faux-concern.

'Well I 'ope your joints hold up over the next week an all. You're on litter duty, starting tomorrow. Nightie night, girls.'

TWENTY

If You Can't Pull the Boy You Want ... Pull the Boy You're With!

Saturday was one of those beautifully sunny days you occasionally get in England in autumn. I couldn't wait to feel the sun on my face but Star and Indie decided to spend the day in one of the music rooms working on their latest track about a girl who feels burdened by the enormity of her privilege. Apparently it was *seriously* coming along, and for the first time I didn't really mind that it was Indie having to share experience rather than me.

Georgina elected to stay and listen, but I'd already heard most of what they were working on and it sounded like a bag of cats being murdered, so I jumped at Honey's suggestion to share a taxi to Windsor with her and Portia. At the back of my mind I guess I thought this might be my chance to make peace with Portia.

'What about your litter duty?' I asked Honey.

'Oh, I paid a Year Seven to do it for me.'

'Frightened one to death to do it, more like it,' I thought I heard Portia mutter, but I didn't see her lips move so I decided I must have imagined it.

I was feeling a bit quiet and self contained myself as I ran through the apology and make up speech I needed to make.

Honey, sitting between the two of us, chatted away merrily. 'Even though I've decided it is too, too tragic to pull school boys at my age, I think, as I'll be sixteen next term, realistically I'm going to have to settle for them during term time, darlings. Such a drag, but there it is.'

Neither Portia nor I responded. Apart from anything else we'd both heard the speech several times already that term. The taxi driver responded, though. 'On the pull are we, girls?' he asked jovially.

'Oh shut up, you village dwelling peasant,' Honey snapped – and he duly did. 'Which is why I thought we may as well go to the Three Swans,' she added to Portia and me.

Portia was as silent as the sphinx.

'But that's a pub, isn't it?' I blurted.

'We *are* allowed to go into pubs, darling,' she reminded me. 'Just not allowed to order alcohol.'

'Oh,' I said, feeling like the fourteen-year-old know-nothing baby I was. 'Don't you have to be accompanied by an adult?'

'Oh Calypso, Calypso, Calypso. That is why, darling air-headed creature that you are, I did you the massive favour of calling Billy. He's going to be there with some of his friends. You know he used to go out with my sister. She dumped him for someone less plebbie of course but he utterly adores *moi*.'

I thought Billy dumped Poppy, I was thinking to myself, but typically I must have said it out loud.

But as it turned out, it can't have been me who said it as the next words that came from Honey's lips proved. 'How would you know anything, Portia? Shouldn't you be busy mourning the death of your mother instead of listening to malicious gossip?'

'Honey!' I snapped leaning over to Portia to show my solidarity but she had turned her face towards the window.

I tried to reach out my hand to her but we were pulling into Windsor and before the car even drew to a standstill, Portia had already unbuckled her seatbelt, jumped out of the moving car and run off through the streets. The driver went mental.

'I think we'd better run after her,' I told Honey. 'That was really poisonous – even for you, Honey.'

Honey fluttered her implausibly long fake lashes and arched one professionally plucked brow. 'Don't be so wet, Calypso. Forget about old Misery Briggs, darling. She's *such* a drama queen.'

Even with all my resentments against Portia, one thing she was not was a drama queen. Honey had no competition for that particular crown.

'Honey, we've got to chase after her. We can't just leave her when she's so blatantly upset. That was really horrible of you,' I repeated.

Honey paid for the taxi and then, taking my hand in hers and swinging it like we were the best of friends, she led me through the sunlit cobbled streets towards the pub.

'She's probably run off to cry on her brother or Freddie's shoulder, darling.'

I pulled my hand away, and scanned the area for Portia, but she had already disappeared into the crowds of tourists around the castle.

Honey wrestled my arm from me and started tugging so hard I thought she'd rip it from my torso.

'Come on, the others are waiting for us at the pub,' she cajoled.

'But Portia?' I insisted as she dragged me through the streets.

'She'll be with Tarquin now. Besides if she wants to find us she knows where to look.'

'I suppose,' I agreed, reluctantly giving into the inevitable reality that Honey always gets her way.

'I don't know why you're so bothered about Misery Briggs anyway. She stole Freds from you.'

'What do you mean?'

'Look, it's all over Eades that they are an item.'

Honey checked my reaction as we were entering the Three Swans.

'But not worry, darling. I couldn't tell you in the taxi with Misery Briggs, but Billy wants to get back with you.'

'Back with me where?' I said as the smell and noise of the pub arrested my senses. I'd never been in a pub before so I didn't know what to expect as we pushed the door open on the low ceiling smoke choked room. I looked around but I couldn't see Billy anywhere. I saw Poppy though. She was sitting in a red velvet upholstered corner booth, smoking with two other Upper Sixth girls. I remembered the Post-it Notes they slapped on my back last July when Honey was running her Post-it Note campaign against me. We made our way towards them. They were all smiling at me as if I was the only girl in the world they wanted to be with, asking me what I wanted to drink and telling me how much they adored my outfit.

'You look stunning, Calypso,' Poppy said, making room for me in the booth. My instinct was to run but everyone seemed so genuinely friendly and I didn't really have anywhere to run to.

'I know! Isn't she amazing for an American?' Honey boasted. 'She's practically got style, almost.'

I scrutinised Honey's face, wondering where this virtual niceness would lead, but she looked genuinely . . . well, genuinely genuine really. I didn't relax exactly, but I sat down. Poppy and company were accompanied by about half a dozen madly fit Upper Sixth Eades boys. Poppy introduced me, and they all stood and air-kissed me before falling back into a conversation about some arcane game of football they play at Eades.

A boy named Charles Von Archmontberg asked me if I wanted a drink, but before I could answer, Poppy dived in. 'Just get her a vod and Diet Coke, darling, and another for me.' She blew him a kiss but he looked to me for confirmation. I smiled and nodded. I wasn't about to disagree with Poppy O'Hare.

'Here's yours, darling,' Poppy told Honey, pushing a glass across to her half-sister. 'Vod and Diet Coke, but say this straight Coke is yours if anyone asks,' she warned, pushing another glass across to her. Then she ignored us and rejoined the conversation she was having with the boys.

'So when is Billy coming then?' I asked, looking about the heavy low-beamed pub full of Eades boys and Saint Augustine's girls. I scanned the room, with its dark oak furniture, plush patterned carpet and walls covered in etchings of Windsor Castle, in the hope of spotting him.

Poppy turned to me. 'God, I hope not,' she groaned, blowing a plume of smoke right in my face. 'That hideous little pleb. Ugh!' She shivered at the memory. 'Goodness knows what I ever saw in him.' She took a long deep drag on her impossibly long thin pink cocktail cigarette and blew some more smoke in my face.

I turned to Honey and tried not to cough. 'But you said . . .'

Charles returned with my drink and plonked it in front of me. 'One vodka and Diet Coke,' he declared, smiling in a flirty way at me.

Honey laughed her hyena laugh. 'Oh, I just told you Billy would be here to make sure you came, darling. I had to save you from Misery Briggs, and I knew you'd come if you thought Billy was going to be here.' She nudged me. 'He really did call me though, to tell me he fancies you though. Whoops! I wasn't meant to tell you that,' she said, putting her hand over her mouth as if she was ashamed.

'Got the hots for the Gypo, have you?' one of the boys asked nastily, and all the others laughed loudly.

One of them, I think his name was Peregrine or something stupid like that, leaned in so closely I could smell the Guinness on his breath. 'You do know his father rents out limos?'

'Well, your father sells mineral water, Grins,' declared another boy, who'd been introduced to me as Sebastian.

The rest of the group, including the girls, found this so hilarious the table rang with guffaws and shrill laughter.

Peregrine defended himself above the noise. '*Owns* Britain's major spring water company, I'll thank you,' he said, taking a gulp of Guinness. 'Been in the family for generations.' With that, he poured what was left of his Guinness on to Sebastian's lap. After that, one thing led to another. The crowning moment came when Cameron and Archer poured their drinks on top of Peregrine's head with the chant, 'Chav, chav, chav.'

It dawned on me that I was in Hoorah Henry Hell. As I looked around me, I couldn't really see a polite or even a mildly civil way of getting out of this aristocratic pub brawl. So I just stood up and legged it like a mugger down Oxford Street.

Sometimes escape is the better part of valour, I always think.

I charged through the cobbled streets, heading towards the tea shop I'd caught the taxi from last time I was in Windsor. Everything had been so clear that weekend, before Freddie mentioned the ball. I was so relieved to see Billy chatting to another boy outside the pizza place that I threw my arms around him in a parody of a damsel in distress. 'Save me, Billy!' I cried.

He laughed as he untangled my arms from around his neck. 'Slow down,' he said, grinning kindly. 'What do I have to save you from this time? Another dog?'

'Hardly, this was far more hideous. I was in the Three

Swans, with Honey and Poppy.'

'Nice company you're keeping,' he added ruefully.

'And loads of Eades boys. It was hideous, Billy, they were all just pouring Guinness over one another and I was just sitting there with Poppy and her friends and Honey, of course. They seemed to find it the most natural thing in the world.'

'Waste of good Guinness,' Billy remarked and in that smile, I saw again all the things that had attracted me to him in the first place. I needed to know if what Honey had said about the way he felt was true. He was squinting into the sun and as he ran his hand through his mussy blond hair, my tummy did what can only be described as a massive back flip.

'By the way, this is Tarquin – you know, Portia's brother? Tarquin, this is Calypso, the one you've heard so much about.'

I went bright red as Tarquin put out a hand to shake mine.

'How do you do?' I said awkwardly as I saw Portia heading towards us.

Billy suddenly looked nervous. 'You *did* get my text?' he muttered to me so that Tarquin couldn't hear.

Tarquin looked uncomfortable.

'Which text would that be?' I asked flirtily as I watched Billy's face redden. I couldn't believe he was still ashamed about not texting me. 'Honey said something to me, though.'

'Only, I didn't mean to give you the wrong idea. Honey?'

Guilt was written all over his face. He'd obviously been too busy to text but he didn't want me to think I'd forgotten him. And now he knew Honey had blown his cover. Bless.

'Forget about texts, forget about Honey anyway. I've got the same ideas I've always had,' I assured him, flirtily grabbing his hands in mine. Before he could respond my witty repartee was interrupted by Portia's arrival.

I waited for her to say something to me. Something like 'Hello' or, 'Oh, I see you've met my brother.' Or even better, 'Why don't we put the past behind us and just be friends like we were at the start of term?'

But she didn't say any of those things. What she actually said was, 'So, should we head off then?' She was looking at Billy and her brother as she said this, not at me.

'Yes,' agreed Tarquin. 'Best be off.'

Billy looked at his watch. 'Yaah, we'd better push off,' he agreed, adding, 'Thanks again, Calypso, about you know, understanding.'

'Oh that's OK, I love understanding,' I blurted and then I thought – what am I supposed to have understood, actually?

'So will we see you later, then?' he asked after the others had already turned to leave.

That was all the encouragement I needed to go blurtatious and a stream of madness came pouring forth as it does when I'm faced with the eyes of a fit boy boring into my soul. 'Yaah, that is, I hope so, Billy. It's just that, well, I'll see what I can do but I'm very busy today and I have to meet my . . . friends.'

'Not Poppy, Honey and the Guinness wasters?' he asked, beginning to move away himself. 'Laters,' was all he said as he turned and joined Portia and Tarquin.

I put the icing on the cake of my rambling blurt and called back, 'Yaah, laters,' only I didn't move because, well, it was just a blurt. The fact was, I wasn't in the least bit busy, and all my friends were back at school in the music room.

It didn't really matter, because none of them turned around. I felt like a crime scene as I stood there in the bright autumn sun for all of a minute before deciding that with Star, Indie and Georgina back at school, I had little choice. I was meant to stay in a group of three at all times. Also I didn't want to take a taxi back to school on my own with a potentially grumpy driver who expected enormous tips from posh school girls, so I wandered back to the pub as if I hadn't ever left it.

I opened the door on the smoke choked pub, remorseful at having to return to a group of people I really didn't like. Also I was nervous about being carded. Even though I was tall I was only fourteen and nine and a half months, and the only ID I possessed was my school library card and it wasn't even forged! I looked guiltily around the packed room full to the rafters with older Eades boys and Saint Augustine's girls. No one appeared to notice me as I made my way over to the guffaws and shrieks of Honey et al.

'Sorry about that,' I told Poppy, Honey, the other two girls and the Hoorah Henrys as I sat back down in the booth. 'I just remembered I had to get some money out of the cash point.'

Yaah, that would be the day. I didn't even have an ATM card.

TWENTY-ONE

Think With Your Brain, Move With Your Body, Slam 'Em With Your Blade!

On Monday, the Eades fencing team loped into our salle with their special, we-own-the-world walks, followed by their security men with their, we-might-look-like-idiots-but-we-spend-a-lot-of-time-following-these-boys-who-own-the-world-about-so-don't-mess-with-us-all-right swaggers.

I felt very alone and strange without Star to back me up and Portia hating me. Bell End was chatting to the Eades fencing master, Professor Eichstiech. If Star had been here we would have debated whether the two of them were going to hate each other or get on like a couple of weird men with beards.

Professor Sullivan, our old master, had always eschewed the company of other fencing instructors. He was a man apart and we liked him like that. Bell End was a different sort of fish – he was much keener to jostle for the top dog spot. The first with the chalk in his hand, the first of the two to slap the other on the back, you know the sort of chap.

Eichstiech had an Olympic gold which, rumour had it, he hadn't taken off since he'd won the wretched thing sixty years ago. At least he didn't wear his outside his clothes like Bell End, but apparently though he even showered in it, slept in it and wore it beneath his vest as a constant reminder of what a golden champion he was. I hope I wouldn't become a seriously tragic creature if I won gold.

Both Billy and Freddie hung back with their team before play. It was just a 'friendly' but we still had to rustle up one of the younger, more promising épéeists to make up our sabre numbers. Bell End presented us with Emille who was seeded out before I'd finished my stretches. This meant that between Portia and me, we could only afford to lose one bout between us if we weren't to lose the match. Good one, Star.

When Freddie and Billy saw Portia, they waved at her like a two-boy fan club. Looking at Billy, I caught his eye, and he smiled. I wondered if perhaps I hadn't been a bit hasty in deciding I didn't fancy him. I mean, he was *soooo* blond and fit and not to mention about four inches taller than Freddie and two years older. Looking at Freddie, I still wanted to fall into a heap of desire, but Star's reasoning wasn't to be so easily dismissed. She was right, Billy *was* far less complicated and maybe he deserved another chance.

With Portia as my unspoken enemy, I was lurking with

the year below, doing my Supermans, which I suppose made me stand out, only not in the way I fantastically cool way I wanted to stand out.

I spotted Billy out of the corner of my eye, loping over to Portia and saying something to her, probably 'Where's Calypso?' to which she probably replied, 'I don't know, but I hope she has that flesh-eating germ don't you?' Only Portia wouldn't have actually put it like that. She would have just implied it with an enigmatic shrug. Just the same, whatever she said made Billy laugh.

Billy's name was called with mine for next first bout by Professor Eichstiech. Normally, Portia would have hooked me up at the back to the electrical apparatus. But given she was now my enemy, I figured I'd have to rely on Emille, or worse, fumble pathetically on my own in front of everyone. But unlike a normal enemy, Portia was too much of a toff to be petty. I realised her aloof demeanour wasn't going to wobble over someone as insignificant as me as she hooked me up in a more or less friendly fashion. She even wished me luck. This made me cross because I wished she *was* petty so that I could tell Star and everyone else how petty she was.

I could feel Bell End's eyes on me as Billy and I touched our gear to make sure it was wired up to record hits properly. In consideration of my reckless emotional game with Portia, I emptied my head of all thoughts. I didn't want to end up in a humiliated puddle at *Billy's* feet. I could feel Billy's eyes on me even though I couldn't see them behind his mesh mask after our salute.

Professor Eichstiech called, 'En garde! Ready! Play!'

I made a compound attack from the start, a feint to provoke Billy into a parry and a *trompement* to deceive the parry. But I lost my right of way with a crossover, which is illegal, as you can't cross your legs in play.

After a yellow card (penalty), I was starting to wish I really was in the infirmary with that flesh-eating disease. Billy anticipated every move I made and successfully riposted. I knew things were going badly, but I soon came forward fast, picked his blade up and made a cut across his chest, after which I began to gather my nerves and concentrate. Just the same, my comeback, such as it was, came too late to win the bout.

Bell End took me aside after I had shaken Billy's hand and congratulated him for rinsing me. 'Bloody, bloody idiot,' Bell End said. He also used another word which, if a pupil used it, would mean a gating. He was shaking with anger he was so rattled, and I suspected it was because this was his first outing to Eades as the new fencing master, and he probably thought he had something to prove. 'Stop being such a bloody girl, Kelly. Now get a grip, think with your brain, move with your body, slam 'em with your blade.'

I went over to the refreshment table and drank a juice so I wouldn't have to watch Portia fencing Freddie. I even chatted to a group of Year Sevens just so I could keep my back to the piste.

Billy came over and said 'Hi,' which startled me so much I spilled the juice down my white jacket. Thank goodness I'd taken my metal lamé off, otherwise it would have been ruined and I'd have had to borrow Portia's.

'How's things?' Billy asked, looking at the spillage.

'You were with me on the piste,' I snapped, imagining he was having a dig at my form as I dabbed away hopelessly at the orange stain lest it spread over my breast.

'Good bout, I thought,' he said.

'Well, you would, wouldn't you. You weren't rubbish.' I was quite glad I had the spillage as it meant I didn't have to look at him and show him my blush.

'Here, let me,' he offered, dipping a paper napkin into his plastic cup of sparkling mineral water and dabbing at the spot on my chest.

Even though I was wearing my breast armour it still seemed incredibly intimate. I looked down at his long fingers as the stain disappeared and then I looked up into his eyes and there it was, that look of adorable protectiveness, just like the time he saved me from the girl-eating dog.

'I wondered if you were going into Windsor this weekend again?' I blurted idiotically.

He nodded. 'I think that's it, don't you?'

I looked around confused.

'The stain,' he explained, pointing to my chest. 'I mean, I think it was a successful operation.'

'Oh yes, the stain. You've done the most incredible job. I mean, you could do it professionally if you wanted. Not that you would,' I added, realising what a hole I was digging. 'I mean, you're madly bright, and, well you probably wouldn't dream of becoming a stain spotter, would you? That would be ridiculous.'

He laughed. 'You always make me laugh, Calypso,' he said.

'You make me laugh too,' I told him flirtily.

He looked awkward then, as if he had to run to the loo. 'Anyway, thanks for being understanding about the text and well, everything.'

'You mean lack of text,' I teased. Only Billy didn't smile back. He looked confused. 'Not that I mind,' I hastened to add. 'I mean, you've been busy with the fever of exams building up. And it's not as if I've been staring at my mobile waiting for it to ring or anything blatantly tragic like that. No, I've been wildly busy myself,' I rambled on. 'Hardly even know I own mobile sometimes.'

That was when I saw Freddie looking at me. Only he wasn't looking at me in a nice way. He was shaking hands with Portia and looking at me like I was the biggest bitch in the world. In that paranoid second, I decided she must have said something nasty about me to him.

While I looking at Freddie, Billy shuffled off, muttering something about Portia winning again. Bloody Portia, I thought, before remembering she was on my team.

'Lucky none of the teachers saw you,' one of the girls from a lower year whispered to me.

I turned to her distractedly, having no idea what she was talking about.

'You and the Eades captain, Billy, isn't it?'

'You were all over each other,' added another. 'We'd never get away with that. It must be so cool being in Year Eleven,' she said dreamily.

I wish.

I didn't get a chance to speak to Freddie before our

names were called because after his bout with Portia he was surrounded by all the fawning girls in lower years. And then when our names were called together I was in an unfit state to fence again. As we touched each part of one another's bodies and blades to make sure the electrics were working, I felt the blush creeping up. Emille had already lost two of her bouts. I had lost one. Portia had won two. If I lost this bout, we'd be counting on Emille which meant we may as well surrender. I had to beat the prince's arse.

Wired up, standing on the en garde, attached to the electrical point recording device, I saluted him casually. Then, placing my mask over my face, I concentrated my mind as best a girl can when she's an emotional whirlpool of confusion over which fit boy she fancies the most or, more to the point, which fit boy fancies *her* the most.

Then the president called 'Play,' and I advanced swiftly down the piste, preparing for a focused attack. I knew Freddie's form well. I just hoped he hadn't shifted it since we last fenced.

What I really wanted to do was break distance (a fancy way of saying run away back to the other end of the piste) to stop from impaling myself on his sword and throwing my arms about him and pulling him then and there in front of the world. I'd seriously be disqualified for that, though.

I was *sang-froid* personified as I advanced towards HRH, though. Billy may have rinsed me, but that only made me more determined to see that it didn't happen a second time. I won my first point, and after that I made damn sure Freddie's target area was continually threatened for the rest of the bout.

I was unbelievable in fact – shocked by my own ice-cold nerves and amazed by my ability as each lunge set the electrical recorder lights flashing and buzzing like a techno nightclub show. I was a veritable Olympian. I'd never played so well, although every move I made felt familiar and right – in fact there was an eerie sense of *déjà vu* about the whole bout. I was indestructible, and what's more I didn't even feel the few cuts Freddie *did* manage and in sabre that's something. After a bout my torso and arms were always covered in bruises and welts.

I made an offensive action so as to draw his counter attack, parry and riposte. When the distance between us was so close that I wanted to rip my mask off and snog-age him senseless, I remained the consummate professional. I was going to fence in the Olympics, and no boy, however fit or royal, was going to hinder my play. I delivered my cut, as Bell End's words rang in my ears, 'Slam 'em with your blade!' And slam him I did, good and hard, setting the buzzers off.

At the end of the bout, I triumphantly tore off my mask and walked toward Freddie to shake hands. I could hear Bell End clapping and yelling like a football hooligan through cupped hands, 'That's my girl! Well done, Kelly. Cut the little prince down to size.'

'Good game,' I said, as Freddie shook my hand formally.

I knew that my head was a sweaty pulp, but for once I didn't care. The clear head I'd maintained during play became a muddle of confused feelings as I looked into Freddie's ink blue eyes.

Portia was detaching me from behind, but the electricity of what I felt for Freddie was coursing through my system. He was still distressingly fit, even with his hair all plastered to his head with sweat, and suddenly I wondered what would happen if I did just kiss him there and then on the piste? I reached my hand out to brush away a lock of hair from his damp forehead.

He didn't move to stop me but he said, 'You and Billy looked like you were getting on well?'

It was a question I didn't know how to answer immediately, and as it happened it was one I didn't get a chance to, because Star came bursting into the salle and started calling my name. I wished she hadn't made her entrance just at the moment because I knew now that I needed to talk to Freddie properly – to see where things really lay between us.

'Darling!' she called out in an OTT drama queen-ish way as she threw her arms around me. At first I thought she was just messing around, and Freddie laughed, but he still left without saying anything really meaningful, like 'I won't go to the Euro-Royal-Bash Thingamee if I can't take you with me, Calypso.'

I didn't even get time to finish my fantasy before Star pulled me away. It was only when we got into the changing rooms that I realised she was really crying.

'It's Brian – he's gone missing!'

TWENTY-TWO

Mayhem in the Pet Shed

'I'm sure he'll be OK, darling,' I reassured her after I'd changed out of my gear. 'Snakes are quite good at looking after themselves, remember?'

Star looked at me pointedly as she replied, 'They also eat rabbits and hamsters, *remember!*'

'Dorothy!' I cried, charging off towards the pet shed, envisioning my poor little rabbit as a bulge halfway down Brian, the reticulated python.

Star grabbed me by the arm, though. 'Dorothy is *absolutely* fine,' she insisted crossly. 'Georgina's waiting at the pet shed in case Brian comes back.'

'Phew.'

'And for the vet.'

'Oh thank god, for a minute there . . .'

'See how you reacted when you thought Dorothy was in danger,' she pointed out, a little self-righteously.

I felt a little guilty, then realised what Star had said. 'What do you mean, waiting for the vet?'

'Well, unfortunately, Absinthe's got a bit missing off her,' she explained, as she continued her trot towards the main building.

My voice was weak with horror as I chased after her. 'A bit missing off *what*?'

Star was running along purposefully, pausing to peer into hedges and shrubs as she replied casually, 'Only her ear. I suppose it's mostly blood, but can we stop discussing Absinthe?' she implored. 'The main thing is to find Brian.'

We dashed a little further along the netball court, checking along the longer grass that ran along the fencing for Brian. Coming out of the chapel, we were stopped by a group of seven elderly nuns who were stepping out holding hands. They were all really small and old but ever so friendly.

'Hello, girls!' they called out in their thin little nun voices. 'Isn't it a lovely day for a stroll?'

'Yes, sisters,' I agreed, joining Star as she fell to the ground to run her hands through a patch of long grass.

'Enjoying the fresh air, are we?' one of them enquired sweetly.

'No, I've lost my snake,' Star explained, desperately.

'Heavens, Star, not dear little Brian!' they exclaimed in one voice. They looked as stricken by her loss as she was as they clutched their rosary beads.

'Oh heavens, I do hope he's not lost,' one of them continued. The others all agreed fervently. Some of the elderly nuns are a bit potty.

'I just told you he *is* lost,' Star insisted, trying not to get cross with them. Looking up at their little soft faces creased with years of prayer and concern, it was hard to be cross.

'In that case we must all go back into the chapel

immediately and say a prayer to Saint Anthony for your snake,' said Sister Joseph firmly.

'What a good idea, Sister,' another nun said.

The others all nodded.

'Yes, Sister Michael, remember he found your glasses this morning before we'd even got down on our knees, didn't he?'

'Did he?' Sister Michael looked a little vacant.

'Yes, Sister, he always does the trick, does Saint Anthony.'

We left them chatting about the marvels of Saint Anthony as we legged it to the next patch of shrubbery.

'Poor Absinthe,' I muttered. 'You don't think it could have been Brian that . . .?' I asked, because she hadn't made that bit clear.

She was scouring a large shrub outside the main building as she replied, 'Don't be absurd, Brian wouldn't hurt a fly. Not that I'd blame him – if he did eat the ear, that is. Absinthe makes the most hateful faces at him when there's no one around to supervise.'

Now she was going too far. As much as I'd love to hate Honey's rabbit, she was a sweet little thing, much nicer than last term's rabbit, Claudine, who was always biting. Absinthe might be ridiculously mauve, but she didn't have a mean bone in her body as far as I knew. 'That's not true, Star, she's just a little rabbit and how's Honey going to feel when she finds out?'

'Honey?' She coughed and pretended to fall over. 'Honey, *feel*? Ha! You of all people know what she's like.'

There was nothing I could really say to that so after

helping her scour all the shrubbery around the main building we legged it up the narrow stairwell towards our dorm rooms.

'He's so incredibly intelligent, Calypso; you're always saying so yourself.'

It's true. I do always agree with Star that her snake is intelligent, sensitive and even cuddly, but I only say those things because I love Star so much. Truth is, I'm a bit afraid of Brian and his beady eyes and flicking tongue. I know he's not poisonous or anything, but if looks could kill, all the pets in the pet shed would be dead.

'So that's why I've been teaching him this special skill,' she announced.

'What sort of skill?'

'Well, I wanted to be sure that he knows his way around the school so he can come and find me if he's upset or something.'

'Brian's a snake, Star, not a homing pigeon.'

'He's always showing Daddy around our manor when he gets lost.'

Given that Star's father is perpetually stoned and spends most of his time lying unconscious on the floor, I wasn't madly impressed by this skill, but I kept my doubts to myself.

'That's why I leave his cage open. So he'll come and find me if something's wrong. Hilda's taken Brian's disappearance very badly, by the way.'

'Hilda?' I repeated, before I could stop myself. I swear, Star's rat, Hilda, thinks of nothing but escaping Brian. She's always running dementedly around in her little rat wheel. I couldn't accept that she wouldn't be throwing her little rat paws in the air at Brian's disappearance.

But as I trotted along the corridor after my friend, I made what sympathetic noises I could. I know it sounds bad, but a part of me was actually pleased that I was the one Star had come to find in her hour of need. It was just like old times.

'This is the main route I've been teaching him, see. I wanted him to know how to find me in the night. He's nocturnal and pines for me. You know at home he always sleeps with me.'

'Yes,' I agreed. Whenever I stay with Star I'm always afraid that I'll wake up with Brian around my neck.

As we dashed into Star's room she began to cry hopelessly. 'I can't stop thinking about him being lost, frightened, dazed and confused. What if he gets run over?'

I put my arms around her. 'He's got a good head on his shoulders,' I told her, as if Brian was some madly sensible sentient being (with shoulders) which I promise you he's not. I mean, for a snake he's bright enough I guess, but. . .

We started to strip search the room. I helped her check in all the cupboards and drawers, tearing all her bedding apart because Star was convinced he liked to cuddle up to her *smell*.

We'd already missed lunch, which was bad enough because we would have to have a talk from Sister Dumpster about the dangers of anorexia. Worse than that though any minute now the bell was going to go for classes. If we didn't find Brian in the next few minutes we were going to have to tell Sister Constance that she had a six-foot reticulated python on the loose.

I repeated this realisation to Star, who started to cry even harder. 'We *can't* do that, Calypso. Sister will totally overreact and ban him from the pet shed.'

'We'll have to, Star, otherwise, well, he could . . .' I trailed off, not wanting to accuse Brian of anything – especially as Star wasn't even convinced that he was actually responsible for nibbling Absinthe's ear.

I was opening Indie's bed drawer when Star cried out, 'Brian!' and her tears of despair turned to tears of joy. But as I went over to cuddle her – Star, that is, not Brian – all was not as well as I'd hoped. Brian was coiled around another rabbit which he was in the process of swallowing.

I screamed in horror, and at that moment Honey came running in, followed by Miss Bibsmore. We grappled with Brian and what turned out to be Tobias, Georgina's teddy bear and lifelong companion. And before you think to yourself 'Oh well, he's just a *toy*,' remember, as far as Georgina's concerned, he's her soul mate with opinions on a wide variety of subjects. Oh, and let's also not forget that Georgina's father pays twenty-five thousand pounds a year in school fees so that Tobias can attend classes.

As we struggled to free Georgina's beloved bear from the jaws of death, Tobias's insides burst, and there, concealed in a muddle of fluff was Georgina's Tiffany flask. Or rather her mother's Tiffany flask, which I suspected contained a stash of vodka.

TWENTY-THREE

One Teddy Bear, Caught Red-Handed . . .

Miss Bibsmore grabbed the flask, opened it up and sniffed the contents. Star was totally oblivious to anything as she rapturously cuddled and stroked her snake. Honey stood behind her nemesis, giggling.

Miss Bibsmore turned to her. 'You think this is funny, do you, madam?'

Honey didn't stop laughing as Miss Bibsmore waved the flask in her face. 'I presume by your inappropriate laughter that this item is yours then, madam!'

Honey sneered so hard that the uneven bubble of collagen in her upper-lip looked like a giant blister about to burst. 'Don't be insane. Why would it be mine? This isn't even my room!'

'I may not have all the whys and wherefores yet, missy, but mark my words, I'm on to you, Miss O'Hare.'

'And my daddy's lawyers are on to you, so I'd be very careful about defaming my reputation if I were *you*, Miss Bibsmore.'

'If you were *me*? If you were *me*?' Miss Bibsmore squealed and then cackled mirthlessly in a mad-ish sort of way. 'If you were me, you'd know what it is like looking after ungrateful spoilt girls like yourself, Miss O'Hare. You wouldn't last a day on my legs.'

Honey, her hands on her hips, rolled her yes and replied, 'Oh go back to your squalid 1950s-decorated flat, you mad old witch.'

Miss Bibsmore ignored her as she took another sniff of the flask and then stuck one of her stumpy fingers inside, tipped it up and licked her finger loudly. She looked around at us, taking in each girl in turn with a piercing look that seemed to reach right down to our very souls – well, that's how it felt to me. Honey merely flopped idly on Indie's bed and started shuffling through the stuff in her bedside drawer. Star ignored her too, as she was still stroking Brian. And as for Tobias, well, he was lying lifelessly on the floor with his inside fluff spewing out, so his soul was bared for all to see anyway.

'Well, is anyone going to own up to this?' Miss Bibsmore demanded, holding the flask in the air. 'Because it didn't get 'ere by magic!'

Honey, looked up innocently. 'How do we know it's not yours, Miss Bibsmore?'

'Don't you cheek me, Missy; I'll have your guts for garters, I will an' all.'

Honey looked the picture of blond-haired, blue-eyed innocence. 'I'm not cheeking you, Miss Bibsmore. I'm being deadly serious. How do we know you're not a secret drunk? Or perhaps you planted it? People like you are always planting things because you're bored and envious. I know it must be hard for you, being surrounded by beautiful teenage girls day and night, but really, Miss Bibsmore, turning to drink is *never* a solution.' Honey said all this casually, without even looking up as she searched more deeply in Indie's bedside cabinet.

Miss Bibsmore shuffled over towards her. 'The only thing I'll be planting, Miss O'Hare, is a mountain of blues on top of you.'

Honey remained unfazed. 'Well, given that the flask was found on Tobias, common sense would seem dictate it is his. After all, he's always been a bit out there hasn't he, darling?' She directed this comment to Star, who predictably enough ignored her.

'I suppose you think that's funny, Miss O'Hare?'

Honey ignored her. 'Oh look, Indie uses a vibrator,' she declared, as she pulled a phallic-shaped pair of hair-straightening tongs out of Indie's drawer.

Miss Bibsmore raised her voice. 'I'll ask again. Who is responsible for *this*,' she yelled menacingly holding out the flask.

'Sorry, are you offering us a drink, Miss?' Honey asked blinking innocently. 'Because I wouldn't want to have to report you, Miss Bibsmore.'

Star and I said nothing. I was hoping that if we stayed quiet for long enough, Miss Bibsmore would grow tired of standing there holding up the flask and shuffle off. Deep down I knew that wasn't likely, but Honey had turned the straightening tongs on and was using them on her hair which created this weird sense that everything was actually completely normal. Just another day in dorm-hell with Honey that would eventually pass just like all the others had.

'Lost the power of speech, 'ave we, girls? Well, perhaps you can tell me who owns the bear then?'

I looked at poor Tobias and wondered how Georgina was going to take it, seeing him splattered on the floor like road kill. But then I reminded myself that she must have opened him up and concealed the flask inside him in the first place. Then Star announced, 'It's my bear, Miss Bibsmore.'

'Yours?' Miss Bibsmore repeated, as if not quite accepting the fact.

'Yes. Mine, Miss.'

'Pass me the bear,' Miss Bibsmore insisted.

Honey bent down, grabbed the ripped Tobias with all his insides coming out and flung him at her. Miss Bibsmore caught him adroitly and examined him carefully. 'Well, I can't see a name tag so at the very least whoever owns the item'll be receiving two blue tickets, one for 'aving a personal item untagged and another for 'aving a pet in the dorm,' she said, pointing to Brian. 'As for this –' she held up the flask again '– we'll have to see what Sister Constance has to say. You can come with me,' she said, pointing to Star. 'As can you, madam,' she added, pointing a gnarled finger at Honey.

'Me?'

'Yes, you, Miss O'Hare. Now hurry along, you can carry the bear and the flask, and no funny business neither.'

'Why me? This isn't even my room, that's not my bear, and I haven't got a pet in the dorm.'

Miss Bibsmore pressed her face close to Honey's. 'Because, Miss O'Hare, I don't like the cut of your jib.'

'I'll come too,' I blurted.

Miss Bibsmore looked at me beadily. 'If you wish. But I don't advise it, Miss Kelly.'

Star shook her head at me, a gesture that caught Miss Bibsmore's eye.

'I don't know what's going on here, but I smell a rat.'

For a moment I thought she meant Hilda, but then I realised the seriousness of the matter and began to contemplate the consequences of what could happen. A sinking feeling fell upon me as I followed Star and Brian, who were following Honey with Tobias and the flask. Behind us was the sinister *tap, tap, tapping* of Miss Bibsmore's stick as we made our way to Sister Constance's office.

As we filed down the corridors lined with a century's worth of photographs of illustrious old girls, and shelves of trophies, plaques and other evidence of their achievements, I felt humbled and unworthy. I'd never really imagined a plaque to Calypso Kelly, but the realisation that I might *never* have one made me feel like I was squandering my life.

I know that probably sounds melodramatic for a fourteen- (and nine and a half months) year-old, but then Bob doesn't call me Queen of the Doomsday Prophecies for nothing.

TWENTY-FOUR

If You Ask Me, it Was Her Brain that Needed Botox!

Sister Constance sat at her desk in that intimidatingly serene way that only a tall, thin nun with decades of practice and a long black habit can pull off. Miss Bibsmore explained the events of the last ten minutes. Sister didn't interrupt or ask any questions; she merely made a sort of steeple with her fingers and nodded as each of the items – Tobias, the Tiffany flask, and Brian – were all laid out, one by one on Sister's desk, only Star had to grab Brian back because he started slithering and knocked over a statuette of Mary.

Sister Constance's ominous silence, combined with the sombre and detailed way in which Miss Bibsmore explained the case, lent the office a court-room-like atmosphere.

Eventually Sister said, 'Thank you, Miss Bibsmore, you can leave this with me. I know how busy your schedule is.'

'Right you are, Sister,' Miss Bibsmore agreed. Clearly she would have preferred to stay. Nonetheless she backed out the door reverentially but stopped short of leaving. 'With all due respect, if you want my opinion, Sister, Miss O'Hare is the most likely culprit. I've had my suspicions about her since I first laid eyes on her, I have.'

Sister Constance nodded as if taking this on board. 'Thank you, Miss Bibsmore. I'll take it from here.'

So for the next hour (well, probably around five minutes, but it felt like an hour) we all sat gathered around the desk, gazing and contemplating the evidence in total silence. Sister Constance appeared to be thinking, or at least praying very hard. I looked up at the giant crucifix on the wall above her and began to wonder about Absinthe and whether I should interrupt Sister's thought/prayer process and tell Honey that her rabbit had been attacked by Star's snake. But just at that moment, Honey pulled a Chanel compact from her pocket and started looking at herself.

'Miss O'Hare?' Sister Constance spoke in a warning tone.

Star and I simultaneously took our lip-gloss from our pockets and began to apply.

'Do you think I need more Botox, Sister? I mean obviously I don't have any lines like you, but it does give your eyes a bit of a lift,' she enquired chattily, demonstrating how she'd look with higher brows by stretching the skin on her forehead.

Sister Constance sighed wearily. 'You are a very silly girl, Miss O'Hare, and rather than looking to a mirror for guidance, you should pray to our Blessed Virgin Mother.'

Honey rolled her eyes at me. I pretended not to notice.

'Let's discuss the evidence here, shall we?' Sister continued. 'A snake.' She gestured to Brian, whom Star was still stroking. 'And a flask of what appears to be vodka.'

'Can I just interrupt for a second, Sister?' asked Honey, continuing without waiting for an answer. 'I frequently smell alcohol on Miss Bibsmore's breath.'

'No, Honey, you may not utter a word unless I ask you a specific question,' Sister said. 'Then of course there is Georgina's bear, Tobias,' she added, as she gently patted his remains which were strewn forlornly across her desk.

'No, Sister, like I told Miss Bibsmore, the bear is mine,' Star cut in.

'Yes, I've grasped the ludicrousness of your claim, thank you, Star,' she said gently. 'But Tobias has been a fee-paying student of this school as long as Miss Castle Orpington has, and I place my reputation on recognising *all* my pupils and their family associations.'

Star blushed and looked strangely stuck for words.

'Perhaps the first thing we need to do is place Brian back in the pet shed so that you can focus on the serious-ness of the matter at hand. You might also ask Georgina to come and see me.'

'Yes, Sister,' Star agreed and backed out of the room with Brian, leaving just Honey and me.

Honey snapped her compact shut and stood up angrily. 'Well, as it wasn't even my room the flask was found in, I don't see why I should be kept from my next class,' she complained. 'Daddy would be furious!' She looked like she was about to explode with exasperation and even though she's the nastiest girl that God ever breathed life into, I felt I had to say something. Honey deserved to know her rabbit, Absinthe, had been injured.

'Actually, Sister, Honey's rabbit's been injured and the vet's been called. Georgina's at the pet shed now waiting for him to arrive.'

'What?' cried Honey, with a look of genuine despair on her face. I felt really, really terrible for a moment, before realising the fallout that would ensue when she discovered that her rabbit's attacker was probably Star's snake.

'How did this happen?' Sister Constance asked calmly, looking directly at me.

I did a little cough. 'Well, see the thing is, Sister. Well. That is, we can't be sure, but we think, maybe, only maybe though, when Brian escaped he might have taken a bit of a nibble . . .' I trailed off, unable to bring myself to directly accuse Brian of anything that would have him banned from the pet shed, because that would destroy Star. 'But we're not really sure, and he's always been such a kind snake, so it would seem very unlikely . . .'

'That bitch!' screeched Honey. 'I knew something like this would happen,' she spat. 'It's ridiculous that you allow a snake in the pet shed, Sister,' she railed. Which is a bit rich given that Star's father had paid for a centrally heated pet shed for all the pets and a separate area for Brian and Hilda to be housed in.

Without waiting for permission to leave, Honey stormed out of the room, and that was that. Sister Constance and I were now alone. We sat for the next few minutes in silence, breathing in the aromas of frankincense, old books and an open box of butterscotch, which was beside a statue of Mary on her desk. Finally the bell went at which time she told me I could go to class and return with the others after supper.

TWENTY-FIVE

Daddy's Plastic Girls

Honey's righteous fury at the attack on Absinthe by
Brian should have been short lived but for the fact
that Honey adores being right and furious more
than cats enjoy stalking mice and licking cream. Enjoying
the combination of both emotions was too delicious for
her. Even though it turned out that Brian wasn't to blame.

'You're too tragic to even speak to,' Star told her when
she came into our room before supper.

'I don't want to believe that people like you even exist,'
added Indie, as she trailed in after her.

There wasn't much I could add to that. I felt ashamed
for blaming Brian when what had really gone wrong was
all Honey's fault. Poor Absinthe had caught her paw in
one of the enormous hoops Honey had pierced Absinthe's
ears with. Also I was in the bed next to Honey's and had
my mattress to consider.

Portia put down her magazine and smiled in her regal
way at Star and Indie, who smiled back, and then we all
huddled on the floor for a confab on Georgina's fate. Honey
was looking at herself in the mirror at the time and didn't
deign to respond, let alone grace the floor with her presence.

'So no one's seen Georgina since she left to wait for the vet earlier in the day?' Indie asked.

'You don't think they've expelled her?' Portia asked in a low whisper as the vet was ushered in to our room by Miss Bibsmore.

This vet was really fit-looking for a grown-up, although his dress sense was a bit tragically retro. He was so adorable though, the way he delivered his diagnosis on Absinthe in the gentlest, kindest voice you can imagine. He looked as genuinely saddened by the whole affair as were we, apart from Honey. She was furious.

'You mean you expect *me* to pay *you* for disfiguring my pet?' she shrieked, her head spinning around on her neck – well, not really, but it looked like it was about to. 'How dare you treat my rabbit without the permission of myself or my guardian!' she screamed. 'What am I meant to do with a rabbit with half an ear?'

'Well, I was called to the school, so I just presumed . . .'

'Ugh!' she grunted. 'That's the trouble with people like *you* and your sorry red brick university degrees! You presume too much. If *I'd* been consulted I would have told you to put her out of my misery.'

Portia, Star, myself and even Indie were used to Honey-isms such as this. All in a day's Honey. But as we looked up at the poor vet with his angelic tousled locks in an attempt to convey our solidarity with him, I could tell he didn't have a clue what he was up against.

'You mean *her* misery,' he corrected. The poor, sad, deluded sod. He really had no idea. He sat down on Honey's bed as if he wanted to comfort her. 'Sorry, Honey, isn't it? Perhaps I haven't explained myself clearly,' he persevered. 'Absinthe will be just fine. She'll make a full recovery. She's only torn part of her ear but it will heal and the main thing is she's retained full hearing capability. I'll drop by in a few days to remove the stitches and she'll be right as rain, I promise you.' He gave her shoulder a comforting little pat.

I caught Miss Bibsmore popping her head around the door and listening in on the scene as it played out but Honey didn't.

Honey turned to him. Her eyes flashing like machine-gun fire. 'And I'm meant to take precisely *what* comfort from the news that I now have a disfigured pet? Are you suggesting that I throw good money after bad to keep a hideous half-eared rabbit alive? I could spend your vet bill on a pair of rabbit-trimmed Gucci stilettos! You monstrous, money grabbing pleb. Now get off my bed, you pervert.'

After the accusation of being a pervert, the vet dived off the bed and looked around at all of us. His plan of breaking the good news to a sweet teenage girl that her pet was going to be OK had crashed against the barriers of Honey's unspeakable nastiness.

He opened his mouth to reply, but Honey cut over the top of him. 'Well, hop to it!' She clapped her hands. 'Down to the pet shed and put the wretched thing out of my misery.'

But the vet didn't look like he was going to 'hop' anywhere. His whole demeanour changed before our eyes from fit, kindly, older man a dangerous force of authority.

I swear a chilling breeze was blowing around him as he said: 'Miss O'Hare, the only misery I know of is the lamentable attitude you and your friends have towards your pets. People like *you*,' he began, but I think he was too angry to go on because he started spluttering.

I felt sorry for him. Apart from Honey I think we all were, so as he turned to leave, I began to blurt, 'Can I just say, that erm, well, it was super of you to come and help Absinthe and erm . . . well, seriously, actually I think. Yes, that's it, personally, and I think an enormous amount of people would agree, you've got a really cool and original dress sense for an old, I mean, a grown up. Yes, those retro corduroys are well, well they're on trend this season, aren't they? So that's really cool, isn't it?'

I wasn't exactly waiting for applause but when my blurt stopped, the entire room was silent. Everyone was looking at me blankly as if I was mental. I mean, his dress sense was seriously horrendous but it *was* original in a retro sad sort of way.

He had already put his hand on the door handle at that point but he turned back to face, not Honey, but me.

I knew my speech wasn't as polished as it could be but I was shocked by the venomous look on his face. 'That's all you spoilt girls care about, isn't it?' he asked me directly. 'Cool clothes and accessories, Daddy's plastic and Mummy's contacts.'

My face stung with the unfairness of his attack. I was only trying to cheer him up. 'I don't like your clothes that much,' I assured him.

Dig, dig, dig Calypso, a voice in my head was heckling.

So I grabbed the shovel. 'I was just, well, I was just trying to be nice to you, to cheer you up. Not that your green flares aren't cool in a retro (I think I actually said 'sad' but I hope I didn't) sort of way. It's just that they're not my sort of thing. See, I wanted to say something kind after what Honey said to you. Besides my mummy, that's Sarah, doesn't have any contacts, and my daddy, that's Bob, doesn't even *believe* in plastic!'

The vet clicked his tongue at me in disgust. That was so going to be the last time I ever complimented an older man, however fit and kind he might seem. Because that's the thing – you never know when grown-ups are going to turn on you. One minute they're all, 'Let's be pals and I really, really, really care,' and the next, it's all, 'Time for bed, lights out, blues all round and I'm filing a report.' Star's right, grown ups only exist to subjugate us.

'I shan't be sending a bill,' he told Honey in a grand voice he hadn't shared with us earlier. 'I can assure you however, that I will be making a full and detailed report about this school and your treatment of animals.' He made the word 'report' sound like a weapon of mass destruction.

We were all cowering as he glared around the room at Portia, Honey, Indie, Star and myself as if we were Honey clones, when really we were as appalled by Honey as he was. The difference was, we'd suffered Honey for so many years we were virtually immune to her toxic psycho toff take on life.

'I can't believe he went off at you like that,' Indie said after he'd gone. 'I thought you were really nice to him,' she told me gently, rubbing my back.

'I even complimented him on his flares,' I added, shaking my head at the injustice of life.

Star said. 'It just proves what I've always suspected. Grown-ups are not to be trusted.'

TWENTY-SIX

The Feverish Age
of Reports

S upper was fish fingers, my favourite, but not tonight
— I had no appetite. None of my friends with pets
did. A rumour had swept through the school that
the pet shed was to be closed, pending an investigation
and that the vet had spoken sternly to Sister Constance
about the animal rights issues of allowing girls to pierce
rabbits' ears and place large heavy hoops in them.

We were in a complete state and none of us could eat
our food. It wasn't just the pet shed we were upset about
either; we were more worried about Georgina's fate.
Sharon, the lady on tray duty that evening, took our names
and said we were all going on report for not eating.

'Fine, report yourself, stupid,' Star told her as she
slammed her full tray into the slot with a crash.

'Don't you take your food issues out on me, dearie, or
I'll report you for disrespecting a dinner lady!'

But Star had already stormed off.

'What is it with everyone and their reports today?'
Honey asked gaily, skipping along beside us happily — just

to wind us up, I suspect. 'Report, report, report, Is it the word *du jour* or something?'

Now was not a time for skipping and I told her so. 'You can imagine how panicked Star and I are about the fate of our own pets,' I told her as we headed off to Sister Constance's office after supper.

As we waited on the bench outside Sister's office for our summons, Honey taunted us for our 'sickly sentimentality,' which in case you haven't heard, is sooo last millennium. Then she blabbered on about not being in the least bit fazed about the possible closure of the pet shed as she was sooo over pets.

'Oh shut up, will you, Honey!' Star snapped – only Honey looked shocked, and she's never shocked by Star telling her to shut up. Also, she was looking at me. That was when I realised that I, Calypso Kelly, unshielded by Daddy's plastic and Mummy's contacts, had just told The Ultimate Psycho Toff, to shut up.

'Sorry, Honey,' I muttered.

Honey merely ignored me and began studying her manicure.

Star was abnormally silent, which made me feel frightened about what was to come. When Star doesn't express herself verbally you just know it's going to come out another way. She was glaring at Honey and Honey was glaring back at her as Sister Constance finally cried out, 'Enter!'

When we wandered in, we weren't invited to sit down. Sister Constance didn't even look us in the eye. She looked stricken. The serene calm that characterised our Mother

Superior seemed to have been drained from the inside of her soul, and her face seemed to have shrunk into her nun habit.

Star and I stood there with Honey between us. I felt Star nudge her because Honey fell into me theatrically, as if Star had used super human force. Actually, knowing Star she might have. Normally I would have done nothing, but hating Honey as I did at that moment I nudged her myself – really, really hard – and she fell right back against Star's elbow.

'Ow!' she complained. 'Sister! Did you see what they just did to me?'

Sister Constance didn't look up, let alone reply.

'I have a preternatural tendency to bruise,' Honey whined, rubbing her arm. 'I wouldn't want to have the nurse look at me and jump to conclusions regarding abuse,' she muttered, knowing that no one gave a damn what she did at that particular point in time.

Again, Sister refused to comment.

Eventually Star asked about Georgina.

'Georgina has left the school,' Sister Constance replied. We waited for a bit for her to go on but all she did was take a butterscotch from the box on her desk and begin to suck on it really loudly.

'What? For good?' Star asked.

Sister Constance nodded. 'Miss Castle Orpington has left the school grounds of her own accord,' she explained, the butterscotch rolling around in her mouth. 'She, along with Tobias, fully accept responsibility for the flask of vodka, but other than that, her father has refused to discuss her future at Saint Augustine's. He's in Morocco at the moment and cannot be reached.'

'But *you* will let her back?' Star demanded to know.

Sister sucked hard on the sweet which made the most revolting noise. 'That is a matter for the school board, Star. More to the point is the spiritual bankruptcy that led her to seek refuge in alcohol.'

Honey rolled her eyes. 'I think she probably just wanted to get drunk, Sister.'

Star and I both had to suppress a giggle.

'Girls!' Sister warned.

But Honey continued, 'I think you're blowing this out of proportion. Why, Eades boys wander about their school sucking on flasks all the time and no one bats an eye. A boy from Marlborough I know said they can even buy it at the school tuck-shop. And the by the way, now we are on the topic of tuck shops, all the boys' schools seem to have the most enormous shops. That is sooo unfair, Sister. They can even buy clothes and order Savile Row suits at their schools, whereas our tuckshop is just a window sill that's only open once a week and even then we can only buy sweets. We can't even buy phone credit! It is sooo babyish.'

Sister Constance, daintily taking her butterscotch out of her mouth between thumb and forefinger replied, 'Miss O'Hare, you do say the most ridiculous things. And the older you get, the less tolerance I have for your ridiculousness. So, for the love of Mary will you just, shut up!'

All our jaws collectively dropped to the floor as Sister

popped the sweet back in her mouth and sucked on it loudly.

After a few minutes of rude sweet-sucking noises, Sister spoke again. 'Georgina isn't my only concern, though. I had the vet in here earlier and he has grave, grave doubts about the attitude some girls have towards their pets, which I must admit I fully share. He furthermore expressed doubts about the viability of the pet shed after the unfortunate fate of your rabbit, Miss O'Hare.'

'Fine, shut the pet shed,' Honey said. 'I'm so over animals anyway. Unless we're talking those little fur trimmed Gucci shoes. I think I'll have them in mauve. I know, maybe if I give them Absinthe, they'll give me a discount,' she added, giggling at her awful joke.

That was when Star thumped her across the back and she fell theatrically across Sister's desk and got a bit of a nosebleed – not because of how hard Star had hit her, but because of her theatrical fall. Plus, after you've had as much cartilage removed from your nose as Honey has, your nose tends to bleed quite easily.

Sister ignored Honey and the spot of blood on the end of her nose as she sucked serenely on her sweet for a moment. I thought she wasn't going to say anything about it at all but then she did. Not to Honey, just to me. 'Take Honey down to the infirmary,' she instructed. 'Star, following Brian's escape from the pet shed, the attack on Tobias, and the events that have transpired here, I feel compelled to contact your father.'

Star remained strangely silent but I couldn't stop

myself. 'Sister, that's sooo unfair! You saw what happened. Honey launched herself and besides there is barely a drop of blood. If we take her to the infirmary, there might be a, well, a report or something!'

Sister gave me a look that spoke volumes – volumes as in, 'don't push it or you'll be the next one launched.'

TWENTY-SEVEN

Fact: Friends Don't Steal Other Friends' Boyfriends

On the way down to the infirmary, Honey, in keeping with her Honey-ness, immediately dialled the police. 'Hello, officer? I have just been attacked by a ferocious girl – a famous rock star's daughter – and I've been badly injured . . .'

I snatched the phone off her and pressed the 'End' button.

'What?' she asked, blinking with innocence. 'This' – she pointed to her now completely bloodless nose – 'is GBH; that's Grievous Bodily Harm. Star will *have* to be charged and I hope incarcerated.'

The only grievous thing about it all was Honey, and I told her, 'You've hardly even been hurt. The bleeding was totally negligible and you used Star's mild whack to launch yourself on to the desk intentionally. Besides, it didn't even bleed properly, it was just a spot and there's no sign of blood now.'

'Don't be ridiculous,' Honey snapped, pinching her

nostrils together as if stopping a torrent of blood. She called the police again.

It wasn't the first time the police had been called by Honey to have a fellow student arrested. Once she'd tried to have Star done for having red hair – in Honey's eyes a crime against aesthetics! And anyway, Star's hair isn't even red, it's strawberry blond – after several sprayings with Sun-In, anyway. The point is, Honey's frantic call about GBH didn't have the police hopping around the way she'd hoped. They arrived but then wandered into the infirmary in a bored sort of way, accompanied by Sister Constance. They didn't seem even mildly keen on the idea of charging Star or anyone else. Honey had to implore them even to open their pads and write something down, and even then they only wrote down her name. By this stage, there was no evidence that Honey had even *had* a nosebleed and Sister Constance, whom they justifiably considered a reliable witness, said it was all a storm in a teacup and offered them butterscotchs. They were more than happy to accept both Sister's version of events and her butterscotch and wandered off back to their police car.

Just the same, a rumour had swiftly spread that Star had been led from the school grounds in handcuffs for assaulting Honey. The truth was that Tiger had picked her up and taken her home along with Brian and Hilda because, as he told Sister Constance, he didn't consider Saint Augustine's a safe environment. He wasn't so easily bought by the offer of butterscotchs apparently. Either that or Sister had downed them all herself by the time he arrived.

For me, Georgina and Star leaving was like the theft of

my two closest friends, although I felt sorriest for Indie because now she'd have to go to bed and wake up alone in an empty room.

'It's worse for you,' I told her. 'You'll have no one to chat to at night.'

'You could always come and stay with me?' she suggested hopefully. That was when I first realised that Indie and I had become proper friends in our own right, as opposed to two girls with shared friends. 'Otherwise I'll sneak into your room,' she promised.

'Why don't we have a moonwalk?' I suggested as the idea suddenly occurred to me. 'We can escape after lights out, take our duvets, vodka and tuck stashes down to Puller's Wood. It's a Saint Augustine's tradition.'

Indie clapped her hands. 'George and Star have told me all about them,' she replied excitedly. 'Let's!'

The first time Indie came into our room on her own, only Honey and I were there. She hissed at Honey, 'You are such a bitch!' exactly like Star would have.

Honey, who was checking her mobile, looked up nonchalantly and replied sarcastically, 'Thank you so much for all your tea and sympathy, darling. I'm the one with the broken nose who'll probably have to spend the rest of my life having corrective surgery.'

'That's if you have any cartilage left after all your other nose jobs,' shot back Indie.

Then I noticed that it wasn't her mobile she was fiddling with at all. It was mine.

'Honey, what are you doing with my phone?' I demanded crossly.

'Just reading your messages,' she responded shamelessly, before turning back to Indie. 'At least I've *had* a nose job! You should think about surgery yourself, Indie. I mean, most people are probably too polite to say anything, but honestly darling, take it from someone unafraid of the truth. Surgery is a necessity in your case rather than an option, if you see what I mean.' Honey held up her Chanel compact to Indie's spectacularly stunning face.

As Honey hadn't responded to my demand that she give me back my mobile, I snatched it from her and began to check my messages.

'Oh, like the surgery you had to remove your brain, you mean?' Indie replied, snatching the compact from Honey and tossing it into the bin.

There were no messages. 'There are no messages,' I said to Honey, holding up my phone.

Portia walked in at that moment but she only said 'Hi' to Indie, ignoring both Honey and me.

'Oh, well there were a few. I read them. Several in fact,' Honey replied idly, shrugging her shoulders. 'I must have deleted them accidentally. Soz, darling, but your phone is sooooo ancient. They were all from Billy, as usual. Probably best you didn't see them actually. Billy's got a very pervy turn of phrase and I know how politically correct you Americans are.'

I stood there opening and closing my mouth both at her audacity and her news that Billy had been texting me. I had been hoping for something from Freddie but this turn of events had me frantically wondering what was going on.

'I didn't know things had heated up quite that much between the two of you,' Honey continued, now smirking. 'I suppose I always thought of you as a little mouse . . . but you're quite the seductress, Calypso.' She laughed loudly at her own turn of phrase.

I just stood there, blinking. So did Indie.

'So you're admitting you just deleted her personal messages?' Indie clarified.

'Hardly! At least not on purpose, obviously,' Honey gasped indignantly.

'Rubbish,' Indie said crossly.

While this exchange was going on I was wondering whether this was the first time Honey had *accidentally* erased my messages. It would certainly explain a lot!

Honey commenced brushing her hair, which involved flipping her head over. 'Why don't you scuttle off to your own room, Indie, things are getting a little crowded in here, don't you think, Portia?' Honey asked.

'I don't think you want to hear what I think,' Portia replied as she focused on sending a text message from her own mobile. I tried to gauge her expression but as ever she was as inscrutable as the Sphinx.

My eyes were burning with desperation to see whom and what she was texting. 'How many times have you tampered with my mobile exactly, Honey?' I demanded, turning my attention back to Honey before I shamed myself by craning over to peer at Portia's screen.

'Oh, Calypso, talk about self-centred!' Honey snapped, flipping her head back up. 'Why does it always have to be about you, you, you? You can't always take centre stage like this. Don't you think its poor Georgina and Star we should be worrying about, darling?' she implored, her lower lip dropping as if she truly cared.

'You're incredible, Honey,' Indie said to as she flopped on to Honey's bed.

Honey fluttered her eyelashes. 'Thank you, darling. I'm sorry I can't return the compliment.'

Indie leaned back on Honey's bed, making herself comfortable by rearranging her pillows. 'All Star did was give you a bit of a slap and after the way you've been behaving, I can't believe she was so restrained,' Indie told her. 'If I were Calypso I'd give you another slap for deleting Billy's texts.'

'Calypso doesn't seem to mind, so why do you?' asked Honey as she grabbed at her pillows. 'Now get your filthy feet off my bed and go back to your own room.'

'I *do* care as a matter of fact, Honey,' I corrected her as Indie left the room.

'Oh, then it must be *me* who doesn't care,' she replied with the ease of someone completely comfortable with her role.

I was so angry I stormed out of the room. When I passed Clemmie and Arabella's room they called me in. Of course I told them all about what Honey had done.

'What a bitch,' Arabella agreed.

'She's done it before with other people,' Clemmie added casually.

'All par for the Honey course,' they both said, sighing.

'I don't know if she's done it before now. I don't know if Freddie or Billy have tried to contact me before and, well, I've been so confused about how I feel because I've been getting barely any texts at all.'

Seeing how upset I was they both gave me a cuddle. Their other roommate, Rosie, had been in the en suite having a shower but as she came out she remarked. 'I thought you and Billy were an item?'

I briefly looked up at Rosie who was still in her robe. She smiled and went back into the bathroom. I turned to my friends. 'I think I only started liking Billy because of all the complications with Freddie, mostly because Freddie wasn't texting me. Well, actually neither was Billy, but he's doing his A-levels so that's understandable. The real issue is that Freddie's going to the ball with Portia. Wait a minute, why did Rosie think Billy and I were an item?'

The girls looked at one another. 'Honey told us, I think,' Arabella said, looking to Clemmie for confirmation. Clemmie nodded. Now I was really confused.

'When you say Freddie is going to the ball with Portia, do you actually mean going with as in *going with*?' asked Arabella.

I shook my head. 'I don't know. That's the thing. Honey's got me confused.'

Clemmie put her arm around me. 'So, it's Freddie you *really* like?'

I nodded.

'Seriously, serious?'

I nodded again because as easy as it would be to like Billy after seeing Freddie at fencing I knew that I felt something much stronger for him. He might be inconvenient, but he was the one I wanted to pull.

'OK, well, you're not going to like this, then,' Clemmie warned me, shaking her head. 'But Honey told us that Freddie and Portia were an item.'

I looked from Clemmie to Arabella. 'What did she say, exactly?'

'Just how mad for one another they were,' Arabella replied vaguely.

'Yes, but it is Honey we're talking about and as she's our only source I wouldn't put much stock by it,' added Clemmie.

I nodded. 'I know but . . . well, Portia hasn't helped.'

'Portia wouldn't be a bitch,' Arabella said firmly. 'I've known her all my life and one thing she isn't is a backstabber.'

'Oh, it's such a mess,' I groaned, putting my head in my hands with the frustration of it all.

'Honey is a witch,' Clemmie said, 'but Portia stealing Freddie, I don't buy. Have you spoken to Portia about all this?'

The tears sprang to my eyes at the obvious sense in this remark, and Clemmie and Arabella took me in their arms for another cuddle. It felt good to finally share my plight with others, and all my doubts and suspicions about Portia came tumbling out, as well as how horrible I'd been towards her and how now I couldn't go to the ball because I had nowhere to stay in London, and even if Portia hadn't been trying to steal Freddie I wouldn't blame her now if she did.

Clemmie and Arabella were really comforting. Arabella offered me some sweets, and Clemmie said she wouldn't even mind if I ate a jelly baby, as Sebastian was growing up now and hardly resembled their little faces at all.

I smiled through my tears. 'Indie and I were thinking of having a moonwalk tonight, if you want to come,' I told them, drying my eyes.

'Hoorah, a moonwalk!' they squealed, bouncing on the bed with excitement. 'We haven't had one since last term.'

'I know, it's been so cold, but the stars are bright and the moon's full and I know I won't get to sleep tonight anyway. I'm too worried about Star and Georgina.'

They were already gathering sweets, fags, Body Shop Specials and duvets as I left their room. On the way back to the Saint Ursula room I was determined to try and sort things out with Portia once and for all.

TWENTY-EIGHT

The Girl In The Iron Beak

I arrived back at my room, set on inviting Portia to the moonwalk. I had a picture in my head that once under the stars, stuffing ourselves with sweets and vodka, I'd have the bottle to apologise for being so horrible and put things back on track. But things had changed in the room in my absence.

Portia was reading *Nun of Your Business* – last year's copy – the one I had co-edited. But I didn't have a chance to speak to her about moonwalking or making up, because Honey dived on me like I was her best friend in the world.

'Darling!' she said as she threw herself on me enthusiastically. 'I am sooooooo seriously sorry about deleting the messages from Billy. Please forgive me,' she begged, seeming genuinely contrite. 'I'm almost certain I remember what they all said.'

What could I do? Apart from hug her back? 'Of course I forgive you,' I told her, not just because I was surprised and curious – although I was – but because I was totally weirded out by what she was wearing on her nose. I guess there is no nice way of putting this. Honey was wearing a big, black metal sharp-pointed beak.

'What have you had put on your . . .'

'Oh, this?' she asked, nonchalantly tapping the monstrosity perched on her face. 'Sister thought, it was best. It's a nose guard.'

'Sister Regina?' I asked, shocked that the adorable lovely little Florence Nightingale of the infirmary would stoop to such artifice.

'Sister Dumpster,' Portia said, from behind *Nun of Your Business*.

'So, Portia, do you fancy going for a moonwalk this evening?' I asked lightly.

'Her name is Dempster, actually,' Honey snapped at Portia – that is, she was trying to snap, but her words echoed inside the iron beak.

Portia hadn't replied to my suggestion, in fact she hadn't even looked at me. I looked at her mother staring out at me from the family photograph then looked at Honey, the ultra aristo-psycho toff. She looked like a monster, a victim of torture. The Girl in the Iron Beak. It was completely bizarre.

'Daddy said I should sue,' she said with a sigh. The metal nose made her sigh sound really nasal and common.

But I didn't laugh.

Portia huddled further towards the wall. I think *she* might have been laughing.

'Poor you,' I remarked, more or less for the sake of it because even though I was furious with her for deleting my messages, and for the trouble she'd brought on Star, she was Honey. 'So, Honey, what were these text messages from Billy you deleted?'

'I told you, just heavy breathing, a little smutty for your wholesome American taste.'

'Heavy breathing? Smut?'

'Darling, you *really* don't want to know.'

'Oh, but I do,' I told her firmly.

Then Portia's voice added, 'So do I.'

'Oh, darling, what's that top you're wearing?' Honey suddenly squealed, which made me jump six feet in the air as the words echoed about her nose. 'It's divine!'

I looked down at the stretched-out-of-shape white-ish T-shirt I was wearing. 'Erm, Topshop, I think it was in the five-pound bin.'

'Oh, don't you just *adore* Topshop?' she enthused. 'It's so tacky and yet so happening. Wrong, but deliciously right and darling on your figure. You make it look like something Lee whipped up.'

'Lee?'

'Alexander McQueen, darling, everyone who knows him calls him Lee.'

Portia loudly flicked the switch on her mobile charger. Honey rolled her eyes dramatically in Portia's direction and the look, combined with the iron beak was really quite alarming. I found myself feeling sorry for poor Bob and Sarah, forgoing the pool and the other luxury treats they sacrificed so that I could live in a room with something the carnival had kicked out.

'Sorry, what was that you said, Honey, I missed it?'

'I was saying, Mummy, Poppy and I sat in the front row

at his last show in Paris and he totally adored us. Well me, more than Mummy or Poppy.' She giggled. 'They were tearing their false nails out with jealousy.' She laughed her hyena laugh, only the iron beak made it sound like an exhaust pipe on an old car exploding.

'He's got a boyfriend, hasn't he?' I hazarded.

'Oh Calypso,' she hooted. 'Even gay men like girls like *me*.'

'Of course they do,' I replied, as I wandered into the en suite to take a shower and smother my laughter.

'I did mean it before though, Calypso. I am genuinely sorry, about before, you know deleting your messages from Billy.'

I came back into the room. Honey had just said the word sorry again and more relevantly she increasingly sounded like she actually meant it. I was so shocked, I said, 'OK, it's fine,' even though I didn't mean it. 'But in future I'd rather you didn't help yourself to my mobile, Honey.'

'I was surprised that there weren't any messages from Freddie, darling?' Honey added, looking pointedly at Portia who was tidying up her area.

I glanced at Portia as I replied, 'Oh I suspect he's seeing someone else.' I was trying to get a reaction, to test the waters, but Portia went on folding her clothes and putting them away in her drawer as composed and regal as ever. So I tried harder. 'Besides, I've gone off him really. Billy and I have got something more special.'

This time Portia looked up but only because she was noticing that one of the evil fluorescent lights was flickering. She pulled over a chair, stood on it tapped the tube back in place. Then calmly she went back to the task of tidying her area. It was maddening.

Indie came running into our room and totally ignoring a bitchy remark from Honey, she handed me her phone – a tiny little purple jewel with her name picked out in diamonds around the face.

'Calypso?' It was Star's voice. 'Your phone isn't working. Georgina's tried to call you as well and she said to check that your SIM card is OK.'

'My SIM card? Why?' I asked.

'I don't know, she didn't say, but she's really insisting you check it.'

I looked over at Honey who was studying her nails with a suspicious amount of intensity. 'OK I will but I'm more worried about you. I hate it here without you. We all do. You *are* coming back, aren't you?'

'Of course I'll be coming back. Daddy just wanted to make a point to Sister. But after this week, it's half-term anyway, which means you won't see me unless you come to my place for the party.'

I tried not to whine but I couldn't help myself. 'I *really* want to go to La Fiesta though, Star. I've never been.'

'No you don't, Calypso. Believe me, they are tragic!' she assured me. 'And full of plebs and we're too old for that rubbish anyway.'

'But the cashmere tops and the skirts – and the shoes. We bought the whole outfit,' I pleaded desperately

'They're just clothes, darling! Please say you'll come; everyone else is coming. We can wear the outfits at my place. We can wear them all week if you like. Imagine it:

we could waft about in them like stunning figurines from the 1930s. Daddy said we can use the recording studio for the last track. I want you to be part of it Calypso, you know, on the CD? It was Indie's idea.'

'But I can't sing for toast.'

'No, on instrumentals.'

'And what instrument would that be, exactly?' I asked, a smile beginning to spread across my face.

'I don't know . . . triangle?'

'Triangle?'

'Don't mock the triangle, darling. It's a very underrated instrument.'

'It does sound fun,' I agreed, almost, but not quite tempted, well not enough to forgo my dream of La Fiesta anyway. I knew I should get over myself, but a dream is a dream and Bob is always telling me to hang on to my dreams.

'So you'll come?'

I was noncommittal. 'Well, the thought of wafting about in bejewelled cashmere, like 1930s figurines and playing the triangle does have a certain appeal.'

The truth was I saw myself as a tragic Cinderella who had forever been barred from the ball. Calypso, the proverbial underdog (that's me), was finally and firmly determined to put a stop to all those who would prevent her from attending the ball, be they Draconian parents or my closest friends.

And though I know Star loved me, she didn't really understand. She's been to loads of balls whereas I'd never been to one. An irrational part of me was even a bit cross with Star for not understanding and being so stubborn when she knew how long and how much I'd wanted to go to this ball. We'd spoken of little else in Los Angeles and Georgina and Star were the ones who'd persuaded my parents to let me go.

Star stuck the emotional thumbscrews on me. 'Kevin's coming to stay and so is Billy. Loads and loads of Eades boys are coming, coach-loads of them and I'm inviting some of the fit boys from the village as well.'

'Billy will be there?' I said it out loud so Portia would hear, but she merely walked into the en suite and turned the water on really loudly.

'Yes, he's spending the whole week and Freddie's going to the Annual Euro-Royal-Bash thingamee. so please come.'

'Maybe I will come,' I agreed. The truth was, though, it was all a pose. Hearing Kevin and Billy's names together only reminded me of Freddie and that just reminded me that he wouldn't be at *my* ball but at the wretched Annual Euro-Royal-Bash Thingamee with Portia. And as lovely and fit as Billy was . . . he wasn't Freds.

'How is Georgina? Is she coming back? There are all sorts of rumours going around.'

'Of course she's coming. Everyone who matters is coming. Indie is coming straight after the Euro-Royal ball,' said Star, misunderstanding me.

I wished I could go after La Fiesta too, but the train fare from London was about a hundred quid more, and all I had was thirty-seven pounds left to last me until after half-term.

I changed the subject back to Georgina. 'No, I mean is she coming back to school?'

Star seemed surprised by my question. 'Why wouldn't she be coming back?'

'It's just that everyone's saying she's been expelled for having that flask of vodka.'

I heard her giggle echoing down the phone. 'Oh yes, I can just imagine, Saint Augustine's waving goodbye to Tobias's school fees as well as hers. Tobias doesn't require a bed, doesn't eat and so it's a twenty-five thousand pound drop in the coffers as far as the school is concerned. And don't forget, Calypso, Tobias was caught with the vodka, not Georgina. They can't pin it on her. Tobias has been suspended for a week for having vodka; Georgina has only been suspended for helping a fellow student conceal vodka.'

'Seriously!'

Our conversation was interrupted by Miss Bibsmore. 'Mobiles! After nine? 'And that mobile to me immediately, Miss Kelly.'

I gave Indie a regretful look as I handed over her jewel to Miss Bibsmore. I expected her to just plop it in her pocket but instead she turned it over and over in her hand as if marvelling at its beauty.

'Well, perhaps you best hang on to this one, Indie. I wouldn't want to be responsible for something so lovely.' She handed it over to Indie and blushed.

'Thank you, Miss Bibsmore.' Indie smiled.

'But you can 'and yours in, Miss O'Hare, right now.'

'What about everyone else?' Honey hooted through her

iron beak. No one else had mentioned her iron beak whatsoever – but everyone knew full well that she was only wearing it for attention and to try and make a point about Star injuring her.

'I'm not talking to everyone else, so mind your own beeswax.'

'Beeswax? Sorry, no idea what that might be, Miss B,' she said, her attempt at sounding innocent rattling through her beak like a coin dropping down a drain-pipe. 'I don't speak *pleb* slang, see.'

'It's the gunk inside your head that you use for a brain, Miss O'Hare. I don't claim to be intelligent and I might well be what your type refers to as common an' all, but at least I don't gad about with a bit of tin plonked on my nose.'

'Ugh!' Honey screamed in outrage. 'I was told to wear this nose guard after being assaulted by a dangerous criminal who has yet been brought to justice.'

'Well, as far as I can see you're on the loose an' all, so unless this other dangerous criminal has a mobile as needs handin' in, I'm not interested.' Miss Bibsmore stuck her gnarled wrinkly hand out for Honey's mobile.

'I'm sooo going to complain to Daddy.'

'I've no doubt you will.'

'How do I know you're not going to ring up all your hideous plebbie relatives on it?'

'You don't, but I'll be taking it just the same an' all, thank you. Though if I were you, Miss O'Hare, I wouldn't go planting ideas like that in a plebbie head like mine,' she cackled.

Honey slammed her mobile in Miss Bibsmore's outstretched hand but didn't let it go. 'Before you take it, I actually need to ring that vet to make sure he's put that hideous deformed rabbit out of my misery.'

Miss Bibsmore clenched her hand around Honey's hand. 'No need. I've spoken to the vet an' all, and a nicer man I've yet to meet. I told 'im I'll be looking after that poor creature from now on and 'e's more or less agreed to drop his report as long as the likes of you are prohibited from keeping pets at Saint Augustine's.'

'Oh, that's really sweet, Miss Bibsmore,' Indie told her and Miss Bibsmore rewarded her with an awkward little cuddle.

'You're a lovely girl you are, Indiamaca – a *real* princess. A girl that certain other girls should look to for guidance. But off to your own room with you now. It's lights out soon. Hail Mary . . .' she began, and we joined her in a few Hail Marys before she switched off our light and shuffled off.

Alone with Portia and Honey in the dark, I turned on my torch and opened up my mobile to check on the SIM card, but there it was, safe and sound.

I went into my mobile's phone book so that I could text Georgina and reassure her all was fine on the SIM card front, but when I went into my address book it was empty.

'This is weird. My address book is empty,' I said out loud.

'I don't see why she didn't take *your* phone,' Honey whined.

'Probably didn't think it was worth taking,' I told her.

'I was speaking to Portia, darling.'

Portia didn't reply.

After a while Honey said, 'Besides, your phone is such a brick, your SIM card is probably dying.'

'I guess,' I agreed, while not entirely convinced. It wouldn't surprise me if Honey deleted my address book. I shone my torchlight in her face, but she didn't look in the least bit guilty or worried but I pressed the point anyway. 'You didn't interfere with my address book, did you?'

'Moi? Darling, what a horrible thing to suggest. What sort of girl do you think I am?' she cried out indignantly.

I didn't dwell on my broken phone for long though because Clemmie and Arabella, cuddled up in their duvets crept into our room. They were followed closely by Indie, cuddled up in hers. 'We've got Body Shop specials and loads of tuck so just grab your duvets,' Arabella ordered. 'Oh, and your fags and torches.'

TWENTY-NINE

Moi? Self-Centred?

It wasn't as easy to sneak out of the Main Building as it was when we were housed in Cleathorpes. Even though we were only two floors up and had the benefit of scaffolding to climb down, we'd definitely be splattered on the lawn below if we slipped and fell. The climb wasn't going to be easy, holding torches, sweets, Body Shop specials, duvets, fags and pillows.

'Let's wrap it all up in a sheet and I'll climb down first,' I suggested gamely. 'Then when I'm safe, toss me the bundle and the rest of you can climb down.'

'I'll climb down with you,' Portia said as civil as ever. 'The bundle will be too heavy for one of us to catch.' I was glad she'd listened and decided to come though.

'This scaffolding is freezing,' I remarked to her as we climbed down, hoping to draw some warmth from her cold civility but she didn't have a chance to reply even if she wanted to, because no sooner had we touched our toes on the lawn, than Indie threw the bundle down and we had to concentrate on grappling with that. Portia was right, I would never have managed it on my own.

Indie was the next down, followed by Arabella,

Clemmie and finally Honey whose iron beak kept chinking on the scaffolding. In an ideal world I would have liked to exclude Honey, but then boarding school isn't an ideal world. We made our dash across to Puller's Wood in super fast time because even though it was quite a mild night, the grass beneath was crunchy with frost.

We made our nest in a little clearing, spreading out our duvets and setting up our tuck. It was just like last year only without Star and Georgina. Even the moon was full, which meant it was so bright we didn't need the torches once our eyes adjusted.

Indie told me that Star had called again. 'She's *really* insisting that you to go to her place for the half-term break.'

'Well, as I've nowhere to stay in London, I'll have to, I suppose,' I conceded.

Honey sat up and prodded me with her foot, 'But I said you can stay at my house. We'll have the whole place to ourselves apart from the servants, obviously.'

'They're called staff now, Honey,' Indie snapped. 'You have absolutely no respect for the people who work for you, do you?'

Naturally, Honey ignored the remark. I hadn't even had a chance to get my head around the prospect of staying at Honey's. I suppose I hadn't actually thought she'd meant it.

'Oh, look, there's a shooting star,' cried Arabella, pointing with her cigarette up at the heavens. 'I'm going to wish that I pull Alfred at Star's party,' she announced.

'I wish I could skip the whole Royal Bore thingamee and go straight to Star's place with rest of you,' Indie added, cuddling under a duvet with me.

'Given the choice I'd rather go to the Euro Ball.' I sighed wistfully as I spotted a shooting star of my own.

Suddenly Portia spoke. 'You should be grateful you even have a choice.'

I was stung by what I saw as a direct attack on me. 'But I don't have the choices I want. Unlike you, Portia, I haven't been invited to the Royal Ball.'

The vodka stash concealed in the Body Shop bottles was being passed around. 'Do you know, Calypso,' Portia remarked lightly as if about to explain weather systems, 'I actually used to look up to you? I actually used to admire you. Last year, when you set up *Nun of Your Business* and raised all that money for charity, all I wanted was to get to know you better. I was so thrilled when I discovered that you and I were sharing this term. I saw it as a chance to get to know you properly. But you're nothing like I thought you were. In fact, as far as I can tell, you and Honey are *the* most self-centred girls I've ever had the misfortune to know.'

I took a big gulp of vodka and almost choked. So much for my plan to make up with Portia under the canopy of the stars. I felt like I'd been slapped across the face. Instead of making up, all my pent-up resentments about Portia going to the ball with Freddie just exploded out of me. 'That's easy for you to say, Miss I-Was-Born-With-A-Silver-Spoon-In-My-Mouth.'

Honey did her hyena laugh, which sounded more peculiar than ever echoing around her metal beak.

'Don't ruin tonight, you two,' Indie pleaded, nudging

me in the ribs with her elbow. 'This is my first moonwalk at Saint Augustine's. I don't want any arguing.'

'Yes, have another drink,' Clemmie urged, passing the Body Shop special flask to me.

'Yes, stop it, both of you,' Arabella added, passing another Body Shop Special over to Portia. 'Boys simply aren't worth falling out over.'

'Exactly,' agreed Clemmie.

I took another long slug of vodka and passed it to Indie, hoping the confrontation was over.

'A silver spoon in my mouth didn't save my mother's life though, did it?' Portia replied emotionlessly.

She was right, and in that moment I fully realised what a tragic piece of work I was, obsessing about a couple of boys when what really counted was being here with my friends and knowing that on the other side of the world Bob and Sarah were working hard to give me all this. I remembered how I'd not even bothered opening the e-mail from Bob and Sarah when there was an e-mail in my inbox from Freddie. I'd been obsessing about all the wrong things. 'I'm really, really sorry, Portia,' I told her as the tears sprang to my eyes. 'Please, Portia, I'm sorry.'

But she continued, her voice pleasant but cold, 'People like *you* will never understand that money and position don't instantly deliver your dreams. Sometimes, you have to do things you'd rather not do. Sometimes you have to put other people before yourself. Do you think I want to go to this stupid ball any more than Indie does?'

I felt the blood rush to my face at her words. For a start I was shocked that she hadn't acknowledged my apology, and then I began to feel angry because even though she could see I was tearful, she was really going for me. Behind her aloof demeanour, which prevented her from showing her true feelings, was the simple truth: she disliked me.

'People like you . . .' she continued.

'Oh, just have a sweet, you two, and lighten up,' Clemmie groaned. 'I didn't risk my life climbing down that bloody scaffolding to hear you two arguing.'

Still, her outburst worked for a moment, at least until the silence was interrupted by Honey. 'You really, really hate Calypso, don't you, Portia?' she said with a reverent awe in her voice.

But I barely listened to Honey. The fragile sense of belonging that I'd built up last term was under attack. 'Anyway, Portia, what do you mean by people like *me*? People without money? People without title and privilege?' I lashed back. 'Just because I'm American and titleless, and not as rich as you . . .'

Portia groaned. 'How typical that you make this about your country rather than looking at yourself. I'm not talking about your nationality, Calypso. I'm talking about the fact that self-centred, manipulative people like you and Honey make the world a colder, more miserable place for the rest of us.'

'Me and Honey?' I repeated. I looked over at Honey in her metal beak and her eyes met mine in a look of horror. 'Honey and me!' I said it again because it wasn't easy getting my mind around our two names linked together like that.

'How *dare* you!' Honey squawked through her beak. I don't suppose she wanted to be grouped with me either.

'Um, this is getting a bit heavy guys. Can we just chill a bit?' Indie pleaded. 'They're *both* just stupid balls full of stupid boys we'll loathe by next year. None of it means anything.'

'At least you're invited, though,' I reminded her.

Arabella interjected. 'Well, I'm glad I don't have to go to the stupid Royal Bore. I can't think of anything worse than dancing with all those old farty men. Yuk.'

Indie giggled. 'That's what it is actually, a Royal Bore.'

'Exactly, it all sounds positively evil to me,' Arabella groaned. 'No, I'm looking forward to pulling lovely fit boys at Star's house party and riding quad bikes around in the mud.'

'I know Daddy needs me, but I wish I could join you after the ball, like Indie,' said Portia, sighing. 'I'd much rather be spending time with Star and, erm, the boys. Just chilling.'

The image of Madame Deportment 'chilling' made me laugh. 'Chilling? You, Portia? You're so cold I'm surprised bits of you don't snap off,' I blurted before I could stop myself.

Portia was right I *was* becoming like Honey. Help!

THIRTY

'You Can Check Out Any Time You Like, But You Can Never Leave'

I spent the rest of the week in Indie's dorm, too, mostly because I was too uncomfortable to be around Portia. Honey, on the other hand, stuck to me like glue, which was creepy, not just because of the iron beak, but I was concerned about the associations the other girls might make about us hanging out together. Indie hated Honey and wouldn't let her in her room, so at least I was safe there. Indie was really kind. She told me not to worry about what Portia had said and urged me to make up.

'But I've tried,' I reminded her, 'and she threw it back in my face.'

'Give her time. You know what Honey's said to you about Portia, but you don't know what she's said to Portia about you.'

'I don't think Portia listens to Honey,' I told her, quite certain I was right.

As far as Honey was concerned, it was now written in stone that I was spending the half-term week at her place, and out of desperation, I let myself be talked into it. Although I dreaded the thought of spending time with Honey, I was still determined to go to the ball.

On Friday, the day we left school, I had to go back to my room to pack my bag. I hoped Portia would be gone already, but despite my careful timing, I was just in time to see her placing the last item in her bag and zipping it up. Dressed in old jeans and a T-shirt, a cashmere hoodie tied casually around her waist, her long dark hair tied up in a pony tail, she walked past me without acknowledging me in her special regal way. Honey high-fived me and I high-fived her back, because, well, I couldn't just leave her hand hanging in midair when I was going to be stuck with her at her house all week!

That was when it hit me. Portia had said she'd much rather be spending the week at Star's when we were on our moonwalk. And what's more, she'd sounded like she actually meant it.

'She said she'd much rather be spending the half-term break at Star's,' I announced as if coming out of a dream – or perhaps it was a nightmare.

'Who cares what Misery Briggs prefers?' Honey shrugged. 'We'll have the best time at La Fiesta. I've arranged caviar and champagne for the ride back to London . . .'

'Yes, but don't you see? Freds is going to be at the Royal Bore, not at Star's, so if she's so keen on Freddie, why would she want to be at Star's?'

Honey shrugged again as she turned her back on me and went into the en suite, slamming the door behind her.

I had been a complete idiot, allowing Honey's suggestions and poisonous whispers to seep into my consciousness. Indie was right, I had to sort this out. I charged down the stairs which were packed with girls and their luggage, all of them making their half-term plans to catch up on the King's Road. By the time I fought my way outside, I was calling out Portia's name as loudly as humanly possible without losing a tonsil. But her chauffeur-driven Rolls Royce was already crunching down the gravel driveway. And then it hit me: all was lost. Thanks to my obsession with attending La Fiesta, I was stuck with Honey now.

In the limo on the drive back to her place, Honey produced those tiny little one-glass bottles of Veuve Clicquot that you see runway models drinking at after show parties. I had never even tried champagne, not that I was going to admit this to Honey or anything. I was actually quite curious to see what the big deal was. Sucking up the contents of our mini-bottles through matching orange straws, driving down the hedge-lined country lanes, I watched in shock as Honey suddenly threw her iron beak out the window.

'What about your nose?' I asked fearfully, because after a while Honey's lies sort of seep into you. Of course I knew all this; I'd known her for coming up on five years, which begged the question . . . what was I doing, sitting in the back of her limo with her, like we were two close girl friends? And then it got even worse. As the bubbles of the champagne charged up through the straw and into my mouth, I looked down and she was actually holding my hand.

She squeezed it warmly. 'Oh, I don't need it now, I was only making a point. If Star thinks she can get away with hitting me, she's about to get a nasty surprise. Daddy said I needed the infirmary to quantify my injuries.'

We had come to a T-junction, and as we took the turn to London, I realised that I was the one who had taken a wrong turn. Instead of heading off to stay with my best friend, Star, in Derbyshire like a sane girl, I was in Honey's limo on the way back to Honey's mansion in Chelsea, where I would be spending the next week. A whole week in Honey World!

There was no chance of escape now, though so I sucked on my straw, hoping the champagne could make me feel more optimistic, but all it did was make me feel like screaming hysterically and tearing at my clothing the way those women do in Alfred Hitchcock movies.

'I've got loads of bleach at home so don't worry about your hair, OK?' she said faux-kindly, giving my head a pat.

Of course she had bleach. No doubt she also had arsenic and cyanide and a whole host of other poisonous toys to try on me as well. I felt like her little pet which is probably how she saw me. With Poppy and her mother in LA, Georgina and all the other girls who tolerated her at Star's estate and her rabbit now in the possession of Miss Bibsmore, I was all Honey had left. Maybe *I'd* end up being turned into a pair of designer shoes!

Looking at it from the other angle, I did have choices, as Portia so accurately pointed out. I could have been at Star's with all the other girls. I could have been riding quad bikes by day and pulling fit boys by night. OK, Freddie wouldn't be there, but I could have met other fit boys, danced, pulled, moved on. But instead I was in Honey's limo en route to Honey's mansion, where bleach and God knows what else awaited me.

It was about five o'clock when we finally dived out of the limo on Cadogan Gardens, a garden square behind Harrods in Knightsbridge where even the plants have trust funds. The door was opened by my old friend: Honey's crippled manservant, Oopa. He was dressed in the usual valet garb, morning coat and striped trousers. He didn't smile but merely wandered out to the limo and started to bring in the bags. The rest of the staff were lined up as if to meet the Queen, curtsying and doffing their caps to Honey. It really was like we were in another century.

'Bring up some champagne, Oopa, Dom, I think, don't you, Calypso?' She asked me as if genuinely interested in my opinion.

'Oh yes, always Dom,' I agreed, even though I didn't want any more champagne, and I definitely didn't want to be alone with a seriously châteaued Honey. Nonetheless, I scuttled up the marble stairs after her, trying to reassure myself that I would be OK. It was only a week after all and at least Honey was being nice to me . . .

She opened the door on a bedroom so palatial that you could get lost in it. She had her own phone and one of those intercom systems so she could contact the staff in any room of the house. But there was something rather sad about it all, as if all this luxury could in someway compensate for being alone. As much as Honey went on about her Daddy suing everyone at Saint Augustine's, he'd never actually attended any of the school functions for parents. I started to feel a bit sorry for Honey. I would hate to go home to LA to a house with no Bob and Sarah – even if I did have loads of people to do things for me and lots of lovely things. The best thing about holidays at home with my parents was being with them – as mad and wholemeal as they were. I was the most important person in the world as far as they were concerned. They loved me.

'We'll have a glass of bubbles and then I'll take you to your quarters,' she babbled away excitedly, flopping on her antique four-poster bed. 'Chopin once made love to George Sand on this bed,' she moaned, as she writhed around ecstatically.

I muttered something lame like 'How splendid,' but I wasn't really paying attention. Everything in her room was so unexpectedly tasteful, and I was envious that she actually owned a bed that Chopin and George Sand had made love in even though that image was a bit gross. I wasn't a great fan of George Sand, but she was still an author and, more importantly, she was brave and wild spirited, like Star.

'Why didn't you go to the première in LA with your mother and sister?' I asked her.

'I don't think that's any of your business,' she snapped at me in the way people do if you've touched a raw nerve. But she soon gathered herself together and added, 'So, I've called in Stephan to do our hair and Mimi to do our nails and then I thought we could just drink champagne, eat sushi and pop out to Calm-a-sutra for a bit of a laugh.'

'Calm-a-sutra?' I enquired as I gazed at the sad, vast gorgeousity of her bedroom.

'The nightclub in Kensington,' she explained, looking at me like she just realised what a big mistake she'd made in bringing an unsophisticated nobody like me into her world.

'Oh, sorry, of course I *love* Calm-a-sutra, it's really cool, isn't it?' I gushed. I'd never been there in my life, obviously, but like everyone, I knew of it through the social pages. I almost said, 'But it's a club and we're only fifteen' – well, I was only fourteen and ten months actually, but I tried not to remind the other girls about that.

'So show me what you're wearing to La Fiesta,' Honey demanded.

'Oh, we bought these adorable outfits in Los Angeles, I told her enthusiastically. 'You know when Georgina and Star were out there.'

I thought I saw a look of irritation flash across Honey's face at the mention of Star and Georgina being in LA with me, but it disappeared quickly as we heard a tap at the knock at the door.

'Come,' Honey called and Oopa staggered in, buckled under the weight of a heavy silver tray bearing an ice bucket, a bottle of vintage Dom and champagne flutes.

'Shall I be of the pouring man? he asked, in heavily accented English.

'Just do what you're paid to do, you wretched little

ungrammatical cripple. I'd hardly ask for champagne if I didn't want to drink it, would I?' she snapped.

I bet she would actually, I thought to myself, already beginning to wonder how long I could keep my secret hatred of Honey secret. I was starting to think the price of going to La Fiesta was going to be very costly indeed. A week seemed like an impossibly long time to spend in the sole company of the most toxic psycho toff in the world. And with Honey knocking back the champagne at this rate, it would be even worse.

I began to make escape plans. The Ball was on Sunday night so there was the possibility that I could make an excuse and leave on the Monday to join Star and the others, except I hadn't any money of course. Maybe I could call Star and plead with her to send me her one of her father's roadies to pick me up. Star would understand. She had probably anticipated my call pleading for rescue, knowing Star.

Oopa did as he was bid and then backed out of the room tugging his forelock (not really, but I bet Honey wished he had been).

After Honey had downed another glass of champagne (I'd taken care to take only take a sip of mine), she showed me my quarters. It was a room in the basement, a quarter the size of hers but still very nice with a massive king-size bed, a fireplace with a plasma screen above, and en suite bathroom even more luxurious than the one at school.

'This is sooo cool,' I told her, looking around.

Honey wrinkled her nose job. 'Anyway, let's go back to mine and work out what we'll wear tonight,' she said, grabbing my hand and leading me back upstairs.

It was actually quite fun preparing for Calm-a-sutra. We put MTV on, and Honey encouraged me try on all her cool designer outfits and we danced about gaily and jumped on her bed. At eight o'clock the sushi, Stephan and Mimi arrived at once. I'd had loads of manicures and pedicures in LA with Sarah but I'd never had my hair dressed!

Stephan and Mimi guzzled the rest of the champagne and picked at our sushi and fawned and chatted away to us as if we were really grown-up clients. After they left, Honey and I helped one another put on our make-up. 'You've got madly long lashes, darling,' she remarked approvingly as she applied a mile of mascara to them.

'Thank you,' I said, even though I was a worried I looked a bit overdone.

I stood up and did a twirl in the full-length mirror stand, thinking I looked amazingly grown up, but Honey threw another strappy dress at me. 'Try this one, actually; it might be a better fit.'

It was a sort of dark-green colour with a copper thread running through it so it spangled, only not in a tacky way. It was longer than the tangerine one I was wearing but completely backless.

I held it up against my figure. 'This is stunning, Honey.'

She glanced at it before turning back to her wardrobe for another rummage. 'It's not a label or anything. I just found it at Vanilla, rummaging around one day.'

I slipped off the dress I was wearing, which was worryingly short and tried the non-label on. 'I love it.'

Honey nodded. 'Keep it. I'm never going to be tall enough to fit into it.'

'Wow, are you sure?' I asked, uncertain about accepting a gift from this girl who until recently had been so cruel to me.

'Don't be mad, it's nothing. Besides, that other dress made you look like a slut.'

'Thank you,' I told her. 'I mean about the dress, not the slut thing.'

She dismissively waved off my gratitude and turned her attention to the pile of jewellery on her dressing table. 'These earrings or these?' she asked, holding up two pairs of wildly glamorous chandelier drop earrings.

They were both fabulous. I pointed to the ones in her left hand.

'Typical, they're the cheap crystals from Accessorize; you can wear those if you want. These are the diamond ones,' she explained, holding up the others. 'One of Mummy's husbands bought them for her at Graff. I *always* get her cast-offs.' She sighed, as if receiving expensive diamond gifts was one of the many crosses she bore.

We arrived at Calm-a-sutra around midnight, tottering out of the limo in our impossibly high Christian Louboutin shoes.

The doorman recognised her instantly, and we were ushered to one of the private booths, which were large white beds with soft white faux fur throws and matching pillows. A flock of fit Eades boys from the Upper Sixth immediately came over and started to chat to us. I recognised Charlie, Sebastian and Peregrine from the pub in Windsor and got the impression they were expecting us. I looked at their cocktails worryingly, anticipating the boys tipping them over one another later in the evening.

I agreed to a try a sip of Peregrine's mojito, which tasted really nasty. Honey, of course, said it was delicious and demanded Charlie get her one of her own. I was bored very quickly, as Honey focused her attentions on heavy flirting with Charlie. All the other conversations at our bed seemed to centre on other trustafarian teens I didn't know and glamorous places I'd never been to.

'Do you ski at Klosters or Val d'Isere?' Peregrine asked me, in a generous attempt to include me.

Honey dragged herself away from Charlie to answer for me, 'Oh don't ask her, darling, she probably doesn't even know how to ski.'

'I do know how to ski, actually, but . . . erm . . . well, I live in America.'

Sebastian, who was sooo seriously châteaued by this stage that he couldn't focus properly, told me I was 'a babe'.

'That's sweet of you,' I said, moving even further away from him in the bed which practically placed me on Peregrine's lap. He was very nice about it though and not at all sleazy. When he asked if I wanted to dance, I saw it as an opportunity to get Honey away from Charles.

'Excellent idea, let's all dance,' I agreed, forcing Honey, Charlie and the others up to join us.

Honey's dancing practice by mirrors actually seemed to have paid off, and soon she was in another world, thoughts of pulling Charlie, and seemingly everything else, far from her mind as she closed her eyes and danced in mesmeric movements to the music. In fact the two of us ended up dancing together while Charlie, Sebastian and Peregrine did that sort of English pubic school boy dance – you know the one – it looks a bit like old men with Zimmer-frames trying to attempt a rugby scrum.

After a few dances we started to head back to the bed booth, when Peregrine took me aside and asked, 'Are you and Freddie an item or what?'

'Or what,' I replied, wishing I had an answer to give him. 'Why?'

'Well, I don't know him that well but he asked me if I saw you, to tell you to call him.'

'Let me get this straight. *He* asked *you* to tell *me* to . . .'

But I didn't get a chance to clarify what Freddie might have wanted Peregrine to tell me because Honey grabbed my arm. 'Come on, we're leaving. The car's outside,' she shouted in my ear, and that was when I realised how wasted she was. Her eyes were glazed and her speech slightly slurred.

'I have to get Honey home,' I told Peregrine. Despite first impressions, I was now beginning to think that Peregrine and the rest of the guys seemed pretty decent for Honey people. And then I thought, maybe they were thinking the same about me.

Charlie and Sebastian offered to see us out, and noticing the paparazzi gathered around the door in force, they were really responsible and had security help hold back the paps so we could climb discreetly into the limo.

The last thing I needed was another episode in the tabloids.

'Make sure she drinks loads of water when you get her home,' Charlie advised, but I wasn't paying attention. Honey was slumped with her eyes closed at the other corner of the limo. I opened up my phone. It was too late to call Freddie but I decided a text-flirt would be OK. That way he would get it when he woke up. I smiled at that thought. I still had no address book but that didn't matter because I knew his number off by heart – and that heart was pounding as I punched in my message.

JUST SPOKE TO PEREGRINE. CALL ME? C

I pressed 'send' and waited but the message came back. NO SERVICE. I checked the signal but that was fine and I knew I still had credit left.

I jabbed Honey with my foot to wake her. 'Honey, can I borrow your phone to send a message to Freddie. My phone isn't working.'

Even though she'd looked me in the eye as I'd asked, she suddenly collapsed back into her seat and started snoring loudly.

'Honey!' I yelled, but she resolutely refused to budge, apart from when I tried to knick her phone from out of her bag, and then she hit me.

'Sorry, darling. I thought you were a pikey trying to steal from me,' she explained, then drifted back to sleep.

'No, I just really need to make a call and my phone is out of . . .' I tried to say, but it was pointless.

She was still snoring when we arrived back at the mansion. I gave Honey some water and asked her again if

I could use her phone, but she firmly dispatched me to my quarters.

I was feeling sleepless, so I took a bath in the luxury of the large black marble Jacuzzi that had steps leading up to it. The Aveda products smelled heavenly, and the towels were all fluffy and enormous. It was like being in a movie, only not one I wanted to stay in. To be honest I'd have preferred to bathe in pond water if it meant I could have a mobile that worked.

THIRTY-ONE

Honey's House of Horrors

I was awoken by a buzzer going off in my room the next morning. I looked for where the noise was coming from and saw a red light flashing above a sign with the words 'Honey's Bedchamber' written underneath in swirly-whirly writing.

I clambered into my jeans and T-shirt and rushed upstairs, expecting the worst – perhaps she'd got trapped in her duvet or was being strangled by her eye-mask.

'Open my curtains,' she screamed hysterically. 'I can't see a thing.'

I stumbled in the dark over to the curtains and tried to open them but they wouldn't budge.

'Use the button by my bed, you idiot,' she howled from another side of the room.

So I crawled over to her bed, found the switch on her bedside light, then found the button for the curtains and let the grey autumnal light flow in.

Honey was lying crumpled in a corner by her bathroom door.

'Are you OK?' I asked when she didn't get up. I could see the tiniest bit of blood coming out of her nose.

'I was trying to go to the loo,' she sobbed. 'I bashed my nose on the door.'

And that was when it happened – when I finally lost my ability to hold in my secret hatred for Honey a moment longer and burst out laughing. 'It's a shame you threw that beak away – it was obviously really handy.'

'You bitch,' she snarled. 'Maybe you'd be more comfortable upstairs with the servants.'

'Sorry,' I said, kicking myself for losing control.

But there was no going back. Oopa was instructed to remove me from my quarters to the servants' floor upstairs, where I was confined. I wasn't actually locked into a cell, but as good as. I didn't feel comfortable leaving the room in case I ran into Honey, so I lay on the camp bed in the tiny box room. It was so small the bed was too long to completely fit, which meant it was a bit buckled in the middle, and I couldn't stretch out completely. I spent the day meditating on the mess I had made of things, and I don't mean with Honey. I mean with everything – with Portia, with Freddie and most of all with the choice I'd made to choose a stupid ball over my friends. I'd been naïve to think that it would be any fun at all at La Fiesta without Star and the others. In the pursuit of a childish dream I'd gone – in the words of my father – too far.

I couldn't remember the exact directions to Star's estate, because if I could, I swear I would have jumped out of the four-floor window and walked there, even though it would have taken two weeks.

Sunday was better, as Honey needed to re-bond with me for the ball. She came into my room and woke me up with a lovely cup of tea she'd made herself. 'Sorry about being such a bitch yesterday,' she said. 'Oh darling, look at this room, it's uninhabitable,' she cried out as if genuinely alarmed and ashamed at how I'd been treated. 'The bed doesn't even fit in the room!'

'I know, I had to sleep with my legs up in the air.'

'Oh, poor Calypso, will you ever forgive me, darling?' she asked, her lower lip wobbling.

'And this blanket seems to have brought me out in a rash,' I told her as I scratched at the bumps that had come up all over my body during the night.

'Ghastly! That's sooo Oopa's fault, darling. He's an evil old devil. That blanket belongs to Mummy's dog, Chanel.'

She went to hug me but I pulled away, scratched and said, 'I'll forgive you if you lend me your mobile to make a call.'

'Of course, darling,' she gasped. 'Anything. You know that.'

I couldn't believe it. 'Really?'

'Absolutely, who do you want to call? Are we missing Billy, darling? Are we missing our boyfriend?'

'No, actually, when we were at Calm-a-sutra on Friday, Peregrine gave me a message from Freddie. He wants me to call him.'

Honey's face clouded over. 'Darling, you can definitely use my phone but, well, I didn't want to tell you, but as you're clearly deluded, I guess I'll have to. Freddie and Portia are an item.'

'No.' I shook my head firmly. 'No, Portia said she'd rather go to Star's. I need to call Freds, Honey, really. I really do,' I pleaded.

Honey took my hands in hers and looked into my eyes. 'Darling! For all my wicked flaws and silliness, you know how much I care for you, don't you?'

No. 'Yes of course I do, but . . .'

'Misery Briggs hates you, Calypso. She never stops going on about how much she *loathes* you with every fibre of her aristocratic body. The simple fact is, she's a snob.'

However muddled my feelings for Portia were, she wasn't really one for bitching. 'That doesn't sound like Portia.'

'Have you already forgotten her outburst on the moonwalk? I almost slapped her for you, darling.'

'No, I haven't forgotten anything,' I said, choosing my words carefully, 'but if I could just borrow your phone and . . .'

Honey held her hand up to silence me. 'No, Calypso. It's for your own good. I'm your *real* friend, probably your *only* friend these days. If I don't look after you, who will, darling? Leave Freddie and Portia to get on with their royal fling. We've got a ball to prepare for. You need all the self esteem you can get, and I've promised myself I'm going to make sure you get it.' It sounded like a threat more than a promise.

Had I really sunk so low that Honey was now my only real friend? I wondered later as I took a long cool bath in the hope of getting rid of the ghastly rash. Honey gave me some calamine lotion to put on it which soothed the itching but made me look like strawberry mousse.

We spent almost the entire day getting ready, and by six o'clock, when Honey called Nobu for sushi, I was actually starting to feel excited about the ball again. And although Honey opened up the Aladdin's cave of her wardrobe to me again, I couldn't find anything nicer than the skirt and bejewelled cashmere top I'd bought in LA.

'What bag are you taking, darling?'

I held up the little Gucci bag Sarah and Bob had given me last Christmas, but Honey wrinkled her nose job. 'Darling, that's not on trend, nor is it old enough to be vintage. Try this,' she insisted, passing me a tiny little bejewelled fur Fendi.

'Oh Honey, I can't – it must have cost thousands and thousands!' I protested.

'Only four or five,' she insisted. She pressed the bag into my hand, even though I didn't really want the responsibility of such an expensive bag, especially as I planned to spend the night dancing and would have to leave it in the cloakroom or on a chair. But I didn't really have a choice. Honey seemed to have a marvellous knack for getting what Honey wanted.

'Darling, it looks perfect with the rest of your outfit. I'm going to do my eyes and just use a dab of lip-gloss, what do you think?' she asked as if she really cared about my opinion.

I leaned over to examine her pallet. 'I love the browns; I think their really sultry and old-movie glamour.'

'Exactly, let's do old-movie glamour, darling,' she agreed, smiling up at me. 'But first you'll have to put some make-up on that rash of yours; with all that calamine lotion you look like you've got measles.'

I took the body foundation she passed me and despite my doubts, I went into her en suite to apply it. When I returned, Honey was holding my phone. 'What are doing with that?' I demanded crossly; I didn't want her deleting any more messages.

She looked surprised and hurt as she put the phone into the fur Fendi she was lending me. 'I was just swapping all your stuff from one bag to another,' she explained.

'Sorry,' I said, but she didn't reply.

We were back on speakers by the time we climbed into the limo, thank goodness. I even accepted another one of the tiny Veuves from the fridge and sipped it through the straw. My heart was racing as to what the evening was going to be like. Honey tried to get me to see the humour in the acute discomfort in which I'd spent the previous night, but I was still all bumpy with the rash.

'Oh darling, don't be mad, the foundation has totally covered them up; you're so paranoid. No wonder you have such bad luck with boys, darling. Besides, who'll be looking at you when I'm there?' she asked, faux-jokingly. Then she pinched me, only not in a playful way.

'My skin has the texture of a relief map, Honey. I look diseased.'

Honey laughed uproariously until not only did the collagen in her lip bubble up, but after a choking fit, she did vomit a little , which she spat in my handbag.

'Sorry, darling, it was the first thing to hand. Don't worry, I'll buy you another one tomorrow.'

I was beyond caring, though. I found myself saying, 'That's OK,' and 'Thank you, that's so sweet of you,' and 'Actually no need – I mean, in fact it's really your handbag anyway.' She looked a bit cross then.

On our arrival I stood with Honey on the long snaking queue outside the Hammersmith Palais, caked in foundation, holding my bag of vomit and trying to summon the feelings of excitement I had felt earlier in the evening. It wasn't easy. I wondered how the party at Star's was going. I imagined fit boys and my friends lounging around Tiger's chill room with the angel of death peeing Jim Beam over the black Japanese stones. I imagined them dancing to Star and Indie's music, and then I looked down the queue at the hordes of Year Eight and Nine girls and boys Star and the others had tried to save me from. There was the odd tragic parent on the other side of the road, sitting in their Range Rover, waiting to see their daughter get into the party safely.

This is when I had my epiphany. I think *hubris* is the word. We had studied the word both with Ms Topler and during Ancient Greek lessons. *To presume that one is greater than the gods.* Well, the gods were having a good old laugh now. I looked up at the sky as a few drops of rain fell on my foundation-coated body.

Honey's phone rang.

'Hi darling, yaah we're here now about to go in. We had the maddest night at Calm-a-sutra on Friday. I pulled Charles, remember we met him . . .'

I tried not to listen in, but then Honey shoved her mobile hard against my ear. 'Here, she wants to speak to you,' she said in a really pissed-off way.

It was Georgina on the other end.

'Hi, Georgina, how is –' I started.

'Demand Honey give you back your SIM card immediately!' she insisted firmly.

'My SIM card's in my phone, I already checked.'

'Believe me, that is not *your* SIM card.'

'I don't understand . . .?'

'So, just trust me because I know Honey a lot better than you do, OK? We always used to knick the SIM card out of one another's mobiles in Year Ten. Well, everyone's mobile, actually, you know, just so we could check who was receiving texts from whom. It's easy to do. We just always kept a whole collection of the various Pay-As-You-Go cards and replaced them.'

'That's horrible.'

'Yaah, I know. Sorry. I don't do it now!'

I whispered into the phone my back turned on Honey. 'Honey's a complete bitch Georgina. I'm having a horrible time!'

'Calypso, you didn't just work that out? Anyway, we don't have time to discuss this now just ask her for your SIM card back, *now*.'

Turning around I casually said, 'Honey, can I have my SIM card back, please.'

Honey rolled her eyes.

'What did she say?' Georgina asked. I could hear a party in full swing on the other end of the line.

'She rolled her eyes.'

'Repeat these three words out loud then: Village. Pleb.

Shag! And then say you know and you'll tell everyone if she doesn't hand it over this very moment.'

I turned to Honey, who was looking at me beadily. 'Village. Pleb. Shag!' I said, enunciating each word carefully, slowly and loudly so I wouldn't have to repeat them. 'I know everything and I'll tell everyone,' I warned her with a bravado I didn't feel.

'Fine.' Honey rolled her eyes. 'It was for your own good, if you must know,' she sneered. But she took her phone back, shut it and, after a scramble in her bag, passed me over what must have been my real SIM card.

'Thanks, Georgina. I'll call you guys later,' I said and hung up. I turned to Honey. 'But why?' I asked, confused.

'It amused me.' She shrugged her skinny sun-kissed shoulders.

'It amused you?'

'Yes – do you know how sickening it was, watching Portia becoming best pals with a pleb like you! Treating *me*, as if *I* were the freak! It was just sooo *wrong*,' she said as if she was being madly logical or something.

'So, you stole my SIM card and deleted my texts to redress the social balance?'

'Yes. I mean no, I borrowed your SIM card occasionally and then put it back occasionally. I didn't delete the messages, well not strictly speaking, anyway. I forwarded the messages to my SIM and just deleted them from your SIM, so you see they're not really deleted. I was just borrowing texts from your text library, really. Think of it that way.' She smiled sweetly.

I was aghast at her total lack of shame – I don't know why.

'And it was going to be a surprise but you may as well know I did you the most *enormous* favour. When you were putting the body make-up on I forwarded all the messages I borrowed back on to your SIM so everything is just as it was now. Don't get so worked up about it. I always nick SIM cards, like any normal person does. Even your precious friend, Georgina. In fact it was her idea,' she added.

'Her idea to steal my SIM card?'

'Not *your* SIM, obviously. But when she was *my* best friend we used to steal everyone's, apart from yours because we wouldn't have had much fun with your SIM before this year, would we, darling?' She laughed. 'We used to do it together before you came along and ingratiated yourself into *our* world and ruined everything!' she explained crisply as she shuffled forward with the moving queue.

As we moved ever closer to the entrance, I tried to absorb what her game had meant to my relationship with Portia as well as with Freddie and Billy. Without Honey's interference how would the half-term have played itself out? I reflected on the first time we went to Windsor and bumped into Billy on the bridge. I remembered leaving him alone with Portia, the two of them chatting away happily. Was that when the two of them realised they liked each other? It explained why Portia wanted to go to Star's party.

'And don't think *you're* so special,' continued Honey, gathering outrage as she ranted. 'I nicked Portia's SIM too. Only of course I had to put hers back more frequently because she has a family who loves her and she gets loads of texts. When I first found out you were text-flirting Billy and Freddie, I thought it might be amusing. Then once I discovered that Billy was keen on Portia, I couldn't resist. Darling, it was like watching a gripping soap opera unfold. You can't blame me, not when you pushed in on my world, stealing Georgina and chumming up with Portia.'

'I bloody well can blame you and I will,' I told her furiously, realising now that she must have deleted that text Billy had asked me about. All the time I had been considering pulling Billy as a second-best, less complicated boyfriend, Portia had already pulled him. Actually, rather than her stealing Freddie, I had been stealing Billy – at least that must have been how it appeared to Portia.

I felt sick.

Honey smiled at me and poked her tongue out. 'So sue, sweetie.' She shrugged. 'I still love *you*!'

At that moment we arrived at the head of the queue and Honey handed her ticket to the door gorilla and skipped in to join the warm, dry throb of the party.

I followed, handing the door gorilla my ticket.

'Stand aside, luv. That's not valid.'

'But my parents bought it online,' I told him desperately.

'Like I said, you isn't valid, move aside.'

'But can't I go in with my friend?' I begged – using the term 'friend' loosely, you understand. 'It's raining.' I did my special little-girl-lost face but it didn't work.

'Stand aside, you're blocking the door,' he repeated without so much as looking at me as he continued to check and take tickets from others on the queue and allowing them through. 'You isn't valid.'

'Honey,' I called out, 'he won't let me in.'

She didn't come out but spoke to me from behind the door gorilla. 'Never mind, darling, just wait there for me. I'll be out at two when Oopa is picking us up. The servants have the night off or I'd suggest you wait for me at home. Big kiss!' With that, she shrugged and disappeared into the noise and bright lights of the ball.

I took shelter with one of the tragic parents standing nearby under an umbrella and watched the girls and boys as they filed into the party. They all looked sooo young! Eventually the parent of the daughter who had offered me shelter under her umbrella waved desperately as her little girl finally disappeared into the party. She apologised to me but said she and her umbrella were leaving. I almost pleaded with her to take me home with her, but I resisted the temptation.

So there I was, the tragic American Freak who had actually imagined Honey, the toxic psycho toff, had liked her. I wiped a tear before it could fall down my face and ruin my make-up, before realising there was no need to worry about that now. I wasn't going anywhere. Why shouldn't I cry my heart out?

I stood in the rain with my SIM card in one hand and my clutch bag of vomit in the other. I opened up the Fendi and tried not to breathe in as I found my phone and wiped it free of vomit. It was a bit of a struggle and I dry-retched a few times, but eventually I managed to swap the SIM cards and start my phone up.

My message bank was near to full. The first few texts

were from Freddie, just the usual flirty text. The next was from Billy, and even though I wanted to delete it and scroll down to see if there were more from Freddie, it was quite long for a text so I began to read.

I KNOW THIS IS A SHITY WY 2 TLL U. BUT AFTER I SAW U IN W I KIND OF PULLED PORTIA. I FEEL REALLY BAD BUT I GUESS THAT DUSNT HELP? SORRY. B.

It was sent the day I'd kissed Freddie in the rain under the awning in Windsor. Which meant the same day I'd decided Portia was stealing Freddie from me, Portia was actually pulling Billy. I felt stupid as I remembered flirting outrageously with Billy the next time I saw him with Portia. To think – I'd interpreted his embarrassment as a sign that he was desperately keen on me when actually he was desperately keen on Portia!

It was hard to absorb the full enormity of how not receiving that text from Billy had destroyed my friendship with Portia. I scrolled down to the next text which was from Freddie.

SORTED THE EURO BALL. WHERE WILL I PCK U UP? TEXT ME OR DO U STLL WNT ME 2 BUGGER OFF? X FREDS

The tears were streaming down my face, and I didn't care that every time I wiped them away I was smearing my eye-makeup even more. Freddie had wanted to take me to the Royal Bore after all. My crying jag was interrupted by a suited door gorilla who came up to me and tapped me on the shoulder. I expect he wanted to offer me a tissue, so I waved him away. Only unlike your average door gorilla he spoke really nicely to me. 'Excuse me, Miss, are you Calypso Kelly?'

'Yes I am and I need to get into that ball,' I told him, resisting the urge to throw myself into his big comforting looking chest. 'I am totally drenched –'

'I understand you had trouble entering the party. Sorry about that, miss, but His Royal Highness didn't think we'd manage to find you in there and . . . '

I looked around. 'Is Freddie *here*?' I asked.

He gestured toward another man in a suit only this suit wasn't a door gorilla; this suit was Freddie, my Freddie. Freds.

'Freds? What's going on?'

How romantic was this? Freddie walked towards me, smiling. How utterly fairy fable-ish, I thought as I swooned with excitement – right up to the point where Freds wrinkled his nose and asked me, 'Have you just vomited on yourself, Calypso?'

THIRTY-TWO

My Royal Wake-up Call

I began to explain about Honey and how she'd vomited into my handbag, but Freddie started to laugh. 'It's *not that* bad,' he teased. 'At least not as bad as your skin, which appears – if I'm not mistaken,' he added, peering closely at my arm, 'to be peeling off you.'

And then he did the coolest thing! He took his hand and ran it down my arm. Only it wasn't cool when he looked at the gunk on his hand and grimaced.

'That's the make-up she made me put on to hide the rash from the prickly blanket . . .'

He put his arm around me. 'You can tell me all about it on the boat. Right now we have a ball to get to.'

'You mean the Royal Bore? I mean, the Annual Euro-Royal-Bash Thingamee?'

'Yes, now put this on,' he instructed, handing me a motor bike helmet and leather jacket. 'Quick spin down to the river and we take a boat straight to the castle pier.'

I wanted to pinch myself as I climbed on to the old Norton behind Freddie and we sped underneath the Hammersmith fly-over. I clasped my hands around him tightly as we rode Bond-like down some old stone steps. I swear my heart was in my mouth by the time we got to the little strip along the Thames called the Lower Mall. I could see the jetty and a giant boat with security guys hanging about it, waiting for us.

Two men in chinos who were chatting into mouthpieces were there to take the bike from Freddie. We handed them our helmets and jackets and walked down the jetty hand in hand. I had to carry my lovely shoes, though, because they kept slipping through the slats.

Just before we climbed on to the boat, Freddie wrapped his arms around me and kissed me, only not for very long as he pulled away to ask, 'Is there actually anything valuable in that bag of yours?'

I looked at the fur Fendi Honey had lent me and shook my head. 'No, I washed my phone in the rain and now it's in my . . .' I looked down at the phone wedged in the elastic part of my bra where my cleavage would have been – if I had any.

Freddie looked too and grinned. 'So, no passport? No valuable item of jewellery, no wallet, no government documents of vital importance, no driving licence, car keys?'

'Nothing. The only item of value is my Lancôme Juicy Tube lip-gloss.'

'In that case,' he said, removing the bag from my hand and tossing it into the Thames, 'I think we can dispense with it.'

'Oh,' I said sadly, as I watched it sink to the bottom of the river. 'I was really quite attached to my Lancôme Juicy Tube lip-gloss.'

'Sorry,' he said, putting his arm around me. 'I was lying about the spew thing, though. It really did stink. Besides, I'm planning on kissing you quite a bit and I hate lip-gloss.'

I smiled. 'It was actually Honey's bag.'

'Really?' He rubbed his jaw in a madly sexy way, appearing to ponder the situation for a split second and then smiled as he announced in a Sean Connery piss-take, 'Well, my dear, the bâteau awaits us!' Then he bowed down, really, really low and ushered me on to the boat.

On the boat he directed me to the shower where I scrubbed the make-up from my body. The redness had gone down and now looked only a little pink and was hardly noticeable. It was like being in a really cool dream – only one I'd never even dared to dream, although I still regretted losing my lip-gloss to the Thames. Being without lip-gloss always makes a girl feel slightly vulnerable, but then I reminded myself that a prince had just whisked me off on a motorbike and now we were en route to a ball. A Real Ball – and not just any ball, the Royal Bore!

There was a knock on the door as I was about to climb back into my soggy clothes. I opened it an inch. Freddie was standing there, only he was facing the other way as he passed me the most stunning ball gown I had ever seen. It was black silk taffeta spangled with tiny multi-coloured diamonds and thousands of sparkles. It looked like a long ballerina's dress, like a summer night sky sparkling with stars.

'Oh Freddie, it's so lovely. How did you know what size I was?'

He scratched the back of his head. 'Well, see, that's where I had to solicit the help of secret agent Portia. I took her out for pizza that day I first saw you in Windsor. You girls can eat pizza till it comes out your ears, can't you? She told me your size and suggested where I'd find such a dress. I almost got her a gating, I interrogated her for so long.'

'Oh,' was all I could really muster saying, for fear of blurting about all the horrible things I'd thought about how suspicious and mean I'd been to her about everything. 'But how did you know you were taking me? I thought it was complicated.'

'Complicated doesn't even come close. Mother quizzed me no end about you before she'd agree to send off for the dress.' By this point I was getting cold so I took the dress from his hand and closed the door to change.

When I came out, he passed me a box which contained black Jimmy Choos with satin ribbons that laced up the leg.

I wanted to say something cool like, 'Oh I can't,' but I didn't have the mettle. Instead I virtually snatched them from his outstretched hands. He helped me sort out all the bows and ribbons as we tied them up my leg. I really did feel like Cinderella being claimed by her prince. I only wish I could stop the feeling of shame about being so ghastly to Portia.

When we arrived at the ancient stone battlements of Windsor castle, the fireworks were already being let off. Freddie and I dashed up the stone steps of the pier and straight through security, through the throngs of glamorous dancing Euro Royals, marvelling at the firework display.

I looked up at the exploding heavens above us but Freddie insisted we leg it, as we were late. As we entered the first of one of the castle's anterooms en route to where I was to be presented to his parents, Sister Michaela's first history lesson from Year Seven started coming back to me – only not the bit where her habit got caught in a nail sticking out of the floor and ripped and we got to see her bald little nun head. No, I mean the part about the castle's history. Even though I saw Windsor Castle all the time, having been schooled not two miles away, for me it had only ever been a landmark, a marker for a nearby pizza place or tea shop. Now I was seeing it as one of Freds's castles, one of his homes. His parents' official residence, in fact. But most of all I was thinking, Calypso Kelly, you are stepping inside nine hundred years of history – and I was thinking in the voice of Sister Michaela.

There, among all the glorious chandeliers, ball gowns and dancing couples, my eyes fixed on the masterpieces by Rembrandt, Rubens, Holbein and Van Dyck. They lined the walls the way framed posters of old films line the walls of my house in Los Angeles. Bob calls them vintage. But Freddie didn't give me time for wonderment as he led me rapidly to where I was to be presented to his parents. My head was swivelling, my heart was racing and before I could take it all in, there they were – his parents: the King and Queen of England. I was suddenly so happy I had spent all these years at an English public school and knew the proper etiquette on forms of address.

And then it got even better! I caught a glimpse of approval pass between Freddie and his mother and father. And then his father asked *me* to dance. We did a lovely waltz, and afterwards he thanked *me*, and before I could tell him that some of the sparkles from my dress had dusted off on his tux, I was whisked off by some old prince – an uncle, I think. Whoever he was, my dress gave him the same treatment as the King, and then it was the King of Spain's turn to get the special Calypso sparkle treatment. I kept praying they wouldn't notice, but then when I danced with Freds's father again he whispered, discreetly in my ear, 'Your dress seems to be spreading its magic all over the ballroom.'

The King of England was actually teasing me!

I spotted Indie in a rich pink taffeta silk gown and tiara that no one but Indie could have carried off. As she waltzed past with some elderly bald man I sort of recognised, she gave me a little wave and a wink. I was so happy I could burst . . . right up until the point that I saw Portia dancing with Freddie. I've never felt so confused about anything in my life because while I was so grateful to Portia for all she had done, I hadn't actually danced with Freddie myself.

I waved at them, but only Portia saw me – and she didn't wave back. The Prince of Sweden was whisking me around and my sparkles were dusting his dinner jacket so it was easy enough to put it from my mind, especially when he started dusting the sparkles off and apologised to me for his dandruff problem.

Later on, Indie and I stood outside in the cool night air

for a bit, sipping on our champagne and looking up at the ink-black sky. We laughed about all the odd people we'd had to dance with. 'Now, you know what I meant when I told you how terminally dull these things are,' she teased.

'Royal Bores, they're all the same,' I said grandly, as if I went to these things all the time, and we both laughed. Secretly, I was having the best night of my life – if you ignore the spew and runny body make-up thing. Even my sparkle disaster seemed perfect.

And then Indie ruined my feel-good fantasy. 'Have you spoken to Portia yet, Calypso?'

'I waved,' I told her, which I knew sounded feeble, even as I demonstrated the friendly little wave I'd sent to Portia. 'But she ignored me.'

'I think you have to sort things out with her, don't you?'

I nodded.

'You know she's madly keen on Billy, don't you?'

'I do now,' I told her. 'I only found out after she left the school on Friday, though. Honey had stolen my SIM card and I don't know . . .'

'You got jealous?' she suggested.

'Yes,' I agreed.

'Well, I know how that feels,' she said, taking a sip of her champagne and looking out over the Thames. And as I watched this beautiful princess in her glamorous gown, I realised that I hardly knew her – well, not half as well as I wanted to at least.

'I was so jealous of you when I first started. All Star and Georgina talked about was Calypso, Calypso, Calypso.'

'All they talked about to me was Indie, Indie, Indie.'

Indie smiled and took my hand as a lump formed in my throat at the shame of my own behaviour these past weeks. Because as much as I wanted to blame it all on Honey, what sort of stupid girl was I to be taken in by a girl who had so consistently made my school life miserable? Also, there was no getting away from the fact that I'd been a serious bitch to Portia without any help from Honey whatsoever. No wonder Portia was so wary of me.

Honey was just being Honey, the quintessential DPG, the psycho toff supreme.

I had no excuse.

'I invited Portia to come to Star's place but she's refused,' Indie told me.

'How come?'

'Her father. She doesn't want to leave him alone now that her mother's dead.'

'Poor Portia.' I looked up at the black sky and remembered our moonwalk and her blunt appraisal of me as a self-centred Honey clone. 'I've been so horrible to her,' I admitted to Indie desperately. 'I don't know what I can do now to make things OK again, though?'

Indie held me by the shoulders and looked me in the eye. 'I do. Make her come to Star's. I know she thinks her father needs her now, but make her come to Star's. She needs it more and the best way to cheer her father up is for her to be happy.' Then she gave me a cuddle and I cuddled her back. 'Promise you'll try, Calypso?' she insisted as she pulled away.

'I'll try now,' I assured her, but as I watched Indie disappear into the throngs of bejewelled, tiara-clad women dancing with men in sashes and medals, I couldn't think of how I was even going to get a chance to approach Portia. I felt so utterly useless.

'So, had enough of all this Royal Bore business yet?' Freddie asked, coming up behind me and wrapping his arms around me.

I nodded, still staring up at the sky, frightened I might start crying or something tragic like that. He took my chin and turned me around and planted a kiss on my nose. 'May I have this dance?'

'I'll have to check my dance card,' I teased as he took my hand and led me back into the ballroom.

He was splendidly graceful as he lead me around the floor and then, just as I was about to burst with happiness, the waltz came to an end and he whispered in my ear. 'Our carriage awaits us.'

I couldn't bear that this night had to come to an end. 'I feel like Cinderella about to turn back into a pumpkin,' I told him, sticking out my lower lip.

He kissed it. 'I think you'll find that it was the carriage that turned back into the pumpkin. Cinderella turned back into herself – only without the meringue-like ball gown.'

'But I don't want to turn back into a girl who smells of vomit and I definitely don't want to go back to Honey's,' I told him, realising as I said the words just how much I *didn't* want to go back to Honey's. In fact, I would rather sleep under the Embankment with the homeless than go back to Honey's House of Luxury Horrors.

Freddie wrapped me in his arms and kissed the top of my head. 'We're going to Star's! It's all sorted. So come on, let's hit the road. We've got a party to go to, people who need us and quad bikes calling out our names. Actually, one of them is calling out its own name.'

I looked at him quizzically.

'Star's named one of the quad bikes, *Calypso*.'

I looked long and hard at this beautiful prince who seemed to genuinely like me and in that moment I realised I wanted to be a better person, which in a nutshell means I never wanted to be compared to Honey ever again.

'Can I borrow one of your security guys for just one sec?' I asked.

'It depends what you want to do with him,' Freddie joked.

'There's someone I need to say goodbye to, and I need to go alone, and I doubt I'll be able to find my way out to the car without him,' I explained.

'And I can't help?' he asked.

'No, it has to be a security guy,' I told him firmly. 'I'll see you in the car.'

I rushed through the ballroom, trailed by my rather large security guy, who wasn't exactly what you'd call nimble or light on his feet. As we ducked and dived our way through dancing couples and chatting groups in my search for Portia, he kept falling over and bumping into people. Eventually I found her dancing with the vaguely familiar bald man Indie had been dancing with earlier.

'Portia,' I panted, 'can I have a word, please?'

She looked at me impassively. 'Sorry, Calypso, now's not a good time,' she replied perfectly civilly.

'But it can't wait. Please Portia . . . please. It won't take a moment.'

'What do you want to say, Calypso?'

I looked at the bald guy and the bald guy looked at me. He looked very, very sad and in that moment I recognised the eyes of Portia's father. His face had changed so dramatically that he didn't even look like the same man Portia's mother had fallen asleep on in chapel. In fact, the last time I'd seen him, he'd had hair!

I looked at Portia. Her own long raven hair was piled up in an elegant chignon and crowned with the oldest-looking tiara I'd ever seen. She looked truly regal. 'Mostly, I want to say I'm sorry,' I explained. 'But . . .'

'It's all fine,' she replied, even managing a slight smile, but it was only a slight one and it didn't quite reach her eyes. I noticed then that she was holding her father's hand.

'No, it's not all right. I've been horrible. Honey stole my SIM card and yours too, actually, and started playing mind games with me, and I fell for it.'

'Why?'

'I don't know. I was totally insanely obsessed that you were stealing Freds and . . .'

'Stealing what?'

'Look, can we just leave it that I behaved badly, madly and even a little dangerously? The point is, at the start of term we became really good friends and I can't bear to think that it can't be like that again. I know it was all my fault, but it was all over boys and do you really want to think boys are that important?'

'Hardly,' she agreed.

'Then come with Freddie and me now to Star's.'

She let go of her father's hand and ushered me to a quiet area.

'I can't, Calypso.'

'Why, because of me?'

'No, because Daddy needs me.' I watched her eyes as they travelled over to her sad father. I watched him return her smile with his own watery one and even though I was ashamed of how I'd treated her, I no longer felt like the most self-centred, selfish girl in all the world because I was determined to make things right.

'I know,' I told her, and then, risking total rejection and humiliation, I cuddled her and kissed her cheek. 'But Billy is sitting in one of Star's wardrobes up in Derbyshire, refusing to come out until you arrive. Star's beside herself! She's had to resort to sliding buttered toast with Marmite under the door, she's so fearful of him fading away from lack of food.'

Portia smiled a proper smile as she whispered in my ear, 'Calypso, have you noticed . . .'

'That I can be a jealous witch? Yes, but I still want you to give me a second chance, because, well . . . because that's the sort of girl you are, Portia!' I looked her in the eye, feeling proud of my little speech. I seemed to have developed into quite the orator in the last few moments. Perhaps when I grow up and fence in the Olympics and win I shall be asked to make a speech and I'll even do it without blurting. Maybe I'll even be all composed, and . . .

Portia interrupted my little fantasy. 'No, Calypso,' she

said pointing around the room. 'Look around you, all the guests are covered in Calypso dust.'

I looked around at the glittering crowd – which was in fact glittering with *my* glitter. 'Oh buggery bollocks!' I exclaimed loudly as Her Serene Highness of Somewhere-or-Other waltzed by and then I pressed my hand against my foul-mouthed New-World lips.

'Calypso!' Portia chided, as she giggled.

'I'm sooo not bred for this sort of occasion. Sorry, I'd better go, Freds is waiting. I'll say hello to Billy for you though, OK?'

'Not so fast,' she said, grabbing my hand. 'How can I trust you not to steal him?' Portia asked, eyeing me up beadily.

I couldn't believe that I'd tried sooooo hard to make up, only to have her mistrust me again. Seriously, these aristos are a bloody tricky lot! 'Portia? I'm going up with *Freds*!' I told her indignantly. 'The whole Billy thing was just a misunderstanding . . .'

'I still think I should come up to keep an eye on you just the same,' she told me, only now I could see she was suppressing a grin. 'Everyone knows what a ferocious text-flirt you are.'

I went bright red with shame and started to justify myself, my brain had started up its *Dig! Dig! Dig!* chant again.

Portia kissed her finger and placed the kiss on my forehead. 'I was only teasing. I'm coming up to Derbyshire tomorrow.'

My head spun around on my shoulders. 'What?'

'Fred's sorted it all out with my brother tonight.

Tarkie's going to stay home for half-term. Besides, what sort of girl would I be if I left Billy to wilt away in a wardrobe with nothing but Marmite toast for sustenance? He doesn't even like Marmite.'

'But Indie said . . .'

'Bugger what other people say,' my enigmatic new friend declared – and quite loudly too.

I laughed as people turned around to stare at the two of us. That was all the encouragement I needed to grab her in a cuddle and smother her in sparkle. Then I kissed her father good night dusting him in sparkles too. 'Sorry,' I blurted, 'I appear to have sparkled you.'

And then her father took my hand and brought it to his lips and kissed it. 'I assure you, young lady, the pleasure is all mine,' he told me and smiled.

I grabbed Freddie's security guy, who was lingering discreetly out of ear shot, took off my shoes and legged it to the car park.

Freddie was waiting by the open door and ushered me into the vehicle in the manner of an ostentatious butler. He could probably get a job working for Honey with that bow.

'My lady!' he said, doffing an imaginary cap.

I climbed inside the black Mercedes. 'Thank you, Jeeves, that will be all!' I told him.

He dived in after me. 'I very it much doubt it, my lady!'

I giggled as he wrapped me up in a big princely cuddle and then strapped me safely into the seat belt.

'Oh my God, I've left all my stuff at Honey's!' I cried as we drove out on to a country lane.

Freddie waved my fears away the way he'd waved Kevin away the day he'd kissed me under the awning in Windsor. 'I'll have someone pick it up tomorrow morning first thing. It'll be with you by the afternoon.'

'And you?' I asked flirtily. 'Will you be with me?'

'To quote Sartre, one of my favourite idlers of all time, "I'm here now, aren't I?"'

'And to quote his miserable mistress, Simone De Beauvoir, "What about tomorrow?"' I shot back.

'*Did* she say that?' Freddie asked, surprised by my awesome literary knowledge.

'I don't actually know,' I admitted, unable to delude him. 'Probably not, but I did,' I told him. 'And I'm here now, aren't I?'

He smiled and ran his hand through his jet-black hair. 'OK, well I'm not sure Sartre said "I'm here aren't I?" But I'm pretty certain that Shakespeare – Macbeth in fact – said, "Tomorrow and tomorrow and tomorrow". Which is how long I'm staying up at Star's place. Although let me text Kevin and check that it was Macbeth. He's the literary one.'

'No one's texting anyone!' I told him firmly, as I grabbed his BlackBerry and tossed it to the floor. I was so over mobile phones . . . at least for a bit. Then I wrapped my arms around Freddie's neck and pulled him in for a big snog-age session. Kissing Freddie is . . . well it's . . .

Well, I'm not going to tell you actually.

Of course, I'll tell Star when I get there, though.

Acknowledgements

Once again, gushing praise must go to the Piccadilly Press team, including the talented and organised Melissa Patey, the debonair Geoffrey Lill, and of course the fabulous Emma O'Bryen, Lea Garton, Yasemin Uçar and Margot Edwards. The lion's share of my gratitude and praise must go to Calypso's first fan though: the inspirational Brenda Gardner.

Although all the characters and situations of the Calypso Chronicles are solely the output of my feverishly mad imagination, I must big it up for the stunning girls of Saint Mary's, Ascot and the fit boys of Eton for their incredible generosity, assistance and sound advice.

Last, but by no means least, I owe an eternal debt of gratitude to my own family and friends, especially the Santospirito boys – Zad for his vivid tales of his own exploits on the fencing piste, Kajj for keeping it real and Simon Peter for keeping it mad. Oh, and to Eric Hewitson for drawing the map and coming up with the idea of Calypso's website www.calypsochronicles.com.

Glossary

FENCING TERMS

attack au fer: an attack that is prepared by deflecting an opponent's
   blade.

bout: one single fight, usually lasting around six minutes, stopped
   each time a hit is made so a point can be awarded, then restarted.

compound attack: an attack executed in two or more movements.

corps-à-corps: literally body-to-body – physical contact between
   fencers during a bout (illegal in sabre).

disengagement: a way to continue attacking after being parried.

en garde: the fencing position, the 'ready' position fencers take before
   play.

épée: one of the three fencing weapons. It has a pointed blade, like a foil,
   but with the blade mounted on either a pistol or French grip. The
   blade is fluted and roughly triangular. The target is the whole body.

flèche: a way of delivering an attack. Literally means 'arrow'. The
   attacker leaps to make the attack and then passes the opponent at
   a run.

flunge: an attack specific to sabre – a type of flèche attack in which
   the legs don't cross.

foil: one of the three fencing weapons – usually the weapon on which
   you would learn. It has a pointed blade with a plastic bobble on
   the end. The target is the body excluding arms, legs and head.

lamé: a woven wire cloth jacket to detect hits on the electronic
   recording device.

parry: a defensive move, a block.

parry of quinte: in sabre, a parry where the blade is held above the
   head to protect from head cuts.

piste: a fourteen-metre-long combat area on which a bout is fought. Opponents are hooked up to an electrical apparatus which enables valid hits to be recorded.

plastron: a padded under-jacket to protect the area of the torso where most hits land.

point: the tip of a weapon's blade.

president: the referee or arbiter of the bout – in the case of school matches, one of the fencing masters.

prise de fer: an engagement of the blades that forces the opponent's weapon into a new line.

pool: in competition, fencers are divided into equal groups, called pools, each fencer meeting someone from an opposing pool until half remain. This is called seeding.

retire: retreat.

riposte: an offensive action made immediately after a parry of the opponent's attack.

sabre: one of the three fencing weapons. It is the only cutting weapon. Points are scored both by hits made with the point of the blade and cuts made with the blade, but most commonly by cuts – for this reason the entire weapon including the guard registers hits even though hitting someone on the weapon's guard is not legal. This means the sabreur is totally wired – unlike other fencers. The sabre target is everything above the leg, including the head and arms. The mask is made of metal, while the mask's bib and the jacket (including sleeves) down to the hips is made of woven metal so that only valid hits are recorded on the electrical apparatus. Before play begins the sabreurs must check that all parts of their electric kit are working – this is done by the sabreurs tapping their opponents on the mask, the sabre, the guard and the metal jacket so that all hits will be recorded – this takes place before the salute.

salle: fencing hall or club.

salute: once formal and involving the kissing of the blade, now a casual acknowledgement of one's opponent and president at the start of a bout.

seeding: see pool.

supermans: an exercise to warm up before combat, a holding stance used for warming up – so called because the fist is raised in the attitude of Superman before he flies.

tierce: a type of parry.

trompement: the action of hitting an opponent after a successful deception.

OTHER TERMS

bell end: the helmet of a penis.

blue: minor punishment. Blue sheets of paper given to write lines on. Time consuming. Older girls regularly get younger girls to perform this task for them in exchange for sweets.

bottle out: lose your nerve (chicken out). Bottle is another word for nerve so you can also lose your bottle.

bursar: schools' financial account manager.

champagne socialist: a rich person who pretends to have left-wing politics while enjoying a luxurious lifestyle (i.e. champagne).

châteaued: wasted, drunk.

chubba: chubby, overweight person.

Co-codamol: an over-the-counter medication to treat high temperatures or pain.

cosh: (verb & noun) a heavy stick or bludgeoning implement. To be under the cosh is to be under pressure.

Coventry (to be sent to): to be ostracised.

cut: to cut someone is to ignore them, look right through.

Daddy's plastic: parental credit cards.

Domesday Book: compiled by William the Conqueror in 1086 as a survey created for taxation. Though unpopular in its day, many of England's oldest families take pride in their ability to trace their lineage back to this book.

DPGs: Daddy's Plastic Girls – girls who are defined by their limitless credit card spend.

dressing down: telling off.

emotional thumb screws: a play on 'thumb screws' – a medieval form of torture, which involved a bolt screwed slowly through the victim's thumb.

exeat: weekends in which pupils attending boarding school go home (in the case of overseas pupils alternative arrangements may be made), usually every three weeks.

fairy bread: open sandwich made with sliced white bread, buttered, sprinkled with tiny, brightly coloured sugary freckles (hundreds and thousands). Usually served to very young children at parties.

fit: (adj) the only word used by posh girls to describe a cute, hot, attractive boy. Girls use the word fit to describe hot boys, but a girl would NEVER compliment another girl by referring to them as fit – she would say 'stunning'. However, boys describe cute/hot girls as fit.

frock up: dress up.

fruuping: all-purpose expletive.

gated: to receive 'a gating' is not to be permitted to leave the school grounds on weekends.

ginga: (first 'g' is hard, rhymes with singer) a derogatory term for a person with red hair.

Gypo: derogatory, racist slang for Gypsy.

high table: the superior or senior table in communal dining.

Hon: as in The Honourable Tabitha Smart-Arse – child of a life peer, baron or viscount.

Horsey Girls: rich, spoiled and posh girls who own their own horses.

House Mother: a woman in charge of a dorm house.

HRH: His or Her Royal Highness.

Jim Beam: American bourbon.

Kev: short for the name Kevin. Suggests someone common/lower class. See **pleb**.

listens: mobile phone messages that you let others listen to. In school, if you have a popular 'listen' you might charge the listeners the cost the service provider charges for the call.

Lomotil: a medication to stop stomach upset.

lookie loos: nosy people.

lycée: French school in which the French curriculum is followed and lessons are taught in French. In countries outside France, the curriculum of the resident country is often offered as well as the French equivalent.

neck: to gulp, as in, to neck your vodka, juice, etc.

NQOC: Not Quite Our Class

OTT: Over The Top, outrageous/extreme behaviour or style.

PA: Personal Assistant.

pikey: an insulting reference to someone's lack of high background or education. See **pleb**.

Pixie Stix: an American sweet. Brightly coloured paper straws filled with flavoured sugar.

pleb: (n) short for plebian – common people lacking breeding and education, no connection to wealth.

plebbie: (adj) for pleb.

pukka: authentic, proper.

readies: slang for folding money, actual notes.

refectory: large canteen where meals are served. Also shortened to ref.

rhyming slang: Cockney rhyming slang – the use of rhyming words rather than actual words. Originally a code language used by criminals in London's East End, so that police and informants wouldn't understand. Now used as general slang.

rusticated: a very serious suspension from school in which the pupil is not even offered the convenience of school work to carry on with at home. This would mean on return to school the pupil would be further disadvantaged by having to catch up.

slack down: to disrespect someone, ignore their instructions.

Sloane: posh, snooty girl (named after Sloane Street and Square, an upmarket area in Knightsbridge/Chelsea in London).

snog-age: (pronounced like corsage) to tongue kiss, long and hard.

social: interschool dance (boys and girls).

sovereign ring: a large, flash ring with a gold coin on it – associated with common people and gangsters.

speakers: as in 'non-speakers' – not speaking to someone.

spliff: a marijuana joint.

squaddie: soldier.

stick: a hard time; to give someone stick is to tease them – also short for walking stick.

Sun-In: a peroxide-based spray, which produces blonde streaks in hair.

toff: snobby aristocrat.

tuck: snack foods you are allowed to bring to boarding school – junk food.

Valley Girl: girl from the valley area of Los Angeles.

Camden Town Tales

The Celeb Next Door

Hilary Freeman

Rosie has lived in Paradise Avenue, Camden Town
all her life. As well as the market to hang out
at and gigs to go to, there are celebrities to spot,
and TV studios where she and her best friends
Sky and Vix might get noticed.

When Rosie finds out that the drummer from a chart-
topping group is moving into the house next door, she
makes it her mission to befriend him.
But things don't turn out quite
the way she expects . . .

'Camden comes to life in this engaging and fun
story of friendship and celebrities.'
Chicklish

Alice in time

PENELOPE BUSH

If you could revisit your past, what would you see?

Things are at crisis point for fourteen-year-old Alice. Her mum is ruining her life, her dad's getting remarried, and Sasha, the most popular girl in school, hates her guts . . .

Then a bizarre accident happens, and Alice finds herself re-living her life as a seven-year-old through teenage eyes – and discovering some awkward truths. But can she use her new knowledge to change her own future?

'An amazing book.
Cleverly written, exciting and fast-paced.'
Chicklish

'An ambitious and successful novel.'
Books for Keeps

Look out for *Diary of a Lottery Winner's Daughter*
by Penelope Bush, released July 2011.

My So-Called Haunting

TAMSYN MURRAY

Skye, a fourteen-year-old who can see ghosts, is stressed. Not only is the ghost of a sixteenth-century witch giving her fashion tips, but she's struggling to settle into life with her aunt, and is developing a crush on the most unattainable boy in the school, Nico.

When her aunt asks for her help with a troubled teen ghost called Dontay, she's glad of the distraction. But then Nico starts paying her attention, and she's soon facing a battle to keep her love life and her psychic life separate.

As things get ever more complicated, it looks as though Dontay's past might cost Skye her future.

'Scarily good . . . and spookily sassy!
A fab, fun read.'
Cathy Cassidy

☆

www.piccadillypress.co.uk

Go online to discover

☆ more exciting books you'll love

☆ competitions

☆ sneak peeks inside books

☆ fun activities and downloads

☆ and much more!